THE PHILOSOPHER KINGS

JO WALTON

corsair

CORSAIR

First published in the United States of America in 2015 by Tor

First published in Great Britain in 2016 by Corsair

1 3 5 7 9 10 8 6 4 2

A CIP catalogue record for this book is available from the British Library.

ISBN: 978-1-4721-5079-0 (paperback)

ISBN: 978-1-4721-5078-3 (ebook)

Printed and bound in Great Britain by CPI Group (UK) Ltd., Croydon, CR0 4YY

Papers used by Corsair are from well-managed forests and other responsible sources

MIX
Paper from
responsible sources
FSC
www.fsc.org   FSC® C104740

Corsair
An imprint of
Little, Brown Book Group
Carmelite House
50 Victoria Embankment
London EC4Y 0DZ

An Hachette UK Company
www.hachette.co.uk

www.littlebrown.co.uk

This is for Ada, who has the best thoughts.

Quid me mihi detrahis?

—OVID, *Metamorphoses*, Book VI

What a wondrous and sublime thing it is to be human, to be able to choose your state, whether among the beasts or among the angels.

—GIOVANNI PICO DELLA MIRANDOLA, *Oration on the Awesomeness of Humanity (Oratio de Hominis Dignitate)*

I am voyaging too.
We will need the foundation as much as the dome
For those worlds to come true.

—ADA PALMER, "Somebody Will"

Nothing befits a man more than discourse on the soul. Thus the Delphic injunction "Know thyself" is fulfilled, and we examine everything else, whether above or beneath the soul, with deeper insight.

—MARSILIO FICINO, letter to Jacobo Bracciolini

I had a queer obsession about justice. As though justice mattered. As though justice can really be distinguished from vengeance. It's only love that's any good.

—ELIZABETH VON ARNIM, *The Enchanted April*

THE
PHILOSOPHER
KINGS

1

APOLLO

Very few people know that Pico della Mirandola stole the head of the Winged Victory of Samothrace. In fact he stole it twice. The first time he stole it from Samothrace, before the rest of it was rediscovered. That time he had the help of my sister Athene. The second time was thirty years later, when he stole it from the Temple of Nike in Plato's Republic. One of Plato's Republics, that is; the original, called by some the Just City, by others the Remnant, and by still others the City of Workers, although by then we only had two. In addition to our Republic, there were four others scattered about the island of Kallisti, an island itself known at different times as Atlantis, Thera, and Santorini. Almost everyone who had been influenced by living in the original Republic wanted to found, or amend, their own ideal city. None of them were content to get on with living their lives; all of them wanted to shape the Good Life, according to their own ideas.

As for me, I suppose I wanted that too, but with rather less urgency. I was a god, after all—a god in mortal form, for the time being. I had become incarnate to learn some lessons I felt I needed to learn, and although I had learned them I had stayed because the Republic was interesting, and because there were people there that I cared about. That was primarily my friend

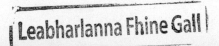

Simmea and our Young Ones. When we'd first come here we'd been doing Plato's Republic according to Plato, as interpreted by Athene and the Masters: three hundred fanatical Platonists from times ranging from the fourth century B.C. to the late twenty-first century A.D. From the time we Children were sixteen, we'd held Festivals of Hera every four months in which people were randomly matched with partners. There were six such festivals before the Last Debate, and all six such matings I'd participated in had produced sons. Simmea had one son from that time, Neleus. And between us we had a daughter, Arete, born after the revisions that made it possible for us to be a family.

Making the Republic work had been harder since Athene stalked off at the end of the Last Debate. She had taken with her both her divine power, and all the robots except two. In the twenty years since the Last Debate a lot of things had changed. Worst was the constant warfare with the other cities.

The art raids had started because we had all the art, and the other cities wanted a share of it, and we didn't want to give any of it up. The real problem was that Plato had imagined his Republic existing in a context where there would be wars, and so training everyone for warfare was a big part of the way he had imagined his city. The guardians, golds, and auxiliaries, silvers, had been training to fight since they were ten, and yet had never fought anyone except in practice until the art raids started. The raids provided a pretext for the warfare it seemed a large number of people had been wanting. While many of us felt they were futile, they were popular, especially with the Young Ones. A city would raid us and take away some statue or painting. Then we'd raid them back and try to recapture it. They began as something like games of capture the flag, lots of fun for everyone involved, but of course the weapons and training were real. By the time it came to real wounds and death, everyone was committed to them. People who had read Plato on war and bravery and the shame of turning your back on the enemy couldn't see any way to back down. So the five cities of Kallisti existed in a constant state of raids and shifting alliances.

The Temple of Nike stood on a little knoll just outside the south gate of the original city. By the time I got there, summoned urgently, the raiders had fled, taking the head with them. I didn't know or care about the head until afterward. Right then I was entirely focused on Simmea. She was still alive, but just barely—the arrow was in her lung, and frothy blood was coming out with every breath. "We thought it best not to move her," Klymene said. I barely heard her, although she was right, of course—moving her would have been fatal. They hadn't even drawn out the arrow.

Simmea's eyes met mine, and they were full of love and trust—and even better, that edge they had that said she loved the truth even more than she loved me. She tried to speak with what breath she had. She said my name, "Pytheas," and then something I couldn't make out.

I made a plan immediately, almost as fast as I would have made it normally. In mortal form, I didn't have access to my powers, and as things were, there weren't any gods who were going to pay attention to me or help, at least not in time. So I drew my dagger. If I slit my wrists it would take minutes for me to bleed to death, but if I slit my throat only seconds. As soon as I was dead I'd have plenty of time—all the time I wanted, once I was safely outside it. I'd go down to Hades, take up all my powers again, and manifest back here a heartbeat after I'd left. Then I could heal her. Indeed, healing her would be fast and easy. I would have lost this incarnation, but I'd been mortal and incarnate for almost forty years now. It had been fascinating and wonderful and terrible, and I'd be sorry to stop, but Simmea was going to be *dead* if I didn't save her.

"Pytheas, no!" Klymene said, and grabbed for the knife. It wasn't that that stopped me.

"Pytheas, don't be an idiot!" Simmea said, perfectly distinctly. And as she said it, or immediately thereafter, she took hold of the shaft sticking out of her chest and pulled the arrow out.

Before I could so much as cut my throat, she was dead, and not only dead but vanished. One second she was there, blood, arrow, and dear ugly face. The next the arrow was lying in blood on the mosaic floor of the temple. Her body had gone back to the time Athene had snatched her from—back, I believe, to the waters outside Smyrna, at the spot where the ship that brought her here had moved through time. Her body would have appeared there, somewhere in the eastern Aegean, and sunk between one wave and the next. She loved to swim, she was a swimming champion, she had taught me and all our Young Ones to swim; but she wouldn't be swimming among the wine-dark billows, she'd just sink down in their embrace. (I've often tried to find her since, to see her for just that one moment more, but it's like looking for one particular helium atom in the sun, trying to find an instant like that without knowing either the exact place or time. I keep on looking now and then.)

Death is a Mystery. The gods can't undo it. Her wound would have been a trivial thing for me to fix if I'd had my powers, but once she was dead, that was the end of it.

Klymene had my knife, and I was prone on the ground clutching the arrow. Simmea's soul too would have gone back to the time she left, and from there it would have gone down to Hades. Unlike most human souls, she knew precisely what to expect. We'd talked about it a great deal. She knew how to negotiate the underworld, and she knew how to choose her next incarnation to maximize her excellence. I wasn't at all worried about any of that. But after choosing her next life, she'd pass through the river Lethe, she had to. Once in Lethe she'd have to at least wet her lips, and once she drank from Lethe she'd forget this life, and me. Souls are immortal, but souls are not personality. So much of personality is memory. When mortal souls pass through Hades they go on to new life, and they become new people with fresh beginnings. I suspect that may be the whole purpose of death. No doubt it is a splendid way for the universe to be arranged. Her soul will continue to pursue excellence for life after life, becoming more and more excellent and making the universe better. But she wouldn't be Simmea anymore, she wouldn't remember this life. She wouldn't remember me and all the things we'd shared.

Once I was back in my real form I'd be able to find her, watch all her different lives if I wanted to, and I did want to. But none of them would be my Simmea. Death of mortals I love is always hard for me to deal with. But this one was worse than the others. Since I was incarnate, I'd been there the whole time. There were no moments of Simmea's life left for me to experience. I had been in time for all of them. I'm bound by Necessity. I can't go back to times I've already visited, none of us can. I'll never be able to speak with her again, or see her rolling her eyes at me, or hear her calling me an idiot. She knew I was the god Apollo. She'd known for years. It just didn't make any difference. When she found out, practically the first thing she said was that it must be why I was so hopeless at being a human being.

It's easy to be adored when you're a god. Worship comes naturally to people. What I'd had with Simmea was a decades-long conversation.

I briefly considered killing myself and going back to Olympos anyway. But her last words and deed had been to stop me—she'd have figured out exactly what I was doing and why. She was extremely smart, and she knew me very well. She probably had some really good reason why I shouldn't do that, which she'd have explained at length and with truly Socratic clarity, if only she'd had time. I might even have agreed. I tried to think what it might have been. My mind was completely blank.

As I couldn't imagine why she'd stopped me killing myself and saving her life, I naturally began to think about vengeance.

"Who was it?" I asked Klymene. "Did we get any of them?"

Klymene has never liked me, and for extremely good reasons. Nevertheless, she is the mother of my son Kallikles. Her expression now was unreadable. Pity? Or did she perhaps despise me? Plato did not approve of giving way to strong emotion, especially grief, and at that moment I was rolling on the ground, clutching an arrow and weeping.

"I don't know," she said. "They came by boat. It could have been anyone. These art raids have been getting worse and worse. They got away—the rest of the troop went after them, except that I sent young Sophoniba for you and stayed with Simmea myself."

"She always liked you," I said. I could hardly get the words out past the lump in my throat.

"She did." Klymene put her hand on my shoulder. "Pytheas, you should get up and go home. Will there be anybody there?"

The thought of going home was impossible. Some of the Young Ones might be there, but Simmea would never be there again. Her things would be everywhere, and the reminder would be intolerable. "I want to find out who they were and avenge her."

Klymene's expression was easier to read now; it was worry. "We all want that. But you're not being rational."

"Are there any bodies?" I asked.

"No, thank Athene," she said. "No Young Ones killed."

"Wounded?"

"Simmea was the only one."

"Then unless the troop catches them, this arrow is the only evidence," I said, examining it. It was unquestionably an arrow, made of strong straight wood, stained with blood now. It was barbed and fletched exactly like all the arrows. We had all learned the same skills from the same teachers. It made war between us both better and worse. I turned it over in my hands and wished I'd never invented the things.

"The *Goodness* has been seen," Klymene said, tentatively. "That doesn't mean it was Kebes. It could have been anyone. But it was sighted yesterday by the lookouts."

The *Goodness* was the schooner Kebes had stolen when he fled from the island after the Last Debate. "You think it was Kebes?"

"It could have been. I didn't recognize anyone," Klymene said. "And you'd think I would have. But if they were all Young Ones . . . well, maybe somebody else in the troop did. I'll check when they get back. Whatever happens we'll be retaliating, as soon as we know who and where. And if you want revenge, I'll do my best to see that the Delphi troop is included in that expedition."

"Thank you," I said, and meant it. The arrowhead was steel, which meant it was robot-forged, which meant it was old. There were still plenty of robot-forged arrowheads around, because people tended to reuse them when they could. Steel really is a lot better than iron. Of course, we were living in the Bronze Age. Nobody else in this time period actually knew how to smelt iron, unless maybe off in Anatolia somewhere the Hittites were just figuring it out. There was no use thinking it might have been pirates or raiders. This was one of our arrows, and the expedition had clearly been an art raid, and that meant one of the other republics.

"Did they take anything?" I asked.

"The head of Victory," Klymene said, indicating the empty plinth where it had stood.

I expect you're familiar with the Nike, or Winged Victory of Samothrace—it stands in the Louvre in Paris, where it has stood since its rediscovery in the eighteen-sixties. There's also a good copy of it actually in Samothrace. The swept-back wings, the blown draperies—she was sculpted landing on a ship, and you can almost feel the wind. It's the contrast between the stillness of the stone and the motion of what is sculpted that makes her such a treasure. But she's headless in the Louvre, because Pico and Athene stole the head, the head which had for a time rested in our Temple of Nike. Her hair is swept back by the wind too, but her eyes and her smile are completely still. Her eyes seem to focus on you wherever you are. The head reminds me a little of the head of the Charioteer at Delphi, although it's completely different, of course, and marble not bronze. But there's something about the expression that's the same. I suppose Athene and I are the only ones who have seen her with the head, at Samothrace, and without, in the Louvre, and then seen just the head, in the City. Nobody else in the City had ever seen any part of her but the head. I tried to comfort myself that in some future incarnation Simmea, who loved the head and had died defending it, would be sure to see the rest of her. It only made me cry harder.

"We'll get it back," I said, choking out the words.

"Yes." Klymene hesitated. "I know I'm the worst person to be with you now, and I would leave you in peace, but I don't think you ought to be alone."

I sat up and looked at her. She was the same physical age as all of us Children, almost forty now. She had been pretty once, lithe and graceful, with shining hair. She was still trim from working with the auxiliaries, but her face had sagged, and her hair been cut off at the jaw to fit under a helmet. She looked weary. I had known her for a long time. We'd both been brought to the Republic when we were ten. When we were fourteen she'd been a coward and I'd said it was all right because she was a girl, and she'd never forgiven me. When we were sixteen we'd shared the single worst sexual experience of my life, then had a son together.

When we were nineteen and Athene had turned Sokrates into a fly and everything had subsequently fallen apart, we'd both stayed and tried to make the revised original Republic work, instead of going off to start fresh somewhere else.

"You're not any worse to be with right now than anyone else who isn't Simmea," I said.

"How are you going to manage without her?" she asked.

"I don't have the faintest idea," I said.

"I wouldn't have thought you'd have tried to kill yourself," she said, tentatively. "It isn't what Simmea would have wanted. Your Young Ones will need you."

"They need both of us," I said, which was entirely true. The difference was that they could have had both of us. If I'd killed myself it would have been temporary. Oh, it would have been different being here as a god with all my abilities. Being incarnate made everything so vivid and immediate and inexorable. But I'd have been here and so would Simmea, and she knew that. Why would it have been being an idiot to kill myself to save her? She understood how temporary death would have been for me, how easy resurrection. If she'd let me do it we could have been having a conversation about it right now. There would even be advantages to being here as a god—there were all kinds of things I could use my powers for. For a start I could get us some more robots, unintelligent ones this time, and make everyone's life easier.

Naturally, I couldn't share these thoughts with Klymene. She didn't know I was Apollo. Nobody did except Simmea and our Young Ones, and Sokrates and Athene. Sokrates had flown off after the Last Debate and never been seen again. We assumed he was dead—flies don't live very long. Simmea was definitely dead. And deathless Athene was back on Olympos, and after twenty years probably still furious with me. If I'd killed myself and saved Simmea in front of her, Klymene would have been bound to notice. As things were, there was no need to tell her. Even without that she had no reason to like me.

"The Young Ones will need you all the more without Simmea," Klymene said.

"They're nearly grown," I said. It was almost true. The boys were nineteen or twenty, and Arete was fifteen.

"They'll still need you," Klymene said.

Before I could answer, she saw somebody coming and stiffened, reaching for her bow. I leaped to my feet and spun around. Then I relaxed. It was the Delphi troop coming out. I bent down and picked up the arrow, which I'd dropped. It wasn't much of a memento, but it was all I had. "I'll go home," I said.

"You won't . . . you won't do anything stupid?" Klymene asked.

"Not after Simmea's last request," I said. "You heard her. She specifically asked me not to be an idiot."

"Yes . . ." she said. She was frowning.

"I won't kill myself," I specified. "At least, not immediately."

Klymene looked at me in incomprehension, and I'm sure I looked at her the same way. "You shouldn't kill yourself because you don't know that you've finished what you're supposed to do in this life," she said.

Not even Necessity knows all ends.

2

ARETE

You don't exist, of course. It's natural to write with an eye to posterity, to want to record what has happened for the edification not of one's friends, but of later ages. But there will be no later ages. All this has happened and is, by design, to leave no trace but legend. The volcano will erupt and the Platonic Cities will be extinguished. The legend of Atlantis will survive to inspire Plato, which is especially ironic as it was Plato who inspired the Masters to set up the City in the first place.

The more I think about this, the more I think that Sokrates was right in the Last Debate. It was fundamentally wrong of them to found the City at all. The story of humanity is one of growth and change and the accumulation of experience. We of the cities are a branch cut off to wither—not a lost branch, but a branch deliberately cut away. We are like figures sculpted of wax and cast into the fire to melt. When I asked Father why Athene had done this he said that he had never asked her, but he supposed that it seemed interesting, and she had wanted to see what would happen. In my opinion that's an irresponsible way for a god to behave. I intend to do better if I ever have the opportunity.

It may seem like hubris, but it really is possible that I might. Others of Father's children have become heroes, and Asklepius is a god. I am the daughter of Apollo, and Father says I have the soul of a hero. Sometimes I really feel as if I do, as if I could do anything. Other times I feel all too human and vulnerable and useless. It doesn't help that I have seven brothers. That's too many. They try to squash me, naturally, and naturally I hate being squashed and resist it as much as possible.

People talk all the time about pursuing excellence, and when I was younger my brothers made a game of this where they chased me. My mother was a philosopher and my father is an extremely philosophical god, and so of course they named me Arete, which means excellence. Maia, who comes from the nineteenth century, says that in her day it used to be translated as virtue, and Ficino worries that this is his fault for translating it into Latin as *virtus*. Maia and Ficino are my teachers. Ficino comes from Renaissance Florence, where it was considered the duty of everyone to write an autobiography, and since Renaissance Florence is almost as popular here as Socratic Athens, many people do. I, as you can see, am no exception.

I'm starting this all wrong, with my thoughts all over the place. Ficino would say it lacks discipline, and make me write a plan and then write it again to the plan, but I'm not going to. This isn't for Ficino, it isn't for anyone but myself and you, dear nonexistent Posterity, and I intend to set down my thoughts as they come to me. My brothers chased me and called it pursuing excellence, but I also pursue excellence, and Father told me that it can only ever be pursued, never caught—though my brothers caught me often enough, and turned me upside-down when they did.

I call them brothers, but they're all half-brothers, really. Kallikles is the oldest. He's Father's son by Klymene, conceived at the first Festival of Hera. Father and Klymene don't like each other much. But Klymene doesn't have any other children, and she and Kallikles have this odd relationship where they're not quite mother and son, but they're not quite not either. Maia says I should think of her like an aunt, and I suppose I do, insofar as I know what aunts are. We don't have any proper ones yet. When my brothers start to have children I'll be an aunt, and my little nieces and nephews will be overwhelmed by how many uncles they have.

Kallikles is the bravest of us. I used to call him "Bold Kallikles" as a kind of Homeric epithet—I have Homeric epithets for all my brothers, which I made up as a kind of revenge for the way they used to chase me. Kallikles fell and broke his arm climbing the tower on Florentia when he was twelve. His arm healed just fine, and when it was completely better he climbed the tower again, and didn't fall off that time. He has a girlfriend called Rhea who is a blacksmith, which means she's a bronze, which is a bit of a scandal as he's a gold. We don't actually have laws about that, the way they do in Athenia and Psyche, but it's definitely frowned on. He lives with her, but they're not married, and so nobody takes official notice of their relationship. Even so, it's awkward, and kind of embarrassing for me.

Next after him comes Alkibiades, whose Homeric epithet is "Plato-loving." His mother is the runner Kryseis. Alkibiades lives in Athenia, and he didn't leave quietly—the rows must have shaken the city. He said he thought Plato's original system was the best—and he said it at great length and with no originality whatsoever. Mother and Father both argued with him. Almost everything I know about how the Festivals of Hera actually worked when we had them here comes from those arguments, as I won't be able to read the *Republic* until I'm an ephebe. Alkibiades thought it was a wonderful arrangement to have a simple sanctioned sexual union with a different girl every four months forever. Mother's question of what happens if you fall in love and Father's question of what happens if you don't fancy some particular girl you're drawn with didn't give him any pause at all. He answered every problem they mentioned by saying that if they'd kept doing it properly, the way Plato wanted, it would have been all right. I had only been thirteen at the time, and about as uninterested in love and sex as anyone could be, but I could see both sides. Having it all arranged without any fuss had advantages. But people did just naturally fall in love. Look at Mother and Father. It would have been cruel to stop them being together.

After Alkibiades left, our house got a lot quieter. I was sorry because he had always been my favorite brother—he was more generally prepared to put up with me than any of the others. He even took the trouble to say goodbye, though I didn't realize it until afterward—he took me to Sparta for a meal with some of his friends, and bade me joy afterward as I ran off to work in the fields. I didn't know until I got home late that night that he had left. He had left on my bed a copy of Euripides he had won as a school prize—they don't allow drama at all in Athenia, or even Homer.

Next in age come Phaedrus and Neleus, who both still live at home in Thessaly. Phaedrus is Father's son by Hermia, who lives in Sokratea. I've never met her, but she once sent Phaedrus an amazing skin drum which we still have. He looks a lot like a darker jollier version of Father. He excels at wrestling—he has won a number of prizes. He also sings beautifully—we sing together sometimes. He's a gold. Phaedrus's epithet is "Merry," because he is—he's the most fun of all my brothers, the readiest to laugh, the fastest to make a joke. It's not that he can't be serious, but his natural expression is a grin.

Neleus is his complete opposite. He's Mother's son by somebody called Nikias, whom I've also never met because he left with Kebes. He must have been dark-skinned, because Neleus is darker than Mother. He unfortunately inherited Mother's jaw and flattish face, so his Homeric epithet could have been "Ugly," but in fact it's "Wrathful" because he's so quick to anger and he bears grudges so well. He never forgets anything. He's a swimming champion, again like Mother, and he can't sing at all. He's a gold. He had a close friendship with a boy from Olympia called Agathon, and since that broke up a few months ago he has been worse-tempered than ever.

I have three more brothers, but I don't know them very well. Euklides and his mother Lasthenia live in Psyche. He visits for a few days every summer. Porphyry and his mother Euridike live in the City of Amazons. He's been here to visit twice. I always feel shy with both of them. I know Euklides better than Porphyry. He is a silver. Porphyry is a gold, and I don't know all that much about him. And I have another brother, somewhere, whose name I don't know and who I've never met at all. His mother Ismene went off with Kebes before he was born.

It's a complicated family, when I write it down like this, but most of the time in Thessaly we've just been five Young Ones with Mother and Father.

To begin again, I was born in the Remnant City fourteen years after it was founded, and I am now fifteen years old. If you consider that is too young to write an autobiography (Ficino does), then consider this an early draft for one, a journal or commonplace book in which I shall record what will become an autobiography in due course when I have more life to record. Though it seems to me that my life has been quite eventful so far, and that there is a lot that has already happened to me that is worthy of note.

I was born four years after the Last Debate. The cities had already divided themselves by then, though they were not in the state of almost constant skirmishing that they are now, and relations between them were generally cordial. Everyone knew each other in all the cities. About a hundred and fifty people had gone off with Kebes and left the island. We don't know what they did, though speculations about it are a favorite topic of conversation. Sometimes people call them the Lost City, or the Goodness Group, after the name of the ship they stole. There keep being rumors that people have seen the *Goodness*, but the truth is that Kebes left the island and nobody knows where he is or what he's doing or anything about his group.

Everyone else stayed on the island, and they all wanted to create Plato's Republic only to do it right this time. This was the case whether they stayed, or left the original city to set up their own. I believe there were fierce debates before everyone sorted themselves out. My parents stayed. By the time I was born, everything was more or less organized again, the new cities were well on the way to being built, and people seldom changed their minds about which city they wanted to live in, because the cities collected people by philosophical temperament, and people's temperaments don't tend to change all that much.

Psyche, the Shining City, was set up by the Neoplatonists, who wanted their city to reflect the mind, and the magic of numerology. It attracted those with a melancholic disposition. Sokratea, which was begun by those who believed that Sokrates was right in the Last Debate, that the City shouldn't have been founded, and that every point needed much more examination, attracted the choleric, though Sokrates himself was nothing like that from all I have read and heard. Athenia, founded by those who believed the opposite, that Athene had been right, and who tried to live even more strictly according to their interpretation of Plato, attracted the phlegmatic. That left the sanguine, who all wound up in the City of Amazons, founded on the principle of absolute gender equality.

Those who stayed in the Remnant were those whose humors were mixed. The other cities characterized us as lazy and indecisive and luxury-loving. At first, because we were the mother city, they came to us frequently to use the libraries and other facilities, but later this happened less and less often. We had a higher proportion of Young Ones than most of the other cities, because many people didn't take their babies with them when they left. This isn't as callous as it may sound, because they didn't know which babies were theirs. Some people could recognize their own babies, or thought they could. Many just couldn't. And none of the Children had been educated to expect that they'd bring up their own children; they'd had them on the understanding that the City knew how to do it best. So there are plenty of people here, like my good friend Erinna, who have no idea who their parents are. Now that we have families there won't be any more people like that, though of course they're still doing that in Athenia, and maybe in the City of Amazons too, I'm not sure.

People did change cities sometimes, as indeed they still do. As young people come of age and find themselves in a city that doesn't suit their temperament, they often leave it for another, the way Alkibiades did. And one of the first things I remember is Maia coming back. My earlier memories are muddled and confused with the cute baby stories Mother told about me—my first word was "beauty" and my second word "logos." (It might sound conceited of me to record that, but honestly, anyone living in this house whose second word *wasn't* "logos" would have to be deaf.)

I must have been about four years old when Maia came back, so it was probably in the eighteenth year of the City, eight years or so after the Last Debate. My parents lived in the house called Thessaly that had once belonged to Sokrates. It was an extremely inconvenient house for a family, as are all the houses of the Remnant. There are enormous eating halls and public buildings, and little sleeping houses designed for seven people to sleep in. There were eight of us, but that wasn't the problem; the problem was that there wasn't room for anything but sleeping and washing and sitting in the garden debating philosophy. Mother

had built a partition down the middle so that she and Father
and I slept on one side and the boys slept on the other. I remember our three little beds all in a row, mine under the window.

One night, long after I had fallen asleep, I was wakened by a
scratch at the door. Father went and opened it, and there was
Maia, carrying a big book. I didn't know Maia then, of course.
Mother was awake, and she went at once to Maia and hugged
her, so I knew it was all right. The three of them went out into
the garden, so as not to wake the boys, and as I was awake and
curious I followed after. We all sat on the grass. I don't really
remember the conversation, though I do remember Mother looking at the Botticelli book Maia had brought, and which I later
came to know and love. I probably couldn't understand all the
words they used, but I knew that Maia had left some other city
and come back to ours, and she had just arrived that night. It
shows how peaceful everything was then that she could do that.
She was probably about forty at the time, and she had come
alone, unarmed and unchallenged, halfway across the island, ar-
riving after dark. The gates were guarded, but she had come in
simply by saying she wanted to. The guards knew her, of course,
because pretty much everyone knew everyone. That was before
the art raids started, and it was the art raids that spoiled everything and led to the present lamentable state of affairs.

I remember sitting on the rough grass in the moonlight, looking at Maia as she talked to my parents. They knew her well,
but I found her fascinating because she was a complete stranger.
There were very few complete strangers in my world in those
days. I remember noticing how white her skin was in the moonlight, whiter even than Father's. Her pale hair was braided and
the braid was pinned up around her head.

"I thought you were all for women's rights," Mother said.

"And don't women have rights here these days, Simmea?" Maia
asked. "Or have I come to Psyche by mistake? Women's rights

are certainly why I went there. But I couldn't stay in the City of Amazons."

I don't remember if she explained why she had come, if they discussed the New Concordance or Ikaros. I only remember the colors and shapes of the three of them under the lemon tree in the moonlight, and the smell of the autumn night with rain coming on the wind.

Maia had been one of the Masters of Florentia, with Ficino, and with Ficino she became one of my teachers. There are three distinct generations in the city. The Masters were those who prayed to Athene to let them help set up Plato's Republic. They were all grown up when they came here, and some of them were old. Ficino was old—sixty-six when he came, he says, and he's ninety-eight now, though he's in better condition than a lot of the younger Masters. He says it's from eating a good diet and not letting his mind atrophy. Maia was only about twenty, so she's about fifty now. (I dared Kallikles to ask her exact age once, and she offered to box his ears for the impertinence.) Most of the Masters are somewhere in between, though a number of the older ones have died, of course.

Then there's my parents' generation, known as the Children. They are all the same age, with very little variation. They were all about ten years old when they came, though some of them were nine or eleven. They're all thirty-eight now, with that same slight range of variation.

Last comes my generation, the Children's children, whom we call the Young Ones. Our ages range between twenty-one and newborn, though far more of us are between twenty-one and nineteen—when they were holding Festivals of Hera three times a year, a lot of babies were born. After that, it wasn't organized, and people had to sort things out for themselves. There are other Young Ones my age and younger, but there aren't great cohorts of us, as there are of my brothers' age and the Children.

I suppose the babies starting to be born now to the oldest of the Young Ones are a fourth generation. I don't know what they'll be called. Do they name generations, elsewhere? I haven't run across it in my reading. Cicero was older than Caelius and Milo and Clodius, but there wasn't a hard line. It would be like us younger Young Ones, I suppose, with overlap and people of all ages. Odd.

I don't plan to have children myself. Partly it's because the whole sex thing seems so awkward and complicated, and partly it's because I am Apollo's daughter, and what would my children be? Quarter-deities? But mostly it's because there isn't any posterity for us. They, or their descendants, would only be born to die when the volcano destroys us all. I suppose I could flee to the mainland like Kebes, and have children there whose genes could join the human mainstream, but there doesn't seem to be much point. What kind of a life would it be, without books or debate, at a Bronze-Age tech level? It's bad enough here when things break down and we have to do everything by hand. Maia says the Workers gave them freedom they didn't appreciate at the time, and that philosophy is harder when you're cold and hungry. What kind of life would it be for children in Mycenaean Greece? Especially as half of them would, statistically, be girls? I'm looking forward to seeing it, but I wouldn't like to live there. So I don't plan on having children. That doesn't mean I'll necessarily lead a celibate life, though I have so far, because there's a plant called silphium that prevents conception, and Mother told me all about it when my menses started.

I suppose it's unusual that my father is a god, and I should write about that. I don't know what to say though, because I've known about it all my life, and take it for granted. I don't know what it would be like to have any other kind of father. It's a secret from most people in the City, though. I used to wonder how it was they didn't guess, but it isn't all that obvious really. Father doesn't have his divine abilities, and while everyone can see how intelligent and musical and athletic he is, they tend to see him as just an exceptional success of Plato's methods. Some people don't like him and think that he's arrogant, but in general, everyone recognizes and admires his excellence. I think it helps that they see Father and Mother together—people have a tendency to see them and speak about them as Pytheas-and-Simmea, as if they were one thing. So they wouldn't think about Father's excellences without thinking about Mother's too. Lots of people in the City, and especially the Masters, tend to see my parents as the closest thing we yet have to Philosopher Kings, as the proof of the success of Plato's methods. It's a lot for me to live up to. Sometimes I feel squeezed by the pressure of expectations.

Ficino's wrong. I've written all of this already and I haven't even got up to where I thought I'd really start, with the day my mother died.

3

ARETE

I ate lunch in Florentia that day. It is an eating hall, as it had always been. When my parents were young and there were plenty of Workers, humans didn't need to do anything in Florentia except take their turn to serve the food one day a month. Now there are rotas for preparation and cooking and cleaning up, and I, along with everyone else who eats there, have to do one of those things every few days. The food is usually good. It was porridge and goat cheese and nuts and raisins that day. Neither of my parents were there, which wasn't unusual. I came in from the palaestra with my friends Boas and Archimedes. We were all exactly the same age, and were training together to pass our adulthood tests in five months' time, when we'd all turn sixteen.

We sat down to eat with Baukis and Ficino. Baukis is three months younger than the rest of us, and she's a friend. Since Krito died, Ficino is the oldest and most generally respected person in the entire city. He's pretty much always in Florentia. He sleeps upstairs and spends most of his days either sitting in the hall talking to people, or teaching in one of the nearby rooms. He seldom leaves Florentia now except to go to the library. He'd been tutoring Baukis while the rest of us were in the palaestra. Boas and Archimedes ate quickly and then went off to work, and my brother Phaedrus joined us. This was awkward and uncomfortable because Baukis started flirting with him, though he's four years older than we are. After a while they left together to look something up in the library, both acting so stupid and coy that I felt myself squirming as I finished my nuts.

"It's quite natural," Ficino said.

I looked at him inquiringly.

"Girls mature faster, and so they are naturally attracted to men a few years older. It's normal. It just seems strange to you because we have had such fixed cohorts that it hasn't been possible until now." Ficino cracked a hazelnut and popped it into his mouth. He had a face not unlike a nut, wizened and brown.

I didn't at all want to talk to him about what girls were attracted to. "Why did you do it that way, then?"

"Plato," he said, and held up a warning hand when he saw me open my mouth to protest. "Plato said to begin with ten-year-olds, and if you do that you will have a generation all the same age. It was one of those things that just happened that way. It was only ever intended to be for the first generation."

"It was only ever *intended* as a thought experiment," I said. Maia had told me that.

"Yes, but here it is, and you and I are living in it." Ficino grinned.

I swallowed the last of my porridge and gathered our plates together to take to the kitchen. "I should go. I have to learn my lines."

"Something Plato really wouldn't have approved of," Ficino said.

"I know. I've never properly understood why he hated drama so much."

"He thought it was bad for people to feel induced emotions, false emotions."

I sat down again. "But it's not. It can be cathartic—and it can be a way of learning about emotions."

"Plato didn't want people to learn those emotions. He wanted his ideal guardians to only understand honorable emotions." Ficino shook his head. "He had a very hopeful view of human nature, when you think about it."

I laughed. "He did if he thought jealousy and grief and anger could be excluded because we never saw *The Myrmidons*. I never saw any play until two years ago, unless you count the re-enactments of the *Symposium* on Plato's birthday, but I still felt all those things."

Ficino nodded. "But that's what he really thought, and so that's why we excluded drama. Or rather, since almost all of the original Masters were people who loved the art of the ancient world, and much of what survived was drama, we decided to keep drama in the library but not allow it to be acted. Reading it quietly, we thought, wouldn't have such an emotional effect."

"Why did you change your minds?" I asked. "Not that I'm not glad you did, because I'm really excited about playing Briseis at the Dionysia."

"We didn't change our minds. It was debated several times, and always decided against, until two years ago."

I was about to ask what happened two years ago, then I realized: the first cohort of Young Ones had become old enough to vote. "Are plays still banned in the other cities?"

"As far as I know they're allowed in Sokratea and the City of Amazons, but banned in Psyche and Athenia."

"And is there any difference in how philosophical people are?"

Ficino laughed. "How would you measure that?"

I opened my mouth to answer, but he held up his hand again.

"No, think about it. Write me a paper on it, either an essay or a dialogue, as you prefer."

I groaned, but only because it was work. It sounded like a really interesting question to think about. I also wanted to talk to other people about it, most especially Maia, and Simmea. I bade farewell to Ficino, gathered up the plates, and took them to the kitchen, thinking about it. How would you measure the general level of philosophy in a population—or even in an individual? There might be simple tests, like how many times books were checked out of the library, but that would only show how many people were studying philosophy, not how philosophical they were. It wasn't my turn to clean up, but they were short-handed so I helped for a while, still thinking about it. Some people were naturally philosophical. Others were not. That's why everyone was divided into their rightful metals, gold and silver and bronze and iron. My friend Erinna said she was glad to be a silver, relieved and pleased.

How philosophical a city was could be simply measured by how many golds it had, except that originally in the City (and even now in Psyche and Athenia) the proportions were worked out numerologically rather than justly. That had been one of the more telling points Sokrates made in the Last Debate. But in Psyche and Athenia they believed that numerology was magical, that numbers described true Forms underlying the world. And Father said he didn't know whether they did or not, and Mother said they had an inner logic and so perhaps they did, but not the way that Proclus and Plotinus wrote.

I hadn't read the *Republic* yet, but Ficino had told us Plato said that a Just City would hold justice and the pursuit of excellence as the highest good. He said that as such a city declined, it would become a timarchy, meaning that the citizens would prize honor above justice. Sparta had been a timarchy, and Plato thought it better than oligarchy, the next stage of decline, where the citizens would prize money and possessions above honor. I wondered what the signs of starting to prize honor above wisdom and justice might be, and how that could be measured.

I went home after the kitchen cleanup was done. I didn't have any work scheduled that day, and I had a calculus class later that afternoon. Mother was teaching it, so it was held in the garden of Thessaly. I knew I had a good hour before the class, and that Mother might be home but nobody else would. I wanted to tell her about being chosen to play Briseis, and I wanted to ask her about ways of measuring levels of philosophy. She wasn't home, but that meant I had the house to myself until everyone arrived for the class, which was good because I had to learn my lines. *The Myrmidons* was to be performed at the Dionysia in just over a month. I had only been given the part that morning, and I was full of the glory of it. I was thrilled to be given a part this year, especially such a good part. I wanted to know all my lines before the first rehearsal and be the best Briseis possible.

I took the book out into the garden. We had a statue of Hermes that Sokrates had carved himself. I raised my hands in greeting to it as I always did. Then I lay down in the dappled shade of the tree, chin on my hands and book open on the ground. I started to work through my lines by brute force memorization, trying to concentrate on the words and not the meanings, and certainly not letting myself be distracted by the thought of what I'd be wearing and how I'd manage my hair, which had to be loosened in mourning disarray for the end of the play. I read each line and then shut my eyes and repeated the words to myself. I was so glad I looked like Father and not like Mother, or I'd never have been chosen for the part of a beautiful woman, even though of course I'd be wearing a mask. I wondered what the mask would look like. "Son of Thetis," I repeated to myself. I opened my eyes to read the next line and saw Father before me, looking absolutely devastated.

I am not using that word lightly. Father's face looked like a city that had been sacked and the fields sown with salt. He has a highly expressive face, the kind of face you see on statues of gods and heroes. Now you could have used it as a study for Niobe or grieving Orpheus. It wasn't just that he had been weeping.

He wept quite easily; I'd often seen him with tears in his eyes at something especially moving. Mother used to tease him about it a little sometimes—she'd say she could tell him a story about a child finding a lost goat and he'd tear up. But now his face was ravaged. I'd never seen anything like it. I sat up at once, closing the book. "What's wrong?" I asked.

"Simmea," he managed to say before he broke down again, and so I knew.

"Mother? Dead? How?" Having thought of Orpheus, my imagination went immediately to Euridike and the snake in the grass.

Father sat down beside me and put his arm around me in the most awkward, tentative way imaginable, as if he didn't know how hard to squeeze, or was afraid of breaking me. "Art raid," he said.

I wanted to cry, I wanted to fling myself on his chest and be held and comforted, but the openness of his grief made mine close up somehow. I felt it as a gulf inside myself, but I didn't cry. An art raid. She had been killed by human greed and folly. And she had despised the art raids. "Instead of raiding each other for art, we should be making more," she had said.

"I couldn't save her, she wouldn't let me," he choked out.

"She wouldn't let you?" I echoed. "Why not?"

"Can you think of any reason? I can't," he said.

I sat there in the awkward circle of his arm and tried to think. "*Could* you have saved her?"

"Easily, if I'd had my powers. And I could have had them before she was dead. I'd have been back in a moment."

I shook my head. "She must have had a good reason." I was only just starting to take it in that she was dead, that she wouldn't be coming in soon to teach the calculus class, that I'd never be able to tell her I'd be Briseis. On that thought I started to cry sudden hot tears. I hadn't really understood even then. I hadn't started to think about the long term. I hadn't even got any further than that afternoon.

Mother and I had fought about all kinds of things, mostly when she thought I wasn't working hard enough, or when I forgot to do things. She could be impossibly sanctimonious and stiff-necked. She never let me get away with sliding along as my friends sometimes did; she wanted me trying my hardest every moment. But we'd been the only women in a household of men, and even when she drove me mad with irritation she was still Mother. I loved her and knew she loved me. If she had no patience with irrationality, she would always listen to reason, and sometimes change her mind. "She was a philosopher," I said.

"She was," Father agreed. "She was a Philosopher King, she was what Plato wanted to produce, the ultimate aim of his Republic. And she was killed in a silly fight for the head of Victory."

"The head of Victory?" I asked, and then I realized what he meant, the statue in the shrine outside the south gates. She was killed trying to stop the raiders from stealing the head of Victory. It sounded almost too symbolic to be true.

"We don't know who it was, but Klymene thinks it might be Kebes."

"Kebes? The Goodness Group?" I pulled away from his arm, which wasn't giving me any comfort anyway, and leaned against the tree where I could see his face. "They've never taken part in an art raid before."

"They've never had any communication with us since they left," Father agreed.

"It was probably Psyche. Or the Amazons." They were the two that raided us for art most frequently. It had been the Council of Psyche who had started the whole thing by demanding that the art be shared out equally to all the cities in proportion to their population. Some of us had wished ever since that we'd just agreed there and then. Plato had set out rules for warfare, but he only ever imagined one Just City, not five of them squabbling over a pile of sculpture.

"Klymene said the *Goodness* had been seen. And she said she didn't recognize anyone."

I shook my head. "I never heard that Kebes wanted art."

"Who knows what he wants? I never did. He broke a statue once, on purpose. He just wanted to get away, and to destroy the City if he could." Father's eyes came into focus. "I remember him sitting where you are sitting now and saying as much."

It was strange to think of Kebes as a real person my parents had known, and not a demon to be afraid of. He had left at the Last Debate, years before I was born. "Maybe—" I began to say, then stopped. I'd been going to say that maybe Mother would understand what Kebes wanted, and I had to face up to the fact that she might well, but she wouldn't be able to tell us.

Father wasn't all that good at knowing what people meant, but he seemed to guess that time. He started to cry again, tears streaming down his face. He was looking at me, but he seemed to be looking through me. "How am I going to manage the rest of my life without her, Arete?"

"I don't know," I said truthfully. I didn't even know how I was going to manage the rest of the day. I couldn't think how I was going to cope with Father being like this. Yes, he's the god Apollo, but that often makes it harder, not easier, not just for him but for all of us. He's not used to ordinary human things. I'm sure he must have lost people before, but the ways he'd coped with that as a god wouldn't be possible for him as a human. He couldn't create a new species of flower and call it after Mother, for instance. And normally when he was having problems that arose out of being human he'd ask Mother about it, and they'd have a fascinating conversation, and she'd help him understand how it worked, logically, and then he'd be all right. Now, without her—was I supposed to help him with it? The thought was terrifying. I wasn't all that good at being human myself yet. I was only fifteen. I didn't know enough about it. It wasn't fair. I wanted to grieve for my mother, not to have to worry about helping my father cope.

"Death is a terrible thing," he said.

"What do I have to do to not die?" I blurted. I'd often wondered about this, but never asked directly.

"Not die?"

"To become a god. I'm your daughter. I could." I hoped I didn't sound childish or hubristic. Fortunately, he took me seriously.

"You could. Several of my sons have." It sounded so strange to hear him mention sons and know he didn't mean my brothers. "You'd have to decide to do it, and you'd have to find your power, and you'd have to find a new and original way of being Arete. Being excellent, that is!" He was still weeping, but his eyes were focused on me now. "You'd still have to die. If you became a god it would happen afterward."

"But you have a body when you're a god?"

"Yes, but it's not the same as a mortal body. Nothing's the same. I'll have to die to get back to being a god. It's the only way. What you should do, if you want to be a god, is to find something to be responsible for, something you can take charge of. That's what my sons who are gods did. It could be something that no god cares about now, or it could be something of mine that I'd devolve onto you. It would have to be something that needed a patron, something you cared about. And then after you died, instead of going on to Hades your soul would go to Olympos and you'd become a god. But you might prefer to stay mortal and go on to have new lives. You get to start again and forget. And there are things humans can do that gods can't—humans can do whatever they can, but we're bound by Father's edicts—or, if we break them, we are subject to punishment. There's a lot to be said for being mortal . . . but it is also awful, I'll admit." He wiped his hand over his eyes and tried to smile. "I would still grieve if I were my proper self, but it wouldn't swallow me up this way."

"If it's awful for you when you know what happens after death, think how awful it is for everyone who doesn't know!"

"I have thought about that a lot, since I talked to Sokrates and Simmea about it, and of course since Athene admitted it to everyone at the Last Debate." He looked at different spots in the garden, as if he could see where they had sat for that conversation. "But while it might be better for individual people to know, it's better for the world for people not to be sure."

"If people knew for sure that they had immortal souls, and that they needed to pursue—" I stopped, because I heard a sound from inside. I thought it was probably the other students come for the calculus class, and I'd have to tell them that Mother wasn't here and the calculus class was canceled not just for today but for always. There wasn't anyone who could take it over, either, not that I could think of.

But it wasn't a student who came out, it was my brother Neleus. He looked almost as bad as Father. His face seemed entirely bloodless. I was delighted to see him—anything to relieve the burden of being alone with Father in this state. I got up and hugged him tightly. "You know?"

"Sophoniba told me," he said. "An art raid."

"Nobody knows who," Father said, without moving from where he sat, staring at the space by the tree where I had been.

Neleus looked down at him and shook his head. "What are you two doing sitting in the garden? We need to find the others, and we need to get drunk."

"Is that what people do?" Father asked.

"Yes," Neleus said firmly. "That's what people do, and it's what we shall do. Come on, let's go to Florentia. Ficino will be there, and they always have wine and won't grudge it to us. I asked Sophoniba to find the others and send them there, and all of Mother's especial friends. We'll gather there and drink and talk about her. Come on."

Father got up slowly. "All right," he said. "If that's what people do."

So that's what we did.

4

MAIA

I am a teacher. I have also worked as a midwife to babies and cities, but it is on teaching that I have spent most of my life. I have the temperament of a scholar. I always have had.

In the years after the Last Debate I had cause to regret a lot of things I had done in the name of Plato, but I never regretted that we had made the attempt to create the Just City. I agree with a lot of the criticisms that have been made of us, of the Masters. Buying slave children was wrong. I always thought so. I should have been more forceful in my opposition. In those days I was young, and too easily cowed by male authority. I grew up in England in the 1850s. It wasn't until I saw the girls who grew up in the Just City that I really understood what free women could be like. That in itself justifies us in what we did, in my eyes— how marvelous they are, their natural assumption of equality. What was a hypothesis to me is an axiom to them. Only Plato in all the thousands of years between his time and my own saw that women could have philosophical souls, only Plato allowed that we were people. Only in the City were women truly liberated, for the first time in history.

All the same, we Masters did and allowed things that were wrong, and I am as guilty as any of us. These days I defer to those whose authority I respect, but I try not to automatically defer to anyone. I accept my share of the guilt for what we did, but I still say that what we tried to achieve was a noble goal, and what we did achieve was wonderful, even if it fell short of perfection. There is no perfection in human things, only in the world of Forms. We tried our best. Our intentions were good.

They don't allow Masters in Sokratea. I suppose they're justified, but I am hurt whenever I think of it. We, and Plato, meant nothing but the best for them! And when I say the best I mean it literally; what we wanted for them was nothing but excellence, virtue, arete. They say you can't want that for somebody else, they have to want it for themselves. Well, perhaps they have a point. But Plato wrote that seeking to increase someone else's excellence is the best form of love. We loved them and we sought their excellence; and if the means were not always ideal, then I contend that we were limited by the constraints of reality. Though Athene, of course, was not.

She turned Sokrates into a fly and vanished, and Sokrates too flew off and vanished, so we had to manage as best we could without either of them.

In the many debates that followed the Last Debate there were more voices crying for going than staying. Trying to fix the City we had seemed less appealing to many than trying to start again, this time with like-minded volunteers. Athenia wanted to do everything exactly the same, only more strictly. Having seen some of the pain caused by being strict, this had very little appeal for me. Sokratea, as I said, excluded Masters from the beginning, when it was only a group of hot-headed children headed by Patroklus. Kebes, with what we came to call the Goodness Group, left immediately that first afternoon, without participating in any of the subsequent debates. That left the Remnant City, which felt at first like a patched-up compromise, and Psyche, and the City of Amazons.

It was Psyche that drove me to the Amazons. Psyche, the city

the Neoplatonists set up, decided to manage without the difficult requirement of allowing women to be full participants in
their city and in the life of the mind. They made women second-
class citizens, as they usually have been, historically. It's amazing to me that any women at all agreed to move there. Psyche is
the smallest of the cities even now, and disproportionately male.
But some women went willingly—and I know it was willingly,
because I argued with them, personally and at length. Some of
my girls from Florentia chose Psyche of their own will. It was
those debates that drove me to the other extreme and the choice
of the City of Amazons—those debates, and the necessity for
them. There were women trained in logic who were prepared
to argue that they didn't deserve citizenship, and that they were
inferior to men.

I know Ficino felt the same way about me leaving the Remnant as I felt about Andromeda and the others who chose Psyche.
He was almost in tears, arguing with me at one point. But in the
end he respected my decision, as I respected his to stay.

The other, less worthy reason I made the choice to go is that
all of my close friends except Ficino were going: Axiothea, and
Klio, and Lysias, and Kreusa. I went despite Ikaros, not because
of him.

I have written already about how Ikaros raped me when I was
young and naive. I had been sheltered and protected all my life
until I came to the city, and I had no instinct for self-preservation.
I went off alone with Ikaros, seeking answers to questions, with
no idea that he imagined this was a sexual tryst. (It's hard to
believe I was ever so stupid.) I saw him as a man from the ro-
mantic and wonderful Renaissance, and I did not consider what
that really meant. He had read Plato and loved the idea of the
Republic, and he was prepared to concede that women had the
philosophic nature. That didn't mean he had entirely put away
the appetites and expectations of his own era. He thought my

protests were conventional. He thought I was saying no because society allowed me to enjoy sex only if it was forced on me in circumstances beyond my control. He believed I wanted it, even when I screamed and fought. He was confused, afterward. He tried to make amends. He gave me a book. I remained furious with him—for raping me, and for continuing to act as though he had done nothing. Others adored him, but I kept away from him as much as I could. I didn't trust him, and I found it harder to trust any men because of him.

I spent eight years in the City of Amazons.

At first it was two thousand people camped out in the fields on the north side of the island. Building the physical city was a challenge. Klio persuaded Crocus to help us. Crocus was one of the two remaining worker-robots. In the debates that followed the Last Debate, both Workers had considered Sokratea, but decided to stay in the Remnant. They had good solid philosophical reasons, but also practical ones—they needed electricity as we needed food, and designing and installing electrical generators elsewhere would be a challenge.

Crocus quarried marble for us and delivered it to the site of the new city, and then we humans wrestled the slabs into roads and assembled the blocks into buildings. Crocus helped—what was difficult for even the strongest of us was trivially easy for him. We built one wall while he built the other three and put on the roof. He cut marble pipes and installed plumbing. We assembled ourselves into teams and tried to learn skills from him and from each other. We did as much as we could. As there were two thousand of us and one of him, in the end more of Amazonia was built by humans than by Crocus, but I don't know how we could have possibly managed without him. We voted him full privileges of citizenship including voting rights, although he never became a resident. We inscribed his name among the list of founders. There is also a bas-relief of him above the main gate, carved by Ardeia.

He returned to the Remnant every night to rest and recharge, while the rest of us planned the city and the work for the next day. We did our planning in the dark. We had all grown used to electric lights in the time we had been in the City, and we missed them. Our old Tech Committee was almost all there, and we assembled to try to deal with problems.

"We need to find a way of having light," Lysias said. "They have refused to let us have any of the solar lights, so we need a proper alternative. What did people use?" Lysias came from the twenty-first century and so, like the Children, he had grown up with electricity.

"Gas lights," I said. "Gas was made from coal in some way. I've no idea how."

"Nobody will know, and there won't be any books on it," Lysias said, savagely. "I don't think there's any coal on the island anyway. What else?"

"Oil lamps," Axiothea said, a calm voice in the darkness. "We have olive oil. We can make glass, or if we can't we can make clay lamps like the Romans had. I wonder what wicks are made out of?"

"If the Romans had them, somebody might know, or it might be written down somewhere," Lysias said, sounding a little more cheerful. "Did they give enough light?"

"Enough to read and work by," I said. "And there are also candles, made from beeswax or tallow. Wicks were made from cotton in my time, which we don't have, but I expect linen would do just as well."

"Candles, of course," Klio said.

"They're just decorative," Lysias protested. "Not that I wouldn't appreciate having one right now."

"Lamps are more effective," I said. I had lived with electricity long enough that it was easy for me to understand how in future ages, candles could have come to be thought of as nothing but decoration.

"Yes, I've heard of things smelling of the lamp, meaning people were up late working on them," Klio said. "And burning midnight oil. So it must give enough light for people to work. We can't make glass, but Crocus can. Except I don't want to impose on his good nature to ask him to do even more for us. There's not much we can do for him in return—only discuss philosophy and read to him, and there are plenty of people in all the cities happy to do that."

"Books," Lysias said. "That's another tech issue we should discuss. We can use the libraries in the Remnant, they've agreed we can. But can we use their printing presses? We should have our own library here. The City Planning Committee have assigned it a place. But should we be building a printing press? Do we have anyone who can set type?"

"And should we be duplicating everything so we have it to hand and don't have to walk ten miles every time we want to look something up?" I asked.

"And if we have only one press, should it be Greek or Latin?" Klio asked.

"It doesn't matter, we melt all the type regularly and recast it—it's only lead." I said. "We'd have to have both sets of molds, but we could print in either language, switching when the type got worn." I had always enjoyed working with the presses.

"Good!" Lysias said, relieved.

When we had set up the original city, most of the tech questions had been philosophical—we had to decide what we wanted to do and what was the best way to achieve it. We had the practical means, unlimited Worker resources, and the presence of Athene to give us divine intervention as needed. We didn't realize what a luxury these things had been until we had to manage without them. Now the problems were almost all practical, and the answers were almost all things we didn't like.

We made the most urgent decisions, and had drinking-fountains and latrine-fountains and wash-fountains enough for everyone, and fields prepared for animals and crops, and shelter from the elements before the first winter came. During that winter we began to manufacture lamps. We had a skilled potter, one of the Children from Ferrara, a girl called Iris. She made the bases, and Kreusa, of all people, knew how to make wicks from flax and instructed others. Crocus was still helping us finish off the city, and it fell to me to ask him if he would make us some clear glass bowls for the lamps.

It was raining. Crocus was putting a roof onto the hall in the southwest corner that was destined for our library. Some of us had, through practice, become quite skilled at masonry, but roofing was still a real challenge. "Joy to you, Crocus," I said.

He stopped work and turned one of his hands to carve "Joy to you Maia!" into one of the damp marble blocks of the library wall. As was his custom, he carved the Greek words in Latin letters, which always looked peculiar.

I beckoned him over to where he could carve his responses in the paving stones of the street outside, some of which already bore his side of dialogues, sadly more practical and less philosophical than those that still lined the walks of the Remnant City. I asked him about the glass globes. "Can make," he inscribed tersely. "How many?"

There were over two thousand of us Amazons, and we all desperately wanted light at night. We were used to it and hated doing without it. Some people had slunk back to the Remnant already for this reason, but most of us were made of sterner stuff. Everyone would want one. "Two thousand five hundred," I said.

"In return?" he carved.

"What do you want?" I asked. How easily it turned to this, I thought, to trade and barter.

"Thomas Aquinas," he carved.

"We don't have it," I said, surprised. "We don't have any Christian apologetics. We didn't bring them. You know we didn't. We'll read you anything we have."

"Ikaros owns forbidden books," he carved.

"He does? How do you know?"

Crocus just sat there in the fine drizzle, huge, golden, mud-spattered. I'd say he was looking at me, but he didn't give any impression of having eyes or a head. With a shock of guilt I remembered my Botticelli book, full of forbidden reproductions of Madonnas and angels, with text in English. Of course. Ikaros had given it to me. What else might he have brought here?

"If he has it, then yes," I said.

"Thomas Aquinas. In Greek," Crocus wrote.

"If Ikaros has it, I'll make him agree to translate it and read it to you," I said. "If not, we'll read you something else you want."

"Display sculpture," he inscribed.

"What? I don't understand."

"I make sculpture, for display in Amazon plaza."

"Oh Crocus, but we'd love that. You don't have to ask that as a favor. We'd regard it as an honor."

"Will make bowls for lamps," Crocus inscribed. He waited politely for a moment to see if I had anything else to say, then went back to his half-finished library roof. And there was his half of the dialogue, there in the marble for anyone to read. "Thomas Aquinas. Ikaros owns forbidden books." Ikaros was no friend of mine. But I felt the urge to protect him nevertheless. No good could come of everyone knowing he had forbidden books. I took a piece of heavy wood from an unfinished house nearby and used it as a crowbar to pry up the heavy marble paving stone. Then I flipped it over so that the carving was on the underside and set it back in place. It was earth-stained and filthy compared to the other flags, but I hoped the rain would soon wash it clean. I went off to find Ikaros.

I wanted to talk to him in private, but I wasn't the stupid young girl who had gone off to the woods alone with him, unconscious of anything but my own burning desire for philosophical conversation. I was over thirty now. I sought Klio about the city. She knew about my Botticelli book, and about the rape. She was pressing olives with a crowd of Children and couldn't come immediately. She agreed to talk to Ikaros with me after dinner.

As luck would have it, I ran into him a few minutes later in the street. He was alone, coming toward me. It was raining more heavily now and my braid was so wet it was coming down from where it was bound up around my head. "I need to ask you something," I said.

"Come inside," he said, opening the door of a nearby house. "This is going to be Ardeia and Diomedes's house."

The house was complete, and held a large bed. "I don't want to go inside there with you," I said.

Ikaros rolled his eyes, half-smiling. "You're not as irresistible as you imagine," he said. "I have quite enough going with Lukretia." Lukretia was a woman of the Renaissance. She had been the other master of Ferrara, and now she and Ikaros were sharing a house here. "But stand in the rain if you prefer. I shall keep dry." He stepped inside, and I stood in the doorway, in view of anyone passing by. "Which of us are you afraid of, you or me?" he asked.

"I have quite enough going with Lysias," I snapped. The trouble was that there was some truth in his accusation. I had always found Ikaros powerfully attractive. But that didn't mean

I wanted to be taken against my will, and he had shown me that he didn't care what I wanted.

"What do you want me for then?" He grinned, and I scowled at him.

"Crocus wants Thomas Aquinas. In Greek. And he says you have it."

Ikaros's face changed in an instant to completely serious, as serious as I had ever seen him.

"I wasn't going to do without books I needed," he muttered.

"You took them when you were rescuing art?" I asked.

"You know I did. I got you that Botticelli book. It was more than anyone could bear, all those printed books, right there to my hand. I bought them, I didn't steal them. And I didn't contaminate the City with them."

"Nobody says you did," I said, but I shook my head. "You think rules are for everyone but you. How did you get them without Athene knowing?"

He ignored my question. "I have done no harm with the books."

"You might be going to now. Who knows what Thomas Aquinas will do to Crocus?"

He grinned irrepressibly. "Have you read Thomas Aquinas?"

I shook my head. "I have never had the slightest interest in him, or anything else medieval. But I hear he's extremely complicated, and you are going to have to translate him into Greek and read it all aloud."

He looked horrified. "Do you know how long it is?"

"No," I said, crisply. "Long, I hope. It's what Crocus wants in return for making us glass bowls for lamps, and without them the lamps won't give enough light for reading and working. So I think you're going to do it, and as the book is still forbidden by the rules of this city as well as the original City, you're not going to have any help doing it. And I think that's going to be an appropriate punishment for bringing the book in the first place."

It might have been unkind, but I couldn't help laughing at the look on his face.

5

ARETE

For a long and terrible time, all that autumn and on into winter, Father insisted on getting vengeance for Mother and everybody else kept arguing with him because he clearly wasn't being rational.

"It's sad, and we're all extremely sorry, but you'd think from the way you're acting that we'd never lost anyone before," Maia said.

Father didn't say so to her, but the truth was that he'd never really lost anyone he cared about before, not lost them permanently the way he'd lost Mother. He said that to me and my brothers after Maia had left. He said it very seriously and as if he imagined that this would have been news to us.

"Who would have thought grief would crack Pytheas that way?" Ficino said to Maia, in Florentia, when he didn't know I was listening.

It was true, though I didn't want to acknowledge it. He was cracked, or at least cracking. It was a terrible thing to see. When he was alone with me he kept asking me if I could tell him why she'd stopped him saving her, and so I kept trying to think about that.

"Might she have been ready to go on to a new life?" I asked.

Father just groaned. After a moment he looked up. "She wasn't done with this life. There was so much we still could have done. Sixty more years before she was as old as Ficino is!"

"Well, might there be something she felt she had to do and could do better in another life?"

"What?" he asked, staring at me from red-rimmed eyes. I had no idea and just shook my head.

Embassies were sent under sacred truce to the other cities. None of them admitted responsibility for the raid, or that they had the head of Victory. This was unusual, but it wasn't unprecedented. They had lied before, on occasion. Only Father took it as proof that Kebes had stolen the head and killed Mother. The *Goodness* wasn't sighted again, and then winter closed in, with storms that made the sea dangerous. When Father proposed organizing a naval expedition to find and destroy Kebes's Lost City, even more people were sure he was cracked with grief. I wasn't old enough to go to the Chamber or the Assembly, but people were talking about it everywhere.

The worst of it was that I was having to deal with Father being like this while also trying to cope with my own grief. It was bad enough that Mother wasn't there to walk in and set everything right with a logical sensible explanation from first principles. But she *also* wasn't going to finish embroidering my kiton or trim my bangs or teach me how to integrate volumes. My throat ached because I wanted to talk to Mother about Ficino's project about assessing how philosophical cities were. But my grief, awful as it was to suffer, was cast into insignificance by the mythic scale of Father's grief. It was all like the first afternoon when he was crying so much that I couldn't cry at all. Her absence was like a presence, but Father's grief was like a huge sucking whirlpool that threatened to sweep everything up and carry it away.

Another thing that didn't help was that every one of the Children, my parents' whole generation, had lost their home and parents when they were ten years old. Compared to that, losing Mother when I was fifteen shouldn't have been anything to cry about. Only Maia seemed to understand. She took me for a walk along the cliffs and told me about losing her father, and how she had lost her whole world and her whole life with him, and all her books. "You still have your books," she said, encouragingly. "You can still read and study. Philosophy will help."

I thought about that. Reading did help, when it took me away from myself, when I had time to do it. But it was history I read, and poetry, and drama. Playing Briseis helped. It was a distraction. Philosophy required rigorous thought and didn't seem to help at all. It all seemed wrong, but refuting it was always hard work. I knew Maia, who definitely had one of Plato's philosophical souls, wouldn't understand that. But there was something philosophical I thought she might be able to answer. "Plato says that people shouldn't show their grief. It seems to me that Father is doing exactly what Plato says you shouldn't do."

Maia put her hand on my shoulder comfortingly. "It's hard to argue that he isn't! But you have to let Pytheas deal with his own grief while you deal with yours. He's a grown man, and you shouldn't be worrying about how he's grieving. Simmea wouldn't have wanted you to bottle it all up any more than she'd have wanted Pytheas to howl his out."

I stared away from her. Clouds were boiling up out of the east and the sea was the color of cold lava, flecked with little white wave-caps. It was hard to believe it was the same sea where I swam in summer, warm and blue. I could see the rocks where Mother and I had often pulled ourselves up to sit for a while before turning back, where I had first been introduced to dolphins. The sea was lashing them now, an angry note of black rock and white spray. The wind was cold and I was glad of my cloak. "It's so difficult," I said. "And I can't just ignore Father. But no ships can sail in this weather."

"Even Pytheas doesn't want to send out his expedition until spring," Maia said.

"I don't think she would have wanted vengeance," I said. I had tears in my eyes, but the cold wind carried them away to fall salt into the salt sea.

"I don't think so either, but I don't know how to convince Pytheas of that. He calls it justice, but it's vengeance he means. He just won't listen—he seems to listen and then he just goes on as if I hadn't said anything. I don't understand it. After my father died I didn't want revenge. But then, there wasn't anything to revenge myself on—he died of disease. If there had been something, maybe it would have been different. It's natural to grieve."

"But it's not natural to howl?"

Maia shook her head. "It may be natural, but it's not philosophical. And Simmea was a true philosopher. I miss her too." She hesitated. "I don't think any of us understood quite how much Pytheas needed her. This excessive grief doesn't seem like what I'd have expected of him. He has always been so calm."

My brothers were no help at all. They had their own grief, of course. "Why did I fight with her so much?" Kallikles asked rhetorically.

"I wish I'd told her how much I loved her," Phaedrus said.

"I keep wanting to tell her things, and then realizing she's not there to tell," Neleus said.

But none of them could really understand how I felt, or how Father felt. They all wanted to join his revenge, once he organized it. I did too. Wrestling and throwing weights in the palaestra gave me a temporary relief. I did feel sometimes that it might have made me feel better to go out with a spear and something clearly marked as an enemy to stick it into. But I knew enough philosophy already to know that it wouldn't help much. Mother would still be dead no matter how many enemies we sent down to Hades after her. And how could it be just to want vengeance, to return evil for evil?

Erinna was a great comfort, when she had time for me. She was nineteen, a silver, and she had real work to do, learning to sail the *Excellence* and fighting in the Platean troop. She was my friend, and she had loved Mother. She was lovely-looking, with olive skin and fair hair, which, since she had been assigned to the ship, she wore cut short on the nape of her neck but still curling up over her broad forehead. When she was free she listened to me talk and often did things with me to distract me. She even organized our calculus class into working on our own. Axiothea, one of the Masters from Amazonia, came over once to help us. Erinna was really kind to me during this time, and I treasured every moment I could spend with her. But she was frequently busy, and much in demand, and I didn't want to waste too much of her precious free time. And naturally, I couldn't explain to her about Father properly, because really explaining about Father would have meant talking about his true nature.

Erinna is the one who suggested that I should try to write an autobiography. She said that writing things down sometimes helped her to come to terms with them. She said that Mother had told her that, years before. Because it was her advice, and before that Mother's, I began it, and I found that like wrestling, it helped at the time. So I dealt with my grief by writing autobiography, working hard at the palaestra, and reading history.

The other person who really helped was Crocus. Crocus is a Worker, a robot, and he had been a close friend of Mother's. We had long ago worked out a way for the Workers to write in wax so there wasn't a permanent engraved record of every time they wished somebody joy, but he always carved what he wrote about Mother into the paving stones. He wanted to talk about debates they had shared, and he took me to the places where they'd had them. His responses were engraved into the marble, and it comforted us both when he engraved what Mother had said beside them, making them into full dialogues. He knew all about death and what happened to human souls—at least as much as anyone else. But he worried about his own soul, and Sixty-One's, and the souls of the Workers Athene had taken with her after the Last Debate. We had enough spare parts for Crocus and Sixty-One to last indefinitely, but he wondered whether he should want his soul to move on. He wondered if he would become a human or an animal or another Worker. He mused about why Plato never mentioned Workers. Crocus could always distract me from my own thoughts. Sometimes he would come into Florentia and join me and Ficino when we were debating.

He had built a number of statues—we called them colossi, because they were so immense. They combined hyperrealism— you could see all the hairs up Sokrates's nose in his *Last Debate*— with strange outbreaks of fantasy—in that same statue, one of Sokrates's eyes is already a fly's multifaceted eye. Parts of them were painted and parts of them were plain marble or other stone. He had decided to make a sculpture of Mother, but he hadn't decided where. We went together to look at various places in the city he thought might be appropriate. I know he tried to talk to Father about this too. But Father was too sunk in grief to give an opinion—though he did sensibly agree with me that having a colossus of Mother in the garden at Thessaly would be a bad idea.

One day when it was my turn to help cook dinner in Florentia, I came out to eat late and saw Maia and Aeschines sitting with Father and Phaedrus. I took my plate over to join them. Father wasn't crying at that moment, but his face still had that devastated look. Maia looked firm. Aeschines was looking troubled. He was one of the Children, and father of my friend Baukis.

He had been a good friend of Mother's, though not especially of Father's. Father found him slow. He was a member of the Chamber, and on a number of important committees.

"Nobody is going to agree to a voyage of vengeance," Maia was saying as I put my plate down.

Father looked up. "Arete. Joy to you."

"Joy," I echoed, though joy was the furthest thing from either of our voices.

"Joy to you, Arete," Aeschines said. "I haven't seen you in a long time. You must come and eat with me and Baukis in Ithaka one of these days."

"Joy, and thank you," I said. There was a fresco at Ithaka that Mother had painted when she'd been young. When Aeschines invited me, I was suddenly filled with a need to see it. She had painted it so long ago, and she had done better work since, as she always said. But I liked it, especially the way she had shown Odysseus in the harbor that was our own harbor. "I'll come one day soon," I promised.

"Baukis will be glad." He smiled at me in a friendly way, as if he genuinely liked me.

Meanwhile Father had turned back to Maia. "Maybe nobody wants a voyage of vengeance. But how about a voyage of exploration? It's ridiculous when you think about it, nonsensical for us to be here and know so little about what's out there right now. Finding Kebes would be an advantage, if we could, whether or not he's responsible for . . . for killing Simmea." His face crumpled up.

"Exploration, yes, maybe," Aeschines said, briskly. "But it would leave us without a ship here."

"What's the use of a ship that takes up so much maintenance but which nobody ever uses?" Father countered.

Aeschines nodded. "We use it for training, and visiting the other cities, but I do see your point. It would also mean a number of people wouldn't be here if we were attacked. I assume you'd want to take a troop?"

"I think so. It could be dangerous. And if we did find Kebes, well, we'd definitely need a troop. But we wouldn't be looking for danger or vengeance or anything. We'd just be trying to find out what was there. If that was Kebes, well . . ."

"What you're a lot more likely to find is a lot of Minoan and Mycenaean settlements," Maia said.

"Well, wouldn't it be useful to see if they're where they're listed as being in the Catalog of Ships?" Father asked.

"I want to come," my brother Phaedrus said. "I want to see something that isn't just this island."

"So do I," I said.

"You're much too young," Maia said.

"Too young for a voyage of vengeance, true," I said, choosing my words carefully. "I'm not yet an ephebe, I haven't taken up arms or been chosen for a metal. But I'm old enough to go on a voyage of exploration."

"Good point," Aeschines said. "Would this be a safe voyage of exploration, safe enough to take children, or would it be a dangerous voyage of vengeance?"

Father looked at me, then back at Aeschines. Before he could speak, Ficino came over to join us. He'd finished eating, but he had a cup of wine in his hand. The red hat he almost always wore was askew. "You all look very solemn," he said, after he'd greeted those of us he hadn't already seen that day.

"We're discussing sending out a voyage of exploration in the spring," Aeschines said. "Arete wants to go, and—"

"Splendid!" Ficino said, unexpectedly, beaming at me. "I want to go too."

"Old men and children," Phaedrus said dismissively.

Ficino laughed. "What better explorers could there be? How far will we go, Pytheas? Do you mean to get to Ithaka?"

Aeschines laughed, and Father actually smiled, for the first time in months. "I hadn't thought we'd go as far as that," he said. "Around the Kyklades, and north to the Ionian islands. Maybe touching the mainland at Mycenae."

"Mycenae!" Ficino said. "I really have been extraordinarily lucky all my life, and now to have this voyage proposed at the very end of it! How about Pylos? Nestor might be there as a young man. Or Troy itself? Imagine meeting the young Priam, perhaps attending his wedding to Hekabe." Maia reached over and straightened his hat.

"We know so much about the future, and so little about this time where we're living," I said. Ficino grinned at me.

"We want to find Kebes," Phaedrus said.

"Kebes is probably the least interesting thing in the whole Aegean," Ficino said. "Though no, it would be interesting to know what kind of city the Goodness Group have come up with, to compare it with the others."

"Kebes couldn't found a city without other people out there hearing rumors of it," I said.

"We have," Maia said.

"Well, but we're on an island, and we had divine help," Father said.

"Kebes may be on an island," Phaedrus said.

Father leaned forward. "He probably is. But he doesn't have enough people or enough resources to stay on an island and entirely out of contact. He must have been trading or raiding, and if he has, we'll hear about him."

"Also, we don't know whether or not there are rumors out there about us. If we're supposed to inspire the legend of Atlantis, there probably are," Aeschines said.

"I don't think Kebes was responsible for the raid," Maia said. "He's never been involved in art raids before, or contacted us at all. It doesn't make any sense."

Father looked stubborn. "Everyone else has denied it."

"They've lied before. Psyche have lied. They just can't be trusted," Maia insisted. "It probably was them. Or the Amazons."

Father hesitated for a moment. "How could we find out? Send spies?"

"Perhaps," Maia said. "But it will be sure to come out sooner or later. Whoever has the head will be sure to display it, eventually, and then we'll hear."

"And go to war," Phaedrus said, fiercely, slapping the table and making the cups and plates bounce.

"Unless it is Kebes," Father said. "Then we'd never hear and there would be no vengeance and . . . nothing. I want a voyage of exploration so we have more information."

"More information would be a good thing, certainly," Aeschines said. "I'll suggest it to the committee."

Ficino raised his cup. "It's my birthday. I'm ninety-nine years old. It seems the perfect time to set out on a voyage. To exploration!"

We all drank.

6

ARETE

I wasn't in the Chamber for the debate, or in the Assembly for the vote, but I was in Thessaly for the family fight.

It was just after the midwinter celebrations. It had been a mild clear day with a promise of spring in the air. The Assembly had voted that the voyage of exploration would take place when spring came, and now the question was of who was to go. Father was going, there was no question of that. Klymene was going with the Florentia troop. Erinna was going, as one of the few people who properly understood how the *Excellence* worked. And Ficino was going, and so was I—I had won that battle without any need to fight. This was to be a voyage safe for old men and children, and Ficino and I were the exemplary old man and child. That I was only a child for three more months didn't matter. I was going!

My brothers all wanted to go. Well, Plato-loving Alkibiades didn't. He had written to us—he had sent a letter to Father with the envoy who went to Athenia. Father let me read it. In addition to saying all you'd expect about Mother, he said to trust that the head of Victory wasn't in Athenia, and that he would let us know immediately if he heard anything. He sent love to all of us and said he had made the right choice and was happy.

Phaedrus and Neleus were at home in Thessaly on the evening when Kallikles came around with a jar of wine after dinner. "We need to talk," he said.

I broke the resin seal and mixed the wine without being asked, using the big red-figure krater decorated with Apollo killing the dragon Pytho, and the cups that matched it. (Apollo on the krater didn't look at all like Father, but I liked the coils of the snaky dragon.) I watered the wine half and half, as Plato recommends, and then gave a cup to everyone.

It was too cold to go into the garden now that the sun was down, which was inconvenient as it was the only space suitable for sitting and talking. There was a reason the houses were known as "sleeping houses." We were supposed to do everything else elsewhere. Most of the year this worked out well enough, and even now it would have been all right if we could have gone to Florentia or another eating hall to have our conversation in public. As it was, we all sat on the beds. I passed around some dried figs and goat cheese and missed Mother, who would have made the boys help.

"I want to go with you on the voyage," Kallikles said, once we were all settled. I sat down beside him on the bed.

"It isn't up to me," Father said. "The Chamber is deciding who goes. Apply to them." Father was looking a little better now that the voyage had been agreed on.

"We all want to go," Phaedrus said.

"You can't all go," Father said. "What if the ship went down?"

"What if it did?" Kallikles asked. "That's part of the hazard of life."

"All of you lost at once?" Father said. "No."

"The city wants to send the best," Phaedrus said. He grinned at me. He was constantly making jokes about my name—it was he who had first thought up the game of pursuing Arete. "And in addition to my little sister, the most excellent people they can find. We brothers are the certainly among the best of the Young Ones."

Father took a deep draught of his wine. "Arete's going," he said. "No more."

"The problem with that is that we're heroes," Kallikles said, spreading his hands. "You know we are. And this is a heroic mission, where we will have the chance to prove ourselves. It's like the voyage of the Argonauts. We all ought to have that chance. The Chamber gives us the chance, on our own excellence. If they turn us down, then they do. But if you speak against us they will turn us down."

Father shook his head. "Not all of you," he began, but wrathful Neleus interrupted.

"I insist on going, even though I'm not a hero!" He looked furiously at Kallikles.

We all looked at him. And suddenly I saw us all looking at him. It was strange. They were all my brothers, and I knew them well, Neleus among them, but now I saw them all with new eyes. Neleus sat alone on his bed, and we were all looking at him, and we were all one thing, and he was another. We all looked like Father, and he did not. We all had Father's calm blue eyes and chiseled features. We had all shades of skin color—or all the shades of the Middle Sea, as Maia put it: Kallikles's chalk pale, Father's olive, mine brown, and Phaedrus's near-black. We had hair that curled wildly and hair that lay flat as silk. Kallikles was short and Phaedrus was tall and I was a girl. We were an assorted set, but we were all Father's children, children of Apollo, of a god. We knew we were all heroes, and Neleus knew he was not. My father and my brothers looked coolly at Neleus, and I looked with them, ranged myself with them in that moment. I had to whether I wanted to or not. I was a hero. I could not make myself be like Neleus. I was human—we were all human. But we all had something else in addition, and Neleus did not, and we all knew it.

"It shouldn't make any difference," Neleus said, into that long silence. His voice wavered a little.

"It shouldn't," Phaedrus said, gently enough. "But you have to see that it does."

"You're not any better than I am," Neleus blazed.

Phaedrus lifted an eyebrow. "You know I am. I'm faster and stronger. We're exactly the same age but I haven't been able to wrestle with you in the palaestra since we were six."

"It's not fair!"

"It may not be fair, but it's the way it is," Kallikles said. He reached out a hand toward Neleus across the space between the beds, but Neleus ignored it.

"It's not your fault," Phaedrus said.

"Being heroes doesn't make you better people," Father said. He sounded immensely weary. "It might even make you worse. Knowing about it might. Simmea was afraid of that."

"What does it mean, exactly?" I asked.

"Arete, even you must see that this isn't the time for a Socratic debate clarifying terms!" Kallikles said, turning on me angrily.

"I don't see that at all," I said, keeping my voice even as Mother would have. "I think this would be a splendid time to discuss it properly. We all know we're heroes, except Neleus, sorry Neleus, but we don't know what that means in real and practical terms. We don't know what difference it can make."

Kallikles looked at Father, but Father was staring down at the blankets and said nothing.

"I'm going on the voyage," Neleus said, in a calm and decided tone. "I appreciate that you all despise me, but I am going. I have more right than anyone, and more need to prove myself than any of you. If the Chamber won't accept me for the voyage I'll stow away. I am her son. I am Simmea's only son, and I am going to avenge her."

I made a little sound when he said he was her only son, because why should gender matter so much? But then I stopped myself from protesting, because he needed to be special, and when it came down to it he wasn't a hero and I was.

There was another long silence. Then Father spoke. "Being a god made me worse at being a human being. She saw that. And she saw that being heroes might be a problem for you. And she was afraid that you would be unkind to Neleus because he isn't, and that he'd suffer from that." She had been right to worry about that, because we had been and he had. Father went on without hesitating, still looking down at the bed and not at any of us. "She thought that people needed more training to bring up children than we had had, but she understood that we had to bring you up and take responsibility for you. Most of the people with the training left after we voted to have families, and the rest were rushed off their feet."

Now he looked up, and it was Neleus he looked at. "You are indeed her only son. She loved you very much. It almost killed her soul having you. She hated to give you up. She was so glad to get you back! I remember it so well, when we first brought all of you here." He looked around the room, shaking his head at the memory. "She loved all of you, but Neleus was indeed her only son."

Then he looked at me, and I saw he must have been aware of the little noise of protest I made. "You are her only daughter, and the only child of her milk."

"What difference does milk make?" I asked, puzzled.

"All the difference in the world," he answered, as if he thought I should know this already. "Mothers give their milk to their children, and with it their strength and their stamina, their ability to survive disease. There's a bond in that milk."

"And I didn't have her milk?" Neleus asked in a small voice.

Phaedrus answered quickly. "You know you didn't. You've read what Plato says, no mother shall set eyes on her own child—they went to the nurseries when their breasts were full and fed some random child who was there." Phaedrus shook his head. "She might have fed me, but never you."

Everyone except me had read the *Republic*. Reading it was now part of the adulthood rite for our city.

"She fed you the night you were born, Neleus," Father said. "She told me so. But after that you were fed by any woman but your mother, and the same for the rest of you. No doubt Plato meant it to even out the advantages given by the milk, so that all could share with all."

"Plato was crazy on some subjects, and that was one of them," Kallikles said dismissively. "Father, where are you going with this line of argument?"

Father hesitated. "I don't remember." He looked over at Mother's bed, where Phaedrus was sitting, and then quickly away. Mother often used to be able to see when Father got ahead of himself and give him his next point. She had a way of laughing as she did it that I could almost hear. Father wiped his eyes with the corner of his kiton. "I just can't lose all of you as well as her."

"You'd be lost too," Phaedrus pointed out.

"I'd be back on Olympos, and you'd all be in Hades after having achieved very little in this life. You're heroes. Arete asked what that means. It doesn't mean anything if you don't live like heroes."

"I'm going," Neleus said, stubbornly. "I'm not a hero, but I am her son, and I am going on this voyage."

"We're all going," Kallikles said. "It won't be all of your sons,

Father. Alkibiades and Porphyry and Euklides would still be on the island even if the ship sinks. And how can we live as heroes if we don't get the chance to join the one heroic venture in our lifetimes so far?"

Father looked from one to the other of them, then he slowly set down his cup, got up, and went out of the street door.

"Where are you going?" Kallikles asked, but Father kept on walking and didn't answer.

"Where is he going?" Phaedrus asked.

Since nobody else was going to, I got up and followed Father. He was walking aimlessly south down the middle of the street. "Where are you going?" I asked.

"To visit the lion," he said.

I put my hand through his arm. "I'll come too." I knew the lion he meant. It was a bronze statue of a lion on a street corner near Florentia. Mother had been especially fond of it. One of my first memories was walking to visit the lion, one of my little hands held in each of my parents' big ones. We walked down briskly through the night's chill that made me wish for my cloak. Father felt warm, but then he always does. I don't know if it was his divine fire burning even in his mortal incarnation or just a natural warmth. We reached the lion, and he patted it the way Mother used to. I patted it too. The lion's face was very expressive, but it was hard to say just what it expressed. It seemed to change from time to time. Tonight the shadows made it seem worried. We turned around and walked back toward home.

It was a cold night and the stars were burning bright and clear, so distinct that I could see colors in some of them. "I can see all the stars in Orion's belt," I said.

"We'll go there one day," Father said.

I looked at him, startled. "You and me?"

"People," he clarified. "They'll settle planets out around those distant suns, one day, far ahead. I haven't been there yet. I'm always reluctant to leave the sun. But eventually I will, and you will too. I promised your mother I'd see her out there one day." He wiped his eyes.

"But what does it mean?" I asked. "She might be out there on another planet far in the future, but she won't remember us, or her life here."

"No," he agreed, sadly.

"And the civilization that settles the stars won't be our civilization. They won't have learned anything from this experiment, they won't know anything about the Just City except the legend of Atlantis in the *Timaeus* and *Critias*."

"Time is so vast—they probably wouldn't anyway," he said. But as he stared up at the stars he began to weep again. We walked on in silence.

"I had not meant this grief to unman me so," he said quietly, when we were getting close to Thessaly.

"It might be better on the ship. Here everything reminds us of her," I said.

"The boys are right. They are men, and heroes, and they have to act as they think best. I can't keep them children, or keep them safe."

"I'm going," I said, guessing where this conversation might be going. "The Chamber have approved me. I'm going!"

"Arete," he said, then stopped and began again in a different tone. "And you have to decide for yourself too. Equal significance means letting people make their own choices. But it's so difficult! Do you think she wanted me to learn this and that's why she stopped me?"

"It's possible," I said. And then I dared to say what I'd been thinking for a long time now. "She would want you to command your grief with philosophy."

"I know," he said, bleakly. "Oh yes, I do know that. I shouldn't be sad and I shouldn't indulge my grief. She is gone on to a better life. I should remember her and love the world for her. I know all that. I really do know it. But knowing it doesn't actually help at all when I want to talk to her so much my whole body aches."

"I know," I said. "I miss her every day."

"I wish I understood why she wouldn't let me heal her. It might all make more sense if I could understand that."

"I don't know," I said. I shivered.

"Come on, we should go in and tell the boys they can ask the Chamber if they can go on the voyage." He was trying to sound cheerful. "And we can have more wine. Arete—do you think revenge will actually help me feel better?"

"No," I said, surprised into honesty.

7

APOLLO

"How now shall I sing of you, though you are a worthy subject for song?" That's from the Homeric hymn to me—the same line is in both Homeric hymns to me actually, the Delphian and the Delian. Mortals find it intimidating to write about me, sometimes. It's as if they think I'll be listening over their shoulder. I find myself thinking it writing this, about Simmea and Sokrates, about Ficino and Maia and Pico. How shall I sing of you? I promised Father there would be songs.

There are already songs on Olympos about the sorrows and miseries of humanity and how badly people deal with death, and certainly there are songs enough about those subjects sung by mortals. I had felt grief myself often before. But this grief resisted being transmuted to art. You have to understand that transmuting emotion into art is what I do. It's one of the reasons I *like* emotions. But this emotion was bigger than I was. It's not that I didn't try to write songs for Simmea. I tried to write them, and for the first time my art failed me. I wrote songs, but they were pale thin things, they would not catch fire. They were true enough, but they left so much unsaid. I wanted vengeance, and yet at the same time as I struggled so desperately toward it I knew that revenge wasn't really what I wanted. I knew that art would come. It always had. The depth of this grief was different and unusual, and so would be the songs that came of it. Her name would live forever, as would her soul. That was the only way I could comfort myself, and it was thin comfort. Meanwhile, I was making an even poorer job of being a human being than usual. I was developing more sympathy for Achilles than I ever had before.

About a month after she died I decided to open her chest and sort out her belongings. She didn't have much—a winter cloak that doubled as a blanket, a pen and ink, some paints and brushes caught up in a scrappy paint-spattered rag, needles and thread, a scraper and a comb, another, finer comb with three broken teeth, a set of menstrual sponges. Underneath these things, all of which I had seen her use a million times and which seemed to miss the touch of her hands, was a pile of paper notebooks. I had seen her writing in them from time to time. "What are you doing?" I'd ask.

"Making notes," she'd reply, shutting the book and putting it away. They were small, the standard little notebooks the Workers had produced and which we continued to produce now with rather more effort. They had buff covers and were sewn together. I had never realized how many of them she had. I counted—twelve. If they were full and each held five thousand words, which would be about right, that was sixty thousand words she had written. I expected them to be notes, perhaps dialogues. They had her name on the covers, and under that they were numbered with Roman numerals. I wasn't sure how to read them—whether to glut myself on them all at once, or to save them. They represented something more of Simmea, which I had not expected. I was excited, and at the same time afraid of disappointment. I picked up the one labeled as number I and opened it and read.

"I was born in Amasta, a farming village near Alexandria, but I grew up in the Just City. My parents called me Lucia, after the saint, but Ficino renamed me Simmea, after the philosopher. Saint Lucy and Simmias of Thebes aid and defend me now!"

Whatever I had expected this was not it. I read the paragraph again. I had never known that her birth name was Lucia, nor guessed that she would have called on Saint Lucy. How little I had known her after all! But this was treasure, an autobiography. Many people in the city wrote one; there was a kind of fashion for them. Simmea had never told me she was writing one. I felt a little hurt, and yet still excited. She would be bound to talk about me. I could see our relationship from her perspective. It was the closest I could come now to talking to her. And yet I hesitated. Lucia, Saint Lucy—what if reading this proved I didn't know her after all? What if she didn't love me? But I knew she had. It was unquestionable. She had said once that she loved me like stones fall downward. I wanted to read her annals of our life together. I wouldn't be able to show it to anyone except our Young Ones, because she was sure to have revealed that I was Apollo. How well I remembered her discovering it, that day in the Temple of Asklepius. How angry she had made Athene! What terrible consequences that had had! And it was all my fault. Yet even so, even in all its consequences that included the metamorphosis of Sokrates and the collapse of the First Republic, I still smiled to remember how well she had dealt with discovering who I was.

I read that first paragraph again, and this time I went on. I was brought up short again reading her pondering whether it might have been a better path to happiness for her to have lived out her life in the Egyptian Delta. "No," I said aloud. I was astonished that she could even have considered that. Had I really known her? She had wanted, fiercely wanted, to be her best self, and surely her best self could only have been in this place and time?

I sat on her bed beside her chest, leaning back against the wall, and read the whole first notebook. When I read that she had said my name to Ficino in the slave market, I had to put the book down because I was sobbing too hard to go on. The first book brought her up to her arrival in the Just City and learning to read. Kebes was all through it, but she did not yet mention me as Pytheas. Every time I saw his name I felt a pang of jealousy. Kebes had known her name was Lucia—it didn't suit her at all. She was Simmea, the name was perfect for who she was. Lucia sounded soft and hesitant, while Simmea's mind had been like a surgical instrument. I remembered her smiling at me. Kebes was nothing. Matthias, she said his original name was. Well, he was gone. I didn't know whether or not to believe that he'd been responsible for the raid in which she had been killed. We hadn't heard anything from him for such a long time. Nobody knew where he was, or cared anything about him.

I took up the second notebook. I touched the letters of her name where she had written them in both alphabets. Simmea, not Lucia. I knew, with my rational self, that if I'd ever asked her what her childhood name had been she would have told me. That she never had showed how trivial it was, not how important. I turned the second book over in my hands. There were twelve books. If I read one a month they could last me a year, and for that long I could have a little more of her. If I had been my proper self that was what I would have done, one a month, or even one a year. But in mortal form, with emotions that pounded in my veins and clutched at my stomach, I could not bear the suspense of not knowing what she had written. I opened the second notebook.

It began with her learning to read, and to love Botticelli. It was far on into it before she mentioned me, and the time she taught me to swim. I was hurt that she had disliked me before she knew me, and then charmed by her description of that swimming lesson, which I remembered very well. I was surprised she was attracted to me so soon. The second book ended with our agreeing to be friends. I picked up the third, hesitated only for an instant, then opened it.

By the time Arete came to find out why I hadn't been in Florentia for dinner I had read all but the last volume, and was up to the conversation we had with the Workers outside Thessaly. I remembered that time so well; Sokrates, and the robots becoming entranced with philosophy, and Simmea discovering my true identity. It was so exciting. It had felt as if we could unravel all the Mysteries and remake the world. The words were still engraved in the paving stones outside, I walked on them every day. "Read. Write. Learn." And she belonged to the city and wanted it. And yes, she loved me, she saw me clearly and loved me. But I had always known that. I hadn't known she felt unworthy of me whether I was god or mortal. And I never doubted that what she wrote was the truth. She never said that she held the truth above me—she didn't need to. It was axiomatic to Simmea. That was the thing about her that was so hard to put into a song.

I went with Arete to Florentia and sat with Ficino as I ate porridge and fruit. He talked to me but I barely listened. My mind was with Sokrates and Simmea and a time that was twenty years gone. I missed that sense of infinite possibility, like a bud coming to flower. Everything after the Last Debate had been compromised. I wanted to go back and read the last notebook, even though I knew now that it would end before our life together, that I would never know more than I knew now of what she had thought of our Young Ones, never read about our one long-anticipated mating. I looked at Arete, the product of that one sexual act, who was eating grapes and talking to Ficino. I felt my eyes mist with tears. I had read about Simmea's matings with Aeschines and Phoenix and Nikias. I hoped the one time we had sex together had fulfilled her anticipations. I thought it had, and she said it had, but unless she had packed more into the last notebook than the others, I would never know for sure.

I wondered who she had written the notebooks for. Not for

me. I was fascinated to read them, but I wasn't their intended audience. Equally they were not for publication in the City and inclusion in the library, certainly not, because not only did she reveal the truth of my identity, but she explained things neither I not anybody else in the City would need to have explained. What audience had she imagined? They were written in lucid classical Greek. Who could read them? Anyone in classical antiquity and truly educated people for another millenium. I considered for a moment that once I was back in my true form, I could take them to Athens and leave them on Plato's doorstep. My mouth twisted. I wouldn't do it, but I was so tempted.

Phaedrus and Neleus were in Thessaly when Arete and I got back. I took the last notebook out of Simmea's chest and saw their interested glances. Before they could inquire, I removed all twelve notebooks and tucked them into the fold of my kiton. Our Young Ones were definitely not Simmea's audience for these, and I didn't want them reading them. Her thoughts and feelings and intimate experiences weren't for them. Arete was looking at me curiously. "Did your mother ever tell you her childhood name?" I asked her.

"No," she said. "Wasn't she always called Simmea?"

"Her parents called her Lucia," I said. "But she never used it after she came here."

"Lucia?" Neleus asked. "I never knew that."

"It isn't important," I said as I went out. I was glad I'd told them. I didn't want Kebes to be the only other person who knew it. Though Ficino would know it too, if he remembered. He probably didn't remember—not that his wits were wandering like poor old Adeimantus, but he couldn't possibly remember the original name every child had given him.

I took the notebooks to the library and sat in the window seat where Athene used to sit. It was dark outside, though the library was lit with electricity, and warmed with it as well. The library stayed at a constant temperature. Crocus and Sixty-One kept the electricity working now as they always had. They needed it themselves, of course. I wondered why Athene had left them when she took all the other Workers. She took the others to punish us, of course, to make us do without them and realize how difficult it would be. To live a life of the mind you need slaves or technology, and technology is unquestionably better. Now we compromised, eking out the technology we had and working ourselves half the time. It didn't leave us the leisure for philosophy we had before. A tired mind can't think as well. But nobody who enslaves another can be truly free.

But why had she left Crocus and Sixty-One? Was it because she felt they had betrayed her in becoming philosophers? But surely that was the purpose of the City? They were Sokrates's friends, and my friends now. Perhaps it was because those two had spoken up at the Last Debate, choosing the City? I didn't know what she was thinking. I wondered whether I ever had. Athene seemed very far away as I sat on her seat in the library. People constantly debated why she had set up the City. I thought I knew that—because it was interesting, and because she could. When it ceased to be interesting she had abandoned it. I had projects like that myself. My oracle at Delphi was one of them. It had seemed as if giving people good advice would help everyone get on better. I hadn't kidnapped people from across time to do it, but I had dragged a shipload of Cretans across the Aegean.

I looked at the last notebook, XII. Had she stopped after the Last Debate? Why? Twelve seemed an extremely round number—and Simmea had distrusted numerology and suspiciously round numbers. It wouldn't have been an accident. But it might be as far as she had reached. I'd seen her writing in notebooks fairly recently—it irked me that I couldn't remember when exactly. The book might not be finished. I opened it and checked. It was full.

I read everything she had written in the last notebook. Then I sat staring unseeingly at the bookshelves. She hadn't written about the Last Debate. She had written about the conversation we had in the Garden of Archimedes, which I remembered very well, and then about the last Festival of Hera, the one in which she'd been paired with Kebes. My fingers clenched into fists reading it. She had told me it hadn't been so bad. She said she didn't want to discuss it, and I hadn't pushed her about it. She had never told me that he had raped her, or I'd have killed him. I really would. I was ready to kill him now. She wrote that it wasn't rape, that she had consented, but I knew better. She had said no, and asked him to stop, and he had gone on. He had bruised her. She had gone there willingly, for the City, like the philosopher she was, and he had tried to take her into his fantasy.

I got up and paced the library furiously. I wanted to kill Kebes, now, immediately, with my bare hands, but I didn't know where he was. Simmea had written that I'd have been upset, but she had no idea how upset I would have been. I had learned what rape was, what it meant. I was also furious with Athene for pairing her with Kebes. It had been aimed at me, and I knew it, and Simmea knew it too. I would have killed him and left his body for the dogs and kites. He had tried to own her, and he had hurt her, my Simmea, my friend, my votary. She had told him I didn't try to own her, and she had told Sokrates that she and I wanted each other to be our best selves. It was true. Worship was easy, commonplace. Beautiful women were everywhere. People who understood what I was talking about and could argue with me as equals were incredibly rare. How could he have done that? And why didn't she tell me? Was it connected to the reason she had stopped me saving her life?

I was also furious that he had called her a scrawny, flat-faced, bucktoothed Copt. It was true, and she cared so little that she had laughed, but it galled me that he had dared to say it to her, to try to hurt her that way, through her looks. I always put up with Kebes because he was Simmea's friend, and all that time he had imagined he owned her, owned some imaginary person called Lucia. She was Simmea, Plato's Simmea, as Sokrates had said to her, as close to Plato's ideal Philosopher King as anyone was likely to get. She had never told me about that conversation either. She had told me about Sokrates's plan for what turned into the Last Debate, but not about the rest of what she had written, and how they had talked about the way they both loved me.

I missed Sokrates. Not the way I missed Simmea, as if half of myself had been amputated so that I was constantly reaching out with a missing limb. I hadn't entirely lost him, either; there were days of his life before he came to the City when I could still visit him, in Athens, once I was back to myself. But I missed being able to just talk openly with him. He would have had wise advice for this situation, and nobody else would. Nobody else could even understand it. There was nobody I could remotely imagine talking to about it, except Simmea and Sokrates, and I couldn't have either one of them. Sokrates had flown to me, after Athene had transformed him into a gadfly, and perched on my chest for a moment, then he had stung me and flown away, and nobody had seen him since.

I went back to Athene's window seat. Nobody was in sight. A few people had been in the stacks, but they had fled when they saw my face. (Even without far-shooting arrows rattling on my shoulder, my wrath can have that effect on people.) I sat down and opened Athene's secret compartment under the arm-rest. All I was thinking was of hiding Simmea's notebooks. I wasn't expecting anything to be there. Athene had been gone for almost twenty years. She'd had plenty of time to cover any traces she wanted to cover. But as I slid the notebooks in I felt that there was something there, stiff parchment, not paper. I pulled it out, curious.

It was a map of the Aegean, hand-drawn and colored, dolphins and triremes drawn in islandless spots on the lapis sea,
but with all the islands and coasts drawn accurately. Kallisti was
shown round, which meant it was a current map. The labeling
was in the beautiful Renaissance Greek calligraphy that everyone in the City had learned, along with the corresponding Italic
hand. Our city was marked, but not the other four cities on the
island. There were cities marked in other places, some of them
known to me, others strange. We didn't have any maps like this,
but anyone could have made it without too much trouble. We
had parchment, we had the tools for making illuminated man-
uscripts, we even had accurate maps.

The thing that surprised me was the circle marked in red ink
around a city on the northeastern edge of the island of Lesbos.
The handwriting was entirely different from the rest of the map,
it was a scrawl and nobody's neat penmanship. This was clearly
a later addition, drawn in after the map was made. "Goodness"
it said. The handwriting was immediately recognizable. It was
mine.

8

ARETE

There's nothing like the feeling of a ship under full sail. It's as if the ship is alive, every rope and piece of wood responding to the wind and the will of the sailor. It feels like magic when you are part of it. Before the voyage I had never been on any craft for more than a few hours. I'd learned the use of tiller and sail on the little fishing boats. I had been taken around the island on the *Excellence* twice, once a circumnavigation when I was quite young, with all the Young Ones my age, and once a year ago when Mother was going with an embassy to Sokratea and she took me with her. That was the trip where I'd really made friends with Erinna. Before that, she'd just been somebody my brothers' age who I saw around sometimes. On that trip we'd talked properly for the first time. I'd been fourteen and she had been eighteen. I knew she saw me as a child. All the same, when I came aboard for this voyage and she waved to me, my heart swelled.

When we left I was wild with excitement, not to avenge Mother but to be moving, exploring, doing something different. Then, as soon as the ship had left the harbor and stood out to deep water, I was filled with the calm joy of the wave, as I had been both the other times I had been aboard ship. Dolphins came alongside and followed us. The water was so clear that I could see the whole pod, and the rush of water breaking along the side of the ship, and the gold and black sand far below on the sea bed. Yet when I looked up and out the sea was, well, wine-dark as Homer puts it. The sea was a deep dark blue of precisely the same reflective luminosity as rich red wine. And the white wave foaming along the ship's side broke it, and the dolphins surfacing, and the shore of the island. I looked back at the City, which looked as small as a model even from this little distance. Above it the mountain was smoking, as it often did. Perhaps there would be a little eruption, a new stream of lava snaking down the side. Or perhaps the great eruption would come, the eruption that would carve away half the island and destroy the City and everything. I hoped that wouldn't happen while I was away.

Phaedrus came over to me where I stood by the rail looking up at the mountain. All three of my brothers who had asked to go had been accepted by the Chamber to make the voyage, Phaedrus, Kallikles and, thank Hera, Neleus. I don't know what he'd have done if they had refused him. "Is there a god of volcanoes?" Phaedrus asked.

"Hephaistos?" I ventured. "He's supposed to have his forge in one. That Titian picture in the temple, remember?"

"But his main area is making things, isn't it?"

"Yes, overlapping with Athene on technology. She designs things and he implements them. Athene overlaps with a lot of people on a lot of things. Ares on war, Fa—Apollo on learning. I suppose knowledge does cover a lot of ground." I looked at Phaedrus, who was still looking at the mountain as the *Excellence* sailed east. I lowered my voice, although nobody was near enough the overhear us. "Have you been talking to Father about how to become a god?"

He flushed. "You must have done the same or you wouldn't know what I was thinking."

"I don't think there's anything wrong with it," I said. "But volcanoes seem like a huge area."

"But there isn't anyone specific for them. Poseidon has earthquakes, and the ocean. It's hard to think of anything that's vacant. I could specialize in volcanoes, learn about them. We've grown up next to one, after all."

"But how would you do it?" I couldn't imagine how such a thing could possibly work, how Phaedrus could go from the young man at my side to becoming a patron deity of volcanoes. I couldn't picture the intermediate steps at all. "It's hard to see how you could develop an excellence of volcanoes." I looked at the plume of smoke, being blown on the same wind that was drawing the ship. "I was just hoping it wouldn't erupt and destroy the city before we get back."

"That would be terrible," Phaedrus said, immediately without any hesitation. Then he stopped. "Why would it be worse than if it did it when we were home?"

"Guilt at surviving." Without meaning to, we both looked at Father as I said that. He was standing by Maecenas at the wheel, looking almost happy. Phaedrus and I looked back at each other, uneasily.

Just then Klymene came along and hustled us into a group learning to shoot from the mast. The first part of this consisted of learning to climb the mast, which was a skill we'd need to acquire in any case. The *Excellence* was sailed by wind-power, and it required a number of people able to scale the masts to rearrange the sails. We had been organized before we left into three watches, and each watch had officers and sailors, who were people like Maecenas and Erinna who already had the necessary skills. The rest of us would learn as we went along. Some of us knew how to sail fishing boats, but the skill of going aloft and managing the great sails was very different in practice, even though the theory was the same.

I loved everything about the ship that bore my name, the taut ropes, the sea breeze, the way she heeled through the water. I loved the solar-powered deck lamps that began to glow softly as dusk came on. I loved sleeping in a hammock and swaying with the sway of the ship. The voyage was the first time I ever slept aboard—the time we went to Sokratea, we slept in a guest house there. I loved learning the new skills, sail-setting and rope-coiling and mast-climbing. From the crosstrees at the top of the mast I could see for miles, in a wide arc as the mast moved. I volunteered to spend as much time there as I could and to be a lookout. "It's good because you're light, but you won't like it so much in a gale and lashing rain," Maecenas predicted. He was Father's age, one of the Children, Captain of the *Excellence*. I was in his watch, the Eos watch, with Erinna, Phaedrus and Ficino. We came up an hour before dawn and worked until an hour after noon, when the Hesperides watch took over. Father and Kallikles were in that watch. The third watch, the Nyx, took over an hour after sunset. Neleus and Maia were assigned to that. There were thirty people in each watch. I have no idea how Kebes managed to fit a hundred and fifty people into the *Goodness*, because the *Excellence* felt crowded with ninety.

The Kyklades are a group of islands that circle Delos, the island where Father was born. At that time Delos floated on the water, but afterward it was attached to the sea-bed like other lands—or this is the story recounted in the Homeric Hymn to Delian Apollo. (Father says it's poetically true, whatever that means.) Tiny Delos is the center of the Kyklades, and the other islands do form a rough circle around it. It's possible to draw them so that they look even more like a circle, and to make Delos seem like the center of the whole Aegean, and the Aegean as the center of the whole world. It depends on your perspective, as Mother used to say. Kallisti is the southernmost of the Kyklades, and to get anywhere from there except Crete you have to sail north.

North isn't a good direction to go in Greece in the spring, because of the winds, so we went northeast, toward Amorgos, which we reached late on the evening of the first day out from home. There were no signs of life ashore, but we weren't really expecting any. No Amorgians were mentioned in Homer's Catalog of Ships.

We put down our anchor and slept aboard. Erinna showed me how to sling my hammock, next to hers, and how to get into it sideways. I slept better that night than I had any night since Mother was killed. Erinna woke me before dawn in time for our watch and I sprang out of my hammock, feeling fresh and ready for a new day.

"You seem better," Erinna said as we came up on deck.

"I feel better. The sea is good for me. And doing different things. I still miss her, but it doesn't weigh on me the same way. And you were right about writing the autobiography, too."

"She was right about that," Erinna said. She hugged me suddenly, and I hugged her back, tightly. "We can remember her without being sucked down into grief."

"That would be wonderful," I said. "If only Father could."

The Nyx watch were ready to hand over to us then, and so we had to work. I swarmed up to the top of the mast and relieved the Nyx lookout there, who that morning was the Captain of the Nyx watch, a Child called Caerellia.

"No signs of life at all," she said.

I was disappointed. I was hoping for people. Amorgos is about the easiest island to get to from Kallisti, in normal winds, and Neleus had made a very convincing argument that it was the most likely place for Kebes to have founded his city. We put an armed party ashore as soon as it was properly light, then we sailed around the island to collect them from the other side. I wasn't allowed ashore. Phaedrus and Erinna went, and I looked down from the masthead with envy.

At the end of the Eos watch I stayed on deck, staring over at the Amorgian shore as it slipped past, glancing up occasionally at the Hesperides watch as they ran about trimming sails. Ficino came up to me as I was standing there. The sea-breeze ruffled his white hair where it stuck out under his old red hat. I saw him every day so I didn't normally think much about it, but he really was the oldest person I had ever met.

He grinned at me. "Not feeling seasick?"

"Not even a twinge," I replied.

"Good. Well then, it's time for lessons, I think," he said.

Ficino was nominally part of the Eos watch, but he had declined learning how to climb the masts and had learned only how to steer, which was both the easiest and the most fun. "Lessons? But surely I'm learning enough just being here. I've learned a lot about how the ship works already. And also geography, and I'll learn history as soon as we locate some people."

Maia laughed, and I jumped, because I hadn't heard her come up and she was right next to me on my other side. "You need philosophy and rhetoric and history and mathematics," she said, as if I wasn't already ahead of her in mathematics.

"But we don't have any books," I said. I had my notebooks, though I had left behind the two I had filled already.

"We have sufficient books," Ficino said. Trust them to bring books, I thought. "But for now, how about calculating the angle the ship's bow makes?"

I calculated angles in my head for hours, until we had rounded the point of Amorgos and were tacking our way up the other side to where we hoped to meet the shore party. Ficino and Maia then began to make me work on rhetoric, aloud. "Plato says young people shouldn't learn rhetoric, it makes them contradict their elders before they have wisdom," I pointed out.

"You wouldn't be studying it yet in Athenia," Maia said. "But we think fifteen is old enough to begin."

"I learn more the older I get," Ficino said. "I'm glad I began so young." His eyes were on the gentle curve of the shore we were slipping past. "I don't sleep much these days. Growing older I need it less, perhaps as I need the time more to learn things and get the most out of every day. Learn what you can while you can. Learn, Arete."

There are times when I wish my parents had given me a different name. Pursuing excellence and learning excellence are puns I am thoroughly sick of. Now we were on the ship there was even more opportunity for such jokes, of course. But Ficino was entirely serious.

Amorgos is a long thin island, and it took hours sailing back east around it before we found the shore party. They had built a fire by a stream as arranged, and the Hesperides masthead lookout spotted their smoke and called out. The shore party signaled that they had seen nobody, so we anchored again to take on fresh water. "We're going to spend the night here," Maecenas told Ficino as he went by. "You can go ashore if you want to."

Everybody seemed to want to, just for the excitement of walking on a different island. There were crowds around the ship's boat. I could see we wouldn't be ashore soon.

"Where will we go next?" Maia asked Maecenas.

"Tomorrow we'll make for Ios."

"Will there be people there?" I asked.

Maecenas shrugged. "Homer doesn't mention any, but that doesn't mean there aren't any. And Kebes may be there. It's the next likeliest place, after here." He moved on, trying to calm the people waiting to go ashore.

"When did the islands come to be inhabited?" I asked.

"I don't know," Maia said. "We don't have anybody here from before Plato, and Plato wrote a thousand years after this. Well, as far as we know when we are. Athene told us that we were here in the time before the Trojan War, but we don't know exactly how long before, and we also don't know the exact date of that war. We're not even sure if it was real or mythical."

"Real!" Ficino said.

"Both," I said, staring over at the pine trees on the Amorgian shore.

I realized they were both looking at me. "What do you mean?" Ficino asked.

"Well, like Athene," I said. "She was real, she lived in the City and brought everyone here and set it all up. But she's a goddess, she's also mythical. She's in a lot of myths, and yet the two of you have had conversations with her."

"I have been on expeditions with her to steal art treasures," Ficino admitted. "I have looted Byzantium in her company. She's real enough. She's glorious."

"But she's also the Goddess Athene, she could move you through time and do all kinds of strange things. She had a mythic dimension. She was both at once." And Father was the same, I thought, even without his powers. I thought of that strange moment when we all stared at Neleus. My brothers and I were also like that, to a certain extent. "And the Trojan War has to be like that too."

"I think it must happen after the City is destroyed," Ficino said, sitting down on a pile of canvas. "Otherwise we would not have been able to resist participating, knowing what we know."

"On which side?" I asked. I also wanted to ask him how he could be so maddeningly calm about the City being destroyed, but I had asked him related questions before and found his answers entirely unsatisfactory. The real problem was that he was ninety-nine years old and he was sure he was going to die this year, and I was fifteen and I didn't ever want to die at all.

"What a fascinating question," Ficino said. "To attack beside Achilles, or to defend beside Hector. The Greeks or the Latins. Which would you choose?"

"Neither side was entirely in the right," I said. "And there's no question that it was all the fault of the gods in the first place. Helen—"

"It's possible that if we went to Argos now we might see the young Helen," Ficino said. The boat had taken two groups of people in, and it was quite clear to me that it would be hours before it took us. I shuffled a little closer.

"Do you believe we're that close in time?" Maia asked.

"It has been thirty-two years since we came," Ficino said. "How long before do you think she would have put us? Perhaps more than that. Perhaps Helen is not yet born. I said we might see Nestor as a young man, and he was a very old man at the time of the Trojan War. I'd love to go to Pylos and see. But we're not sailing in that direction, at least not this time. Perhaps we'll see Anchises as a young man. That would be marvelous."

"I too would love to meet Homer's heroes," I said. "But which side would you want to fight on, really?"

"I'm torn, but it would come down to the Latins and Troy," Ficino said. "The beleaguered city holding out against the sea of enemies."

Maia put her hand on his shoulder. "Florentia?" she asked.

Ficino smiled up at her. "Perhaps. My Florentia, like Troy, left a great legacy."

"But our Florentia—" Maia began.

Just then a group of Young Ones including my brothers Neleus and Kallikles came running to the side of the ship, stripped off their kitons and dived into the water. They went racing off toward the shore. "Oh!" I said. I measured the distance between the ship and the shore. It wasn't all that far. "I'm going to swim too! Would you bring my kiton?" I shrugged it off and offered it to Maia.

"Let's all swim," Maia said, dropping her kiton on the deck.

"It's too far for me," Ficino said. "I'll go in the boat and bring your kitons to protect your modesty once you get ashore."

People were diving all along the side of the ship. Maia and I joined them and began to swim toward the first shore I had ever seen that was not that of the island of my birth. All the while I was swimming, quickly outpacing Maia and almost catching up with my brothers, I kept thinking about which side I'd want to fight on. Troy, or the Achaeans? To rescue Helen, or to defend the city? For Agamemnon or for Priam? It wasn't a fair question. We knew Troy was doomed. But Ficino would have fought for her anyway. I ran ashore, and the land felt strange under me. It seemed to be rocking. Earthquake? Or was the island, like Delos long ago, not tethered to the sea-bed? Then I realized this was something Erinna had told me about: when we were used to the motion of the ship, solid land would seem to move. I got up and immediately hurt my feet walking on pine needles. I hoped Ficino would bring my sandals too. I looked back at the *Excellence*, sitting gracefully at anchor, and although I had longed to explore this new island she looked like the most beautiful and dearest thing imaginable. Troy, I thought, and then no, the black ships.

It was just as well we probably wouldn't be given the choice, when it was so hard to decide.

9

ARETE

After Amorgos we sailed to Ios, and from there to Naxos. We found no people on Ios, and no sign of Kebes. Life aboard became almost routine, up before dawn to take my watch, which I mostly spent up at the top of the mast. Watching the sun rise from up there was always incredibly beautiful. The sky slowly lightened and became pink, and the sea echoed the color and was rose-pink dotted with jade-green islands. I could see so far from the mast at dawn that the islands looked like leaping dolphins. Then sometime in the day we would come close to an island. A party would go ashore to explore, find nobody, and come back. The rest of us would go ashore to cook, hunt, and take on water. Then we'd come back aboard and either sail on overnight or stay in our fairly protected anchorage, depending on winds and what the captains thought.

The night on Amorgos we sang at the campfire, both kinds of songs, Phrygian and Dorian. Some songs we all sang together, and some people took turns singing. Father played the lyre and sang a new song he had written about Mother's excellence and love of truth, which made everyone cry. Erinna and Phaedrus and I sang some of the choruses from *The Myrmidons*. It was like a festival, only better, because we hadn't been preparing and rehearsing, it was all spontaneous. Then we all went back to the ship to sleep.

On Ios the shore party had killed a boar that ran out of the woods and attacked them. We roasted it and ate it under the stars, which seemed brighter from there than they were at home. We sang again after we had eaten. Phaedrus persuaded me to do Briseis's duet with Patroklus. When we sat down again, Erinna leaned over from where she sat whittling and patted my arm. "You have a great voice." My soul soared at praise from her.

"We're fortunate that all of Pytheas's children seem to have inherited his singing abilities," Maia said. Neleus frowned at that, because he could never seem to sing in tune. I didn't think singing was a particularly heroic ability. Erinna's singing voice was clear and true.

Naxos at first seemed no different from Amorgos and Ios. When the shore party signaled that they had found people we were astonished, as if we had believed we were alone in the time of the dinosaurs. I didn't meet the Naxians or see their settlement, so at first their presence felt like a disappointment, because they prevented me from going ashore. Those of us left aboard waited impatiently for the shore party to return, running through all the facts about Naxos we knew. "Isn't it where Theseus abandoned Ariadne?" Erinna asked. "Could that have happened already?"

Ficino nodded. "It should have happened in the last generation. Theseus's sons by Phaedra fought at Troy. Ariadne might still be alive."

"We don't know exactly when we are," Maia reminded him. "We might have a better idea when they come back. Ariadne might be there, or she might not have come yet, or she might be dead. How long did she live after being abandoned?"

"Dionysios is supposed to have come for her and taken her away," Ficino said. "So she might be gone."

Father was staring fixedly at a little island just offshore as if he were remembering something. I wanted to ask him about it, but there were too many people about. It was hard to get privacy aboard, and even harder when everyone was lining the rail impatiently waiting for the shore party.

"We don't know when we are at all," he said. "I have a feeling it might be much earlier than you're assuming. 'Before the Trojan War' doesn't necessarily mean immediately before."

Even though I'd been thinking about dinosaurs, I was surprised and disappointed. "No Anchises?"

"We'll have to wait and see."

"Here they come!" Erinna said.

The official report was that they had made contact and the locals didn't have any useful information. "Miserable primitive place," Maecenas said, pushing through the crowd of questioning people. "Council meeting. Now."

The ship had a council of six that was supposed to make decisions, and Maecenas called them together in his cabin. The rest of us had to wait. As we weren't going ashore and therefore couldn't cook, dinner was cold, smoked fish and olives washed down with water lightly flavored with wine. After the feasts and singing of the previous nights it felt like a letdown. A group of us sat down to eat in the bows, where we could watch the sun setting over the sea. Erinna and I sat together on a coil of rope. "If we leave soon we could reach Paros in a few hours," I said. "I can see it from the top of the mast."

"Do we know if it's inhabited?" Phaedrus asked.

"Not in the Catalog of Ships, but they quarried marble there, so it seems it might be," Maia said. "I expect we'll stay here until morning."

Kallikles came up to join us. He had been in the shore party, so we greeted him with enthusiasm. "Tell us what it was like?" I urged, as Erinna moved toward the rail so that he could sit down beside me.

"It's not a proper city, it's very small, maybe a village is the proper term. They live inland, out of sight of the shore, though they have boats. They keep chickens and goats and pigs, and let them run in and out of their houses. The houses are really primitive, not much more than huts. There's a wooden palisade around the village, and an entry blocked with thorn bushes. We didn't go inside, but it isn't very big and we could see everything. There's just one plaza, with houses around it in a circle—no roads at all, no paving stones, just dirt. There are strange statues set up in the plaza, half-carved marble, sort of flat, with huge heads and weird noses, painted, dressed and decorated with beads. They're not like anything I've ever seen. Very bright colors. I can't even decide whether or not they were beautiful."

Ficino looked away from the sunset and stared at Kallikles. "I want to see them!"

"I don't know whether you'll be able to. Maecenas wasn't talking about going back. The people weren't friendly at all. They ran into the village and barricaded themselves in when they saw us coming. The men were armed with bronze spears with weird flat blades. They wouldn't speak to us, they kept waving their spears. Then an old woman came forward to talk. She had a huge sore on her face with pus coming out of it. She spoke Greek of a kind, but it was hard to make ourselves understood. She kept telling us to go away, that she wouldn't give us anything, and she couldn't seem to understand we didn't want anything except information, which she didn't want to give either. Maecenas offered her a silver cup, which she snatched, but even after that she didn't want to be friendly. They didn't let us in or offer hospitality at all. They held on to their weapons and we held on to ours."

I was trying to picture it. "What were the houses made of?"

"Stone and wood. It wasn't the materials that were primitive, it was the style."

"You've never seen anything that wasn't classical," Ficino said, smiling.

"I've been to Psyche," Kallikles said.

Maia laughed. "Psyche is also classical. All our cities are."

"It wasn't built by Workers," Kallikles protested. "But you're right, this was a different style entirely. No pillars. Primitive. Odd. I was really uncomfortable looking at the place. Chickens pecking around their feet, a toothless old woman bent over grinding wheat by hand in a quern, and everyone frightened, the men with their weapons, half cringing and half defiant. I've never seen poverty like that."

"It sounds like a village in India or Africa in my time," Maia said, thoughtfully. "I'd never imagined Greece like that, full of savages. But I suppose it must have been once."

"Don't build too much on one primitive fishing village," Ficino said. "There were places not too far from Florentia in my own day that the boy would have described the same way— toothless peasants with sores, and animals running in and out."

"I can't even imagine it," Erinna said. I couldn't either. When I'd thought about the difficulties of Mycenaean Greece it was in terms of women not being equal, and lack of books, not sores and poverty. Homer talks about cities, and I had imagined cities like our cities.

"Did they give any useful information about the date?" Ficino asked.

"They'd heard of King Minos, but not of Kebes, nor Mycenae nor Troy, at least as far as we were able to make ourselves understood."

"Minos," Ficino said thoughtfully, turning back to the west. The sun was on the horizon now, gilding the rippling sea and lighting the clouds purple and gold. "Crete. Maybe we should go there."

"Pytheas wants to go north," Maia said. "He's sure Kebes

went that way, though whether from something Kebes said years ago or just out of his obsession I don't know."

"Father isn't a fool," I protested.

"You have to admit he hasn't been entirely rational since Simmea died," Maia said.

"This crushing grief is strange in a man with so much excellence, a man who we've all been accustomed to look to as one of the very best among the golds," Ficino said.

I nodded. Erinna, who was behind me, put her hand on my shoulder and squeezed in a comforting way. It did comfort me, but it also sent an unsettling jolt of energy through me. My breath caught in my throat. I liked it too much. Everything I'd ever read about bodily love came back to me, and I moved away as she dropped her hand. I could feel my face was burning hot and there was heat too between my legs. I stared out over the sea. The first star appeared in the east, silver against violet. "Let me not be unworthy," I prayed to it. Kallikles was still talking, and I tried to concentrate on what he was saying.

"It wasn't clear whether the old woman properly understood what we were asking, or if she thought we were saying we were from Minos," Kallikles said. "It was horrible. I wanted to help them somehow. Give them my knife, or better, teach them how to make iron and wash. Teach them philosophy! But at the same time I couldn't wait to get away. The way the old woman was talking to Maecenas, ducking her head as if she thought he'd strike her!" He shook his head.

"You can't help them, it could break history," Maia said.

I turned to her, surprised out of myself. The deck lights had just come on, giving everything a warm golden glow. "What do you mean break it?"

"If Kallikles taught them how to make iron it could change everything. Not that village, maybe, but imagine if the Trojans had iron weapons and the Greeks only bronze! Trying to help them could ruin everything!"

Ficino laughed, and we all turned to him. "We don't know that. It could be what sets history right. Nobody knows much about what happened in Greece before the Trojan War. Maybe the Age of Iron began because Kallikles taught these primitives how to make it."

"I don't actually know how," Kallikles admitted.

"I expect it's in the library." Erinna said. I wanted to turn to look at her, and I normally would have, but I kept still.

"We could send out expeditions to teach them medicine and technology," Kallikles said. "We could really help them."

"That would be wonderful," Erinna said.

Maia tutted. "And if Troy had iron and didn't fall?"

I was breathless again at the thought. I had imagined Ficino going to Troy's aid despite knowing they would lose, now I imagined him going and changing everything.

"And what would happen then?" Ficino asked. "A different history starting from here where Troy never falls and Rome is never born? I don't think that's possible. We're here, we're free to act, anything we do is already part of history. We won't change everything. We're embedded here. We're in a secret forgotten part of history, but history can't be changed. We know what's coming. We're safely tucked in the margins of history. Athene saw to that."

"You have a lot of faith in her still," Maia said, sharply.

"In Providence," Ficino said. "If these people need help and we can give it, perhaps that should be part of our mission. If we're going to do it then it's already part of what we will do. And it might relieve some suffering."

"But what would happen if we tried to change history?" Erinna asked. "If we deliberately did something—if we told Paris what would come of him stealing Helen. If we told Helen?"

"They'd do it anyway. Lovers are idiots!" Ficino said. I felt my cheeks heat again. "It would be better to warn Priam about the wooden horse."

"I wonder if they're discussing helping the village in the council now?" Phaedrus mused.

"I wonder what Father's saying," Kallikles said.

"Why aren't you on the council?" Ficino asked Maia.

"It's only six people, so they can make decisions quickly," she said. "But why aren't you?"

"They're all Children," Ficino said. "There aren't many Masters on this expedition, and while there are plenty of Young Ones, you wouldn't expect them to have positions of responsibility yet." He turned to Kallikles. "You should tell your father what you've been saying to us, about wanting to help. It's a question for the whole Chamber back home, but it's a question we shouldn't forget."

"And we should debate whether what we do can change history," Maia said. "It's another thing we should have asked Athene while we had the chance."

"I'll definitely tell Father," Kallikles said. "But if we can change things, it wouldn't necessarily make them worse. We could make them better."

"But it's all connected. We can't change anything without changing everything. If Priam knew about the wooden horse, there would be no Rome," Maia said.

I resolved to ask Father about history as soon as I could safely get him alone.

The ship stayed at anchor that night. I didn't go down to my hammock beside Erinna. I wrapped myself in my cloak and slept on deck, badly. When I was awake I fretted about my inappropriate response to Erinna's hand. She had meant friendly comfort, and my body had undoubtedly felt lust. I wrestled with the twin horses of my soul, as Plato urges. When I fell asleep, I dreamed about history as a broken rope, lashing about and pulling the sails out of trim as the ship prepared for a storm. Every time I woke the real ship was barely moving beneath me, and I fretted about my feelings for Erinna. I liked her. I respected her. She was a wonderful friend. Maybe I even loved her. She seemed to like me, but of course not in any inappropriate way. She was four years older than me. Then every time I slept again it was the same dream, the cut rope, the uncontrollable sails, the oncoming storm clouds. A light rain woke me an hour before dawn, a little early for my watch but I got up anyway, re-draping my blanket into a cloak to keep off the weather.

Only a few of the Nyx watch were awake, as the ship at anchor didn't need much attention. We nodded to each other. One of them was my brother Neleus, who came forward to wish me joy of the morning. "Do you know where Father is?" I asked him.

"Asleep down below, I think. But he'll be up soon." Neleus nodded to the east where the sky was starting to pale. Father inevitably woke at sunrise. Naxos was a dark bulk immediately to the north of us. The rain was chilling me. I walked over to the rail. Neleus walked beside me. "They're out there somewhere," he said.

My mind was full of Erinna and the Naxians, and I frowned at him, puzzled. "Who?"

"The Goodness Group," he said, his hands clenching into fists. "We'll find them. We'll avenge Mother. I know you want that as much as I do."

I put my hand on his arm. "I grieve for Mother, but I don't know whether vengeance will help."

"It'll help me," he said. "I feel I let her down."

"Oh Neleus, you didn't," I said.

"She was always so exacting, and I didn't meet her standards." He was staring out over the dark water, not looking at me.

"It's true what Father said. She loved you. I often felt I didn't meet her standards either."

"You and I are all that's left of her now," he said, turning toward me.

"Well, genetically," I agreed. "But all the people she taught, all the pictures and sculptures she made, that lives on." For as long as the City lives, I thought. Not into posterity, because there is none. Unless we can change history. If we can change history, then her legacy could really last.

Father came up from below, yawning. I waved to him and he came over to us. "Joy to you both," he said, and we repeated the wish.

"I need to know something about how the universe works," I said.

He looked over to the little island he had been looking at the day before. "There'll be a temple there one day," he said, quietly. "A temple to me. It'll be there by Homer's day. We're here early. But I don't know exactly when."

"Can we change history?" I asked.

He and Neleus both stared at me. "What do you mean?" he asked.

"Can things we do, here and now, change what will happen in the future?"

"Yes. Of course. But not things that the gods know about, not things that are already fixed."

"So there's only one time?" I asked.

"Right. It's as if time's a scroll, and we haven't read all of it but it's all there, and once we've read it, that's fixed. But it all scrolls along in order when you're inside it. From outside, it's different." His chin wavered. "I remember explaining it like that to Simmea and Sokrates."

"So for instance we could teach the people on Naxos medicine and iron working and navigation and philosophy, and it wouldn't change the outcome of the Trojan War?" I asked.

"No."

Neleus looked at me in astonishment. "What a great idea!" he said. "Let's do all that. Let's give them more choices and make all of their lives better."

"It was Kallikles's idea, when he saw them yesterday," I admitted. "But I agree: if it doesn't break history we have a moral obligation to help them."

"Wait," Father said. "It won't break history, but it can break you if you try to go against Fate and Necessity. And you can't teach philosophy to every starving peasant in the Aegean."

"Why not?" Neleus asked. "Mother would have."

Father stared at him for a moment. "She would have," he admitted.

10

MAIA

One of the strangest things about the multiplication of cities after the Last Debate was that we were all doing variations of Plato's Republic, and so we came to feel that attempting to create Plato's Republic was the normal thing people did. It might have been different for some of the older Masters, like Ficino. I had only been nineteen when I came to the City, and the Children had been no more than ten. When I thought about it, of course, I remembered a world of people who went from one year to another without thinking twice about Plato, but I did not care to think about them often. There had been no place for me in that world. So the argument in my mind was never whether to set up the Just City, always how best to do it.

With the founding of the City of Amazons I found myself doing things for the second time, and trying to fix the errors we had made the first time. For the Children, of course, it was the first time, and they viewed the errors they had found growing up in the City quite differently from the way we Masters did. One of the first decisions we made was that there would be no more Masters and Children. We all agreed that the Children were much closer to what Plato wanted than we were. Nevertheless, we were the ones with the experience of setting up the original city, and with working on committees, and with making decisions. It was decided that Masters ranked with silvers, auxiliary guardians, but that we could serve on committees, which were otherwise for golds alone. The Children were used to deferring to us.

We had to work hard, without Workers, just to have enough to eat. All the same, we spent more time in debate than anything else. We debated everything in committees and then before the whole Assembly—and the Assembly here consisted of all those over eighteen, though they were not all equal within the Assembly. Irons and bronzes were given one vote each, silvers three, and golds four. The age of eighteen was chosen because it was the traditional age of adulthood in Plato's Athens. We would have gone with Plato's thirty, but nobody was thirty yet except for Masters. I was only a little over thirty myself. To start with we had practically nobody who was not an adult in our newly defined terms. A few of the Children had brought their Young Ones, and a few of them were pregnant. The first baby born in the City of Amazons was Euridike's Porphyry, born the first winter. I delivered him myself, the first baby I ever helped deliver who was not immediately taken away from their mother to grow up in anonymity.

Porphyry encapsulated in his tiny person our first two great debates—over names, and over families. Klio and some others wanted us all to take back our original names and allow eclectic naming of new babies. This divided everyone. Lysias and I were against it. "It's not that different, and I've been Lysias so long it feels like my real name now," Lysias said, and I nodded.

"Why would I want to be Ethel? Ethel feels like another person, a person from another world. It has been more than ten years. I'm not Ethel anymore. I've grown up as Maia."

"I can't think of you as Ethel," Lysias agreed.

"And I don't think I even knew you were Li Xi," I said. "It's a name from another culture. It would make you seem different from everyone."

"I think Klio thinks that's a good thing, to point up the differences."

For once Ikaros and I were on the same side. "Naming ourselves and our children from the classical world unites us; using naming customs from other times and places would divide us," he said in debate. The vote was close, but we won. Porphyry was named after the philosopher, who had been one of us and had recently died. He was also named for the purple stone that had symbolized Roman technical prowess in the Middle Ages and the Renaissance, and thirdly for the idea of being *porphyrogenitos,* born to the purple, being the first baby born in the new city and the heir to our traditions. It was a lot of weight for a name to carry.

The other great early debate was over marriage and families. None of us wanted to carry on Plato's idea of arranged matings at festivals. We had all seen the misery and complications it caused. But some of us wanted traditional marriage and families, while others wanted to try other varieties of Plato's idea of having wives and children in common. I was torn on this subject. We Masters had been very loose about this. Klio and Axiothea might as well have been married, except that they were both women. Lysias and I had a friendship that included some sex. Ficino had been strictly celibate while openly admiring all the beautiful youths. Ikaros, in addition to his spectacular public Platonic relationship with Plotinus, had an ongoing private arrangement with Lukretia, and sex with anyone he could charm into lying down with him. We masters were not a good example. I felt that this was an area where Plato should perhaps have stayed with tradition.

This time Ikaros was firmly on the other side. He wanted to

keep everything fluid and flexible, where people could live together if they chose but everyone should be available to everyone else with no exclusivity. Ikaros read Plato's passage on this aloud, very movingly. Many Children spoke about their love for each other and their desire to form families and bring up their own children. Lukretia expanded on Athene's point in the Last Debate about the damage done to cities and states by families and factions, with chilling examples from her own experience. Eventually we came to a kind of compromise where families would be permitted but not marriages or inheritance, and those families could be of any number and any gender, and could form and reform at will. Thus Porphyry was born into the family Euridike had formed with Castor, Hesiod, and Iris, although his father was Pytheas, who had stayed behind in the Remnant City.

I was sharing a house with Lysias, and if the vote had gone the other way we had agreed to marry. When I came home exhausted after Porphyry's birth, he brought me apple porridge and rubbed my feet.

"We could have children now," he said, looking up at me. "You're not too old. If you stopped taking the silphium."

I shook my head. "It's not what I want."

He looked disappointed and got up from the floor to sit beside me on the bed. "Why not?"

I had seen a great deal of childbirth, enough to put anyone off, but that wasn't it. "I want a life of the mind, not to be mired in domesticity. All that milk and washing."

"But you have maternal instincts. You're such a good teacher."

"I put my maternal instincts into being a teacher. The whole City is my baby—this city and the original. I don't want my own baby to love more than all the others. I think Plato's right that I would favor it."

"I want children," Lysias said. "I was prepared to do without to make the Republic, but what we're doing here is all compromised anyway. I want to help everyone, you know I do, but I want my own children to grow up here too, now that it's possible."

"Would you want that if you had to be the mother rather than the father?" I asked. "If you were the one to stay home and sing them to sleep?"

"Yes," he said, with no hesitation whatsoever. I was astonished. "Is that what you want?" He looked into my face.

"I was just being rhetorical. I never imagined you would agree. In the nineteenth century it would have been unthinkable for a man to do a woman's work that way." I put my hand on his.

He smiled. "In the twenty-first century it was unusual but not unheard of. And we assigned some iron boys as nursery attendants. I would do it if that's how you wanted to arrange things."

"I don't want to shrink my horizons to a baby," I said. "In my own time, that was the end of all independent thought."

"It needn't be that here," Lysias said. "If we decided to have children, I'd certainly be willing to be the one to stay home with them. But we'll also have crèches to provide flexibility. Nobody's going to be forcing you to be a nineteenth-century mother."

"I see that. But even so."

"I truly want this. I want children. And I can't do it without your help. You have a womb and can grow a new person. I can't."

I had never before thought of this as a form of female power that men lacked. No wonder they tried to control us in so many societies for so many years. (And no wonder Athene remained a virgin.) I still didn't especially want to have babies. But I didn't want to lose Lysias, and it seemed so important to him; and if he would take charge of the parts I didn't want to, then I thought that perhaps it didn't have to be something huge and life-changing for me.

So I agreed to stop chewing silphium, and I did stop. The next month when my blood came on time I was astonished, and the same the month after and the month after that. I knew that even at the festivals not every girl became pregnant every time, but I had expected Lysias's fervor to have had results. He had never wanted me so much or so enthusiastically. I saw now that he had seen sterile coupling as hardly worth doing. I wasn't comfortable about this change, but I didn't feel I could talk to him about it.

After six months with no result, I talked to Kreusa, and she reassured me that sometimes it could take many months to become pregnant, and that I shouldn't start to worry until it was a year.

After a year, I talked to her again, and she recommended green leaves, sunlight, relaxation, and prayers to Hera. I tried all of these, and never had my monthly blood arrive more than a day late. "Am I too old?" I asked her, a year after that, on a sunny autumn day while we were alone together on the shore smoking fish.

"What are you now, thirty-five, thirty-six? No, that's not too old. Old for a first time, but there shouldn't be any trouble. Lysias is a few years older, there might be problems on his side. Have him eat red meat when he can and abstain from fish."

"Have you ever had a baby?" I asked her as I tossed some more wood onto the fire.

She frowned and paused, with a single fish in one hand and a stick with five more threaded on it in the other. "One, when I was young. My mistress beat me for being so careless with the silphium. I was lucky not to find myself out on the street. It was a boy, poor thing, and had to be exposed." I remembered the baby I had exposed and how terrible I had felt, even though it couldn't have survived and it was not my own. I put out my hand toward Kreusa, but she didn't seem to see me. "I cried for days. By the time I had a house of my own and could have afforded a child, I'd found philosophy and didn't want one. I'm surprised you do, honestly." She plunged the stick through the fish abruptly and turned to put it on the smoke rack.

"I don't, all that much," I said. "Lysias really does. Now I've been trying for two years without getting anywhere, and he still feels strongly about it and I'm still ambivalent."

"That's probably your problem," she said, her face still turned toward the fish and the fire. "Your ambivalence. If you truly wanted it, you'd get pregnant."

"But you didn't want to, that time back in Corinth." I strung more fish onto another stick.

She shook her head without turning around. "I don't know why it should be. Lots of girls get caught when they don't want it at all, but lots of women trying without really wanting it can't manage it. And some who do desperately want it can't, and that's the saddest thing of all. I'd give up trying and fretting and just see what the gods send if I were you."

"Lysias—"

"He's a funny one," Kreusa said, turning back and picking up the stick I held out to her. "He's not Greek."

"Neither am I," I said.

"No, but you're not what he is either." She sighed and put the fish on the rack. "It probably makes no difference. Some men want sons to be their heirs. If he comes from that kind of family, well. Or even if not, if he wants children so much there's nothing you can do about it. You're not too old. But time is not on your side."

I picked up another fish and another stick. "He says he'll do all the work with the baby and leave me free for philosophy and teaching. Well, as free as I am now."

She laughed. "Perhaps he will, but what will you do if he doesn't? Men, eh?"

"We're equal here," I said. "In the City of Amazons there are more women than men, especially among the guardians. We can make a real difference."

"And yet you're still trying to have a baby because your man wants one?" She laughed bitterly, then began to turn the fish before they started to scorch.

"It's very difficult," I said.

I persuaded Lysias to eat more meat and less fish, even though he preferred fish, but it didn't make any difference. My blood continued to come with infuriating regularity. At first we consoled each other, and then we stopped talking about it, until at last we only talked about philosophy and politics and other neutral subjects. All in all we tried to conceive a child for six years, with no result at all. Other women seemed to have no difficulty conceiving, even other Masters. I continued to help as a midwife as our birth rate rose, along with teaching and working and serving on committees. Ikaros and I opposed each other almost as a matter of course all this time. Axiothea joked that if we ever did agree then the matter was sure to be settled.

I knew how important having children was to Lysias, so I wasn't at all surprised when he left me in the seventh year, though I was surprised that he left me for Lukretia, who was older than I was, and who had never shown any interest in him before that summer. I missed him surprisingly much. Even as we had been drawing apart he had always been courteous and friendly. Now I came home alone to a house that felt colder.

11

ARETE

That day for the first time I saw some other ships, three big ones with rows of oars, away to the east, heading southward. I called the news down, and there was some excitement, but we didn't change course to intercept them. We reached Paros about mid-day.

At first it seemed deserted, because we reached it from the southwest, and the settlements were all on the northeastern coast. The shore party didn't find anything inland, but we all saw the ones along the shore after we had sailed all the way around. I saw three of them, much like the one Kallikles had described on Naxos. I looked at them as hard as I could as we sailed by them, and so did everyone else aboard who wasn't tending to the ship at that very instant. I didn't see any people clearly, because they fled at the first sight of the ship. Paros was thickly wooded, and they ran off into the trees, mothers carrying wailing babies and everyone clutching their most precious possessions. "They must be expecting raiders," Neleus said. "Maybe Kebes is nearby."

"Or maybe more people like them. What would Kebes find to raid in a place like that?" The huts looked flimsy enough to push over at a touch. There was one square-built stone house on a little eminence, but even that looked filthy and shabby. The statues were strange, as Kallikles had said, festive and brightly colored when all the rest was so drab. They stared out at us with their huge painted eyes.

"That one has an owl," Maia pointed out at the second village. The owl was not carved but painted onto the side of the statue. "Do you think it's supposed to be Athene? Do you think they're meant to be the gods? The Greek gods?"

"Who else would they worship?" Erinna asked.

"It seems so strange," Maia said. I squeezed her hand, to show I understood what she meant. It was hard to think of these villagers as Greeks.

The shore party managed to speak to some Parians, but with no more conclusive results than we had had at Naxos. We left as soon as they came back. That night we sailed on. I had managed to suppress my erotic longings for Erinna, or I thought I had. I was sure she didn't feel like that about me, and I knew that I wanted to increase her excellence, as Plato says, so it was all right for me to love her as long as I didn't act out of lust. Mostly it was nice to just think how much better the world was because she was in it, and to see her sometimes, adjusting the sails or teaching people how to steer. When she smiled at me, my heart turned over.

We came to Delos at sunrise on the fifth day out from home. I was at the mast-top, in the crosstrees where there was a little platform for sitting. There was a huge wing of thin cloud in the eastern sky, striated like wool pulled out for carding, and the sun had lit it pink and then gold. The sky was paling from pink as we came into the natural harbor of Delos and dropped anchor there below the temples. I could feel somebody climbing the mast below me so I scooted over to make room for whoever it was. My heartbeat faster thinking that it might be Erinna. I was surprised when it turned out to be Father.

He looked out over the island. "It's such a long time since I've seen it," he said. "No lions yet."

"It looks deserted. Or is everyone still asleep?"

"It's only used for the festival at this date. There'll probably be a few priests, I should think."

"The temples look like proper buildings."

He smiled his kouros smile. "They may have had inspiration."

"But not those poor villagers on Naxos and Paros?"

He looked impatient. "I can't be everywhere taking care of everything all at once. Yes, I could spend all my time curing people of boils and teaching them to read, but instead I set up centers of healing and learning, to teach doctors and scholars. I gave Greece an oracle where they could come and ask their questions. I sent Sokrates a daimon to watch out for him, but I can't do that for everyone. I'm constantly inspiring people, but only people who can do something with the inspiration. I do the best I can within what Fate allows. Don't confuse me with Ficino's ideas of God, Arete!"

"Sorry," I said.

"Besides, I didn't know anything about them. They didn't pray to me," he said, still staring out over Delos, toward the mountain in the center of the little island where he had been born long before. "Those people in the Kyklades. I didn't know they were there. There weren't any statues of me, did you notice?"

"But this is so close," I said, gesturing at Delos, the first and oldest center of the worship of Apollo in the world.

"How often do you think they leave their petty islands?" Father asked, shaking his head. "Probably they haven't ever been any further out to sea than they need to catch fish. I'll do what I can to help them, now. I'll argue in Chamber in favor of Kallikles's idea of sending out missions to them. You're absolutely right that it's what Simmea would have wanted to do."

"And it won't change anything?"

"It might get the Naxians to build that pleasant temple I remember on the little island," he said. "But it won't change the future. There's only one world. We're in prehistory here. We hardly know the names of kings. Nobody knows for sure what happened on any given day, or when people learned about sanitation or philosophy, or even metal smelting. This isn't the generation before the Trojan War, it's more like four or five generations before. And even Troy—ask Ficino exactly where it was. He doesn't know. They forgot where it was until it was rediscovered late in the nineteenth century."

"Really?" I was astonished. "How could they lose Troy?"

"There's a lot of history. When it isn't recorded, things drop out. There are entire civilizations that are forgotten. Troy's lucky. It had Homer."

"Why do you suddenly seem so sure about when we are? I thought you didn't know either?"

"I didn't until now. But look at Delos," he said, gesturing. "I pay attention to Delos. It's *mine*. I know when things were built here. This is early Minoan. I should have guessed Athene wouldn't have put us immediately before the eruption."

I looked at the island. "I really want to go ashore," I said. "It's so beautiful. I want to explore it. I feel connected to it, even from up here, as if it's calling to me."

"You're my daughter. The island knows you." He sighed. "It knows me too. But I probably shouldn't go ashore, just in case. People don't usually recognize me, incarnate. They're not expecting to see me. But Sokrates did. And priests of mine, on Delos— they probably are expecting me at any moment. And if the island knew me—no. It's a little unkind to the priests, being so close and not letting them see me, but better not to risk it."

"Why do you keep your real nature secret in the City?" I asked.

He kept on gazing out over the island as he answered. "Because I want to live an incarnate life that's as normal as possible. It makes people uncomfortable if they know who I am, normal people. Your mother—Simmea was different. And I didn't tell her. She worked it out for herself." He wiped away tears, unself-consciously as ever. "If I tell people, they'll treat me differently. As it is, they think I'm a credit to Plato, and to them. They treat me as one of them. If they knew, they would expect me to be able to do things, and to know things. I don't have my powers, so there's not much I can do. And I do know some things, but I'm here hoping to learn, not to teach. And there are a lot of things I don't know, and they'd find it hard to believe that I don't. Some of the things I do know it's better for people not to know, to guess and work out for themselves."

"But you tell me?"

"That's different. I couldn't have kept it from you Young Ones. You have a right to know. I'm your father. And being a parent, up close and every day, is one of the things that has taught me the most."

"But you're also a god."

"You were asking about becoming a god." The sun was up now, blazing a gold path on the azure sea. He gestured to it. "That's *mine.* And Delos is mine. And inspiration and healing and poetry and all those things. Those are responsibilities. But they're not what's important. Being a god means being myself forever, and that means knowing myself as well as I can. Seeing the sun rise over Delos makes me feel all kinds of things, and they are different now because of what I have experienced since the last time I saw it. So I feel at home, and yet not at home, and the contradiction there is fascinating, and I can explore that feeling and make it into something."

"But not all the gods do that. And humans can," I said. "Humans can make art."

His eyes were precisely as blue as the sky, and his expression wasn't human at all. "They can. But they have such a brief span to do it. And a lot of their life is misery, and while that's a productive subject for art, it's a limited one. And then they die and

lay down their memories in Lethe and go on to become a new person. They come to the end of themselves and change and start again. Gods may or may not make art, but they can't come to the end of themselves. Not ever. And we *are* art. Our lives are subjects for art. Everything we are, everything we do, it all comes to art, our own or other people's. Mortals can forget and be forgotten. We can't. Everything we do has to be seen in that light. There's no anonymity. If you're a god, your deeds will be sung. Even the ones you would prefer to forget about."

"And I can choose, whether to be a mortal or a god?" I felt as if the whole world was holding its breath before he answered.

"Going ashore on Delos might help you. But time is the best gift." He stared out over Delos again. "I don't understand why she wanted to die. How she could have been ready. She told me not to be an idiot, but I don't understand how I was wrong."

We'd had this conversation a hundred times already, but this time I thought of something new. "Why are you assuming she was right?"

"What?"

"You're assuming she was right. Mightn't she have been wrong? Mistaken?"

He looked stricken. "But that would make everything worse! If she'd been wrong then I should have done it, and now it's too late."

"Somebody's coming up," I said, as I felt it through the mast.

It was Klymene. "Good to see something that looks halfway like civilization," she said, after she had greeted us. "I'm leading the shore party today. I thought I'd come up and see if I could spot any signs of life."

"There's smoke rising from the altar over there," Father said, gesturing. It was a thin thread of gray smoke, almost invisible. I hadn't seen it until he pointed it out. "I expect you'll find a priest or two."

"Somebody who isn't too terrified of us to talk would be good," Klymene said. "And Kebes can hardly have avoided coming here if he came this way at all."

Father went down shortly after that, and Klymene followed him before long. I saw and announced the sails of fishing boats away to the northeast, where another island loomed in the blue distance. My eyes kept being drawn back to Delos. I longed to walk on it. I watched enviously as the shore party left. It was Erinna's turn to go. Phaedrus and Kallikles had both contrived to join them, although it was not their turns. No doubt they felt the same affinity with the island I did.

At last my watch was over and I joined Ficino and Maia on the deck to watch the boat return. Erinna was rowing. "There are two priests," she called up to us, "and they say we can come ashore and cook and take on water and worship Apollo, but we should be back on the ship before dark."

Maecenas set a watch, for which Father volunteered. Those of us young and fit enough to swim hastily gave our kitons and sandals to friends old and frail enough to want to go in the boat. When my bare sole met the soil of Delos I felt a shock of joy that brought tears to my eyes. I felt I knew the place already. I knew where the cave was where they said Apollo had been born, and the plane tree on the mountain where he really had. I knew the altars and the temples, those already there and those not yet built. I found the words of the Homeric Hymn to Delian Apollo in my mouth as I came out of the water.

Delos did not seem to move unsteadily beneath my feet. It felt like the most solid earth I had ever trodden, as if Ios and Amorgos and even Kallisti were hollow shells and Delos alone was firm.

The sun was hot, and as I walked I saw lizards darting away from me. Kallisti was home, Amorgos and Ios felt like adventure,

Naxos and Paros felt like somewhere I wanted to rescue. Delos felt like somewhere my soul had known before birth. "Mine," Father had said, possessively. I felt that it was mine too; not just that it belonged to me, but it was mutual. I also belonged to it.

I didn't wait for my kiton but walked on, naked as in the palaestra, leaving the others behind. If we had to be back on the ship by nightfall, I didn't have long. There was a spring I needed to find, and I knew where it was. I kept walking around shadow-buildings that didn't exist yet, like the opposite of ruins, potentials. The spring was in a grove of trees, exactly where I had known it would be. I heard it before I saw it and pushed through the trees to come to it. When I came out into the clearing around the spring my two hero brothers were there, grave-faced, waiting in silence. Everything felt right, even that I was naked and they were clothed. We did not speak. Kallikles brought out a cup from the fold of his kiton, which he held out to me. I took it in both hands and dipped it into the pool, raised it high so that sunlight reflected into the water, then poured out a few drops on the ground and drank. I passed it to Phaedrus, who drank and passed it on to Kallikles. We kept on passing it around between the three of us until the cup was empty.

All this time, since my foot had first touched the shore, I hadn't thought, only acted, and everything I had done had been inevitable, necessary, and right. Once the cup was empty that changed, and I was only myself again, not a vessel of divinity, but I didn't want to speak and break the silence. Phaedrus put his hand on my shoulder, and without discussing it we all began to walk back toward the ship. By the time the sea was in sight I felt more nearly normal, though I noticed that we all kept avoiding the future-ghosts of temples.

Ficino handed me my kiton, and I put it on. Unusually for him, he didn't ask any questions, though his gaze was sharp. I sat down next to him. There was food ready, nut porridge and baked fish, and I ate it hungrily. The priests of Apollo, a man and a woman, came and blessed us, sprinkling water on us from branches with green leaves. I accepted their blessing with the others, avoiding my brothers' eyes.

Klymene came over and sat down by Kallikles, who made room for her. "Joy to you, son," she said.

"Joy," he muttered.

Klymene rolled her eyes and turned to Ficino. "They know Minos, and Troy, and Mycenae, but no names of kings we could offer," Klymene said to Ficino. I was listening, but like my brothers I didn't want to talk yet. I just sat there eating in silence.

"Have they seen Kebes?" Ficino asked.

"Not by name, but they know the *Goodness.* They say the captain is called Massias. Some people from the *Goodness* have been here for the festival, and behaved appropriately. They said they thought our ship was the *Goodness* at first. They don't know the location of their city, but they come here from the northeast, so that gives us a direction."

"Northeast. Interesting," Ficino said. "What's northeast of Delos?"

"Well, Mykonos close by," Klymene said. "Beyond that, nothing much for a long way. Due east gets you to Ikaria and Samos. Northwest are Tinos and Andros. Northeast, well, a biggish gap of sea and after a while you get to Chios and Lesbos."

"And on the mainland, Troy," Ficino pointed out.

"Why would Kebes have gone to Troy?" Klymene asked.

Ficino shook his head, as if to ask why anyone would go anywhere else.

We went back to the *Excellence* before nightfall, as the priests had asked. Phaedrus was in the same boat I was. "What was that?" he whispered to me.

I shrugged. "The island? We should ask Father, maybe."

"Our souls?" he asked.

Ficino was looking at us curiously. "We should ask Father, when we can be quite sure we've got him alone," I whispered.

12

ARETE

I couldn't sleep that night with thinking about what had happened. We sailed northeast to Mykonos, which had some scattered fishing settlements a little more civilized than those of Naxos and Paros, but only a little. A party tried to talk to them, again without success. I didn't go ashore, and I couldn't catch Father alone. We sailed on east to Ikaria, which we reached late on the next day. There was no sign of life visible from the ship. We anchored for the night and the next morning put down a shore party, which now felt routine. We sailed around another long thin island, and met up with the shore party in the late afternoon. They had seen nobody, and we concluded that Ikaria was deserted like Ios and Amorgos. We therefore went ashore as we had done there, and began to build fires to cook a meal.

While we were ashore, the three of us cornered Father and took him off into the trees away from everyone to ask about Delos. There was a wonderful scent of pine needles all around us as we walked and scuffed up the droppings of years, a thick layer of pine must which felt as if it had never been disturbed before. Although it smelled amazing, it was uncomfortable to walk on the strange surface. My feet sank in at every step and it took a real effort to move them. Old needles kept finding their way into my sandals and scratching my feet.

"I'm glad to see you found the spring," Father said, once we were well away.

"Why didn't you warn us?" Kallikles asked.

"I didn't know for sure Delos would affect you," Father said. "And I didn't want to disappoint you if it didn't. I did tell Arete that it might help."

"Was it our souls?" I asked.

"Your souls and my island," he said. "What happened?"

"Nothing much, really," Phaedrus said. "We went to the spring and waited, and Arete came and gave us water. That's all. But I've never felt anything like it."

"It felt right," I said. "It felt like knowing what was right and doing it because it was inevitable. There wasn't any choice."

"Then you were in the hand of Necessity, at the edge of your Fate, doing what was inevitable," Father said. "All of you. Once you were on Delos, you had to go through that ritual, and you knew it and you did it. The sprinkling on the shore is the echo of that."

"I hated it," Kallikles said. "Not at the time. At the time it just felt right, the way Arete said. But the more I think about it the more it felt like having my own self taken over. I wasn't in control of what I did. And afterward when Klymene spoke to me it took a real effort to answer. I felt drained, even though all I'd done was walk through the woods and drink some water."

Father put his hand on Kallikles's shoulder. "It's hard for anyone to resist Fate and Necessity."

"I didn't even try," I said, and saw my brothers nod. None of us had tried.

"What did it do?" Kallikles asked.

"Connects you to me, to the world. If you weren't my children it would mark you as votaries. As it is, it marks you as what you are. My children. Heroes."

"How does it work?"

"It's a Mystery."

"Mother always said you said that when you didn't understand something," I said.

"That's exactly what a Mystery is, something the gods don't properly understand," he said. "Fate and Necessity are the bounds set on us. All of us. Fate is the share our souls chose before birth. Necessity is the edges of that."

"If we were marked as heroes, did the others notice?" Phaedrus asked.

"I don't know, I wasn't there. Did they?"

"Ficino noticed something, but he didn't say anything," I said. "And maybe Klymene—she was looking at Kallikles in a funny way. But nobody said anything. Is it going to happen again?"

He spread his hands. "I don't know. If you go back to Delos, probably. And in Delphi, perhaps."

"You said it marks us," Phaedrus said, coming back to that. "Who does it mark us to?"

"The gods," Father said, casually. "If you meet them, they will know what you are, now."

"But not Porphyry and Alkibiades and Euklides back on Kallisti?" Phaedrus asked.

"I don't know. The gods might recognize them as my sons. But they'd definitely know you three now." Father put his hand against an especially large pine, patted it, then turned and started walking back toward the shore.

"So we could have resisted it?" I asked, following, the pine must underfoot still resisting my every step. "What would have happened?"

"If you'd been strong enough, you wouldn't have gone through the ritual. If you'd tried to resist and not been strong enough, you'd have done it anyway. Why didn't you resist?"

"It felt so right," I said, and my brothers nodded, though Kallikles was biting his lip.

"But it wasn't you," Phaedrus said. "You're here, you were on the ship. It wasn't you making us do that."

"It was my power. Things done with my power keep on working, even though I'm here. I can't intervene. But things that have been set up keep on working. Delos is full of my power." He frowned. "I don't have any power right now, myself. So I couldn't give you any. But Delos could."

"We have power?" Phaedrus squeaked. I didn't laugh at the way his voice came out because I felt the same myself.

"You said it marked us, you didn't say it gave us *power*," Kallikles said, rolling his eyes, though you think he'd be used to Father by now. "What *kind* of power? Power to do what?"

"Power according to your souls," Father said, in that infuriating way he had, as if it were the most intuitive thing in the world and everyone knew it already.

"To do what?" Phaedrus repeated.

"To do whatever you want to, under Fate and Necessity," Father said.

"Heal people? Walk on lava?" I asked.

"Yes, those sorts of things," he confirmed. "But feel confident in your power before you try walking on lava! I don't know how much power you have, I can't tell without my own power. It may not be enough."

I looked at Phaedrus, who was the one who wanted to control volcanoes. He was staring at the backs of his hands as if he'd never seen them before.

"I don't know exactly how it works," Father went on. "Whether Necessity woke up what was there already, or if some of my power from the island came into you. But right now you can do things I can't."

"We could have healed Mother," I said before I thought.

"Too late," Father said. "If I'd taken you there years ago, perhaps."

"Why didn't you?" Kallikles asked. "If you knew it would do this?"

"I didn't know. I thought it might. And you were all so young. And we wanted you to be your best selves. I didn't know what that would be. It wasn't until you said you wanted to come on this voyage that any of you said you wanted to be heroes."

"So we could do the kind of thing gods do? Like transforming people into things?" Phaedrus said, pensively.

"Yes, but it's not usually a good idea," Father said. I saw an expression on his face that I hadn't seen since before Mother died. He was worried. "You have power. You might be able to do that. But please don't!"

"How do we use it?" Kallikles asked.

Father's brow furrowed a little. "You just reach out and use it. You'll work it out. You've all learned logic and self-control."

"Not like the gods," Phaedrus said, and laughed.

"How about time travel?" I asked.

"Don't try that!" He looked really worried now. "That does take experience. It isn't time travel. You step outside time and then back in. Being outside time isn't like being in it. Look, please don't try that until after I have my own powers and I can show you how to do it. Terrible things could happen to you. You could get lost forever." He laughed suddenly. "This reminds me of when the boys were all starting to walk at once! Suddenly nothing was safe, and we had no idea what you could get into or do. Simmea—am I ever going to stop missing Simmea?"

"Ever is a long time for a god," I said. "Can we use this power to keep from dying?"

"Your body will have to die, eventually. But you can keep it healthy meanwhile. And you don't have to stay dead, if you choose to be a god."

It was such a scary thought. "You'll help us?" Phaedrus asked.

"What, I have to run entry-level divinity classes now? Of

course I will." He hesitated. "You're heroes. In some ways, you have more ability to use your powers than I do mine, even when I have mine. Gods are bound by Fate and Necessity, of course, but we're also under the edicts of Zeus—we can't use our powers to interfere in human affairs unless we're asked. You can keep right on interfering as much as you want because you're still mortal for the time being."

"What?" Phaedrus sounded affronted. "What about what Athene did setting up the Republic? Wasn't that interfering in human affairs?"

"The Masters prayed to her for help doing it," Father said. "She could grant their prayers. She couldn't have done it alone."

"And buying the Children?" I asked.

"The Masters decided to do it. She just chose to help. It was all human action and the consequences of human action." He looked helpless.

"And what she did to Sokrates?" Kallikles asked.

"He was her votary. You can do whatever you want to your votaries. And no other gods can do anything to them." He looked ashamed. "We don't always behave as well as we should."

"And it'll be made into art?" I asked.

"Eventually, inevitably, yes," he said. "Everything we do will be."

"What?" Kallikles asked.

"I told Arete this. Our lives are art. It's part of being a god."

"And for a hero?" he asked.

Father shrugged. "It depends on their deeds."

The three of us looked at each other, and then back at Father. He shook his head. "Just be careful. And try to be careful what other people see. They'll react to you very differently if they know. Think carefully."

"Rhea," Kallikles said. Of course, she would be his first thought. "I'll have to tell her as soon as we get back."

Father looked at him sympathetically. "Maybe she'll under-stand the way Simmea did."

Erinna, I thought, sadly. There were already too many gulfs between us. My age, and Father's nature, and her silver rank, and now this.

Then Phaedrus gasped, and we turned to him. He was a little way behind, and he was walking a handspan or so above the pine must of the forest. It didn't seem strange, and then it did, to see my brother walking on air unsupported. Bold Kallikles took a leap and joined him. I hesitated, but Phaedrus put out his hands to me, grinning. I reached for his hand and took a step up onto nothing, and the nothing held me up, and we were all standing above the ground, walking on air. The strangest thing was that it didn't take any effort and didn't feel unnatural. It was as if I'd always been able to do it but had been shuffling away on the ground out of habit. I ran a few steps up the air, laugh-ing, until my head was almost at the top of the pines. Then I saw Father, still scuffing his feet down in the must, and stopped.

"All right," he said. "Now before you go any further up, show me how you're going to come down."

Coming down was difficult, much harder than going up. We couldn't do it for a moment. I figured it out first—I took big exaggerated steps downward, as if descending an invisible stair-case, and the boys copied me. When my feet touched the earth I felt unexpectedly heavy and almost fell. It reminded me of how walking on Amorgos felt strange after the motion of the ship. I took a cautious step, and then another. The boys were down now too, staggering and shaking their heads.

"What else?" Phaedrus asked. "What else can we do?"

"I really don't know," Father said. "You'll have to find out for yourselves, find your limits. You should be looking for your do-main, what you care about, where you have excellence. I told you about that. It's different for everyone. And go slowly, be care-

ful. Test what you do. Think like philosophers. Pursue excellence, in this as in all things."

I wanted to try things. But I was afraid, too. I wanted to be a
god, or I had thought that I did. Now I wasn't sure. I could see
a chasm opening between me and everyone but Father and my
brothers. I didn't need the warning to hide my new powers from
the others. It was the same way I felt about growing up. I wanted
to be grown up, of course I did, to vote in the Assembly and be
assigned a metal—gold, of course, and there wasn't much doubt
I'd make it. At the same time I didn't want to stop being a child,
secure, looked after. There were ways that was comfortable. I'd
always been the youngest in the family, and there were advantages to that. There were advantages to being human. Not the
only one Father ever talked about, dying and being reborn as a
completely new person. I couldn't see that as an advantage at all!
I liked being me, and I wanted to keep on doing it. The advantages I could see were more to do with being like everyone else,
living the kind of life we all lived. Having somebody love me one
day, even if it couldn't be somebody as wonderful as Erinna.
Being excellent but still relatively normal. Like Mother, I thought,
instead of like Father. But I had the power now. I couldn't pretend I didn't.

"I want to be free and choose for myself," I said, as we came
out of the trees again just above the beach. I hadn't disliked feeling in the hand of Fate. But the more I thought about it, the less
I wanted to feel that again. Fate and Necessity are what binds
the gods. I wasn't sure I wanted to be bound that way.

"Then keep away from gods," Father said, looking over his
shoulder at me, half-smiling. Then suddenly he looked serious.
"One thing you will have enough power to do now, all of you, is
reach the gods with your prayers. Be careful what you pray, and
what you ask and whose attention you draw."

On the beach some people were preparing food, and others

were racing and wrestling on the sand as if they were in the palaestra. The *Excellence* was bobbing sedately at anchor. Clouds were
blowing up out of the west and glowing rose and violet in the rays
of the lowering sun. (Since I'd left home I seemed to spend a lot of
time looking at the sky. It was always changing, yet it was the
one thing that was the same everywhere.) Nobody took any notice of us coming back, except Erinna, who waved happily as she
caught sight of us, and Neleus, who raked us with a dark-eyed
glance before turning back to the fire he was building.

13

APOLLO

I had guessed that Delos might have an effect on my Young Ones, but had not quite thought through what that would mean. I knew it when I saw them coming back aboard to sleep that night. The three of them had a new look about them that I nevertheless recognized. They were always beautiful, and always moved well—everyone brought up in the City knew how to move well. But now there was something about them, a certain sleekness, a not-quite-hidden glitter, as of a scarf draped carelessly over treasure. They looked like Olympians in disguise.

After the Last Debate, Simmea and I set up housekeeping together in Thessaly, which had been Sokrates's house. We took all the children belonging to us—Neleus, and my three boys. I took Kallikles, Alkibiades and Phaedrus from the city crèches. Many people wanted their babies but couldn't identify them. There was no difficulty with mine. I'd have known them by their heroic souls, but anyone could tell at a glance from their eyes and bone structure. Phaedrus's blue eyes looked strange against his dark skin, especially then, when he was five months old. Alkibiades was nine months old, and Kallikles was just over a year.

We also collected Neleus, who was also five months old. Simmea frowned when I carried him into Thessaly. "I swore to Zeus and Demeter not to treat him differently from the others," she said. "They're all my children."

"They're all your children, and you won't be prejudiced in his favor in any way, but here he is," I said. Then she took him and hugged him as if she'd never let him go.

It only took a couple of days for Simmea to decide that Plato was right, or at least that the two of us couldn't manage four lively boys all day and all night. We took to leaving them in the nursery for several hours in the day so that we could get things done. There they were being brought up according to the precepts of Plato, communally, by people trained in early infant care. It didn't hurt them, or at least I don't think it did.

I had always known all my children were mine, always known they were heroes, always been able to pick them out of a crowd. Power didn't make any difference to that. I looked at them across the deck, trying to see where it did make a difference. Arete met my eyes, and as I looked away I recognized and identified my emotion.

I was envious, something I had rarely experienced. Envy is like jealousy, but quite distinct. Envy is when somebody else has something and you wish you had it too. Jealousy is when they have something and you wish you had it *instead*. I have felt jealous of people, usually when the thing I wished I had was somebody's attention. It's hateful, far and away my least-favorite emotion, because it makes me less than I could be. I dislike feeling it, and try to avoid it. Envy has been much rarer for me, because apart from people's attention there's normally very little that I want that I can't just have, and very little of that is something anyone else could have anyway.

But at that moment when I saw my Young Ones coming back aboard full of power, I wanted access to my own power. And I could even have had it, if I really wanted it, far more power than my children had. I could return to being my whole self at any time, at the cost of this mortal life. I considered it for a moment, there on the deck. I could swim to where my priests were standing on the Delian shore watching the ship maneuvering out. I could sacrifice myself there—dying, as was poetically appropriate, where I had been born. I could return moments later in my full power. I just had to want it enough to give up my incarnation—and that meant wanting it more than I wanted to fulfill Simmea's dying wish.

It was tempting, but only fleetingly. I looked down at the choppy sunset-hued sea between the ship and the shore. Simmea had taught me to swim. And Simmea had wanted me to stay in mortal form. She had some reason, and I felt sure she was right, whatever that reason was. Until I understood it and fulfilled it, or until I happened to die naturally, I would stay incarnate, even if it was inconvenient. Even when it hurt. Envy wasn't pleasant, but it did teach me something about myself, even if it was something I didn't much like. I was glad to have time to compose myself before there was a chance to talk to the Young Ones. I wouldn't want them to know I suffered from such a mean emotion.

My priests were still standing on the Delian shore, looking toward the *Excellence* as the watch on duty brought her head around so her sails could catch the wind. I leaned out on the rail, smiling, and waved to them. They looked at each other in consternation, then back at me in dawning affirmation. They waved back emphatically. I was glad I'd been able to make somebody happy.

I was tempted to take up my powers again on Ikaria—not out of envy for the Young Ones' power. I had thoroughly dealt with that annoying emotion by then. No, on Ikaria the urge came purely out of a desire to protect them. They were children, and there was so much trouble they could get into! With divine power there were so many things it was easy to get into and difficult to get out of. The things they thought of—walking on lava!

Time travel! I didn't want them burned up by lava, but far less did I want them stepping outside time and not being able to negotiate what they found there.

I tried to remember my own childhood. I'd had Mother and a whole set of goddesses shielding and teaching me. (That may be why I have always lived solitary since.) What I chiefly remembered were bounds set around my power, bounds for me to test, to encourage me to develop safely. From the moment I was born I had the power to destroy the world (I had the *sun*), and they shielded me until I had the judgment to understand that destroying the world would be unutterably stupid. They knew what I was to be. The other Olympians wanted me—well, except Hera, who didn't want me or anything like me. They shaped me to fill the place in the pantheon meant for me. I like to think I have done better than that already, fulfilled far more than the promises and prophecies. And I am still trying to increase my excellence, and the world's excellence.

If there were places destined for my children I did not know what they were. I wasn't aware of any prophecies or expectations. They had to find their own way. I could give them advice and prohibitions and information. I couldn't use my power to teach them, or to give them safe boundaries to work in, because right now when they needed it I didn't have any power. It felt like letting them down. And yet, Simmea had wanted me to stay incarnate, at the cost of her own life. Could this be why? Could they need to learn without boundaries? As soon as I thought it I knew that this was insane. Simmea hadn't known anything about the powers of a god except what I'd told her. She hadn't known about Delos or what they would need. She was going on the information she had at the time, most of which I must have and some of which I might be able to discover if we ever caught up with Kebes. (Or whoever had killed her, if it wasn't Kebes.)

I did feel like an idiot whenever I thought about it. What

could I do, incarnate, that I couldn't do as a god? I usually asked the question the other way around, for there were so many things I could do as a god that I couldn't do as a human. I had become human to learn about will and consequences and the significance of mortal life. There were things I had learned, and no doubt there was more to learn. But as for things I could do better incarnate—beyond learning that it seemed to amount to suffering, and waiting. Perhaps there was something else Simmea wanted me to learn. But she had seemed so urgent—don't be an idiot, she had said, as if her reason was obvious and imperative. She let herself die, she gave up her memories and our life together and the future we could have had. The least I could do was try not to be more of an idiot than I could help.

From Ikaria we sailed to Samos, and there we had our first solid news of Kebes. (I had the map with me. But I hadn't shown it to anyone or even spoken about it.) There were no Samians in the Catalog of Ships. And the priests in Delos hadn't known anything beyond "northeast" for Kebes. There was no sign of the *Goodness*. But there was a settlement here, where the city of Samos would one day stand. It wasn't a mud-hut encampment either, like the primitive ones we had seen on Naxos and Paros and Mykonos. The buildings were made of well-mortared stone, with familiar pillars in the style it amused me to call archaeo-classical. Nor did it have the strange flat Kykladic statues, but rather a solid Renaissance-style statue of a goddess. The people didn't run away or immediately attack us, though we saw a stir in the streets.

Maecenas dropped anchor just outside the harbor and immediately called a council meeting. Everyone who wasn't part of the council looked enviously at us as we went down to Maecenas's cabin. I was on the ship's council because the Just City was an aristocracy—rule was by the best. And by the standards they were using, I was going to be selected as among the best on almost all occasions. I sometimes felt a bit of a fraud about this, as they were judging by human standards. But I was glad to be included in the council and have my voice heard.

"What do we do?" Maecenas asked bluntly. "This could be Kebes. Probably is. Do we attack? Or talk first?"

"Talk first," Klymene said, a hair before me.

"We need to find out more," I said, when she spread her hand to yield to me. "We don't see the *Goodness*. It seems like a small place."

"It's as big as Psyche, and it has the same kind of look about it of something built without Workers but with our sensibilities," Maecenas said. "And Kebes only took a hundred and fifty, and no Young Ones."

"I don't think this is it," I said.

Everyone disagreed with me. As I didn't want to tell them about the map, I couldn't explain why I didn't think so.

"It's logical that it is," Klymene summed up after a while.

"What we need is more information," I said. "Whether this is Kebes or not, we need to talk. And if it is, we need to find out whether they raided us and took the head of Victory. We might be able to set up friendly relations, if not. And if it isn't Kebes, we need to find out who they are."

"Let's go in then, and see," Maecenas said. "If I send you, Pytheas, will you stay calm?"

"If I am an envoy, I will behave as an envoy," I said, standing up and bumping my head on the cabin roof.

"I wasn't challenging your honor, man," Maecenas said. "Sit down. You go, and Klymene, and take Phaenarete and Dion. We'll stay anchored right here, in bowshot. If there's trouble, we'll hear. But if there's trouble, get back here as fast as you can." Phaenarete and Dion were older Young Ones, strong, and well-trained with weapons.

"That place doesn't have a palisade," Klymene said. "And they didn't run off. We ought to be able to talk."

"Wear armor," Maecenas said.

So I had to put on a cuirass, and endure the envy of the entire ship's company as I was rowed ashore. Samos has a natural deep harbor, and they had built a wooden wharf with poles—they were clearly used to receiving a big ship like ours. There was a crowd waiting to receive our little boat, and the armor didn't feel like much protection.

Nobody looked familiar. Most of the crowd were young, and so I wouldn't have expected to recognize anyone, but some of them were older, indeed aged. They were also the wrong mix of people to be the Goodness Group—all of these had what I think of as typical Ionian Greek looks. They could have been carved in marble. "Joy," one of them said, a middle-aged man. "You have come early. Why do you stand off from shore? Is there sickness aboard *Goodness*?"

His accent was unusual, but he spoke good Greek.

"Joy to you. We're not the *Goodness*," Klymene said. "Our ship is called *Excellence*. We come from Kallisti. Who are you?"

The answer was surprising, and took a long time to elicit clearly. It turned out that they were a group of assorted refugees from wars in Greece and the islands who had been settled here by Kebes and his people to found a new city, which was called Marissa—after, they told us, the name of the mother of God. God himself was called Yayzu. They traded regularly with the *Goodness*, giving them food in return for manufactured items such as bowls and statues. They did not recognize the name Kebes, though when I said Matthias there was a general sigh and a smile of recognition. The thing they most wanted to discover from me, once I had said the words "*Excellence*" and "Kallisti," were whether we were still in contact with Athene. When I told them that we hadn't seen her since the *Goodness* left, they seemed very relieved, and admitted that they had two people in Marissa from the Goodness Group, the doctor and the teacher. These two came forward now through the crowd, visibly of our people. The teacher was much paler-skinned than anyone else, a Master I had known slightly called Aristomache, now in her seventies. The doctor, Terentius, was clearly one of the Children, much swarthier than most in the crowd. He seemed only vaguely familiar. They hugged us and asked for news of friends left in the City.

"Is it safe for us to bring the *Excellence* in?" Klymene asked.

Terentius looked surprised. "Of course! Why wouldn't it be? Marissa is a civilized city. Well, semi-civilized. As civilized as any of our colonies," he finished proudly.

"You have colonies?" Phaenarete asked. "How many?"

"Lots," Terentius said, slightly cagily, though the appalling arithmetic positively leaped to mind—if they had two people in each one they could have seventy-five colonies like Marissa up and down the Aegean. "Are you all still on Kallisti trying to do Plato's Republic?"

"Yes," I said. "Though we have five cities there now, and lots of Young Ones. This is our first exploratory voyage."

If I made us sound like five united cities, who can blame me? Kebes had been founding colonies. Who could imagine how large an army he might be ready to field if he thought we were divided and easy to conquer? I didn't doubt that he would still hate us.

Klymene and Phaenarete started to signal to the ship that it was safe to come in. "One thing, Aristomache," I said. "Marissa. Yayzu. Is this some primitive religion I'm not aware of, or are you really teaching them Christianity?"

"Christianity, of course," she said, with a twinkle in her eye.

"What's Christianity?" Dion asked.

"It's the one true faith. It has been kept from you, so you could worship Plato, but it's the only thing that can save your soul," Aristomache said. Heads were nodding around her. Dion's eyes widened.

"It hasn't been kept from you at all. It's that crazy religion Ikaros has in the City of Amazons," I said, dismissively.

Dion was a sensible lad. He nodded politely at Aristomache. "Oh, that," he said.

"God sent his son, his only son, down into the world to save everyone," she said.

"Right, and Athene's one of his angels," Dion said. "I remember now. It's popular in the City of Amazons. Here too, I see."

Although we had thought a lot about what Kebes and the Goodness Group might have been doing, collecting refugees from Greece and settling them in colonies on uninhabited islands had never crossed our minds. And of course they were doing just exactly what everyone else I knew was doing, trying to live the Good Life in Plato's Republic. It also hadn't occurred to anyone that Kebes would try to do this in a Christian context, more than a thousand years before Christ. Ficino and Ikaros had managed to reconcile Christianity and Plato, and also in Ikaros's case Christianity and the inarguable presence of Pallas Athene. I wondered how Kebes had done it. He wasn't stupid, and he'd been trained by Sokrates, but didn't have most of the structure they were starting from. He couldn't have. He'd been *ten*.

"No, actually Athene's a demon," Aristomache said.

Dion shrugged as if he didn't care either way. I hoped this would be the general reaction aboard, at least among the Young Ones.

I don't have anything against Christianity. It's a wonderful story. Indeed it's a wonderful story that has been mostly wasted by Christians. It produced some incredible architecture and music, and some splendid visual art, especially in the Renaissance. But they have made surprisingly little art about what it's like to be an incarnate god, suddenly subject to the pains of humanity, and then being tortured to death, before returning to sort things out in divine form. It's the heart of the story, and I'd been thinking the whole time I'd been incarnate myself that they could have done so much more with it. Michaelangelo, Rembrandt, Bach, yes, but who else had truly entered into the Mystery of it? For every *Supper at Emmaeus* there are thousands of Annunciations and Nativities, as if the interesting thing is that Jesus was born. Everyone is born. There's a lot of focus on the Crucifixion, again mostly in the visual arts, but surprisingly little about how he experienced his life, before or after death. Fra Angelico came closest, I think. But you'd think in that whole era where Christianity was dominant, they'd have thought about the whole thing more, instead of getting obsessed with sin and punishment.

Faced with Aristomache's pious mouthings here, I felt shaken for the first time. I knew time couldn't be changed. But if it could . . . if it could and if Christianity could have taken root here, at the very beginning, then the world I cared about most deeply might never exist. Christianity was a religion with a good story and an appealing simplicity—forgive and be forgiven, be washed in the blood of the sacrifice and be saved. If it could catch on in the Aegean before the Trojan War then everything would be different. I knew time was fixed and unchangeable. I had lived outside it. But even so, I felt a chill.

Our ship was warping in toward the wharf. "Do you want to trade?" the old man asked me.

"Certainly we do, though that will be for our captain to negotiate," I said, smoothly, still thinking about Christianity and Kebes.

"Tonight we will feast the *Excellence!*" the old man announced. The crowd cheered.

"Where are your other colonies?" I asked Terentius, as casually as I could. "Where's your main city?"

"What are your intentions toward us?" Aristomache asked.

"Exploration, a little trade," I said, spreading my hands peacefully. "Unless you raided us last autumn. Somebody raided us and killed Simmea."

Aristomache looked shocked and put her hand on my arm. "Oh, that's terrible. I'm so sorry. I remember you two were inseparable. I remember when she gave birth, you didn't want to stop holding on to her hands. She told me how you were both practicing agape. What an awful thing to happen! It must have been pirates. There's so much turmoil on the mainland, and some of them have ships. But we'd never do such a thing. It's true we have been avoiding Kallisti to keep away from Athene, and philosophical trouble. But we'd never do anything like that."

Terentius was nodding, looking appalled. They both seemed utterly sincere. I exchanged a quick glance with Dion. I didn't like to think that Kebes was doing better at civilization than we were.

14

ARETE

I seemed to spend half my time at the top of the mast looking far out at the sea and thinking, and the other half at the rail looking at close-up islands. Usually my time at the masthead was peaceful. I suppose I should have been contemplating philosophy, but my mind had a tendency to wander.

The day we left Ikaria I wanted to think about our powers, and what they meant, and what father had said about the gods, but there was no time for contemplation. We had our first squall on my watch. I stayed at the masthead looking for rocks, and calling them out when I did see them. The others were worn out adjusting sails and changing tack—all our practice had been in smooth weather. When your sails are wet and the wind backs as you're trying to adjust them, canvas feels alive, as if it's trying to get away from you. Erinna nearly fell into the sea helping Nemea wrestle with a sail. She saved herself by swinging on a rope. My heart nearly stopped when I saw it. There was no time to do anything, but my impulse in the moment before she caught the rope was to fly down from the mast and snatch her up. I had risen to my feet and was about to leap. On sober reflection I had no idea whether I could fly, let alone carry another person as I did it. I resolved to ask Father. But it felt like the right thing to do, the thing my instincts prompted, and in another instant I would have tried it.

In the excitement I nearly missed seeing a fishing boat scudding before the wind. Fortunately, it saw us and veered off. I kept watching for rocks and calling them out. By the time the clouds lifted our watch was almost over, and Samos was close at hand.

When Thano, my replacement lookout, came up I went down to the deck and hugged Erinna, intensely aware of the feeling of her body and fighting down the sensations in my own. "I'm so glad you're safe!" I said.

"My own clumsiness that I slipped in the first place," she said, but she did hug me back for a moment before letting go. "It shows how important all those drills are. My body knew what to do when there was no time to think."

I felt nothing but relief that I hadn't yielded to my own instincts. Whether I could have flown and caught her or not, I'd have revealed what I was to everyone. That wouldn't have mattered if I could have saved her life, but what would she have thought? "I'd never been aloft in a storm before," I said.

"That was no more than a little squall. If there's any sign of a real storm we'll find somewhere sheltered to anchor, I should think. Real storms can be bad for sailing ships. Like the one at the beginning of the *Aeneid*."

"Or when they open the bag of winds in the *Odyssey*," I said.

She grinned. "Isn't it fun to think we're sailing their very seas, before they sailed them?"

"What would have happened if you'd gone overboard?"

"I can swim. The water was rough, but I'd probably have been fine. Maecenas would have put the ship to, which would have wasted time, but we're not in a life or death race."

I was even more glad I hadn't flown down off the mast and perhaps killed myself when she wasn't in real danger.

"But my head might have hit the deck, or a rock," she went on. "You can't help thinking about that kind of thing. I'm glad the rope was there and I caught it."

"Oh yes," I said, wholeheartedly. Just then I caught sight of something over her shoulder, on the shore. "What's that?"

It was a city, a proper city. We sailed closer and anchored near it, and a small shore group was sent in. It was a real city, which seemed homelike after the places we had seen. It had columns and broad streets and it was clean. There was even a colosseum, which we didn't have at home, though of course I recognized it from paintings. There was an unpainted marble statue on the wharf, a goddess with a baby on her knee. The style was familiar, although of course I hadn't seen that particular statue before. It made me feel welcome after the strange decorated heads on Paros and Mykonos. There hadn't been any statues that I'd seen on Delos, only immense columns and future ghosts.

"Auge," Maia said, coming up to us at the rail. I turned to her questioningly.

"Auge must have carved that," she said. "I recognize her style."

"I suppose that means that this is definitely the Goodness Group." We were quite close to the statue, which was bigger than life-size so I could see it well. The goddess was looking down at the baby, who was looking out at us, with his hand stretched toward us.

Maia nodded. Erinna was also looking at the statue. "Who is she?" she asked.

"Auge was one of the Children," Maia said. "She left with Kebes."

"I meant, which goddess," Erinna said.

"Hera—" Maia said, with much less certainty. "No, Demeter, or perhaps—"

I looked questioningly at Maia. Her voice sounded strange.

"Aphrodite with baby Eros?" Erinna suggested. "But he doesn't have any wings."

"Surely Kebes wouldn't . . . ? Where's Ficino?" Maia turned to me. "Can you see if you can find him?"

Erinna and I went to look for him. He was asleep in a hammock, looking so old and tired that I hesitated to wake him. Erinna clapped her hands softly, and he woke at once, instantly alert. "What is it?" he asked.

"We're at a city that might be the Goodness Group city, and Maia wanted you to look at a mysterious statue," Erinna said.

"That's worth waking up for," he said. I remembered him saying he didn't sleep much these days, and was sorry to have disturbed him. He swung out of the hammock and pulled his kiton on. I looked away from his old-man's wrinkled skin, like a plucked chicken. I drew Erinna away, hardly noticing until afterward that I had touched her arm. Ficino had earned his dignity.

He came over to us as soon as he came out on the deck. Neleus had joined Maia by the rail and we all crowded together. "Holy Mother!" Ficino said.

"Literally and specifically, I think," Maia said. She sounded furious about it.

"This can't have anything to do with Ikaros," Ficino said. Erinna raised her eyebrows at me. I shook my head. I had no idea why he would say that.

"It could just be a goddess we don't know," Neleus said.

"That's exactly what it is," Erinna said. "I don't know her. It seems as if you two do?"

"It's the pose," Ficino said. "It seems Christian."

"Like Botticelli," I said, seeing it at once now that he had pointed it out. The statue resembled Botticelli's Madonnas, the ones in the book we had at home, the book Maia had brought with her. The child on her lap, her head bent over him.

Ficino looked at me sharply. "Not like any of the Botticellis we have in Florentia," he said.

Maia blushed. "Remember, I had a book," she said. "Ikaros brought it from one of his art expeditions with Athene. It has the Madonnas."

"Did you show it to Auge?" Ficino asked.

"Yes," Maia admitted. "When she was just starting to sculpt seriously. That's probably all this is. Influence. It probably is Hera." She sounded as if she were trying to convince herself.

"Where is that book now?" Ficino asked.

"In Thessaly," I said. "My mother loved it."

"Simmea always loved Botticelli," Ficino said, sounding sad. "In the dining hall at Florentia she'd always sit so that she could stare at one or another of his paintings."

On the quay Father and the others were talking intently with a group of locals. They were wearing kitons that were each dyed in one solid color, mostly blues and pinks.

"So what goddess do you think it might be?" Erinna asked, patiently.

"Maria," Ficino said. "The mother of God in Christianity."

"That thing the Amazons are into?" Erinna asked. "How would the Goodness Group know about it?"

"Where did you get Kebes?" Maia asked Ficino abruptly.

"The slave market at Smyrna," he said. "The same place I found Simmea. They were chained together." I shuddered. I knew that all the Children had been enslaved, but knowing it was different from hearing a detail like that dropped casually. That was my mother he was talking about. Thank Athene he had been there to rescue her!

"What year was it?" "Oh Maia, honestly! You can't expect me to remember that! So long ago, and so many children."

"But was it after Christianity?" she asked.

"Oh yes. They both had saints' names, I remember." He stared at the statue. "But they were only ten."

"Simmea used to say that we should have started with the abandoned babies of antiquity," Maia said. I had heard her say so myself.

"Ten-year-olds are not wax tablets that can be wiped clean and written afresh," Ficino agreed.

"I can't understand how Plato could have thought they were," Neleus said.

Just then the shore party sent a signal that it was safe for us to come in. "Are you sure?" Maia muttered, but Caerellia began to give orders for the Hesperides watch to take the ship in to the wharf, where there were poles for us to tie up to as we did at home. Proper docking facilities, no doubt intended for the *Goodness*.

"There were some masters among the Goodness Group," Ficino said. "It isn't necessarily a case of what ten-year-olds remembered." There was a cheer from the shore.

"Somebody, some Jesuit or Dominican I think, said that if you gave him a boy until he was seven he'd be theirs for life," Maia said.

Ficino barked a laugh.

"So Christianity was a big thing?" Erinna asked. "In the bit of history we don't hear about?"

"It was the dominant religion of Europe for fifteen hundred years," Maia said. "We just try not to mention it much."

"Even Rome became Christian," Ficino said.

Erinna and I looked at each other, astonished. "Rome!" It seemed entirely implausible.

"They even counted their years from the birth of Christ," Neleus said. He was scanning the crowd on shore intently as we came in closer. "Father mentioned that once."

"And where did you get Pytheas?" Maia asked.

Ficino laughed. "Pytheas is something else. He came from the slave market in Euboia. One of the earliest expeditions. Athene named him herself, the only one she ever would."

"But what year?" Maia asked.

"Four or five hundred years after the founding of Rome?" Ficino said, uncertain.

"So how would he know that?"

"Somebody must have told him," Neleus said. "Maybe one of you let it slip. Or one of the other Masters."

We were tying up. I realized I'd be able to step ashore, no need for swimming this time. Father was still talking to the locals, but Klymene and Phaenarete strode over toward the ship.

"Interesting that Athene named him," Maia said. "Did she know what she was doing, and did she have the right to do it?"

"That neatly sums up the Last Debate," Neleus said.

"It seems so strange to think that you've actually met a goddess," Erinna said. Neleus's eyes met mine. It didn't seem strange to us at all.

"She rescued me from a life where I was stifled, and gave me a life I wanted to lead," Maia said. "And we did all have the very best intentions for building the Good Life."

Klymene swung herself onto the *Excellence*. Caerellia and Maecenas were there to greet her. "This is Marissa, a colony founded by the Goodness Group but mostly consisting of refugees from the wars of the mainland," she said concisely, to them but loudly enough that the rest of us pressing around could hear. "They are friendly and want to talk about trade. They have other cities, we don't yet know where."

"Marissa," muttered Ficino. Maia nodded, as if it meant something. Too close to Maria? She seemed a benevolent goddess from what I knew of her, which was entirely pictorial. Of course I had not read the words of the Botticelli book, which were in the Latin alphabet but some language I did not know. I hadn't heard much about the religion she was part of. *Even Rome*, I thought, still amazed.

"You said it's safe?" Maecenas asked.

"Safe enough. Leave a watch aboard, I'd say."

Caerellia nodded and started giving orders, that the watch on duty would stay aboard. Everyone not part of the Hesperides watch started for the rail.

"Safe for old men and children," Ficino said, taking my arm. I was surprised how thin his hand felt. I swung over the rail and he followed me more slowly.

"Wait," Maecenas said.

We stopped and turned.

"I want you to help with negotiations," Maecenas said to Ficino.

"That's never been one of my areas of interest," Ficino said.

"No, but you're good with people," Maecenas said.

Ficino sighed and took his hand off my arm. "Very well. But I insist on having time to explore Marissa, at least as much as we did at Delos."

"I don't know how long we'll stay, but I won't keep you in negotiations every minute," Maecenas said.

Ficino nodded and went with him.

I could see Father still surrounded by people. Erinna and Neleus had both stepped onto dry land, and were staggering a little, the same way I was. Maia was already striding off toward the statue. We followed after her.

Looking around, I found myself remembering the visit I had made to Sokratea with Mother a year ago. I touched Erinna's arm—it just wasn't possible to avoid touching her, but even the most normal things were charged with tingling erotic potential that I had to fight down. She turned to me. "Remember Sokratea?" I said, keeping my voice as even as I could. She nodded.

"This feels the same, sort of. It's like the City but not like it, and everyone is a stranger."

She nodded again. "In some ways it's stranger than those weird primitive villages, because it is like home. But it's not like Sokratea either. We've been in constant contact with Sokratea. We're allies. We have diplomatic relations, and trade. We were there on a recognized mission."

"I was thinking that," Neleus put in. "We haven't heard anything from the Goodness Group in all this time. How did Klymene decide to just trust them and bring the ship in?"

"Klymene and Pytheas," Erinna said. She put her hand to her side where she kept a little knife for cutting ropes and whittling wood. Neleus did the same with his, and I realized as their eyes met that they were ephebes, they had gone through weapons training, and that whatever other uses they had every day, the knives at their sides were also weapons. I felt useless and young and unarmed. "Your father wants vengeance more than anyone," she went on. "He wouldn't have called us in if he thought they were responsible."

It was true. I looked over to him, still surrounded by Marissans. An old woman at his side said something and came toward us, or rather toward Maia and the statue. "Maia!" she called, clearly delighted. "Joy to you!" It must have been true what Ficino said about the Goodness Group having Masters in it, because she looked very old, almost as old as he was.

Maia turned. "Aristomache! Joy! How lovely to see you. What have you been doing?" They hugged each other

"Teaching, as always," Aristomache said.

"Here?"

"Here, and in Hieronymos on the other side of the island. And before that in Lucia, our first city, on Lesbos. And you?"

"Teaching too, in Amazonia and now back in the original city. You have three cities?"

"We have eight, on three islands. And you have five, all on Kallisti, Pytheas says?"

"That's right," Maia confirmed. "We've been calling you the Lost City, we never thought of you having so many!"

"Well, with only a hundred and fifty of us we had to find recruits, and when we saw how many people needed help we just kept on with it," Aristomache said. "War's such a terrible thing. We do what we can." She smiled. "Now who are these?"

"These are Neleus and Erinna and Arete, pupils of mine."

Aristomache nodded to us in a friendly way. "I'll introduce you all to some pupils of mine."

Maia smiled at her. "We'd like that."

Aristomache peered more closely at Neleus. "Are you Simmea's son, young man, or don't you know? In any case, I was there the night you were born."

"I am," he said. "And Arete is my sister."

She leaned forward and peered at me. "Good. There's a definite resemblance. I'm glad she left descendants. Pytheas told me what happened to her. Terrible."

Erinna was looking up at the statue. Close up, it towered over us. It wasn't a colossus like Crocus's statues, but it was much larger than life size. Maia glanced up too. "What's this?" she asked Aristomache.

"Come on Maia, you *know* that Jesus Christ is your lord and savior," Aristomache said. "You might have turned your back on him to worship demons and given Plato more honor than is due a philosopher, but you know in your soul that He is the resurrection and the life."

"Demons! Nonsense. And for that matter, you must have prayed to Athene yourself," Maia responded.

As Aristomache opened her mouth to answer, I realized that they had spoken in a language I didn't know, and that Neleus and Erinna's faces reflected their incomprehension. I had never heard this language before, but I understood it as clearly as if it were Greek or Latin. It must be one of the powers that Delos had awakened in me, though I had no idea how or why. I'd have to ask Father, and talk to Phaedrus and Kallikles to see if it was the same for them.

"Do you deny that he is your savior?" Aristomache asked, fiercely.

"I've had this same fight with Ikaros," Maia said, turning red in the face.

Aristomache frowned, then nodded. "Ikaros . . ." she began, and then suddenly went back into Greek. "Yayzu came down to Earth to save us all." Aristomache smiled all around, including all of us in the conversation.

I nodded politely.

"Tell me about him?" Erinna asked. "I love the statue."

"Well that's a good place to start," Aristomache said. "His mother was a virgin, and God sent her a son, his son and himself. He was born human, like all of us, and grew up, and taught, and was killed for his teaching, and then arose from the dead and taught again. He went through a human life and understands us. He's not playing with our lives for his own amusement like Athene. And through him we will have eternal life, in heaven."

I'd heard about heaven from Ficino, so I knew it was a place like Hades that some people thought was an interlude between incarnations and others thought was the end-point of all incarnations, for souls that had purified themselves. It's mentioned in the *Phaedo*, though not with that name. My eyes went to Father, still deeply engaged in conversation on the other side of the agora. He had come down to earth and become mortal, and was learning about understanding human life. So there was no reason not to believe that Yayzu had done the same. And his mother, especially as Botticelli had painted her and Auge carved her, seemed like a perfectly nice goddess. The statue had a book in one hand. And I could certainly understand anyone who had been at the Last Debate being angry at Athene. I nodded and smiled at Aristomache.

15

ARETE

We were feasted by Marissa, and I believe in the process Maecenas came to some trade agreement, but I don't know the details. I know there are too many things that only the Workers
can make, and everyone wants those things. But in Marissa they
were making some of them and getting others from the *Goodness*,
like glass. We trade Worker-made glass to all the other cities.
But they didn't have any Workers and they were making their
own. I saw it in some of their windows, and while it was thick
and streaky, it was still pretty impressive that they were making it themselves. They were also making iron. And they had
plumbing—they didn't have wash-fountains in every house the
way we did, but they had public baths, and public drinking foun-
tains, like Rome. I thought they were doing pretty well.

I also admired their outreach to the refugees. It was what I'd
wanted to do the moment I'd seen the villages of the Kyklades,
and the Goodness Group were doing what we'd talked about—
rescuing people and teaching them hygiene and technology and
how to read and think independently. They didn't have printing presses, but they had literacy and fairly advanced math. Aristomache was a good teacher. I was impressed by how much they
had achieved, especially when we got Aristomache off the sub-

ject of Yayzu and his mother and onto the subject of how they'd done it.

We were all sitting in their eating hall—they only had one. Most people, most of the time, cooked and ate in their own houses, which had little kitchens for that purpose, unlike ours. When they had a big feast, the important people ate in the eating hall, which also served as their Chamber. It was a big room with a pillared portico that held about a hundred. The rest were feasted outdoors in the agora, where they held their Assembly. The feast began at sundown. It consisted of a savory wheat and milk porridge, followed by fresh sardines, followed by roast ox, which had been roasting all afternoon, of course, and piles of absolutely marvelous honey cakes, also made with wheat. We didn't have wheat cakes or porridge often at home, as most of the wheat we grew was made straight into pasta. Cakes made from wheat were quite different from cakes made from barley and nut flours, much lighter and more fluffy. Wine was served, about three-quarters water, the strength I usually drank, weaker than adults usually had it at home. It took us most of the meal to get Aristomache off religion and onto the subject of what the *Goodness* had done.

We were seated at tables of ten, all nibbling honey cakes. Father and Maecenas and Ficino were at the top table with Terentius and some of the kings of Marissa. Aristomache, Maia, Erinna and I were with some of the members of the Chamber. All of the tables were mixed that way. Klymene and Neleus and the rest of the Nyx watch were back aboard, but we were assured that food was being sent to them.

"When we left, we sailed north. We wanted to get away from Kallisti, and we didn't know where we wanted to go exactly," Aristomache said. "We went to the mainland of Ionia, near Troy, and found a war going on. Not a Persian invasion, or even a Trojan one, just a petty civil war. The ship was really full, so we ferried most of our people over to Lesbos and set them down, then went back to rescue refugees. It was a purely humanitarian mission, we weren't thinking about anything else. They were mostly women and children who would have been enslaved. Of course we thought about Hekabe and Andromache, but we seem to be too early for them. The King of Troy is called Laomedon." She took a sip of wine.

"We founded Lucia pretty much where we'd landed, without doing any surveying or anything. There was water, which was all we really needed. There were olive trees too, which may mean there had once been a settlement there before, because olives usually mean people. We rescued goats and sheep from the mainland, and fortunately a lot of our refugees knew how to look after them and milk them and process wool, because we didn't." She laughed. "We had a lot to teach each other! That first winter was hard. Some of the girls were pregnant, some of ours from the festivals, and some of theirs, mostly from rape. They were all grateful because we'd rescued them—but what else could we have done? We had the weapons that were on the ship, of course, and we'd all had training."

"Of course," Erinna said, her eyes shining. "And you founded a city?"

"It wasn't a proper city at first, but we all worked on a constitution, and building it, of course."

"Why did you decide to call your city Lucia?" I asked. I knew I'd heard the name before, and I'd just remembered where. Father had said it had been Mother's birth name. It seemed like a peculiar coincidence, but I couldn't think of any possible connection.

"I think Matthias proposed it," she said. "It means Light of course, and new light was what we all wanted. It was only afterward we thought of Saint Lucy and seeing everything with new eyes, which is what the name means to us now, our fresh start and our turning back to God. It was Providence, I suppose."

"So how was it in the beginning?" Maia asked.

"We debated everything, like the philosophers we were, but sometimes the practical people we'd rescued had better ideas than any of us." Aristomache smiled at one of the locals at the table, who looked down, clearly embarrassed. "They brought us back to Earth whenever we floated off too far. And it was that winter that we came back to God. That was Matthias's proposal too."

"Who's Matthias, one of the people you rescued?" Maia asked.

Aristomache laughed and took another honey cake. "No, he's the one who used to be called Kebes. He took his real name back. Some of us did that and some didn't, according to what made us more comfortable. I didn't want to be Ellen again."

"We discussed that in the City of Amazons, too. I didn't want to be Ethel," Maia said, astonishing me. She seemed so very much a Maia that it didn't seem possible she could ever have been called anything else. Ellen was clearly derived from Helen, but Ethel came from that strange language they had spoken together briefly. Maia was right, it emphatically didn't suit her.

"We didn't force anyone to worship God, but Matthias wanted to build a church and become a priest, and most of us had originally been Christian and many of those who hadn't saw the light and wanted to be saved. I don't think any of us had worshipped the Greek gods seriously back in the Just City, and if we had it was because of being taken in by Athene."

"And your local recruits?" Erinna asked.

"They saw the sense in it, after the cruel things their gods had done to them. They understood the value of a god of forgiveness who understands us."

Some of the locals around the table were nodding. "A god who accepts everyone, even slaves and women," one of them said, shyly.

"So how did you go from one city to many cities?" Maia asked.

"We kept sending the ship out with a troop to rescue people, and eventually Lucia was running well and we had so many people that it seemed like a good idea to start a second city around the coast. Then we founded Marissa, here, when there was another war three years later, and we filled in the others. Usually the *Goodness* spends half the year sailing between the cities, trading, and the other half rescuing people and bringing them to whichever city needs people. We may found another city this year, on Ikaria. The *Goodness* tends to stay with a new city, and lots of experienced people stay to help things get going at first—people who know how to build and plant and everything like that. It takes quite a while for a city to get going properly. But Augustine is at that stage now, where it can grow naturally. We're ready to found a new city."

"And how many of you—the Goodness Group—stay in each city?" I asked.

Aristomache refilled her cup, considering. "It depends. There are lots in Lucia, of course, which is still our main base. Then there are lots wherever a city is new and needs help. Otherwise, well, the ideal is to have our cities working alone. Marissa doesn't really need anyone from *Goodness* now. It could have local doctors and teachers." There was a murmur from the locals at the table to the effect that they couldn't manage without her. "Nonsense," she said, but she looked pleased. "I stay because I'm getting old and my friends are here. Terentius stays because he's married and his children are growing up here. But Marissa doesn't need us. Hektor could do my job, he's teaching most of the younger children as it is. And Ekate is as good a doctor as Terentius now, and she has an apprentice of her own. She may go to the new city on Ikaria if we do get it going this summer. Locals move around and share their expertise too."

"So your ideal for your cities is self-sufficiency?" Erinna asked, swallowing another honey cake.

"It takes a while," Aristomache admitted. "And they're not big cities, compared to the Just City, never mind the Boston I remember. Most of our cities are about a thousand people. Marissa has eight hundred citizens, and almost that many children."

"Do the children have to pass tests to become ephebes?" I asked. I was thinking about my own looming adulthood tests, to be taken on my return.

"Just swear their confirmation oath," Aristomache said. "And we sort them into Platonic classes, of course. And they can vote in the Assembly then, the golds and silvers, and they're eligible for election to the Council when they're thirty. And nine of the Council are elected Kings every three years, and they make up the Committee of Kings. You have tests?"

"We have an oath too, but we also have to pass lots and lots of tests in all sorts of things. And then we swear, and do our military training, and read the *Republic*, and after two years we can vote in the Assembly, when we're eighteen, all of us, not just the guardians. But only the guardians serve in Chamber. My brothers are all adults, and I'll become an ephebe this year."

Maia was looking about the hall. It had frescoed walls that showed pleasant farming scenes with nymphs and shepherds lolling in fields and under trees, feasting on food very like the food we were enjoying. "You know, Plato was right," she said.

This was such a characteristic remark for Maia to make that I giggled, and so did Erinna beside me. We might have been drinking too much of the excellent wine.

"What was he right about?" Aristomache said. "A great many things, indeed, but what specifically are you thinking of?"

"He's right that there was a golden age in his past when people in Greek cities governed themselves properly according to the precepts he described. Nobody has ever believed a word of it. But he was right. It happened. And this is it." Maia laughed with an edge of hysteria. Ficino looked over to us, concerned. She took a sip of wine and went on. "It will deteriorate to timarchy, and then oligarchy, and so on, exactly as Plato wrote."

"Well, maybe," Aristomache said. "But for now it is the Good Life. For now it is definitely aristocracy. And besides, we're sure we've changed the world, introducing Christianity here and now, introducing civilized ideas and sanitation and medicine in the time before the Trojan War. We're not hiding away expecting everything we do to be destroyed by a volcano. Athene put us on Kallisti so we'd make no changes, cause no ripples, have no posterity. But we're out here making a difference, keeping the peace, helping the poor and the hungry. This is a new world. Maybe everything will be different and the Age of Gold won't vanish and there'll never be a Plato."

Maia hesitated, and I remembered that she had worried about breaking history if we intervened in the Kyklades. Father had reassured me that it wasn't possible, but I couldn't pass that reassurance on, at least not with proper citations. It might not be all that reassuring anyway, to think that Plato was right about everything degenerating. She closed her mouth as if she'd changed her mind about speaking, and when she did open it again what she said was: "You're right to be rescuing people."

Aristomache smiled at the rescued people around the table. "You know what you should do," she said, looking back to us. "You should go to Lucia for Passion Week. In addition to the religious celebration we have a music festival. You'd love it. And that's when the majority of the people who left the city are together, in Lucia at Easter. If you want to find out what we've been doing and see everyone, that's where you ought to go."

"When's Easter?" I asked.

"It's—" Aristomache and Maia began together, then caught each other's eyes and giggled, exactly as if they were both ephebes. "It's the first Lord's Day after the first full moon after the spring equinox," Aristomache finished alone. "So it's soon."

"What's the Lord's Day?" Erinna asked.

The locals clucked, but Aristomache explained quickly and easily. "Instead of having Ides and Nones, we call each seven-day period a week, and the days of the week have names, and the seventh day of each week is the Lord's Day, and a day of rest and religious worship."

"How can you celebrate Easter before Yayzu is even born?" Maia asked.

"He is our *eternal* savior," Aristomache said, serenely confident.

16

MAIA

People say I left the City of Amazons because I wanted comfort, but I have never loved comfort, only learning. I left for reasons of conscience—religious reasons.

I suppose the whole New Concordance was partly my fault, or rather Crocus's, making Ikaros translate Thomas Aquinas. The *Summa Theologica* is really long, and of course because Ikaros shouldn't have had the book he could only work on it in private, and when he had free time. It took him years. He still hadn't finished it by the time I left. Ikaros was the ultimate synthesist, but he had a fast mind that was always racing ahead to the next thing. Needing to translate Aquinas for Crocus, slowly, over a long time, and then reading his translation aloud, and answering Crocus's questions, forced him to keep coming back to it and thinking about it, instead of leaping on to something new.

Ikaros had found a way, in about 1500 A.D. from what I gather, to reconcile all the religions and philosophies in the world. He got into some considerable amount of trouble over this with the Pope and the Inquisition, and was saved, bizarrely enough, by Savonarola. I only know most of this secondhand through Lysias, who had heard of him before we came to the City. I barely know anything about Savonarola, or about the controversies of the Renaissance, and I can't look it up because it falls into the

area we decided to exclude from our library. We have plenty of
Renaissance art, and Renaissance people, but not religion and
politics, because we wanted the Renaissance re-imagining of the
classical world, not what Lysias described as the "medieval rem-
nants" of Christianity. So Ikaros's *Oration on the Awesomeness of Humanity*, as Lysias calls it, saying that I could substitute "Pico
della Mirandola" and "Dignity of Man" if I preferred, is not in
the library, and neither are his nine hundred theses. His work
was too Christian for the Library Committee. But excluding
them didn't keep them out. They were still in Ikaros's head, and
Ikaros's brain was in Ikaros's head, and what Ikaros's brain did
when it was idle was make up perfectly logical but utterly insane theories of religious reconciliation.

He had been thinking about this on and off the whole time,
from the moment when he saw that Pallas Athene was real. He
had told me before the Last Debate that he had found a way to
make it all make sense. But it wasn't until the first years in the
City of Amazons, when he had to go through Aquinas line by
line to translate it, that he came up with the rigorous and philosophically defensible thesis he called his New Concordance.

In the original city, where Sokrates and Tullius and Manlius
and Ficino and all the other older Masters were there to sit on
him, Ikaros couldn't do much about his religious theories except have occasional debates. His debates were always very popular with everyone, but he had to find people who wanted to
debate with him, and his metaphysical theories were never a
particularly popular topic. Athene never showed up for them,
though she almost always came to his debates on other topics.
Most Platonists are quite happy with Plato's metaphysics. Tullius was a Stoic. Even so, Ikaros is such a powerful orator, im-
passioned and fast-thinking and funny, that he could sometimes
find people prepared to take on the more esoteric subjects. Even
here, where everyone is trained in rhetoric, he stands out as

surpassingly excellent. He's good at coming up with memorable images and working them all the way through an argument. He has always been a joy to listen to, in either language.

Once we were in the City of Amazons there was nobody better—nobody even as good. Klio was very good, and so were Myrto and Kreusa. Myrto was his most effective opponent. It wasn't until after she died, in the sixth year, that he gained complete sway over the city.

I could live in a city that has Ikaros in it, even though I disagreed with him a great deal. But I couldn't live in a city that required me to follow his crazy religion. I could be a Christian—I had been for the first eighteen years of my life. Or I could be a Platonic pagan, as I had been for the next eighteen. I had met Pallas Athene, talked to her. I had no doubt that the Olympians were real. I knew the way we worshipped them in the City was acceptable to Athene, who existed, who had set up the City and brought us the Workers, and then lost her temper and turned Sokrates into a gadfly and took the Workers away again. In Athenia they think she was right. I don't go as far as that, but I think what she did was understandable in the circumstances.

Athene thought we should be grateful to her for the opportunity to be in the City—and I was. I can't imagine any life that could have been better for me personally that led on from the nineteen years of my life I lived in the nineteenth century. I would never stop being grateful for the rescue that allowed me to be myself, to be respected as a scholar and a teacher. My feelings about Christianity were conflicted, while my gratitude to Athene was unfailing. On the other hand, Sokrates made some valid points in the Last Debate. I continued to question whether she had the right to do what she had done. But I still prayed to her nightly, and to the other Olympians on appropriate occasions.

What Ikaros did was to build a whole logical edifice reconciling everything—Plato, Aristotle, Christianity, Islam, Judaism,

Buddhism, Stoicism, Epicureanism, Hedonism, Pythagoras, and sundry other ideas he'd picked up here and there. Bits of it were brilliant. For instance, he deduced from Athene saying that the City was just that justice must be a process, not a Form, and that reconciled contradictions between Plato and Aristotle's views of justice as well as being a fascinating idea about dynamic ideals. In fact, all of it was brilliant, if you considered it as pure logic. The problem was his axioms.

He set about the whole thing properly, I have to admit. He wrote it all up, ordered his theses, and announced a great debate. He sent invitations to the other cities and arranged a festival. He debated everybody who came prepared to argue against his points, and when they won on any issue he accepted that and incorporated that into his argument. It's just that the whole edifice was built on such terrible axioms. At first I had wanted it to be true, wanted the loving Father and Son I had grown up with to be real, as well as Athene. I wanted Jesus to be my savior, as I had believed as a child. But the more closely I looked at what Ikaros was doing, the less sense it made. His axioms were twisted. It was incredibly ingenious, and it all made perfect logical sense, each piece of the structure balanced on each other piece. But it was a castle of straws balanced on air. Athene just wasn't an angel, and wasn't perfect. Errors can be refuted, and as his errors were pointed out, by me and by others, he patched them. But his leaps of faith were not errors, and they were inarguable. I tried. Many of us tried. And it was all right as long as it was just a case of what Ikaros believed and tried to persuade people. It was when, after the festival, the Assembly of Amazons voted to make his New Concordance the official religion of the City of Amazons that I knew I had to leave. It would be practiced at festivals. I couldn't believe it. And I couldn't possibly teach it.

I'd told Klio and Axiothea that I was leaving, and they'd both tried to persuade me to stay. Axiothea was quite happy with the

New Concordance. Klio had initially been even less in favor of it than I was, but once she began to study the logic she had been won over by the way Ikaros had integrated Platonic thought all through, and especially with his theory of dynamic ideals, which fit everything she believed. Klio had always disliked Ikaros, but now they began to work together on this project. They spent a lot of time together and became close. She told him about the religions and philosophies she knew about that were unfamiliar to him, and they worked together to reconcile them with everything else.

The New Concordance was generally very popular in the city, though I wasn't sure how many people even among its adherents really understood it properly.

I announced generally that I was leaving, though it hurt me to go. I had put eight years of my life into this city, this second attempt to do what Plato suggested, and I had a new generation of students growing up. I packed up my few possessions in my cloak: my comb, the notebooks where I was writing this autobiography, and my Botticelli book. I opened it and looked at the angels clustered around the *Madonna of the Pomegranates*. They were beautiful, and perhaps they were real, but Athene wasn't one of them. She was too much herself. She was real and imperfect and divine. She had rescued me from a life of unfulfilled emptiness and brought me to the City. I prayed to her now for guidance, and found myself thinking of my old house in the Remnant, and the rich colors of Botticelli's *Autumn* on the wall in Florentia, and Ficino's welcoming smile. I was right to leave. And I'd give this book to Simmea. That felt right too. I closed it and put it into my cloak, and went off to one last day's teaching. Other people would be taking over my classes the next morning.

"I've done you an injustice and I want to apologize," Ikaros said.

"What?" He had surprised me, coming up behind me after a gymnastics class. I had been teaching the littlest ones how to fall and roll and come up again, while the older ones were practicing with the discus. Then I had escorted the children through the wash-fountain, and handed them over to another teacher for their lute lesson. I was standing alone in the palaestra drying my hair on my kiton. It was autumn, almost olive season, so my damp bare skin was covered in goosebumps. I felt at a disadvantage, and quickly twisted my kiton back on, which left my damp hair dripping down my back. I never seemed to have any dignity around Ikaros. But when I looked at him, he wasn't looking at me but down at the sand.

"I like you, Maia, and perhaps Providence meant us to be together, but I messed everything up between us at the beginning. I didn't understand that you were truly saying no. I thought you were making a show of modest protest. Klio has explained to me that you were not. I'm really sorry."

I glared at him until he looked up at me. He wasn't laughing at me. He seemed sincere. "Klio had no right—why were you talking to her about me?"

"Because I want to understand why you oppose me so much."

I was astonished that he was taking me so seriously. "And you're finally acknowledging that you did something wrong?"

"Yes. I said so. I truly misunderstood all this time." He sat down on the wall that separated the palaestra from the street.

"I was screaming and struggling!"

"But your body—I thought—Klio has explained to me how I was wrong. It was a long explanation, but I do finally understand now." He smiled ruefully up at me. "Perhaps I shouldn't have been talking to her about it, but I'd never in a hundred years have understood without all that. I was wrong. And I have been punished by being deprived of your friendship, and Klio's friendship, all this time."

I didn't know what to say, so I just stared at him.

He sighed and rubbed his eyes. "Klio tells me that in her day, philosophy has discovered that people have two minds, a reasoning mind and an animal mind. Your reasoning mind believes that you have logical disagreements with me, but it is your animal mind driving what you feel. You have to get them into alignment to become godlike. That's what Plato meant with the metaphor of the charioteer."

"That is not what Plato meant!" I snapped, infuriated. At that moment, I'd have cheerfully turned him into a fly if I could. There's nothing more irritating than having somebody misinterpret my intentions and Plato's at the same time!

He went on. "Your animal mind wants to love me, the way your body wanted to love me that night under the trees. But your rational mind says no to love, because it's afraid to love, maybe because of what I did. So I want to persuade your rational mind."

I crossed my arms and leaned back against a pillar. "Go ahead. My rational mind only listens to rational arguments, not all this animal mind nonsense! And I think saying that part of me loves you is the most arrogant thing I've ever heard, even from you. And I am not afraid to love!"

"Who do you love?" he asked, rhetorically. "Lysias? No. He's your friend, you sometimes used to share a bed, but that's all. There's no love, no real passion. He has told Lukretia, and she told me."

I was furious with Lysias. "He had no right—"

Ikaros shrugged. "He feels passion for Lukretia, and she asked him about you."

I still didn't understand what was going on with Lysias and Lukretia. I missed him.

There were more women than men in the City of Amazons,

but not by a huge degree—the city was about sixty percent female. I've heard ridiculous stories in other cities about harems and men being waited on by women in return for sexual favors. This seems to me to say rather more about men's fantasies than about anything real in Amazonia. There was a slight surplus of single women, but when you consider women who prefer other women, and families that have more than two adult partners, and men who maintained relationships with each other or with several women—Ikaros among them—it didn't amount to much. Heterosexual men were not a scarce resource. I'd had one or two discreet offers myself since Lysias moved out. It wasn't sex I was feeling deprived of.

"He shouldn't have said anything to her about me, and even if he did, she shouldn't have said anything to you," I said, as evenly as I could, braiding my damp hair and twisting it up on top of my head. "Is there any point to this scurrilous gossip?"

Ikaros ignored this. "So who do you love? Klio and Axiothea? Friends only, although they love each other. The children? You like them, you care about them, but you don't really love them. There's no love in your life, because you have closed off your soul, and that closes out the possibility of God's love. And that's why you won't consider the New Concordance."

"Nonsense," I said. "I love all those people. And the kind of love you're talking about is specifically what Plato tells us to avoid."

"No it's not. It's what he thinks you can use to bring yourself closer to God." He was leaning forward now, passionate. "It is by loving each other that our souls rise up and grow wings to approach heaven. It's in the *Phaedrus*." He pushed back his hair, which was starting to silver now, making him better-looking than ever. "For a while, before I read Aquinas again and realized I was mistaken, I thought that love was enough. Now I see it isn't, that we need reason even more. But we do need love."

"I don't oppose you because I don't have enough love. I oppose you because I *disagree* with you. Because you're *wrong*. I started off half-wanting to believe Athene was an angel, and that God was still there. The more I hear your proofs and arguments, the less I'm prepared to consider it."

He rubbed his eyes again, and I noticed that they were red-rimmed from too much rubbing. "Maia, you're one of the few people here who really can follow my thought, who's really capable of being an equal. So it's very frustrating when you disagree without a logical reason behind it. Won't you forgive me and let us start again?"

I considered that. "I don't know whether I can trust you," I said. Perhaps it was true that before Klio explained he just wasn't capable of understanding. His world had shaped him as badly as mine had shaped me. In a better world, in the City we both wanted to build, we could both have been philosopher kings. Perhaps then we could have loved each other as Plato wanted.

"Are you afraid of me? I don't want you to be afraid."

The children were mangling their scales behind us. Crocus went past carrying the window glass for the new crèche. "I'm not afraid that you're about to ravage me here and now. But you make me very uneasy. Today is the first time you've ever acknowledged what you did. You always laughed about it and dismissed it."

"I didn't understand. In my time women had no way to say yes to anything except marriage and keep their self-respect, so they had to make formal protests without really meaning them. That's what I thought you were doing. Klio had to explain to me that if people can't say yes, they can't say no either. It was a new idea."

"I understand that," I acknowledged. "But I'm afraid you're apologizing now because you want something, that you're trying to manipulate me. And you're making up all these theories about why I disagree, just like you make up all these theories about the gods, and none of it has any basis in reality. What do you want from me?"

"I want you to be my friend," he said, with no hesitation at all. "And I would like you to forgive me, if you can. And I don't want you to leave this city."

I stopped and thought for a moment, trying to examine my own feelings with philosophical rigor. It wasn't easy. I asked myself whether I could forgive him. I found that I could—I did understand what he had been thinking, and also I appreciated the effort he had made now to understand what he had done and accept that it was wrong. "I don't know whether it's possible for me to trust you enough to be your friend," I said, after a moment. "But I do understand what you did, what you were thinking. And I suppose I forgive you." He closed his eyes for a moment when I said that and his face went slack. I realized that my forgiveness really did matter to him. He was so naturally playful, even at his most serious. It was rare to see him this unguarded.

He opened his eyes again and looked at me. "So if I'm wrong about my theories about why you disagree, and you disagree logically, what's wrong with my logic?" he asked.

I let out a breath I hadn't known I was holding, and sat down tailor-fashion on the wall, leaning back against the pillar. "It's not your logic-structures, it's your axioms. I've said this before. Examine your assumptions. You say Athene is an angel, and you say angels are perfect. I can't see how you can believe that after the way Athene behaved in the Last Debate."

"She's an angel, and she's perfect. What she did may seem imperfect to us, but that's because our perceptions are imperfect. If we had complete knowledge, we'd be able to understand what she did."

"That doesn't make any sense. We know she exists. We know we can trust what she told us directly. And she said in the Last

Debate that the gods don't know everything, and that part of her motivation in setting up the City was to see what happened. That's not something we don't understand because we're not perfect."

"She's of a lesser order of perfection than the Persons of the Trinity," he said. "But she's still perfect."

"She turned Sokrates into a gadfly!" I said.

"If we understood more, we'd understand why."

"I have no difficulty understanding why. How can you possibly argue that she was justified in what she did to him? She lost her temper. I have lost my own temper with students often enough to recognize that. It isn't the slow ones that make me do it, it's the insolent ones. Sokrates had some good arguments, but he was behaving like an insolent ephebe pushing the limits. He wanted to make her angry, and he did. But anger and power go badly together, and she is a goddess. Power comes with responsibility. She killed him, or the next thing to it. She was wrong to do what she did and walk away."

Ikaros rubbed his eyes again. "She is wisdom. She had reasons we don't understand. She must have."

"Why is it hard to understand that she lost her temper?" I asked. Kreusa went by with two of her apprentices, all carrying baskets of herbs. She nodded to me, and I waved.

"You're trying to understand her as if she were human. But she's an angel," Ikaros said.

"It seems to me that she's a Homeric god, acting exactly the way Homer described the gods acting. We know that gods exist, gods like Athene, who have incredible powers that nevertheless have limits. We know they can make mistakes, and lose their tempers. We might think they should be more responsible, but we can't affect that. We also know they can be open to persuasion. For instance, Athene agreed to take us to rescue art treasures for the city, though she hadn't wanted to at first. She changed her mind. We know they can be kind to their worshippers. Athene brought all of the Masters here because we prayed for it. For me it was a rescue, and for most of the others too."

"For me, certainly," he acknowledged. "I was dying. She brought me here and healed me. But this is part of her goodness, her perfection."

"But we also know she can be unkind and imperfect, as witness losing her temper. You have to acknowledge that too."

He frowned, and reached toward his eyes then drew his hand back. "We don't understand everything she did, so it seems to us unkind. But if we knew more, we would understand. Exactly like the way Klio explained my actions so that I understand I committed an injustice, only the other way around. If it were explained to us properly, we would see that what she did was just, however it seems."

"I don't think there's any need for such an explanation—" He rubbed his eyes hard and I broke off. "Is there something wrong with your eyes?"

"Just a little tired and sore from so much close work. It's getting all the theses straight all day, and then working by lamplight translating Aquinas. I'm nearly done. At this rate I'll be done by spring. Or next summer anyway." He sighed, and squinted at me.

"You should try bathing them in warm milk at night," I suggested.

"Does that work?"

"It's what my father used to do." I could remember him so clearly, dabbing at his tired eyes when we'd been poring over a book all day.

He smiled at me. "I've been using oil. But I'll try it. Go on. You were going to give me the reason you don't believe the angelic orders are perfect. Do you believe that God is perfect?"

"Plato talks about the world of Forms and the nature of

reality, and the perfect God that is Unity. You think that's the same God as the Christian God the Father, but I see no evidence for it."

"It makes logical sense. Why do you want evidence?"

I shook my head. "Why do you deny the need for evidence, and try to explain away evidence that doesn't fit your structure? We know Athene exists, and we know she's pretty much the way Homer describes her, and so we can make a reasonable guess from that and from the way she behaved and the way she talked when she was here and from things like encouraging us building temples and having festivals and sacrifices, that the Olympians exist and are pretty much, if not exactly, the way the Homer described them. Plato was wrong about that. Plato would have censored Homer because of showing the gods behaving exactly the kind of way Athene behaved."

"But the angels, and Homer's gods if you want to call them that, are on a level between us and God."

"Perhaps. What I think is that in the Allegory of the Cave, where we are the prisoners watching shadows flickering on the cave walls, perhaps the gods are the things behind the fire casting the shadows."

"There are entire hierarchies of levels, with different angels, and the Forms are part of that." He reached toward his eyes again, and again stopped himself.

"I've read your theses. I agree that the internal logic makes sense. You don't have to go through it all again for me now."

"But if you can follow the logic—"

"I can follow the logic and still continue to disagree, when the logic doesn't fit the facts! What we know about Athene does not lead us to be able to deduce anything about unlimited omnipotent deities that may or may not exist, and may or may not be in overall control of the Olympians. You didn't ask her about this, did you? You had plenty of chances. She came to almost all your debates."

"All of them unless they were about metaphysics," he said, and smiled. "She never wanted to talk about that. And I like to work things out for myself." Suddenly the palaestra was full of children, running and shouting, as they were released from their lute lesson.

"But you must see that when you build huge complex structures of dialectic that purport to reconcile Christianity, Judaism, Islam, Platonism, Aristotelianism, and Buddhism with the presence here of Athene, it has to fit the evidence as well as making logical sense." I raised my voice a little and leaned forward eagerly as the children streamed past us.

"It fits the facts if you acknowledge that all the wise are in agreement about everything essential. It's just a case of understanding how and reconciling supposed contradictions. And the reason we see supposed contradictions and don't understand everything about what Athene did is because we're too imperfect," he said, also leaning forward until our foreheads were nearly touching.

I moved back and sat up straight again. "In saying that, you have left the path of philosophy. Literally. You're denying sophia, betraying what she really was."

"If we became angels ourselves, which in my system we might be able to achieve, then we could understand what she was. For now, we don't fully understand. We can't."

"I can't believe that," I said. "And that's why I'm going to leave this city, because this isn't just a disagreement where I can accept the majority vote was against me, this is about our own beliefs and practice. I can't believe it, and I can't practice it."

"You don't have to leave, even though you disagree. We've voted to accept it as the majority religion and practice it at festivals, but we'll have freedom of conscience. You can believe what you want." He reached out to pat my arm, then thought better of it and drew his hand back.

"But I'd have to teach it, and I can't do that," I said.

"You wouldn't have to believe it to teach it!"

"You might not, but I would." I stood up. He stayed where he was on the wall.

"Don't go. Plotinus and Sokrates and Tullius and Myrto are dead, and I almost never see Ficino. Klio's marvelous, and some of the Children are coming along, but there are too few people here who can stretch my mind."

"Are you really suggesting I stay here just to argue with you?"

"Yes!" He laughed suddenly. "How absurd this is."

I laughed with him. And then I left the City of Amazons and went to the Remnant, to start again.

17

ARETE

All my life I'd heard people talk about Kebes and the Goodness Group and the Lost City as if they were all one thing, and it took a lot for me to take it in that they weren't. Kebes was a person, a person now calling himself Matthias, and the Goodness Group consisted of a hundred and fifty people with divided opinions about things, and they weren't one Lost City, they were a whole network of civilization. It was a bit of a shock. The other thing I had never thought about until I talked to Aristomache was that of course they had left during the Last Debate, or at the very end, at the moment when Sokrates turned into a gadfly. They didn't know anything about what had happened afterward. They didn't know that we hadn't seen Athene since, until Father told them so. They didn't know that theirs was only the first defection, nor that the rest of us had lived in a constant state of warfare. They hadn't taken any art when they left, they hadn't taken anything but the *Goodness* and their own skills. All this time they'd been doing what Mother had always said people ought to do and making more art instead of squabbling over the art we had. They'd been doing the same with technology too, starting with what they had and knew and going on from there.

I slept in my hammock on board, ready for my watch that

began at dawn. I woke early and went up on deck before the sky began to pale. I had thought of a safe way of testing to discover whether I could fly, but I needed to be alone with my brothers to try it. Of course, wonderful as sea voyages are, being alone is almost impossible to manage. Even conversations are constantly being interrupted. I wanted to try diving from the deck, which I had done several times to go ashore, but instead of diving, fly. If it didn't work then I'd hit the water as normal. I had forgotten that the deck lights would be on, and that Neleus and the other members of the Nyx watch would be around, even with the ship safely tied up at harbor.

I took my turn on watch, though it was as unlike the watch of the day before as anything could be. I sat at the masthead with nothing to see but Marissa on one side and the rippling sea at the other. Phaedrus came up part way through and told me the ship's council were meeting, which didn't surprise me. I hoped we'd go to Lucia and the music festival. I liked music, and I wanted to meet more of the Goodness Group. "Mother would have liked them," I said to Phaedrus.

He nodded thoughtfully. "I think she would. Except maybe for the religious stuff."

"But why couldn't it be true? If Father's incarnate now, why shouldn't Yayzu have done the same thing in Roman times, the way Aristomache says?"

"Oh, interesting, I hadn't thought of that." Phaedrus put an arm around the mast and leaned out, looking over the city.

"Can you fly?" I asked, seeing that.

"Walk on the air like we did on Ikaria? I haven't tried it this high up, but I'm sure I could."

"No, really fly, swoop about like a bird. I feel I can, but I haven't tried it because I don't want anyone to see me."

"No, it would be pretty conspicuous." He grinned. "I don't

feel that I could, but I don't feel that I couldn't either. Have you found anything else you can do?"

"Understand languages I don't know. Maia and Aristomache started speaking some strange language yesterday and I understood it clearly, though I'd definitely never heard it before."

"Wow." He looked impressed. "Hard to test. Though I suppose you could go around asking the Masters and the Children to say something in their birth languages. But they're supposed to have forgotten them. I've never heard anyone speak in them. Maia's usually so properly Platonic, too. Which of them started it?"

"Aristomache. I suppose in the Goodness Group things are different."

"I don't think they were the ones who raided us. They don't even have any art that isn't Christian, why would they want the head of Victory? But I hope Father believes that."

"Who do you think it was?" I asked.

"Psyche or the Amazons, like normal," he said. "I believe Alkibiades that it wasn't Athenia, and Sokratea has never broken a treaty without a declaration."

"Do you think Father will believe it?"

"There would have to be good evidence. But it should be easy enough to find out where the *Goodness* was at the time, once we catch up with them. I hope he will accept it. If not, it's going to be exceedingly awkward. And if he does start to believe it, I hope he doesn't want to go straight home and immediately get vengeance there. I hope we go to the music festival."

"So do I. Will you do me a favor? When we get the chance, I want to go off somewhere and test flying, and test lifting you when I fly," I said.

"Sure. I want to try that too. And the language thing. I wonder if we all have the same powers or if we all have different ones." He sounded excited to find out. "The only thing I've tried is healing."

"Who did you heal?"

"Caerellia had a bad tooth, and I fixed that. And one of the women at the feast last night had a growth in her belly. It felt uncomfortable being near them, and I knew what to do, so I just did it."

"I haven't felt anything like that. But maybe I just haven't been near anyone who's sick. Though Ficino's awfully old and frail, there isn't anything actually wrong with him, at least not as far as I know."

"I'll try walking by him and see if I feel anything, and if there is, put it right. By the dog, this is great!"

"Aren't you worried about our powers at all?" I asked.

"I'm worried about Fate and Necessity, and screwing things up badly, like getting lost if I try to go outside time and that sort of thing," he said, after a moment's hesitation. "I'm excited about the powers, though. I want to find out what we can do and how it works and have fun with it. I understand why old Kallikles is worried about telling Rhea. But we've never been like everyone else, really. This just makes it more solid."

"Do you still want to develop an excellence of volcanoes?"

He took a step up onto the air and then back down onto the masthead beside me. "I really do. Imagine being able to direct the lava. Imagine bathing in it. Imagine having control over it."

I shuddered, imagining burning up. The volcano had always frightened me. "You can definitely have that."

Erinna called him to stop loitering and get about his duties, so he went back down to the deck, where she had him coiling rope. I stayed at the masthead. Now I was finally getting my free time to think, and I was a little bored.

When my watch was over and I went down to the deck, Phaedrus came up to me. "Nope," he said. "Nothing wrong with

Ficino that I can tell. Also, I got Maecenas and Ficino to say things in their old languages, and they were completely incomprehensible. But we're going to the festival."

"Good. What did you get Ficino to say?"

"Some poetry. It sounded a bit like Latin, but more sing-song. I could make out the occasional word that pretty much was Latin, but that's all."

I found sitting Ficino in the agora of Marissa, drinking wine and talking to a group of locals about Plato. He drew me deftly into the discussion, which was examining the question of whether this was a republic. It seemed to me quite clear that it was, and that it was as Maia had said the night before, one of the fabled republics Plato had heard of.

Sitting there, though, I realized that their classes were much more pronounced than ours. There's a thing people say, that you can tell somebody is gold without checking their cloak pin. It means they are truly excellent, so much so that their quality really shows. People used to say it about my parents. In Marissa, you really could tell, but not because of shining excellence. The people talking to Ficino were all golds, and they were all free to sit drinking wine in the middle of the afternoon. They were cleaner and somehow glossier than the people working around us. I watched a man carrying a sack and a woman buying vegetables. Both of them wore bronze pins. Their kitons were shabbier, more faded, frayed at the edges. Of course, there are always people who let their clothes fall into disrepair. But this wasn't a case of sloppy individuals or personal idiosyncrasy. The people sitting with us all had more embroidery on their kitons, and while none of them were fat they tended to be a little plumper than the others. I thought back to the feast the night before. Had everyone inside the hall been a gold? I thought perhaps they had. This visible class difference was nothing like the poverty in the Kyklades. But it was strange to me.

Just then a woman came up to our table with a pitcher. Because I'd been thinking about it I noticed that she was wearing a bronze pin, of the same design we used at home. I also saw that there was something odd about her attitude. She seemed somehow lacking in confidence. She refilled our wine cups, deferentially, and one of the men paid her—paid her with a coin. I had read about money, but not seen it before. I tried not to gape.

After a while, I persuaded Ficino to walk through the city with me. As we walked I drew him around to the subject of the verses he'd recited to Phaedrus. He repeated them to me patiently, they were by Petrarka on the subject of someone thinking about how people in future ages were deprived by not being able to see a woman called Laura. He then translated them into Latin for me. I had understood them perfectly. So, clearly my divine language ability worked on all languages. It seemed as if there would be places it would be more useful than on Kallisti, where everyone spoke Greek and Latin and nobody spoke anything else, but it still seemed like a fun ability. I wondered whether Father could do it. I wondered whether I could speak the other languages or only understand them. That would be hard to test without giving myself away, but maybe I could try it with Father.

"Why are you and Phaedrus suddenly interested in Italian poetry?" Ficino asked.

I gaped at him, entirely without an answer. If I'd known Petrarka had written in Italian as well as Latin, I could have said I was interested because of that, but I'd had no idea. "We were just wondering what it sounded like," I said, feebly. "It's beautiful. And that's such an interesting thought. Did you see her?"

He smiled. "She'd been dead for almost two hundred years before I read the poem."

"It's hard to understand the time things take, chronology, that kind of thing. The vast expanses of history."

We had walked through the streets so that we were now out-side the marble pillars of the entrance to the colosseum. Ficino stopped. "It's especially hard because we're at the wrong end of it, and because you've met people from so many different times. Why shouldn't I have seen Laura, when we both lived in Florentia in the Renaissance, as if it was all one big party?"

"She could be here, or Petrarka could at least," I said.

"Too good a Christian, for all that he loved classical learning," Ficino said. "And he didn't know Greek, so he couldn't have read Plato. Before I translated his work, Plato was only a legend in Italy."

"It's so hard to imagine," I said. "Ages without Plato. How wonderful that you could bring him back." I wondered if my language gift could be used in that way.

Ficino smiled, and gestured to the colosseum. "Shall we go in?"

Inside, the colosseum descended in banks of earthwork seats down to a raked sand oval. They clearly used it as a palaestra, as there were weights stacked up ready for use. It was empty, and Ficino and I walked down the steps that divided seating sections from each other. I walked out onto the sand and sang a couple of lines from one of Father's praise songs. "Good acoustics," I said. "I expect they use it as a theater too." Looking up, I saw that it was built of earth and marble, not concrete the way the colosseum in Rome is described.

"Probably they use it for all kinds of things," Ficino said. "There are grills on the gates there, look."

We walked over to the gates. There was a strange smell there too, musky and acrid. "Animals," I said. "Do you think they have animal fights in here?"

"The Romans did," Ficino said. "And clearly they do." He was peering in through the grill. "I can see what might be a trident. Maybe they have Roman gladiatorial combat too."

"But they seem so nice," I said. I had to step back because the smell was making me feel queasy.

"Well, the Romans did it, and most of these Marissans are from the mainland and would be used to watching violent kinds of entertainment." Ficino wasn't as disturbed as I was. "I wonder what Aristomache thinks of it."

"I don't like to think of them raking blood off the sand," I said, looking at the sand, which seemed so clean and innocent. "I don't like to think of the Romans doing it either."

"The problem with only giving you art that shows good people doing good things is that it makes you uncompromising, and doesn't give you useful examples," Ficino said. "This isn't a dark secret. It's open to everyone."

As if to demonstrate this, a group of ephebes came in and, after greeting us politely, started to race around the outside of the circuit, exactly as my friends and I would in the palaestra at home.

We walked back through the city. I realized this time that the houses near the agora were larger and better-built than the ones further away. The smaller ones didn't have glass in their windows, just wooden shutters. I saw a woman in a courtyard bent over, turning a stone on another stone. "What's she doing?" I asked.

Ficino looked. "Grinding wheat."

"They don't have Workers, or electricity," I said.

"They don't even have wind or water mills, which we used to grind wheat to flour in my time. They're starting without our technological base."

Just then another woman came out into the courtyard and started to berate the woman turning the stone. We moved away.

"They have social classes," I said.

"Yes," Ficino agreed.

"And money. And wealth and poverty."

"They started with adults who knew those things," Ficino said. "That must have made it difficult."

"Are they pursuing excellence?" I asked.

Ficino looked at me approvingly. "That's the question I've been asking myself. They haven't said they are. They talk about rescuing people and spreading their civilization. But they haven't mentioned excellence at all. And in the discussion just now, did you notice how much of what they said was about politics?"

"You kept asking about philosophy, and they always answered in terms of politics," I said. It was clear, now that I thought about it.

Ficino nodded. "I can't help thinking about Kebes, how stubborn he was. These cities are more than just Kebes, and they're clearly very influenced by the culture of the people they rescued, as well as what the *Goodness* brought. Do you remember your project on how to tell how philosophical a city is?"

I remembered it very well. I nodded.

"How would you assess this one?" We stepped out of the way of a man leading a laden donkey.

"The people you were debating with seemed to understand rhetoric, and to want to debate. But they don't have a library," I said. "Of course, one of the things they want from us is books, and it must be very difficult without."

"It may seem strange to you, but is possible to hand-copy books," Ficino said. "We did it in my day. They've done it too. They have versions of the Bible, the holy book of Christianity, as best they can remember it. And they have versions of Plato, the ones Aristomache knows by heart. There are some books in the school. But you're right that they don't have a library, and that's significant. There's a school and a church and a colosseum." Ficino gestured to a house we were passing, one of the ones with window glass. "They're doing well on a material level, not compared to us, but compared to what we've seen in the islands."

"But maybe not so much philosophically?"

"I keep reminding myself that it was justice Kebes cried out for."

"It was?" I'd never heard that.

"At the Last Debate. I was trying to hold him back but he leaped up onto the rostrum and started yelling out. 'These pagan gods are unjust.'"

We were almost back in the agora. "Athene had just acted very unjustly."

"Yes. But the gadfly that had been Sokrates spurned Kebes and flew toward your parents, which has always seemed to me an indisputable sign. Still, Kebes started rallying people, and off they went." He looked around him. "And here they are, and we'll have to make the best of it."

We spent two more days in Marissa. On the second of them there was a bull baiting in the colosseum. Neleus and Erinna went, but I volunteered for duty aboard to avoid it. Erinna said it was disgusting, and Neleus said it was kind of fun but he wouldn't go again. Maia, who also hadn't attended, said she was glad that at least they ate the bull afterward. Father just shook his head.

We left Marissa with a plan. We'd sail to Chios and spend a night at the Goodness city there, Theodoros, the gift of God, and then sail on to Lucia. We should arrive there just before the festival began. Aristomache asked if she could sail with us, and so did half a dozen other Marissans. They only had one ship, and so moving between islands only happened when the *Goodness* called. In addition, the *Goodness* made a circuit of their eight cities, so taking a voyage meant being away from home for a long period. We intended to return to Kallisti immediately after the festival, and could bring them home to Marissa on the way. There was also talk of sending a diplomatic mission to Kallisti. I happened to be present when this was discussed. "Won't that be for Lucia to decide?" Caerellia asked Deiphobos, who was one of the elected Kings of Marissa.

"Oh, I don't think it would be a problem if we want to send somebody. They can send somebody too, if they want to. We wouldn't speak for them, only for ourselves. We're not subject to Lucia. Though of course, we know how much we owe them, and we're all good friends."

Our sailing plan did not allow for bad weather. The weather, which had been good all the way from Kallisti, now let us down badly. The first day I was reminded of the storms in the *Aeneid* and the *Odyssey*. Many people were sick, and we had to manage the ship short-handed. I fell once wrestling sails, and did instinctively fly for a moment until I could regain the yard. I don't think anyone saw anything more than a well-recovered stumble; they were all too busy with their own tasks. The second day, when there was no letup in the gale, it reminded me of my dream where the ship was history being blown out of control by stormwinds. After that the days blurred together and the storm didn't remind me of anything except itself. I was quite sure we were going to founder, and worried about how long I could fly and how many people I could carry. There were just too many people aboard I loved. I finally understood Father not wanting all of us to come. It wasn't even possible to stay near one person I cared about. Too much of the time, if we'd breached I wouldn't have been able to save any of them. I decided that Phaedrus and Kallikles could save themselves, and if Erinna and Maia and Ficino and Neleus and Father weren't near enough I'd just grab whoever was and save them, even if it was sarcastic Caerellia or grumpy Phaenarete. I slept in exhausted snatches and took water to those too weak to fetch it for themselves. I discovered I had no divine abilities to heal, no sense of what was wrong with people the way Phaedrus described.

When I woke on the fourth or fifth morning to smooth sailing, and clear skies with visible stars, I actually wept.

18

ARETE

We had been blown in all directions, too far from safe harbors, and had sailed with the wind, avoiding islands as hazards. We were sure we were far to the northwest of Chios. We had no idea where we were. We hadn't seen any islands for days except as chaotic shapes whose rocks could destroy us. Now we had an even wind, and we were sailing east. Some people said we should head back to Marissa, or home to Kallisti, but Maecenas was set on visiting Lucia.

So, to my surprise, was Father. I wanted to talk to him about my powers, but the first time I caught him anything like alone he was standing at the rail with Neleus, looking out at the waves. Neleus had been extremely ill all through the storm and still looked wobbly. He was one of the very last people I wanted to know about my powers. It was unfair enough as it was. "I want to go to their city to see Kebes. Or Matthias if that's what he wants to call himself," Father said, as I came up to them, sounding as grim as ever I had heard him.

"But do you really still think he killed Mother?" I asked. "They don't have any of our art, and they said they avoided Kallisti until now for fear of Athene."

"Perhaps he didn't kill her," Father agreed. He looked at me and then at Neleus. "I still want to know where the *Goodness* was that day. The Marissans may not know everything. But even if he didn't—I didn't want to tell you. But she wrote in her auto-biography that he raped her."

"What?" I thought for a moment that he meant Kebes had raped Mother on the day she was killed.

"When? Before the Last Debate?" Neleus asked.

"Yes. At the last Festival of Hera." Father was staring out at a shadow of a shoreline on the horizon. *Before I was born*, I thought, *and only a few months after Neleus was born.*

"But if it was the Festival of Hera, weren't they supposed to . . . ?" Neleus asked.

"They were supposed to try to make a baby. He wasn't sup-posed to take her against her will when she was saying no." Fa-ther sounded vehement enough to bring the storm back. I saw people turning to look from across the deck.

"If they'd been married in front of everyone . . ." Neleus trailed off again.

"That's why she didn't tell anyone. She didn't tell *me*." There was a lot of pain in his voice, but it was quieter now. "It was rape, and he hurt her, and I'm going to kill him."

"Right," Neleus said. "I'll help."

"The punishment for rape is flogging," I said. I had been read-ing the laws in preparation for my adulthood tests. "And it would be very hard to prove now, even with her direct written testimony."

"We're not going to take him to court in the City, we're go-ing to kill him in Lucia," Father said, looking irritated. Neleus nodded.

"But—" I opened my mouth and then stopped. But the rule of law, I'd wanted to say, but the terrible things that happen when bloodfeud replaces it? And why had Mother kept quiet about the rape except to prevent exactly this? Then again, the idea that she had been raped and hadn't told anyone for so many years was awful. The thought of it made my stomach churn. "I want to kill him too. I think rape should be considered a more serious offense."

"When you're an adult you should argue that in Chamber," Father said. "Lots of us would support that. It has the death penalty in the City of Amazons."

"Maybe we could drag him back and try him there," Neleus said. "And look for the head at the same time."

"No. I couldn't bear being on the ship with him for that long. I'm not sure I'm going to be able to bear having any conversation with him at all. I'm going to kill him as soon as I possibly can." Father bit his lip hard, but even so tears ran down his cheeks. "I hate the thought that he's still alive and breathing after he did that to her."

So did I. "But what about trade agreements and diplomatic relationships between us and the Goodness Group?" I asked.

"Once Kebes is dead, we can make agreements."

"But you can't just walk up to him in the street and run him through, and then carry on with the others as if you didn't do it," Neleus said. "You'll have to either make it seem as if you didn't do it, or else tell everyone why. Unless you could find a pretext. Or fake an accident somehow."

"You're right," Father said. "I need to find a way of killing him that's personal and acceptable and doesn't destroy all possibility of friendship between our cities later. I wonder whether they allow duels?"

"It doesn't seem likely," I said, appalled.

"Kebes probably wouldn't agree to one anyway. He's fought me before, he knows I'm better."

"Does he know that you hate him?" I asked.

"Yes. Though he has no idea how much more I hate him now that I know what he did to Simmea. I wish I'd killed him long ago when I had his neck under my hand in the palaestra."

"Why didn't you?" Neleus asked.

"He was her friend and she valued him," Father said, sobbing openly now. Maia was coming toward us. I waved her away, but she kept coming. "She thought he was her friend and he did that to her."

He put his hands up to his face, pushed away from the rail and went below before Maia reached us.

"What's wrong with Pytheas now?" Maia asked.

Neleus and I looked at each other. "Just missing Mother," I said.

"I miss Simmea myself, but—" she shook her head. "I had thought the journey was doing him good."

"It is," I said, truthfully. "He hasn't been like that anything like as often since we set off."

"I suppose it's hard for him to deal with knowing it wasn't the Goodness Group who killed her," Maia said, staring after him. "He was so hoping for spectacular revenge. You'd think he'd realize it does no good. It wouldn't matter how much he avenged her, he wouldn't get her back."

Neleus grunted and went off after Father.

We were lost for two more days and stopped for water twice before we found somewhere that matched our charts. Father told me that he knew exactly where we were all the time, but of course he couldn't let anyone know, other than by suggesting a direction, and they wouldn't always listen. I didn't have that sense, and neither did Phaedrus or Kallikles, but Father said it probably was just familiarity with the geography.

Once we knew our location we crept south along the shore of Asia until we passed Lemnos, which was full of savage villages. We didn't go ashore. Then we reached Lesbos, where we arrived at a well-built city of marble columns and whitewashed stone houses with red tile roofs on the north shore. The *Goodness* was tied up at the wharf. It looked just like the *Excellence* except that it seemed to be missing a mast and the sides were visibly patched with wood of different shades. I wondered how difficult it was to maintain her without Workers.

"We have missed the festival," Aristomache said sadly, as we tacked into the harbor under a blazing noon sun. "Today's the last day. There'll be nothing left but gladiatorial combats. And I was hoping your father would compete. I remember his music."

"If his lyre didn't get drowned in the storm I'm sure he will compete if there's a chance," I said. "And even if we have completely missed it, I'm sure he'd play for you. There's nothing he likes better than singing, except maybe composing."

We were close enough now to see that people on shore were rushing about in evident surprise. "We're not going to be able to tie up the way we did at Marissa, there's only room for one ship," Erinna said.

After the envoys went ashore and negotiated with the Lucians, we arranged to anchor in the harbor, keep one watch aboard ship at all times, and send everyone else ashore in the little boat. "And no swimming!" Caerellia said, firmly. "We're in civilization here and don't you forget it!"

I went ashore with Aristomache and Maia and Neleus. Erinna had gone in an earlier group, with Ficino, though she had patted my arm and nodded when Ficino had said he'd see me ashore. Father had also gone ahead, his lyre slung over his shoulder, but he was talking to somebody on the quay. He finished his conversation and came over to join us. "The *Goodness* was in Troy when Simmea was killed," he said.

"Oh Pytheas, you didn't still think we might have done it?" Aristomache asked, putting her hand on his arm.

"I wanted to be sure," Father said.

"He's been a little crazed with grief ever since it happened," Maia said, in that language she and Aristomache shared.

"Death is a terrible thing without salvation," Aristomache replied, in the same language.

"What's that?" Neleus asked, perplexed.

Father and I exchanged glances, and I saw that he understood, as I did.

"Sorry," Aristomache said. "Come on. Most people will have gone to the agora. It's Easter day, we celebrate Yayzu risen. Tonight we will eat lamb and bread."

Lucia was decorated for festival, with flower garlands set on pillars, just the way we did it at home. It seemed very familiar, laid out on the same pattern as our cities and as Marissa, with broad streets leading to a central agora. On the top of the hill was a colosseum. We passed another huge marble Madonna, also garlanded with flowers. "Auge?" I asked.

"She's our best sculptor," Aristomache confirmed, clearly proud of her. "She lives and works here, but her work stands in all our cities. This is Our Lady of Peace." It was lovely. I could hear choral singing as we came toward the agora. A man passing handed me a honey cake from his basket. Everything seemed peaceful and pleasant. Father took a honey cake but tucked it into his kiton. I wondered suddenly whether I'd seen him eating in Marissa, or just sitting at the table moving food around? He took hospitality very seriously. Well, I had bitten into my honey cake, so it was too late. These people were my friends. I took a colored egg from a smiling girl, and Aristomache gave her a coin. I'd never get used to paying for things.

In the agora, outside a temple, there was a gruesome wooden statue of a man being tortured. He was fixed to a cross by nails through his palms and feet, he had scars of whipping, and his face was distorted by pain. It was painted in full color, just to make the blood and everything more obvious. It was hideous, and yet also beautiful. I couldn't look away from it. There were a couple of paintings in the Botticelli book that I now realized were also depictions of this story—in one he's flanked by an angel and a person dressed in long hair, with a sad old man and a dove hovering behind. In the other a person and an angel are flinging themselves around at the foot of the cross. I had always wondered what was going on in those pictures. But Botticelli's man pinned to the cross seemed peaceful and happy, and also the least interesting thing in the pictures. Here he was clearly in agony.

"Who is that?" I asked.

"Yayzu," Aristomache said.

"They did *that* to him?" I said, appalled. I looked at Father. Clearly he had very good reasons for not letting people know he was really a god.

He smiled down at me. "Not a nice way to die," he said. "Suffocation is what actually killed them. It took days sometimes. It was a Roman method of extreme punishment."

"Why do they have that there?" I asked, as Maia opened her mouth to defend her beloved Romans.

"Yayzu returned from the dead," Aristomache said. "And through him, so will we all. He conquered death, not just for himself but for all of us through all of time. He went through that to save us all. Looking at the cross reminds us not that he died, but that he went beyond death, and so will we all." Even Maia looked moved. Father smiled again, a smile that made me uneasy.

Just then I spotted Ficino and Erinna on the other side of the agora, deep in conversation with a group of strangers. Ficino was always easy to pick out in a crowd because of his red hat. I waved, but they didn't see me. I was looking at them, so I was surprised when I looked back and saw that a burly man in a floppy Phrygian cap had joined us. He was wearing leggings and a tunic, not a kiton. Since it was a festival, I assumed it was a costume for a play. He was about Father's age, clearly one of the Children.

"Aristomache, Maia, Pytheas, joy to you," he said. "What a surprise to see you here."

"Kebes," Father said, nodding. I took an involuntary step backward. This was Kebes? Apart from his fancy dress, he seemed so ordinary.

"Joy to you, Matthias," Aristomache said, seeming delighted to see him. "I've been doing my best to explain to everyone what we've been doing, but you'll be able to do it so much better."

"And what have *you* been doing?" Kebes said, mostly to Father.

"Walking in the steps of Sokrates," Father said, calmly and evenly, and, typically, speaking perfect truth even if it wasn't very helpful information.

I took a step forward again, so I was next to Maia, who hadn't said anything at all. She glanced down at me, looking worried, and that drew Kebes's attention to me for the first time. He looked at me, and then quickly at Father, and then he laughed. "Not so much with the agape, then, Pytheas?"

I didn't see Father move, but suddenly Kebes was on his back on the ground with his cap in the dust. He had a shaved circle on the top of his head.

Maia grabbed Father, and the crowd that had been moving to and fro across the agora crystallized around us, and other people also grabbed Father. Aristomache bent over Kebes as he was starting to get up. "Simmea was killed by pirates recently," she said to Kebes, directly into his face. She was about half his size and more than twice his age, but she clearly wasn't afraid of him.

Kebes froze as he was, up on one elbow, clearly shocked. "Killed?"

"Also," Father said, calmly, as if continuing a debate, standing quite still and ignoring the people holding onto him, "What did you imagine you were doing calling your city after my wife?"

Kebes face immediately closed up again.

"What?" Maia asked, puzzled.

"Lucia was Mother's childhood name," I said. Maia looked down at Kebes and let go of her grip on Father.

"I had no idea she was dead," Kebes said, getting up. He was a head taller than Father, but I hadn't noticed it until now. He dusted himself off, then picked up his hat. He looked at me again, and didn't laugh this time. His expression mingled grief and anger.

"So why did you call the city after my mother?" I asked, while I had his attention.

"We all wanted light," Kebes said, looking truculent. "It's a coincidence."

Aristomache and most of the strangers in the little crowd around us looked satisfied. Father looked as if his face was carved from marble and couldn't change expression. I didn't believe Kebes. Moreover, even though I didn't know him and couldn't possibly tell, I knew he was lying. It was certain knowledge—another divine power unfolding itself in me.

"Look, no hard—" Kebes stopped, looking at Father. "I suppose there are hard feelings on both sides. But she's dead. Let's agree to leave each other alone."

"I don't suppose you'd care to wrestle a bout in the palaestra?" Father asked, the essence of politeness. People were still holding on to his arms, but he wasn't struggling at all.

"No, I really wouldn't," Kebes said. "But I'll tell you what. The music competitions are over. But we could have another, just the two of us, tomorrow. Extend the festival a little. Compete in a different sphere. That way there will be no damage done."

Father was smiling one of his most terrifying smiles now. "But what if I want to do damage?"

"Do it with your lyre," Kebes said.

Father had won every musical competition he had entered in my lifetime, and probably before it as well. If Kebes knew how good he was in the palaestra, Kebes must also have also known how good he was at music. I didn't understand why he would even make such a suggestion, unless he was hoping to deflect Father's anger by giving him a victory that wouldn't hurt.

"I know what you did to her," Father said, intent on Kebes, ignoring the people still holding his arms and the large circle of people gathered around us listening.

"I didn't do anything to her you didn't do too," Kebes said, deliberately glancing at me. "Did I give her a child?"

I stepped between them before Father could throttle Kebes in broad daylight in the agora before half of Lucia and half the crew of *Excellence.* "You are talking about *my mother,*" I said. "And she's dead."

"Nothing against you, little one. And I'm very sorry she's dead," Kebes said, looking down at me. "I loved her. And she loved me." He meant what he was saying. But that didn't mean it was true, only that he believed it.

Father put a hand on my shoulder, and I realized they must have let him go and that he was ready to thrust me aside to get to Kebes. "This music contest," I said, quickly. "What's the prize?"

"A heifer," somebody in the crowd said. I hadn't asked because I wanted to know. I didn't take my eyes off Kebes. Now that he was looking at me, I could see by his eyes that he hadn't offered it thinking it was an easy way to lose. He was sincerely confident of winning. But I was just as confident that nobody could beat Father at music. (He is the god Apollo. He *invented* music.)

"No," Kebes said, looking at Father over my head. "Not a heifer. How about if, instead, the winner gets to do what they

want to the loser? That's what this is about, isn't it? We've always hated each other. This way we both have a fair chance."

Father's hand on my shoulder seemed to become heavier. There
was a hiss of drawn breath from the crowd. Maia was frowning.
Saying *do what they want* seemed better to me at that moment than
saying *kill*. But why would Kebes suggest it? He was lying when
he said they both had a fair chance. He believed he would win.
How could he?

"I can agree to that," Father said. "What should it be? Original lyre composition?"

"Any instrument," Kebes said. "Original composition. I have
an instrument you may not have seen."

I could almost hear Father's sneer. "Who judges this competition?" he asked.

"Four of yours and four of ours," Kebes said, then he glanced
down at me again. "None of our children."

"Nine judges," Father countered. "Four of yours, four of ours,
and one chosen by lot."

"Very well," Kebes said. "And the winner does what they want
to the loser, and the loser doesn't stop them?"

"Without a judgment? That's barbaric," Aristomache put in.
There was a muttering of agreement in the crowd. "It's one thing
when somebody has been condemned, but we've never done it
without that."

"We're all civilized people," Kebes said, lying again, and still
staring over my head at Father.

"Pytheas has been unhinged since Simmea's death," Klymene
said. I hadn't noticed her there in the crowd. "This is madness.
We know the Goodness Group didn't kill her. The ship was in
Troy last autumn, nowhere near Kallisti." She was speaking the
truth as she knew it, even about Father being mad.

"I believe that," Father said. "This isn't about that. It's about what he did to Simmea before he left." Father didn't ever lie, I realized. He sometimes deliberately said things that could be misinterpreted, but as far as I could see he always told the truth.

"What did you do to Simmea?" Maia asked. She had a soft voice but it sounded hard now.

"Nothing you didn't personally sanction," Kebes said, looking at her for the first time since he had greeted her. "You chose the partners for the Florentines for the Festival of Hera. You yourself matched me with her."

Maia made an inarticulate choking sound.

"He raped her," I said, into the silence, to make it clear, since it seemed nobody else was going to. "She wrote about it."

Klymene looked shocked. "Is this true?"

Kebes looked at me, then at her. "No. She wanted it. She loved me." He wanted to believe what he was saying, but he couldn't quite manage it. There was guilt behind his words. I wished everyone could hear it as clearly as I could.

"But there's a written record?" Klymene asked, glancing back at me.

"Whatever she may have said later, she didn't report it as rape at the time," Kebes said, speaking the whole truth now. "There were procedures, if she had wanted to complain about me. You know that. Did she tell you about this, or are we taking Pytheas's word, and his daughter's? This was all twenty years ago."

"But Kebes—" Klymene began.

"Matthias," he interrupted. "That's always been my name."

She waved this off. "Matthias, then. This contest is insane. Pytheas—"

"We've agreed," Father said. His hand was still on my shoulder. "He suggested it himself. A musical contest. What could be more civilized?"

"But the consequences—one of you is going to kill the other one!" Klymene sounded appalled.

"That's going to happen anyway," Father said, gently.

"I could tie you up until we're back on Kallisti," Klymene said, and she meant it. "You always take too much on yourself, you always put yourself forward, you think you're the best and that gives you the right to do whatever you want, but it doesn't. You're not sane, Pytheas, and I can't let you go ahead with this. It's unjust!"

"It doesn't involve anyone but the two of us," Father said.

"He has always hated me, it's not the madness of grief," Kebes said, to the crowd. "But I have proposed this fair contest. It's the best way. The winner to do what they want." He seemed so sure that he could win. There was a kind of gloating in his voice.

Klymene shook her head. "We want peace and trade with your cities," she said.

"That can happen without Pytheas or myself being involved," Kebes said. "We can give assurances. This is a personal matter." Then he turned to me. "You may not believe me, but your mother and I loved each other. Nobody answered my question, and I have a right to know. Do you have older brothers?"

I didn't believe him. He wasn't lying, he believed what he said, but it was something he had convinced himself of, not the truth. I knew my mother. "I have lots of older brothers, but none of them are your sons," I said.

"You wouldn't necessarily know. She said she'd give it up to philosophy," he said, half to himself.

"Simmea didn't have a child after that last festival," Maia said, forcing her voice out.

Kebes nodded, looking disappointed. He looked at me again. "And what's your name, little girl?"

"Arete," I said, putting my chin up. I have been embarrassed and teased about my name all my life, but never have I been prouder to declare it than that day. It was like declaring my mother's true allegiance, proclaiming the name she gave me. It encapsulated the choices she had made in her life, her allegiance to philosophy, to Father, to the City, to her own excellence, and mine, and the excellence of the world.

Kebes looked at Father, and back at me. "Arete," he said, as if he hated the word. It seemed to me that he should have known then and by that alone that he had lost.

19

APOLLO

Mortals can be wonderful and maddening and fascinating, and sometimes all three at the same time.

Every single member of the company of the *Excellence*, except my children, came to try to persuade me not to kill Kebes after I won the competition, even dear Ficino and lark-voiced Erinna. None of them doubted that I'd win. I'd been winning musical competitions since the first years of the Republic, after all. They took it utterly for granted. They just didn't want me to kill Kebes afterward. They had different reasons.

Klymene didn't want me to kill Kebes because he had been her friend, and Simmea's friend. She also didn't believe me about the rape. "Even before this you always misjudged him. Exactly what did Simmea write? She never said anything to me about it, and I saw her that night. Can I see it? Do you have it here?"

Maecenas didn't want me to kill Kebes because he wanted to trade with Lucia and Marissa, and he was afraid it would mess up diplomatic relations. "It might just be that we've been conflating Kebes and the Goodness Group all this time, but he really is important to these people, and if you take him out then it'll make everything harder. I appreciate that you want to hurt him for what he did to Simmea. But you can do what you like—it's your choice, eh? You could just beat him up. Break his nose! That would be satisfying. Break a couple of bones if you have to. Or how about if you rape him, if you could bring yourself to? Humiliate him. But leave him alive, eh?"

Ficino didn't want me to kill Kebes because he thought it would be bad for my soul. "You don't want to have that stain on your soul when you go on to your next life. Killing somebody in battle is one thing, but deliberately setting out to kill them for revenge is different. I'm not thinking about Kebes here, Pytheas, I'm thinking about you. Killing him doesn't avenge what he did to Simmea. It won't bring her back, or change what he did. Vengeance isn't justice. You understand that."

I thought I understood it. I'd taken vengeance before. It certainly isn't justice, or restitution, let alone changing what had happened. I agree that those things would be better, if they were possible. Not even Father can wind back time, though he can wipe it out as if it had never been. But vengeance, inadequate as it may be, is sometimes better than having people get away with what they've done. Kebes was going to go on to a new life, and I sincerely hoped he'd learned something in this one so that he'd do better next time. It was the thought of leaving him alive to enjoy the memory of what he had done to Simmea that was intolerable.

To carry through Ficino's argument, killing Kebes was the best thing I could possibly do for him, for the only part of him that was important, his soul. Kebes had demonstrated over and over again that in this life he would turn away from chances to become his best self. He held tight through everything to his narrow Christianity, his supposed love for Simmea, and most of all his hate for the Masters and the City. He refused reason and justice and excellence. He had turned away from all his opportunities. A new life might give him new chances, with less ingrained intransigence.

Most of the arguments the crew made to me were variants on these three. Erinna was entirely pragmatic, asking what would happen to Arete if they took against us and attacked the ship. Maia was extremely Platonic. She told me that Ikaros had raped her when they'd been setting up the city, but she believed he didn't understand what rape was. She hadn't told anyone because she didn't want to cause trouble, so she understood why Simmea hadn't talked about it.

"When Kebes said I'd personally sanctioned it, I felt as if he'd hit me," she said. "Those Festivals of Hera. It didn't give the girls any choice. I hadn't thought of it that way."

"It didn't give the boys any choice either," I said, remembering that awful time with Klymene. "Sometimes Plato had an idea that seemed good to him, but just doesn't work at all when you try it with actual people."

"But it was a long time ago, and we *had* sanctioned it—we, the Masters. Me. I had sanctioned it." Maia was never a coward; she faced her own responsibility squarely. She was pale but she went on. "And Simmea might not have made a complaint because she didn't want everyone to know. But she didn't tell you either. You know that means she didn't want vengeance." She hesitated, assessing how I was taking it, and then went on. "And Kebes might have learned better since. He seems to be doing good work here. Ikaros understands now. I have forgiven him."

This was the one argument that made me hesitate. *I* had learned better since Daphne had turned into a tree. I hadn't understood what was happening with Daphne. Kebes gave every sign of failing to understand what he had done. But he wasn't sorry. He had hurt her and gone on when she asked him to stop, and afterward he had insulted her. Now he seemed to have deluded himself again into believing, in spite of all the evidence to the contrary, that she was really his. He had named his city after her. He had insisted on knowing whether she'd had a child.

He said she loved him. He kept on claiming her, over and over, when in fact she was . . . her own. (And, yes, all right, mine, but mine because she wanted to be. One of the reasons I hated Kebes was because he was my dark and twisted mirror, and forced me to confront these things. I do try to be just and pursue excellence.)

I struggled to say some of this to Maia. "He didn't sound as if he has learned better. He wasn't acting as if he believed she had equal significance and was her own self. He thought he owned her. She wrote that he said that to her at the time, and I believe from what he said today that he still thinks that."

"But Pytheas, do you truly think it's just to kill him for thinking that?"

"What is justice, Maia? It took Plato ten books, and it's taking us decades, and none of us has a proper answer."

I don't know what she would have replied, because at that moment Ismene came up, and with her my son. He looked like me, and like his brothers. He was much taller than his mother. She was still pretty. I had never known her well. "Joy to you, Ismene," I said. Maia turned to greet her.

"This is Fabius," she said, presenting the boy. He wished me joy gruffly, not knowing where to look. I looked at him, almost as much at a loss. I had met sons before who had been strangers, but they had always known who I was. Should I tell this boy he had a heroic soul? How could I, in front of Maia and his mother? And what could he make of the information in any case? He might not even believe me. It seemed kinder to leave him to make what he could of himself. So we had a limping uncomfortable conversation, and after a little while he and his mother went away together.

"Another son," Maia said, watching them go.

"I can't do anything for that one," I said.

"Oh Pytheas, do you really think you might lose tomorrow?"

"That's for the gods," I said. "Are you thinking of going to talk to Kebes to urge him not to kill me if he wins?"

"Yes," she said, biting her lip. "But as he hates me just as much as he hates you, I can't imagine it doing much good."

At sunset Arete insisted everyone leave me to rest before the competition, and she and the boys and I walked off up the beach. She had brought food from the city, roast lamb with herbs and colored eggs for Easter, but wise Neleus had brought dried meat and raisins from the ship which he shared with me. I had brought a jar of wine. We built a fire of driftwood and sat down by it

"You're not accepting their hospitality, then?" Arete said. "I thought not."

"They'll forget the name Lucia," I said. "This place was called Mithymna." The sun was sliding into the sea before us, lighting the clouds a thousand shades of red and violet and gold. I looked along the curve of the hill where the moon, two days past full, was due to rise. I opened the wine and took a sip. Neat, it was as sweet as honey, and as strong. I handed it to Kallikles, who was on my right.

Arete looked sideways at Neleus. "I can tell when people are telling the truth," she said.

Kallikles and Phaedrus looked interested. Neleus grunted, taking the wine. "Useful ability," I said, carefully.

"Kebes thought he might well win," she said.

"I noticed that," I said. "Interesting, isn't it? He was never known for his musical ability. But he didn't act as if he was committing suicide, and the Lucians in the crowd didn't act that way either. He said he had a new instrument. I wonder what it is?"

"What happens if he wins?" Neleus asked, passing the wine on to Phaedrus.

"He kills me, then he'll get a real surprise when I kill him immediately afterward." I smiled. I almost wanted it to happen. It would make everything so much simpler.

"Isn't that cheating?" Kallikles asked.

"He raped Mother!" Neleus said.

"Right, not cheating," Kallikles said.

"What will you do to him if you win?" Arete said. She was holding the wine jar, but she didn't drink. Plato said nobody under the age of thirty should drink unmixed wine.

"I'll cut his throat. Get it over with as fast as possible."

"Why would he suggest this?" Phaedrus asked. "The winner doing what they want?"

"I expect he wants to torture me to death," I said.

To my surprise, they were all shocked.

"Kebes hates me," I explained. "He always has. It's partly because Simmea loved me, and partly because he hates excellence." I knew this was right. Simmea had explained it to me.

"How can anyone hate excellence?" Arete asked.

"Ah, you didn't realize quite what a wound your name was to him?"

"I did, but I thought that was because of Mother choosing it, choosing you and the City and excellence over him and his choices."

"Yes. That too. But he hates Plato, and all of Plato's ideas. He said he couldn't become his best self because his best self would never have been enslaved or brought to the city, and what he had left was revenge." I remembered him saying it. Kebes was older now, closing on forty like all the Children, but he was still exactly the same as the bull-headed boy he had been that day in the garden at Thessaly. "He wasn't prepared to go on from where he was and make the best of what he could be. And he hates me because I do pursue excellence, and because Simmea chose me and excellence over him and his idea of freedom."

"He hates Plato?" Kallikles echoed, as if the words made no sense.

"I've heard that they say harsh things about Plato sometimes in Sokratea," Phaedrus said.

"Most of the Goodness Group don't hate Plato," I said. "That's clear. But Kebes does."

"But won't the rest of them object to his torturing you?" Kallikles asked.

"I'm sure he's done it before. I expect they do it to criminals. I think that's what Aristomache meant when she said it was barbaric without a judgment," Arete said. "They have that statue. They have gladiatorial combats. They probably think it's all right."

I nodded. "Yes, and Kebes introduced Christianity—which is about to put him in a bad spot. He's a priest. They're likely to be telling him it's his Christian duty to forgive me. At least nobody offered me that kind of pap."

"What will you do if he does forgive you?" Arete asked.

I took the wine jar from her and drank again. "If he could forgive me he wouldn't be Kebes. He won't forgive me. And he won't win. And I'll kill him."

"Is it what Mother would have wanted?" Phaedrus asked.

"Not really," I admitted. "If she'd wanted revenge she'd have told me right away and I'd have killed him then, that day, before the Last Debate. I'd have come up behind him in the dark and got a hold and told him who it was and what I was doing and then broken his neck and left him there, making it look as if he tripped." It would have been so easy.

"If she were here she'd be arguing about the nature of justice," Arete said. "Though maybe she would want revenge. How dare he look at me and say you weren't practicing agape!"

I didn't say anything. If Simmea were alive, we wouldn't have been here. And if we had been, and she'd been here, Kebes would have been civil to me in her presence, as he had promised years ago. And besides, I have never truly understood what Plato meant by agape, especially when it came to men and women. I wasn't sure that Plato even really understood that men could fall in love with women, or that women could fall in love at all. It wasn't until the Renaissance that Platonic love was interpreted that way. There aren't any simple words for what Simmea and I were to each other. She was my friend and my votary. That was enough.

"Why didn't you just kill him?" Phaedrus asked. "When he said that and you hit him?"

"I didn't think," I said, and it was true. I'd smashed him to the ground with a blow. I could just as easily have crushed his throat and watched him choke to death. I had acted entirely without thinking, and on that instinctive level I was used to drawing back and not killing Kebes.

Neleus had the wine. I waited until he had swallowed. "I need you to help me," I said to him. "You haven't accepted their hospitality."

He nodded, eager. "I haven't. Not here, and not at Marissa."

"Good. That was well thought through. The rest of you did accept it, didn't you."

"Sorry," Phaedrus said.

"I didn't think," Kallikles said.

"They're not all Kebes. They're good people, doing good work. Mother would have liked them," Arete said.

"They'll be utterly forgotten," I said, confident of it. I'd been shaken for a moment at Marissa, but I knew the future couldn't be changed, that anything done here was nothing more to history than a marginal note. I'd been to the future, after all. On the beach where we were sitting there would one day be a wonderful little restaurant that made mouth-watering kalimari and grilled fish, crisp outside and moist within. "Forgotten. Kebes and all his works."

"Maia says they're the cities Plato heard about. The ones that lived according to his rule, and then degenerated to timarchy and so on," Arete said. "And they do show signs that way."

I laughed, amused. "Then maybe they are."

I looked back at Neleus. "Kebes said the judges couldn't be our children—by which I assume he's not practicing clerical celibacy and he has some children here. But you're technically not my child, which is a good thing, because it means you can be one of the judges. And because you haven't accepted their hospitality, you're not restricted in what you can do. If Kebes tries to cheat, you're free to act without any inhibitions."

Neleus grinned at me across the flames. "Do you think he has any chance of winning, though?"

"He's certainly seems to think he can. And he's definitely going to try to get biased judges. So we may as well do what we can. He must think he has a chance, or he'd never have suggested it."

"I don't understand how the judges are going to be able to judge fairly," Arete said. "They'll know they're condemning one of you to death."

"It will all be done in public. Everyone will see. It will affect how relations go in future between Kallisti and the Goodness Group. They'll want to be seen to be fair. So I think it will be a real competition." I was actually looking forward to it. "And even if I lose, it doesn't matter. If he kills me, I'll just kill him right after. If that happens, don't stand right next to him."

"Will you blast him with lightning?" Kallikles asked.

"No, only Father can do that. But I will have the arrows of my wrath, which cannot miss." I missed the weight of the quiver on my back. "I won't use one of the ones that brings plague. But there won't be much left of him. There may be a crater." That would be very satisfying. But it would be even more satisfying to defeat him first, so that he had to understand before he died that I was better than he was.

Kallikles was clearly pondering saying something. He looked at Neleus and then away.

I went on. "The other thing, Neleus, is that your other father, Nikias, is here—I saw him in the crowd this morning."

"I had thought he might be, or if not here then in one of their other cities," Neleus said, looking down.

"It's a good thing. Simmea liked him, and he liked her. They were friends, the same as she was friends with Aeschines. He'll probably be pleased to meet you and know you. But he'll also be an ally. If you can find him tonight, you might be able to persuade him to be one of their judges—there can't be much competition for the job. And he might be able to tell us about Kebes's mysterious instrument, and what things are really like here."

"Did you think Aristomache was lying?" Arete asked. "Because she wasn't."

"Aristomache would no more lie than lay an egg," I said. "But good people can be deceived, more easily than bad people sometimes."

"You can tell whether people are lying, can't you?" she asked.

"I can tell whether they're sincere," I said.

Neleus looked at her, and at me. "You're not talking about something people can do. You're talking about some kind of hero thing? Because I can also usually tell when people are telling the truth just by the way they talk, and where they look when they talk."

"I can do that too," Arete said. "But just recently I've started being sure."

"Yes, that's a power," I said. "I can't do that."

"We've all been getting powers," Kallikles said. "I don't want to keep it from you, Nel. I don't want to hurt you by making you feel different either, but keeping it secret is worse. Ever since we went to Delos, we've been able to do some things."

"Like what?" he asked, looking at the three of them. "I knew there was something."

"Healing," Phaedrus said. "And heat." He put his hand into the fire and left it there. "I don't burn. And I can walk on air."

"I can walk on air too. And I have lightning, just a little." Kallikles held his hands a few inches apart and a tiny bolt of lightning jumped between them. "I found out in the storm. I can control weather. I think that's why the storm was so bad. I was drawing it by mistake. I think I have it under control now, though."

"And you?" Neleus asked Arete.

"The truth thing. And I can understand other languages. I can walk on air too, and I can also fly. And I think I could fly carrying somebody, if I had to. That's all." Fly? Simmea and I had imagined that she'd be a philosophical hero. There's never any control over how children will come out. I thought again of the unknown boy Fabius.

"That seems like enough!" Neleus said. "Fly?"

"I've only tried it once, but yes," she said. She looked along the beach. We were still in sight from the ship, if anyone was looking. "I don't want anyone to see me, but I'll show you when it gets darker, if you like."

"It won't get much darker. The afterglow is fading, but the moon's close enough to full that when she's up people would be able to see you." There was already a silver glow behind the hill where the moon was about to rise.

"I'll show you another time, then," Arete said. "It's not weird—it's just like being able to do math in your head, or knowing how to swim."

"Not weird? Being able to walk on air and heal people and

fly?" Neleus's voice rose. "It's about as weird as things get!" He looked at me suddenly. "I've never seen you do anything like that."

"I gave up my powers to become incarnate," I said. "You know that. I can't do anything like that now."

"So in one way, you and I are the only normal ones on this beach," he said.

I blinked. It wasn't a way I'd ever looked at it. The moon was rising now above the colosseum where the contest would be held tomorrow, silvering the pillars. It would eventually become an acropolis, and later a Venetian castle. The moon looked like a great glowing coin poised on the ridge. I remembered going there to talk to Artemis, standing on the dusty plains beside the lander from the ship that bore my name. "The gods have power. But humans have wonderful dreams and make them real, sometimes."

Phaedrus took his hand out of the fire. "If only we had some fruit we wanted to bake," Kallikles said. He put his own finger toward the flame and darted it back at once. "It's funny how we all have different things."

"Different freaky abilities," Neleus said.

"Are you jealous?" Arete asked.

Neleus nodded. "How could I not be jealous? You all have magic god-powers, and you'll get to live forever while I die. But on the other hand, I'm not a freak. You've always been faster and stronger than me. You're weird. You scare people. I'm just strong and smart and, outside of this family, people like me."

"We'll have to die too," Arete said, wisely sidestepping the issue of what happens afterward.

"And we like you," Phaedrus said. He handed him the wine jar. "Or we do when you give us the chance."

"That's true," Kallikles said. "When you give us the chance."

"It just feels as if I have to be twice as good to be normal," Neleus said.

"That's what Simmea was afraid of," I said. "When we brought you home. But you were smart enough to keep up. Not surprising, being her son." I wasn't good at this kind of thing. But it seemed to work. He smiled.

"So tomorrow," I said, and their attention all switched back to me at once. "What do you think I ought to sing, to completely flatten Kebes, so much so that the judges will have no option but to be fair and give me the victory?"

20

ARETE

Phaedrus and I walked in with Father, a few minutes before the appointed hour.

Everyone was there from the *Excellence*, except for the watch that Maecenas had absolutely forced to stay aboard. Kallikles was one of those, though he had complained and protested until the last moment. It seemed as if the whole population of Lucia had turned out as well, even those who were old and sick. I saw people carried there in blankets, old people barely able to hobble, newborn babies, and pregnant women who looked on the point of popping. Everyone gathered in the colosseum, which was just like the one in Marissa.

It was a big space, but crowded now. The seats were packed with people when we arrived, more people than I had ever seen in one place before, perhaps more people than lived in the Remnant. Some were sitting on blankets and sharing picnics. A girl with a little piping flute was wandering through the crowd and being given presents—or no, I reminded myself, money. They used money here.

The nine judges were sitting on raised seats down on the stage. Neleus was among them. The other three from the ship were Klymene, Ficino, and Erinna. From the city were Nikias, immediately recognizable as Neleus's father, Aristomache, and three strangers. I wondered if it would be good or bad that the ninth judge was from Lucia. It was the most likely outcome of choosing by lot. There were ninety of us and more than three thousand of them.

Father was wearing his cloak, pulled back over his shoulder to show the two swords through his belt. Phaedrus carried the lyre. Everyone fell silent when they saw us and then a murmur went through the crowd, which parted to let us pass. It was like a play, and I felt that we should have had time to make costumes before our grand entrance, or at least re-dye our kitons so that we all matched. I would have put us all in black and gold, but any unified color would have done. As it was we were hopeless. Father's cloak was pink, embroidered with scrolls and suns, one of Mother's favorite patterns. His kiton was plain white, as he generally preferred. Phaedrus's kiton was blue, embroidered six inches deep with four different patterns, and mine was a faded yellow embroidered with red Florentine lilies.

There was no sign of Kebes.

We walked down one of the clear aisles and onto the stage. The judges were sitting toward the farther side, on a row of chairs. In the center was a strange piece of wood, almost as tall as I was and about half that broad, with two iron loops bolted into it at the top and another two near the bottom. It was just one straight upright, not a cross, but it had something of the same feel as the crucifix outside the temple. I had no idea what it was for.

Aristomache came forward and introduced the judges to us. The three strangers, two women and a man, were strangers to Father too, it seemed. Their names were Sabina, Erektheus, and Alexandra. Everyone wished each other joy. Erinna was biting her lip, looking very serious.

"I wonder if Kebes is even going to show up," Phaedrus muttered, but just then there was a stir in the crowd, and there was

Kebes at the top of the slope, still dressed in his costume from the day before, with the Phrygian cap pulled down on his broad forehead. A woman and a boy came with him, carrying a strange assortment of things I couldn't quite figure out.

"Why would she have given him those?" Father murmured.

"Who? Mother?" Phaedrus asked.

Father laughed shortly. "No indeed. Athene. It's an instrument she invented and then discarded because it made her look so ugly playing it. It's called a syrinx, or pan-pipes."

I'd never seen anything like it. It consisted of a set of hollow tubes of different lengths bound together. "Like a whole set of flutes?" I asked. Wind instruments were banned at home, because Plato thought they made people soft.

"Yes, sort of," he said. "And what do the others bring?"

The woman was carrying a little folding stool. The boy had a bag, which he set down on the left of the wooden thing and unfastened. Inside were a set of leatherworking knives and a number of leather straps.

"Afraid, Pytheas?" Kebes asked.

Father laughed, because of course he wasn't afraid at all. I wondered if he half-wanted Kebes to kill him so that he could go back to being a god and stop needing to figure out mortality from first principles. But what was the threat in a wooden pole and a set of little knives? The crowd seemed to know, because they had fallen silent as soon as the boy undid the bag. Torture, I thought, just as Father had said. Erinna was frowning at the bag. She asked Ficino something and screwed up her face at his reply. Klymene shook her head.

Kebes's eyes swept over the judges. He nodded to the woman, and she and the boy moved back and climbed up the first set of stairs to sit down in a clear space on the first bench on the edge of the crowd. Father set down his swords on the opposite side of the wood from the bag, took his lyre from Phaedrus, and nodded coolly to us. "See you later." Phaedrus moved back, but I moved forward to embrace him, being careful of the lyre. "Win," I said. "What he said was an insult to the honor of all three of us."

"I'll do my best," he said. "Fascinating as it might look in the art of later times, I find I have very little desire to be skinned alive." I looked back at the tools with a start of horror. Once he had pointed it out I could imagine it all too easily. Bound to the wood by the iron rings and the straps, and then skinned alive. How horrible! Even worse than crucifixion. Surely all incarnate gods didn't have to end up dying in horrible ways? Surely? Aristomache said Yayzu had come back in his divine form, but she hadn't mentioned what he'd done to the torturers afterward. I hoped it was something really appropriate.

I swallowed, nodded, and climbed the stairs to sit in the front row by Phaedrus, on the other side of the arena from Kebes's friends. I looked over at the judges. Neleus smiled at me reassuringly. Erinna was frowning again. I looked down at the little knives where they were laid out so neatly. Everyone in the crowd seemed to recognize them. This must be something they did often enough to have the tools for it. And, most disturbing of all, they came crowding into the colosseum and brought their children to watch.

Kebes had seated himself on a camp stool and was tapping his fingers impatiently. Father stood still and looked at Aristomache.

Aristomache came forward and said something quietly to both men. They both shook their heads. She sighed, and held both hands forward to the crowd, palms out. "You are here to witness a formal musical challenge of one original composition, for any instrument," she began. Everyone immediately fell silent, except one baby whose crying sounded loud in the sudden stillness. The acoustics were wonderful. "Between Pytheas of the Just City and Matthias of Lucia. The victor is to do what he wants to the vanquished. Will you two show mercy, as this is just a personal quarrel, and give up this enmity and compete for a prize?"

"Never," Kebes said.

"There is a place for vengeance in my religion," Father said.

Aristomache looked pained, and so did some of the other judges from Lucia.

"An eye for an eye and a tooth for a tooth," Kebes said, clearly quoting something. "Christianity has room for vengeance too, especially upon heathens and heretics." At the word "heretics" there was a stirring and muttering in the crowd.

"Can't you forgive?" Aristomache pleaded.

"And what have I done to you anyway, beyond existing?" Father asked, mildly, his words pitched perfectly to be heard everywhere in the colosseum. Even the crying baby fell silent.

"This isn't a trial," Kebes snarled at Father. "We're not here to rehearse grievances. And while Lucia is a Christian city, this is permissible by our laws. It's a free contest, freely entered into."

Aristomache sighed and raised her hands again. "The judges are chosen and will swear." Weirdly, she now put her palms together. "I swear by Yayzu and his Heavenly Father that I will judge fairly and by the laws, and not be swayed by prejudice, friendship, or the feeling of the crowd."

It was the strangest oath I ever heard, halfway between the oaths judges take in a capital case and an artistic competition. It became clear as the others swore that the matter of which gods would hold the oath had been left to personal preference. The odd mix of phrases didn't sound any more normal when Ficino swore by all the gods, or Erinna by Apollo and the Muses. Klymene swore by Zeus, Apollo, and Demeter, which was the conventional trio at home for holding significant oaths. Neleus swore by all gods on high Olympos, which cleverly left out Father, since he was right here. Nikias swore before high holiness, which could have meant anything. Alexandra swore by Yayzu and Marissa,

Sabina by Marissa alone, Erektheus by blessed Yayzu and Saint Lucy. Father, who had stood impassive through all the rest, even when he was named, winced a little at that.

Then Kebes came up, putting his palms together. "I swear by God, and Marissa, and Saint Matthew, and by my own true name, that I shall abide by the decision of these judges. Whether it be for me or against me I shall submit myself to whatever follows." His voice boomed out confidently. I couldn't understand what he thought he was doing. He was swearing in truth, without reservations. He believed he would win and get to skin Father alive, but how could he?

Father followed him forward and swore the same oath, calmly and clearly, calling on Zeus, Leto, and the Muses. It seemed an odd choice of gods, but not inappropriate. He couldn't exactly swear by himself.

"We shall draw lots for who will begin," Aristomache said.

"No, you go first, Pytheas," Kebes said.

"No, you." Father made a gesture of elaborate courtesy and the crowd laughed.

"We will draw lots," Aristomache said again, firmly. She shook a bag. "Black or white?"

"White," Father said.

Aristomache sat down again and held out the bag out to Nikias, who pulled out a stone without looking and held it up to the crowd. It was white.

Without waiting for anything more, still standing where he was, in a graceful pose with his cloak draped neatly to leave his arm bare, Father began to play.

I've said that Father invented music, and it's true. I wasn't really worried. All the same, we'd spent a long time the evening before discussing what he ought to play. For an audience that contained a large number of Yayzu worshippers, it shouldn't be a religious theme. Similarly, it shouldn't be something overtly

Platonic. Phaedrus had suggested he play his song about the Last
Debate, and it would have been a good choice, except that it was
a subject that excited strong feelings for and against. We discussed elegies and love songs and praise songs. Father had written them all. "What we want is something everyone except Kebes
will like," I had said. We'd pretty much agreed that he'd play a
song he had written years ago about the sun going down and
a bird flying on toward the dawn. It's a song about death and
hope, of course, but it's also about a bird and a sunset, and the
tune is marvelous.

Of course, Father being Father, he didn't play that at all. He
had written it, yes, but lots of the people there had heard it already. Erinna quite often sang it herself. What he sang was
completely new. I'd never heard it before, and I'm fairly sure he
composed it especially for the occasion, maybe even on the spot.
It had a pretty, complex melody, with chords that would be much
too hard for most people, and then the words made a harmony,
twining around it. It was in the Phrygian mode, of course. From
the first note everyone was caught in the silence. The song was
about me. Or rather, it was about arete, about personal human
excellence, and how it was what we all wanted to attain, and how,
being human, we so often fell short but went on from there, and
kept on trying, and achieved amazing things. The images were all
about building cities and lives, using Plato's parallel that sees
cities and souls as analogous. I had tears in my eyes by the end of
the first verse, and that was before the incredibly uplifting chorus.

It was such a wonderful song, and such a wonderful perfor-
mance of it, that I almost forgot to look at Kebes. He stayed
sitting there, smiling slightly, not at all worried. It made no sense.
However good he was with his pipes, he couldn't possibly top
this. Did he think Father would hesitate to kill him? Or did he
have a deeper plan?

When Father finished the crowd surged to their feet, clapping with all their hearts. Father bowed to them and stepped back, his face calm and composed, opening his hand to Kebes. And Kebes didn't even wait for them to settle down, he grinned, blew a note, and then another, and then a whole ripple of clear fast notes, puffing out his cheeks.

Of course he couldn't sing while he was playing. The syrinx is a breath instrument, so Kebes's tune had no words. But he was good. He had me tapping my foot almost at once. As for the crowd, already on their feet, half of them were dancing. It wasn't Phrygian or Dorian, it was some other mode altogether, a music I'd never heard, one Plato banned from the Republic, a music made of night and laughter and swaying rhythms. How could Athene have invented such an instrument? It was erotic, haunting, dangerous. Father's song had been a call for Platonic excellence. This reached out to the parts of people Plato most wanted to suppress. And yet, these impulses were undeniably part of life too. I looked at Erinna, and looked away again. I don't know how long Kebes played. It wasn't the kind of music that has measures. It built to a climax, hung there, and toppled back with a sigh. The crowd sighed too, and then clapped and stamped and cheered. Phaedrus and I were the only ones sitting, apart from the judges. Father's face was completely expressionless, as if carved from marble.

"That was the strangest thing," Phaedrus murmured as the crowd slowly subsided. "Do you think Father had heard one of those before?"

"He knew what it was," I said. "He knew Athene made it. He must have."

"I've never heard any music remotely like it," Phaedrus said, more loudly.

One of the women nearby leaned over, breaching the space between the two of us and the rest of the crowd. "Myxolydian, that was, and it's a syrinx," she said, helpfully. "It is different when you're used to calm Platonic music."

It certainly was.

The judges were disputing and couldn't seem to come to an agreement. I could see hands being waved. Erinna was shaking her head. Klymene was frowning hard. One of the strangers was pointing at the crowd, and Aristomache was looking reproving. "Who do you think will win?" I asked the woman who had explained about the Myxolydian.

She was a middle-aged woman, and she had two children sitting with her. I couldn't tell whether she was one of the Children or one of the rescued locals. "It's terribly hard for the judges," she said, "because they're condemning one of them to death, and there's no getting away from that after that exchange at the beginning. I'm glad I wasn't chosen. They're judging between such very different things. Matthias has been winning all the musical competitions here for years. Everyone loves the syrinx. Once you have a syrinx and a drum and somebody with a low voice singing, you can have wonderful dancing after dark. But what Pytheas sang—who could vote against that?"

"Do you know my father?" It was something about the familiar way she said his name that made me ask.

"Oh yes. I'm Auge. I used to share a sleeping house with your mother. She was doing agape with Pytheas even back then."

I didn't want to break the news about Mother's death to another of her old friends. "You're the sculptor? I love your work. The statue in the harbor in Marissa especially."

She blushed. I introduced her to Phaedrus, and she introduced me to her children, a boy of fourteen and a girl of twelve. The judges were still arguing. She introduced me to a few more of the people in the crowd, and insisted on sharing her picnic with us—cold lamb and cucumber yoghurt rolled in flatbread, delicious. I hadn't thought I'd be able to eat while Father's life hung in the balance, but once I smelled it I was ravenous. "I think they'll call it a draw," Auge said. "What else can they do? Then everyone will have to be satisfied."

The judges were still arguing when we finished eating. "What do you usually use this colosseum for?" Phaedrus asked.

Auge looked uncomfortable. "Competitions. Drama. Animal fights. Gladiator fights. There are a number of Romans among us. They suggested it. And the locals we recruited enjoy things like that."

"We have drama in the City now," I said. "And some of us went to an animal fight in Marissa."

"And of course we hold assembly here, and we also use it for punishments and executions," Auge said.

Phaedrus looked at the wooden post. "So your punishments are public?"

Auge nodded. "As for drama, we've often wished we'd brought copies of plays when we left. That's something we'd be very keen to trade for. How did you start allowing performances?" Phaedrus started telling her about the vote that allowed drama.

The shadows were growing long when Aristomache stood up again.

"We want to hear you both again before we come to a decision," she said.

"The same work, or something else?" Kebes asked.

"The same original composition," she said. She gestured to Father. He had been standing quite still and expressionless all this time, though Kebes had been exchanging sallies with people in the crowd. Now he smiled, still calm and perfect but deadly. He swung his cloak deliberately so that it draped from the other shoulder. Then he picked up the lyre and turned it carefully upside-down. He then began to play, the same complex tune as before, perfect, even though all the strings were in the opposite places, and he was using his left hand. He sang again, lifting up his voice and filling the space.

Kebes sat stunned for a moment, then roared to his feet. "This is blatant cheating!"

Aristomache raised a hand to cut him off. Father had not missed a note. He raised an eyebrow, and she nodded to him to continue. He played the upside-down lyre, left-handed, through all the complexities of the song, flawlessly, just as if it were the natural way. This time there was perfect silence as the last note died away.

"It's not against the rules of a musical competition to make things more difficult for yourself," Aristomache said, answering Kebes.

"Nobody expects you to do as well," Father said, smoothly. "Your instrument isn't made for it."

But Kebes for the first time looked uncertain. He guessed that if he played as he had before, the judges would find for Father, who had done something more difficult. He frowned hard and turned the syrinx over. Of course he shouldn't have tried. It wasn't meant to be played that way, and he hadn't practiced, which Father certainly must have. Kebes blew, but what came out wasn't the same rippling hypnotic music as before but a discordant babble. The crowd laughed, with an uncomfortable edge. Kebes righted his instrument and played as he had the first time. But he didn't have the same confidence, and without the energy of the crowd the Myxolydian music felt hollow.

There was no doubt what the judges were going to decide. They didn't take long in their deliberations this time. Aristomache stood. "We have a majority," she said. "We will each give our votes. I vote for Pytheas."

"Pytheas," Erinna said.

"Pytheas," Ficino echoed.

"Matthias," Klymene said, staring straight in front of her and not meeting anyone's eyes.

"Pytheas," Neleus said, very firmly.

"Pytheas," Nikias said, in the same tone.

"Matthias," Sabina said.

"Pytheas," said Alexandra.

"Matthias," concluded Erektheus.

"That's six for Pytheas and three for Matthias, so Pytheas has won. But I beg you Pytheas, be merciful."

And as she spoke that word, Kebes shouted "Fix!" He grabbed a sharp knife from the collection on the ground and rushed at Father. But I hardly noticed, because throughout the crowd people were drawing weapons and attacking those of us from the *Excellence*. It was what Erinna and Maecenas had predicted. The whole colosseum erupted into chaos.

21

ARETE

The shape of the colosseum, the steps where people were sitting and the clear aisles for moving about, were on our side. The preparation and the weapons were all on the other side. Kebes's people had been ready and planning angles of attack, picking out victims in advance. It all seemed to happen in a split second.

Phaedrus drew his knife. I had no weapon. Auge leaped to her feet, scowling, and I shrank away, but she was bellowing "Is this what we call guest friendship?" She took a hammer from her belt and knocked away a blade that was coming for me. She thrust me down toward her children, who were clinging together and cowering under the step. "Stop this at once!" she bellowed. "These are friends. There are children here. Are we savages?"

Father and Kebes seemed to be wrestling by the wooden pole. A woman was lying dead at Phaedrus's feet. There was shouting everywhere, a cacophonous din that roared in my ears. I looked around. There was fighting here and there in the crowd, but no more near me, where people seemed to have listened to Auge and were looking ashamed of themselves. The man who had attacked me was backing away, sheathing his sword. But on the other side of the colosseum I could see a group of people with blades charging down the clear aisle toward the stage, making for the place where the judges were sitting. Without thinking I leaped down toward them—it began as a leap and ended as a flight, or I would have smashed to the sand.

I landed beside Father's swords, still lying neatly where he had put them down. I bent and picked them up, one in each hand, and ran toward the attackers. Erinna saw me coming and stood, taking a step toward me. She reached for the bigger sword in my left hand, and I gratefully gave it up to her. She put it up just in time to block an attacker. I blocked another, much more clumsily, and ducked away from a third, kicking at his knee as I did. I didn't have any idea what to do in a fight that wasn't just friendly wrestling in the palaestra. I was too young for weapons training. The smaller sword felt very heavy in my hand. Neleus came up beside me and punched an attacker hard in her side. "Give me the sword," he said, and I did. He swung it at her throat as she came forward again, nearly severing her head. She vanished at once. The one I'd dodged fell over as he was coming for me again—I discovered later that Nikias had thrown the white stone at his temple.

All through the crowd people were shouting out for peace and friendship and civilization, and even for excellence. I flew over a man with a sword who was coming at me and pushed him back onto Erinna's waiting blade. Neleus was still fighting the last of the group, but his opponent looked desperately around and then threw down his sword to surrender, and that was the end of it.

Kebes was bound to the pole, where he had wanted to bind Father. It seemed as if people had been falling everywhere, but in fact we learned later there were only nineteen dead from *Excellence*, and fourteen from Lucia.

As the last man surrendered, Erinna and I grinned at each other. Then an instant later I realized that one of the bodies at our feet was Ficino. His hat had fallen off and was lying on the sand. I knelt beside him and Erinna knelt at his other side. He had taken a sword thrust and was bleeding but still alive. "Amazons," he said, trying to smile. "Trojan heroes couldn't have done better. Don't grieve for me, my dears. I've had a wonderful life, and what a way to die, at ninety-nine, fighting to defend arete."

"We'll get you home to Florentia, and you'll live another ninety-nine years and fight plenty more battles for Plato yet," Erinna said, but there were tears in her eyes.

"Phaedrus!" I called, as loudly as I could. "Ficino needs you!" Phaedrus could heal him, mend whatever was wrong. Phaedrus came down the stairs running, but Father heard too, and he was nearer and got there first. Father bent over, and Ficino saw him.

"Apollo!" he said, surprised. For a moment I couldn't tell if he was swearing or recognizing Father. "Of course!" He sounded the way he did when I made a really conclusive point in debate. Then he laughed delightedly, and coughed up a bubble of blood. A flood of bright red blood followed it, bursting out of his mouth and taking his life with it. By the time Phaedrus reached us he was gone, leaving nothing but blood on the sand, and his battered old hat beside it.

Phaedrus wiped his eyes, and turned to Aristomache, who was clutching her arm. "Are you a doctor? I think it's broken," she said to him.

He set his hand on it. "Just a bad bruise, I think," he said. "But let me strap it for you."

"Aristomache, now that the riot seems to have died down, I want you to speak to Kebes," Father said, as Phaedrus was finishing.

"Good heavens, is he still alive?" she asked.

Father gestured to the pole, where Kebes was writhing against the iron rings, where Father had bound his wrists and ankles.

Aristomache took a step toward it. Auge came down the stairs and onto the stage. "You, Timon!" she roared, pointing at a man in the crowd. "You're a king this year, and you weren't fighting. Come here."

The man came forward. The crowd hushed. "If you're a doctor, go around to the left. If you're wounded, go there where the doctors are. If not, sit down," Timon said, firmly, taking charge. People obeyed him. Phaedrus went over to the left where some other people were gathering. He started helping the wounded.

"Are you responsible for this disgraceful behavior?" Auge asked Kebes.

"For the fixed contest?" Kebes answered, loudly enough for everyone to hear. "No. For my friends who weren't ready to watch me murdered? No." He was lying.

"Yes he was," called the man who had resheathed his sword before Auge's anger. "He told us to be ready to fight if he shouted fix."

"And he had us ready to attack the judges," the man on the ground confirmed.

Timon looked at Aristomache. "Death is the penalty for attacking guests," he said. She nodded. "Those who surrendered or thought better of it are condemned to iron for ten years," he went on. The man near me collapsed in sobs. "As for Matthias—"

"Don't I get to speak?" Kebes asked.

"Ficino is dead," Aristomache said, as if that were sufficient to convict him, as indeed it was in my eyes too.

"Good," Kebes said. "I hated him, hated all the Masters, you included. I hate Kallisti and everyone who stayed on it. I wanted to be ready in case Pytheas cheated, that's all, and as you can see, he did. For us, seizing the ship and killing the sailors was the best way. Now we can sail to Kallisti, where they're weak and divided, and conquer them all."

He wasn't looking at her, he was looking at the crowd, at his people, who had loved him. Some of them looked at him with agreement, but too few.

"This isn't what Yayzu would have done," Auge said.

"It's what the Knights of St. John would have done," Kebes replied.

"I won the contest," Father said. "And even leaving aside guest friendship and inciting riot, he broke his oath to abide by the decision of the judges."

"I did not break my oath!" Kebes shouted. "We attacked because you cheated. I told them to be ready if I shouted fix. I kept my oath, and would have accepted a fair verdict against me, but not this!"

"Kill him, Pytheas," King Timon said. "This is a civilized city. Do to him what he was going to do to you." The crowd cheered loudly.

Father looked to the tools, spilled on the grass now, then at Kebes where he writhed on the pole, and lastly at the crowd in the stands. "If this is your justice," he said. He looked over toward me, and then past me. "Neleus? Help me please."

Neleus went over to him and gathered up the knives. Then he knelt beside him holding them as Father began to cut.

Erinna and I stayed where we were, crouched on the blood-stained sand beside Ficino's hat.

Kebes began swearing at Father, calling him names, accusing him of all kinds of vile crimes. Father began with a shallow cut down the breastbone, and then began carving the skin off. Kebes kept on yelling and taunting. Father didn't respond and just kept on cutting, until Kebes shouted out "And Sokrates didn't love you! And Simmea didn't love you!" Then Father paused for a second and looked at him evenly.

"Both of them loved you, in their ways, but both of them loved me more." Then he lowered his voice so the crowd couldn't hear and said, "Now tell me, did Athene give you the syrinx? Why? When? And how did you learn that music? Tell me, and I'll kill you quickly."

"Oh you're enjoying this!" Kebes shouted, and began another torrent of abuse.

I'm sure it's not true that Father deliberately used the dull knives to make it take longer. It's just that he didn't have much experience with flaying the skin off a living man. Who does, except Kebes himself? I'd never considered before the way skin folds over muscles and fat and bones, certainly never seen it. Kebes abused him on and on for as long as he could, and Father kept asking his questions, patiently, but after a while it was mostly screaming.

I picked up Ficino's hat and left then. I'd seen enough—too much. I don't know how Father could stand it. He stood there skinning him alive, with parted lips and a half-smile, remote, intent on the work, peeling back the skin, seeming as calm as if he were composing music, repeating his questions. Neleus stayed beside him, spattered with blood, handing him new knives when he reached down for them. I couldn't have done it. Kebes deserved to die, yes, and I would have killed him myself. But if I had been Father I'd have let my knife slip when I was near an artery, and ended it quickly.

Erinna left with me, and Auge entrusted her children to us. "I don't think I could torture anyone to death," I said as we went out. "Not even Kebes." I could still hear his screams echoing around the marvelous acoustics of the colosseum.

"Kebes must have done it before. To other people," Erinna said. "Did you know there were Young Ones killed today? And locals? There are *bodies.* Somebody will have to *bury* them."

"Only murderers and heretics get flayed," Auge's daughter said.

"They'll burn the bodies and put the ashes in urns," Auge's son said.

I nodded. It was a sad necessity we'd experienced a few times at home after art raids. "What are heretics anyway?"

"People who think the wrong thing about God and Yayzu," she said.

My eyes met Erinna's and we both grimaced. "And this seemed like such a nice place," she said.

"How often did Matthias flay heretics?" I asked.

"Not often. Every year or so, here, less often in the other cities," Auge's son said. "Some people like it, but I think it's horrible to watch. I hate screaming."

"It's horrible. But Kebes deserves to end up that way," I said.

The sun was setting as we came down to the harbor, sinking peacefully and splendidly into the sea, which spread out gold and blue like a bolt of shot silk, an even more beautiful sunset than the day before. Auge's children had invited us to their home, but we wanted to get back to our ship. The *Excellence* was still bobbing safely at her anchorage in the bay, but to our astonishment the *Goodness* was a smoldering wreck at the dockside.

I hadn't understood from what Kebes said about attacking the *Excellence* that this was something that he had arranged to have happen during the contest. Flaying suddenly seemed too good for him.

It seemed our little boat had been burned in the fighting, but Erinna persuaded one of the women who had a fishing boat ready to go out that she could do better ferrying people back to the *Excellence*. She gave her a coin. "Where did you get that?" I asked as the fisherwoman rowed us to the ship.

"Maecenas gave me a handful at Marissa, for buying stores. I have a few left."

There had been a battle aboard, very bloody, but we had won and beaten off the Lucians. As in the colosseum, not all the Lucians had wanted to fight us, and the small number Kebes could organize to attack weren't all that many more than the watch Maecenas had left aboard.

Maia was standing at the rail with a bow slung as we came aboard. She had a cut on her forehead which had bled a great deal, staining her kiton, but she was otherwise unharmed. "I killed two people," she said, shaken.

"I killed one in the fighting in the colosseum, and so did Neleus," Erinna said. "I also wounded two people, but of course I don't know if they'll recover." I was sure the man I'd pushed onto her blade would die. Maia hugged her, and then me too. She gave her bow to somebody else and we sat down together on the big coil of rope on the deck.

"What happened?" she asked. We started to tell her, the contest first, and then the fight. I was relieved that Erinna's description of my flight was that I took a great leap in the air and landed as easily as a cat.

"Ficino's dead," I said, realizing for the first time that Maia didn't know. "He said he'd had a wonderful life and he had died defending excellence and we shouldn't grieve." I began to weep as I remembered it. I pulled his hat out of my kiton and gave it to her.

She took it and turned it over in her hands. "He always said he'd die at ninety-nine," Erinna said.

"Idiotic numerology," Maia sniffed, wiping her eyes on her kiton.

"He said we were Amazons," Erinna said. "And Trojan heroes."

"It wasn't the way I imagined fighting side by side," I said, only then realizing that we had indeed fought side by side, in a battle.

"It's one of those things that's better in stories," Erinna said.

"We can put up a monument to Ficino when we get home," I said, trying to comfort Maia, who was trying to stifle her sobbing. "In Florentia, which he loved so much."

"I've seen his tomb," Maia said, wiping her eyes again. "Years ago, of course, before I came here. He's buried in the Duomo, a temple in the heart of the original city of Florentia. It's a Renaissance building based on a classical original, which couldn't be more appropriate for him. He was buried with the greatest honor his people could give him."

"Good," I said. "And we will do the same. But I miss him. I miss him like I miss Mother. Of course we'll honor their memory, and of course their souls have gone on to new lives, but I hadn't finished talking to them in *this* life." I knew what death meant now. It was conversations cut off.

"I know what you mean. He was my friend from the first day I met him," Maia said, steadying her chin with her hand. "Without him both the Renaissance and the Republic would have been poorer. But that we can honor. It's the twinkle in his eye that I'll really miss."

I hugged her. It was odd, but in a way I felt closer to Maia than anyone else. Father was Father, with all the advantages and disadvantages of that. And for Mother, of course, he came first, second, and third, while the rest of us came somewhere around ninth. That's why Maia and Ficino were both so important to me. I'd realized that since Mother died. They both really did put their pupils first, after philosophy and the City. I was on the edges of Father and Mother's lives, but I was in the heart of theirs. And that was reasonable, was all right, because after all Father was the god Apollo, and how could I possibly be as important as that? Even if now I had divine powers, and maybe I was going to be a god. (But a god of what? Flight was taken. Was there a god of translation?)

The deck lights came on. The *Goodness* was plainly sinking, but a few of her lights also flickered on even as she foundered. "What happened in the fighting here?" Erinna asked.

"They used a fireship," Maia said. "But the wind changed.

And they came to board us, but we stood them off. I shot one. Only a few of them got aboard. Caerellia was killed, fighting, and young Phaenarete."

Maecenas came back just then, with Phaedrus and our wounded. "We need to get everyone back aboard and do a head-count so we know how many we're missing," he said. "You four get started, find out exactly who's aboard and what condition they're in."

"Is Kebes dead yet?" Erinna asked.

Maecenas shook his head. "Not when I left. It might take half the night. He started screaming 'why are you tearing me apart?' over and over, as if he hadn't meant to do it to Pytheas, and as if he hadn't done it to other people before. It's one of their stan-dard methods of execution, they tell me. They had one of those colosseums in Marissa too, didn't they? I don't know that we want to trade with these people after all."

22

APOLLO

On one of the last days of the Weimar Republic, I ran into my brother Dionysios unexpectedly in a nightclub in Berlin. He was leaning against the wall, half shadowed, a cup in his hand, talking to the piano player. He looked up as I came down the steps and greeted me with a half-smile. He was dressed in black leather, topped off with a leopardskin scarf. He was there for the same reason I was, to save as many as we could, in the teeth of Fate and Necessity. He said something quietly to the pianist, who looked to the saxophonist and played a low D. My brother and I danced together there, cheek to cheek, in that crowded little underground room on the desperate edge of destruction, amid the smoke that was like, and not like, the smoke of sacrifice, and the music that was like, and not like, the music Kebes played on his syrinx that day in the colosseum of Lucia.

Kebes was an enemy, a breaker of guest friendship, a rapist, and a torturer who set up institutional torture in his republic. But none of that is why I turned my lyre upside-down in order to defeat him, or why I killed him in that horrible messy way. The contest was for original composition, any instrument. What Kebes played was not an original composition, it was Gershwin's "Summertime." It's not that he broke the rules of the competition, although he did. He was a plagiarist. He cheated on art, passing off someone else's work as his own, believing no one would know. Naturally, I would have had to punish that even if he had done nothing else. I sickened of the skinning early on, but I believed that if I kept on inflicting the agony with a promise of the release of death, he would tell me why Athene had given him the syrinx, and how he had learned the music. There were no Masters among the Goodness Group who came from late enough that they would have known or recognized jazz. I couldn't reveal my knowledge of his plagiarism without giving myself away. Torture is irritatingly ineffective: he taunted me for as long as he could, but he refused to answer my questions and died without telling me. (How I eventually learned the answers is part of another story, which I may tell you one day.)

After he was dead and vanished, and his tattered separated skin, removed with so much slow effort, had vanished with him, I plunged into the clean Aegean to wash off the blood. I emerged again to mortal problems and complications and the relentless mortal timescale where everything has to be dealt with in the instant, with no time to think through the consequences. I had a tiny cut on my thumb where the knife had slipped, and it stung with the salt of the sea water. All my human interactions felt just like that at that moment, raw and stinging and petty. It was all tension—between Lucia and the *Excellence*, between Kallikles and Klymene, and in the souls of my Young Ones as they tried to deal with their dual nature.

I had been skinning Kebes all through the hours of darkness, and it was weary work; my mortal body needed sleep. But the sun was growing higher in the sky and sleep was far from me. I wanted to be away from the ship and mortal trivialities. I needed to recover from the contest, and the aftermath. I swam again, with Kallikles and Arete.

Swimming always made me feel close to Simmea, because she taught me, because it was the first thing we had shared and the way we came to know each other. I hadn't done it since she had died. Now, swimming, in a state of physical and mental exhaustion, felt almost like being with her, and yet painful because she wasn't there and never would be.

We swam out of sight of the ship and the city. I pulled myself up onto a rock, and the Young Ones climbed up and sat beside me, all of us naked in the warm light of my beloved sun. The rock was gray, but turned black where the seawater ran off our bodies to make it wet. The sea broke about it in a little frill of white foam on sapphire. Simmea would have wanted to paint it.

"Clean at last," I said, inspecting my hands.

"Do you feel any better now that Kebes is dead?" Kallikles asked.

I thought about it for a long moment. "Yes. No. I'm glad I defeated Kebes and I'm glad I killed him, even if it was so slow and messy. He deserved it even before he cheated and broke guest friendship." I had wanted him dead, and he was dead, and off to a new beginning. Meanwhile, everything else was still here, and more complicated than ever.

"Did he even break it?" Arete asked. "Auge immediately started shouting that he had, but we were formally welcomed to Marissa, not here, and they are independent cities in the same league."

"They offered us all guest friendship when we arrived," Kallikles said. "I was one of guards with the envoys. That was clearly and plainly stated."

"I never accepted it, but they offered it to all of us, and when they attacked everyone they definitely broke it. You had eaten their food, and they attacked you anyway. Kebes organized that attack, so he broke it," I said. "Besides, that music wasn't original. It came from the twentieth century. He was cheating and he thought nobody would know."

Arete drew in her breath sharply, and Kallikles gasped. "How did he know it?"

"He wouldn't tell me. It must be some god interfering."

"I'm glad you punished him for it," Kallikles said.

"Yes. And now that's over. Done with. Settled." I tried to feel it was true as I said it. But no matter how much I wanted it to be, nothing felt settled by Kebes's death, and it gave me no relief.

"What about the *Goodness*?" Kallikles asked.

"Let them build triremes," I said, lying back, deliberately trying to relax. They weren't my people, or my responsibility, or anything to do with me. "Let Yayzu look after them. How surprised he will be when he takes notice of them praying to him from here!"

The sun was warm, and after a little while I did begin to relax a little. The Young Ones sat quietly in the sun. I kept feeling that I had left something unfinished. Not skinning Kebes. I had done that thoroughly, made a proper job of the whole messy business. And now he wasn't walking around gloating about raping Simmea, or sneering at Arete, or passing off other people's art as his own. His soul was free for a new beginning, and the world was a better place without him. All the same, I felt as if something was missing. Absent or present, Kebes had been a rival for a long time. I felt emptier without him.

Just then, surprising me utterly, Arete rose up off the rock, neat as Hermes, and flew through the air. It had been such a long time since I'd seen anyone really fly. When in my proper form I could hover in the air, and walk on it, naturally, but I've never been able to swoop about like a bird the way she was doing.

"Stand up and let me try carrying you," she called to Kallikles. He stood up at once and held his arms out. "Don't drop me!"

"I won't. But you'd land in the sea! Or if you don't want to, you could just walk down the air. Don't be a baby!"

She swooped down from behind and carried him up with her.

I'd never seen anything like it. She made several loops in the air, with him dangling from her arms.

"Is he heavy?" I called.

"No! It's not difficult at all. I can barely feel his weight—not like holding up a person, more like carrying a baby."

Kallikles blew a raspberry, and she swooped low and set him gently down beside me on the rock. Then she made one last circuit and perched again by my other side.

"I'm glad I had the chance to try that," she said. "I don't feel tired at all. I think it's less tiring than running or swimming the same distance."

"You did it yesterday," I pointed out. "I saw you fly down onto the stage, and also fly over an attacker."

"Erinna said it was a mighty leap," she said. "Nobody understood it was flying."

"Be careful if you want to stay secret," I warned. "You all three used your powers yesterday. You need to be careful, even in front of people who believe in the gods. Once they know, there's no going back from it."

"I didn't know whether the lightning would come," Kallikles said. "They were getting ready to swarm up the side of the boat. I was out of arrows. I just struck out."

"I think it was a splendid thing to do," Arete said, admiringly.

"You weren't wrong to do it, but it's good you didn't blast all the attackers that way," I said. It was difficult to have powers and not use them, and they were very young. If they revealed themselves, they'd also be revealing me.

"It's electricity, you know," Kallikles said. "When we get home I'm going to experiment cautiously with what I can do with electrical things."

"Be careful around Crocus and Sixty-One," I said.

"I won't hurt them. But I want to try something with their

feeding stations. There are enough stations to feed all the workers we had at the beginning. If I mess one up it won't hurt them."

"It would hurt all of us and kill them if you destroyed all the electricity in the city, and you could. I think it all links together. Or you could kill yourself the way you killed the attacker yesterday." I knew that lightning was akin to electricity, but I had never thought about it in that way before. "Be careful experimenting."

"I will. But I think it can just flow through me."

"And I'll talk to Phaedrus about being careful about people noticing the healing as well," I said.

"He couldn't just let people die," Kallikles said.

"Too many died as it was," Arete said. "Poor Ficino."

That reminded me that she had had her back turned and she might not properly understand what had happened. "Did you see what he did?"

"Who do you mean? Phaedrus or Ficino?"

"Ficino. He deliberately put himself in the way of a blow meant for you. The attacker was ignoring him and going for you from behind. I'd just got Kebes safely pinned to the stake, but I wasn't close enough to do anything to help you. Ficino put his body in the way of the blade." I had been thinking about this ever since.

"For me?" she said, awed and amazed. "He died for me?"

"To protect you," I clarified. "He didn't have a weapon or anything he could use as one. He probably didn't know how to use one anyway. I never saw him in the palaestra. He wasn't in the troop, he was too old. He just put himself in between you and the blade."

Arete started crying. "He said he died defending arete, and I thought he meant excellence, but he meant me."

"He meant both," Kallikles said.

I put my arm around her, just as Simmea always did when people cried. "Would you have done that for him?" I asked.

"Yes," Arete said through her tears, with no hesitation. "I'd have tried to do something more effective to stop the attacker, but if that's all there was to do, of course I would." She paused. "I couldn't have answered that as clearly before the battle in the colosseum. I wouldn't have known. Now I know."

"And for me?" I asked.

"Yes, of course," she said, just as fast, and then stopped, and pulled away from me as she realized what I meant. "Do you think that's what she was doing? Mother? But she knew you're a god." She stared at me.

"So do you," I pointed out.

"It's a strong instinct, to protect," she said, thoughtfully. "I know you're a god, but I'd have put myself between you and a blade."

"You flew down from where you were perfectly safe with Auge and her hammer," I said.

"Leaped," she corrected. "And it wasn't just you. They were heading for the judges."

"Ficino, and Erinna," I said.

"And Neleus," she added.

"A very strong instinct," I repeated, thinking about that. "A human instinct. One I don't possess at all."

"But it's exactly what you were doing," Arete said, surprised. "You were about to kill yourself for Mother, when she killed herself to stop you. If that's what she did."

"It isn't the same," I said, irritated. "I wouldn't have died. Well, yes, I would, but I wouldn't have lost *my life* by doing it, only this temporary mortal life. I'd still have been here, and remembered everything."

"She had time to think," Kallikles said. "The battle was over. She had an arrow in her lung, yes, but it wasn't the middle of a fight and going on split-second instinct."

"It hadn't been over for long," I said. "And she was wounded, and I surprised her, drawing my knife, and maybe she just went with instinct, protecting me, getting between me and danger. Like Ficino. Like you. Like I did when I didn't kill Kebes in the street the first day."

"What a very human thing to do," Arete said. "Poor Mother. Betrayed by instinct."

"But we'll never know," Kallikles said, shaking his head. "It might have been that. She might have done that. Or she might have had some reason, the way you've been thinking. She wasn't afraid of death, not the way so many people are. Ficino wasn't either. They both knew they have souls that go on. She knew from you, and Ficino from Athene. And Mother knew how important you are. She'd been helping you be incarnate for years. She might have thought it would be good for your soul to understand human grief and sacrifice and . . ."

"And how to skin an enemy alive?" I finished, sarcastically. "All the *useful* things I have learned since she died."

"She lived while she was alive, and she wasn't afraid of death," Arete said.

"She told you not to be an idiot. That means she was thinking," Kallikles said.

"She could have just instinctively been telling me not to be an idiot," I said glumly. "I am an idiot all too often."

As I said that, I wished Sokrates could have been there. He'd have said "Apollo! What hyperbole!" and we'd all have laughed, even Kebes. Now I was the only one who could remember those dialogues in the garden. I couldn't be missing Kebes, it wasn't possible. I'd always hated him. Simmea never had, though, even after what he had done to her, even after she had made her definite choice of me and the City, she still spoke of him as a friend. She was a true philosopher. And now I had killed Kebes in the most revolting way, and he hadn't told me anything, and the only good it had done had been to his soul, and perhaps to the Lucians who might lose their taste for public torture without the chief torturer. He might be better in his new life, and the world might be better without him. But I had thought vengeance would make me feel better, or anyway not worse.

Ficino had said it would be bad for my soul to kill Kebes, and I'd dismissed the thought because I'd killed people and taken vengeance before. But maybe it had been. Had it made me worse, instead of better? I kept trying to be less unjust, but did I ever really improve? All my deeds will become art. Now that this was done, I wondered how later ages would see it: the god of music against a man with a syrinx, and then such a slow unpleasant death.

I thought again of Ficino, putting his body between Arete and the blade. And Simmea had done the same for me. I was anguished all over again. There was no question that she'd have sacrificed her life for me if it were necessary. It's just difficult to envision a scenario in which it would be necessary. But she would also give her life for my excellence. That's the first thing she ever did for me: when she was teaching me to swim, she risked her life to increase my excellence. I could see how she would believe that enduring all this would increase my knowledge and my understanding of mortal life, and therefore my excellence. And that's agape, that's what Plato wrote about and Simmea believed, the love that wants to increase the excellence of the beloved. But I also wanted to increase her excellence. She hadn't come to the end of herself. And she *knew* I needed her. Needing her and not having her was such a hard thing to have to learn.

How could she have deliberately left me alone to go through all this? But caring as she did about my excellence, how could she have let me go back to being a god without learning something so important? I put one foot down into the cold clear water of the sea, then drew it back up, making a wet black footprint on the hot gray rock. It was distinct for a moment, then immediately began to fade and dry. Soon there would be no sign that it had ever been there.

I had always protected myself against mortal death. When time is a place you can enter at will, it's easy to do that, to save some moments so the ones we love are never wholly lost. Even with Hyakinthos there are moments left I can visit and savor. I can see him smile again, and if I choose I can spend decades of my own personal time illuminated by that smile, working, planning, contemplating, knowing there will come a next instant, another breath, when I am ready to take it. There are whole days I did not spend with him that I hoard against my future loneliness. That has always been my strategy, and it has always protected me. Simmea knew that, we'd talked about it after we lost Sokrates. She loved me. But that never made her go easy on me. And that was one of the best things about her.

She wouldn't have killed herself just to have me endure mortal grief. But she drew out the arrow rather than have me go back to being a god without learning about it. I couldn't understand it until I saw Ficino, old and unarmed, unhesitatingly put himself between Arete and a sword. He died of the blow. Simmea did the same for my own personal arete. Of course she did. What else would she have been willing to die for?

That was a very good question. I sat up with a jerk. Kallikles and Arete turned to me in surprise "I've been an idiot," I announced. They exchanged glances. "What did she put her body in the way of?"

"You?" Kallikles hazarded.

"What I mean is, what did Simmea care most about?" I asked, Socratically.

"Philosophy, and the City, and art, and you," Arete answered promptly.

"All of us," I corrected. "She cared about our whole family, not just me."

"She did, but she cared more about you," Kallikles said. "And that's right, that's how it should be. We're growing up, we have our own lives, the two of you would have gone on together."

"And you're Apollo," Arete said. "You're more important than we are."

"You seem to be choosing to become gods yourselves," I said. "But whether you do or not, she'd have put herself in front of a blade for you. For Neleus as fast as any of you."

"Yes," they both agreed, with no hesitation.

"And of those things she cared about that much, the one she put her body in the way of was art."

"Yes," Arete said.

"Whoever killed her didn't want to kill her the way Kebes and I wanted to kill each other. Not personally. They just killed her because her body was between them and art." I stopped, to make sure this made sense. They nodded. "So we have to stop the art raids," I concluded. "That's what she'd want, far more than vengeance. They didn't kill her because they wanted to kill her. They killed her because she put her body between them and the head of Victory."

"Stopping the art raids would be a really good thing, but I don't know whether it's possible," Arete said. "People have tried before. Ficino and Mother tried. Manlius did."

"We'd have to go to all the cities," Kallikles said.

"We're going to have to do that anyway, to tell them about the Lucian civilization," I said. I sighed. "It won't be easy. But it's what she would have wanted, and it's what we need to do."

We swam back to the ship. Even though I understood now why she had chosen to die, I *still* couldn't die myself and go back to Olympos. There might be other things I needed to understand from incarnation to become my best self—there probably were, and most of them awful, to do with old age and grief. And now I had to stay alive and go through them and learn, without having Simmea to help. I felt tired thinking about it. But beyond that I had the terribly complicated task of resolving everything Simmea would have wanted resolved, the art raids, relations between the Republics, the situation with the Lucians. It was the kind of thing Simmea was really good at, and I really wasn't. But that was the work that needed to be done.

23

MAIA

Simmea and I were turning cheeses in brine when the mission
from Psyche arrived. It was a hot summer day and we had been
working hard. Cheese wheels are heavy, and if not turned they'll
start to rot. It was the kind of thing Workers had done for us,
but which people can do perfectly well; the kind of thing Lysias
used to try to persuade people to do, but which we never did as
long as there were plenty of Workers to do it for us. The disap-
pearance of all the others did mean that there were plenty of spare
parts for Crocus and Sixty-one, but we only asked them to do
the most important things, things that people couldn't do.

The smell of cheese was overpowering in the storehouse. It
was good strong sharp goat cheese and I knew I'd be glad of it
when winter came, but I wasn't sorry to be interrupted.

The messenger was one of the older Young Ones, a girl of
about ten. She brought a written message for Simmea, and it was
Simmea they wanted; she was on the Foreign Negotiations Committee. "A mission from Psyche," she said, looking up from the
note. "I'm going to have to go, I'm afraid."

"I'll finish up here," I said, with a sigh.

"No, come with me," Simmea said, picking up her kiton from
the heap where she had tossed it. "I want to talk to you. We can
both come back and finish up afterward. Pytheas will watch

Arete." I had been back in the Remnant City for a couple of years. Arete was six. Simmea was just over thirty, all taut muscle and sinew. White stretch marks showed as fine seams on her flat brown belly and the sides of her breasts, the legacy of her two pregnancies. She had a very distinctive face, which many people found ugly but which I was so entirely used to that it just seemed to me Simmea's face.

"I think we should go through the wash fountain before appearing to visitors," I said.

Simmea laughed. "I got so used to the smell of the cheese that I'd stopped noticing it. But you're right. You know, you taught me how to use the wash fountain on my very first day in the city."

"I always did that with new Florentine girls," I said. "Easing them in."

I picked up my own kiton and we walked out together. It felt hotter out in the sun. "I don't know how you coped with all of us," she said. "I had a little taste of it when we brought the boys home, but they were so small. Ten thousand ten-year-olds doesn't bear imagining."

"It was terrible," I agreed.

"And it's not even what Plato suggests. He says take over an existing city and drive out everyone who is over ten—so you'd have had nine- and eight-year-olds, and so on down to babies."

"It seemed more practical," I said, defensive as always when Children criticized the decisions the Masters had made. "It was Plotinus's idea."

"If you'd got children of all ages from ten to newborn, that wouldn't have been any easier," she said, opening the door into Thessaly.

I followed her across the room, tightly packed with beds, empty now because Pytheas was busy somewhere else and the children were at lessons. We went into the spacious fountain room, tiled in black and white diagonals. She turned on the water and we both stepped under. The shock of the cold water on my hot sweaty skin was delicious.

Clean, I dried myself on my kiton and wrapped it around me. Simmea did the same. "I should wash this one day soon," she said, looking critically at a stain. Then she looked directly at me. "I was hoping to do this over a cup of wine after we'd finished with the cheese, but I wanted to ask you about the New Concordance," she said.

I opened my mouth, but she held up a hand.

"I know you hate it. I want to understand. You know more about it than anyone here. Ikaros wants—well, the City of Amazons want—to send people here to preach. In the Foreign Negotiation Committee we're debating whether it will do more harm to allow it or forbid it. We're going to take it to Chamber."

"I was a Christian before I came here," I said.

"So was I," Simmea said, surprising me.

"You remember?"

"Of course I remember." We went out into the street again. "You told us to forget. Ficino said it had been a dream. But ten years of life isn't a dream, and you can't forget it."

"I sometimes almost forget the years before I came here, and I was nineteen," I said.

Simmea looked at me sideways with a patient expression. "New Concordance?"

"Sorry. It's wrong. Literally and specifically wrong. Ikaros has built a whole complex structure based on incorrect axioms. He'll debate any individual point, but I couldn't get him to examine his axioms." We walked down the broad diagonal street of Athene, passing others and nodding greetings to them from time to time.

"So what's so appealing about it? Why did people convert, both historically and in the City of Amazons? Why was my village Christian? Why did Botticelli convert? He wasn't an idiot. Anyone can see he thought hard about things."

I blinked. "Botticelli was always a Christian. What made you think he converted?"

"Didn't he paint the Seasons and the Aphrodite first, when he still believed in the Olympians, and then the Madonnas and things after his conversion?" she asked.

"No, he painted some pagan scenes even though he was always a Christian," I said. "I don't know all that much about Botticelli's personal beliefs, but in the Renaissance almost everyone was Christian, although of course they admired the ancient world. They used pagan stories and imagery just as stories. But Christianity was the majority religion, and it was hardly even questioned. It was the same in my time."

"Aphrodite wasn't just a story to Botticelli, or the seasons either," she said, sounding absolutely sure. "But go on, tell me what it is about it that's appealing. I was a child. I remember chanting and prayers and some of the stories, but none of it was ever really explained clearly."

I thought for a moment as we walked past a smithy, with the scent of quenched iron hanging heavily on the air. "I think what's so appealing, both then and now, is the idea of forgiveness for sin. If you're genuinely sorry for what you've done, you can be forgiven and your wrongdoing taken away."

"You give up responsibility for it?" She was frowning hard.

"Yes. You're washed clean of it."

"Without making restitution to people you harmed?" she asked.

"It's the spiritual side of it," I said, feebly. "But you're right of course, it's between you and God, not you and whoever you wronged." But Ikaros had come to apologize to me. My forgiveness had been important to him, not just God's forgiveness.

"And God is all-powerful?"

"Yes. That's appealing. And of course, there's the whole thing where everyone is really sure, and there's the hope of an eternal afterlife."

"We're really sure about Athene." She was still frowning. "And Jesus incarnated himself as a human?"

"Yes, that's also part of the appeal. Think of a god doing that, giving up his powers, to live like us, to redeem us."

Simmea laughed. "If that's why he did it! Maybe he just had questions he wanted answered."

I was startled. "Questions?"

"About being human. Assuming he was ever real and actually did it. But thank you, I do see now why people might like it. Do you have an opinion on whether we ought to allow it?"

We walked past Crocus's colossal statue of *Sokrates Awakening the Workers.* I was almost used to it by now. "Banning it gives it too much power. And it would be impossible to keep it out entirely now that it's the official religion of the City of Amazons, if we're going to have any contact with them at all. Forbidding it might make it seem attractive to rebellious Young Ones," I said.

Simmea sighed. "Alkibiades is being rebellious, though not in religious directions, which considering everything is a good thing."

"I think we ought to allow it but laugh at it, and keep showing how silly it is. Because it is silly. There are a whole lot of absurdities. And we know Athene is real and has real but limited abilities and knowledge. We can deduce certain things from that, but not that there's an omnipotent, omniscient and omnibenevolent deity who wants us all to become angels."

"I've read some of Ikaros's theses, but only some of them. They make my eyes cross. And of course they don't have their holy book. Having a holy book nobody can read but which you can quote from whenever you want is a bit too convenient!"

"Lots of people here would know if Ikaros were misquoting,"

I said. "I would myself—except that the Bible was a long book, longer than the *Republic*. If he misquotes the Sermon on the Mount, he's going to be corrected, even after twenty years. But he's much less likely to be caught out on verses from the book of the prophet Amos." And of course, Ikaros probably did have a copy of the Bible among his forbidden books. But he wouldn't be able to admit that.

Simmea sighed. "Will you talk to the committee and say what you've just said?"

"Of course I will."

"We're meeting next on the day after the Ides." She grinned. "Letting them in and ridiculing them seems like a terrific strategy. Forbidden fruit is sweet, but nothing is appealing if people mock it."

The mission from Psyche had been housed in an empty sleeping house near the agora. Maecenas, one of the captains of the *Excellence*, and another member of the Foreign Negotiations Committee, was entertaining them. They looked relieved when we came in, and so did the envoys. The envoys were all men, of course. Psyche did not admit women to full citizenship. But they accepted that the other cities did, and dealt with us when they had to. Two of them were Masters, whom I knew, and the third was one of the Children whom I only vaguely recognized.

"Joy to you," Simmea said.

"Joy to you, Hermeias, Salutius," I said, then inclined my head to the third man. "I'm Maia."

"Aurelius," he said.

We all sat down. I fetched wine and mixed it. "Have you had a pleasant journey?" Simmea asked, when we had all drunk a toast to Plato.

"Very smooth and comfortable," Hermeias said, inclining his head to Maecenas. "We called at the City of Amazons, where I had a dispute with Ikaros."

Simmea laughed. "Maia and I were just discussing the New Concordance."

"It's the most ridiculous misunderstanding of Iamblikius you could possibly imagine," Hermeias said, stroking his beard. "I'm glad he didn't live to see it. I managed to refute a few of Ikaros's theses, and he was good enough to thank me for it."

"Will you allow them to preach in Psyche?" she asked.

"We'll agreed to allow them to debate, which is a slightly different thing," Aurelius said. "It's hardly likely to win many converts in a city made up of Platonists."

"It does seem unlikely," Simmea said.

"So what brings you here?" Maecenas said, blunt as ever.

Hermeias and Aurelius looked at Salutius, who had been quiet since exchanging greetings. "Art," he said, and took a deep breath. "Simply put. You have it all, except for what has been produced by us since we left. The original art was brought to the City by Athene and the Art Committee." He nodded to me, as the only member of the original Art Committee present. He had been serving on the committee designing the physical shape of the city at the time, and the one on Children. "It stayed in the Remnant City by default, and you have no more claim on it than the rest of us do. We of Psyche have decided that we ought to have a proportionate share of it. We have just over a thousand people, and we should therefore have ten percent of the art."

I could hardly believe his effrontery in coming here and asking for it. Maecenas's eyebrows were lost in his hair, and Simmea blinked several times before answering. "That's a question we'll have to debate in full committee, and probably in Chamber too," she said. "I'm sure you see that it's something where we can't be expected to give an immediate response."

"Indeed," Salutius said. "We've done without it for ten years, after all. We're not in a tearing hurry. But we have various proposals about how it could be equitably distributed." He turned to Aurelius, who brought out a notebook which he handed to Simmea. She took it but did not open it.

"Am I right in thinking you mean that all the cities want a share in the art, not just Psyche?" she asked.

"Ikaros was most interested," Hermeias said.

"How is this different from when the Athenians asked for a share of the technology ten years ago?" Maecenas asked.

The Psychians exchanged glances, and Aurelius replied. "We agreed about technology because we don't really understand it, and because it's all one thing and difficult to distribute. You argued that if we tried to share it out we'd risk losing what we had, and the very life of the Workers. And you agreed to help us make printing presses, and other such necessities."

"Which you have done, according to treaty," Hermeias put in. "But art is different. A statue can be in one city and a painting in another city. It isn't all needed in the same place to get any of it working properly like technology."

"I see," Maecenas said.

Simmea was chewing her lip with her big front teeth. "I think—I can't say anything until I've talked to the whole committee. But I personally feel it would be better for all of us to be making new art than arguing over the art we have."

Salutius nodded courteously. "I know your own work. But we do feel very strongly in Psyche that we're entitled to our proper share of the rescued ancient art."

"I'll put it to the committee," Simmea said. "And meanwhile, be welcome to the Just City. This sleeping house is at your disposal. You may eat in Florentia, or anywhere you are invited by friends, of course. I'll call an immediate meeting of the committee and talk to you again tomorrow or the day after."

We all parted with great courtesy and formality. Once back in the street, Maecenas turned to Simmea. "You sounded as if you were considering it!"

"Well, what's the alternative?" she asked. "I think we're going to have to give it to them, if they insist. Some of it, anyway."

"Never!" Maecenas said. "Nobody made them leave, nobody makes them stay away. If they want to share our art, they can come back."

Simmea looked at me. "How do you feel about it?"

"Much the same as Maecenas," I admitted. "Think how horrible it would be to divide it all up. Think of only having half the Botticellis in Florentia."

Simmea winced. "I'd hate that. But would you fight to keep them?"

"Yes, I certainly would," Maecenas said, without a heartbeat's hesitation.

Simmea shook her head. "Being on the Foreign Negotiation Committee I've developed a sense for when people will and won't give way on issues. This seems to me like something they won't give way on."

"Surely it would never really come to fighting over art?" I said.

"I don't know," she said. "It's hard to imagine. But Plato gives rules for warfare. And it could come to that."

24

ARETE

Father came back at dawn. I saw him from the masthead where Erinna and I were both looking out. Maecenas had sent us both aloft as soon as we came on watch. "Let me know of anything unusual, on land or sea," he said.

Erinna was very quiet.

"Are you all right?" I asked.

"Of course I am," she snapped. "Sorry. I'm just trying to deal with the fact that I killed at least two people yesterday."

"But you're an ephebe," I said. "You're trained."

"Knowing how to do it is different from actually doing it," she said. "Is that—no, it's just a dolphin."

"They were trying to kill us," I ventured.

"Maybe Plato's right and we should have been going out to battles since we were little children, so that we could get used to it."

"Is that really what he suggests?" I was horrified. "Slaughter is such a horrible thing that it's hard to imagine thinking it right for children to watch. But the Lucian children were there yesterday."

"Yes. And I don't think having seen it would have helped when it came to killing people myself. Didn't it bother you at all?"

"I didn't kill anyone. I gave the swords to you and Neleus, because I didn't know how to use them."

"You pushed that one man onto my sword. And how did you do that anyway? You leaped right over him from a standing start."

"I don't know." I was uncomfortable. I didn't want to lie to her. "It felt natural, like the normal thing to do when he was coming at me."

"They tell us to jump in the palaestra, but not like that! You'll have to teach me."

"I'm not sure I can." The sky was starting to pale behind the city and the fading stars seemed to be listening to me lie. "I never leaped that high before. It was fear I suppose, or battle frenzy."

"So you were afraid? Even though you rushed straight in?"

"I didn't have time to think about being afraid. I saw them running toward you with swords, and I saw Father's swords on the ground, and I just leaped for them." Just then I saw Father come walking down toward the harbor with Neleus, Nikias, Timon, and some of the other Lucians. I called the news to Maecenas below.

"I was terrified," Erinna said. "Until I saw you coming with the swords, I was frozen where I was. I didn't think of going for them, though I'd seen Pytheas put them down earlier. I'd have just sat there and let myself be spitted." She was still staring at the horizon, not looking at me.

"You might have been afraid, but you did everything right. You knew how to use the sword, you killed them, and when that one surrendered you stopped."

She nodded. Father had reached the side of the quay, where I could see him clearly. He was covered in blood, but he seemed unconscious of it as he stood talking to the others. They were gesturing at the wreck of the *Goodness*, which had sunk further overnight.

"You saved my life," Erinna said.

"You saved mine. We fought side by side. You knew how to use the sword. I realized as soon as I got there that I was useless."

"You're not an ephebe yet. You haven't had training. And you were safe where you were up on the stand," Erinna said.

"I couldn't just stay there while you and Ficino and Neleus and Father got killed!" I was indignant. On the quay everyone was waving their arms around. Clearly, the argument was getting heated.

"You came straight toward me," she said. I didn't say anything. I had, and I couldn't deny it. "Thank you."

I still didn't know what to say. "You were in danger. Anyone would have—"

"You really like me, don't you?" she asked.

Now I really didn't know how to answer. "Yes." I stared down at the argument on the quayside.

"I like you, but not like that," Erinna said.

"Like what?" I muttered, feeling the heat rising in my cheeks. "I know," I went on, making it worse.

"You're so much younger, and losing Simmea—I was looking out for you a bit. That's all."

"I know," I said, more loudly. "It's all right. I understand. I don't want anything but to go on being friends the way we have been."

"Good," she said, but I knew that everything was spoiled. Tears stung my eyes. On the quayside, Father shrugged and dove neatly into the sea.

"You should go down to talk to him," Erinna said.

I slid down the mast. The blood was washed off his hair and skin by the time he pulled himself onto the deck, but his cloak and kiton were still stained. He pulled them off and stood naked on the deck, dripping sea-water, with a strand of seaweed caught over his shoulder.

Maecenas looked at me and raised an eyebrow. "Erinna's still up there watching," I said. He nodded. I embraced Father, getting myself wet in the process. Kallikles and Phaedrus came up the ladder onto the deck and embraced Father one at a time, and we all wished each other joy. The sun was up behind the hill and the sky was bright. Again I thought that this was like a scene in a play. But in a play, the gods show up at the end to sort everything out, and let the people who love each other be together. I picked the seaweed off Father's shoulder and dropped it back into the water.

"Kebes is dead?" Maecenas asked, as Phaedrus stepped back.

"Dead," Father confirmed. "Dead and gone back where he came from. And after all the trouble I had getting the skin off in one piece, it vanished with him."

I shuddered. The worst of it was that he said it so calmly. There were times when he wasn't like other people at all. Maecenas started to speak, then swallowed hard and began again. "How are the rest of them?"

"They want reparations because we burned their ship," Father said. "Zeus burned it," Maecenas said. "Literally, by all accounts. They tried to burn us, but the wind changed all in an instant and drove the fireship back on the *Goodness*."

Father glanced at Kallikles, who smiled. "The winds do back unexpectedly sometimes," Father said.

"Yes, but they tell me also that the first man to try to board was struck by lightning, out of a clear sky," Maecenas said. He too looked at Kallikles. "You saw that, didn't you?"

"I was right there," Kallikles agreed.

"I didn't want to believe it either, but you see there's no question about it," Maecenas said. "It discouraged the rest of them, as you can imagine."

I looked with admiration at Kallikles. Without him we might

have lost the ship and everyone aboard. My own powers weren't anything like as useful.

Neleus and Nikias came aboard, dry, from the fishing boat that had been acting as a ferry. Nikias came over to Maecenas at once. "I want to go back to Kallisti with my son," he said. "Will you give me passage?"

Maecenas looked from Nikias to Neleus, and then to Father, who nodded. "Well, of course I will, but this could be a problem if there were a lot of people who wanted to leave Lucia and go with us."

"We promised to take Aristomache and the others back to Marissa," Phaedrus pointed out.

"That's easy. The problem is that without the *Goodness* these people aren't going to be able to keep on doing as they have been doing," Father said. "Timon was starting to say that when I dived into the sea. They want the *Excellence*."

"So they can keep on rescuing people and founding cities," Kallikles said.

"That's a matter for Chamber," Maecenas said. "Did they offer compensation for Caerellia and Ficino and the others they killed?"

"They think we took it out of Kebes's hide," Neleus said. This remark was followed by an awkward silence, broken after a moment when Klymene came on deck.

"Pytheas," she said, by way of greeting.

"No thanks to you," Neleus said.

"If Klymene prefers the Myxolydian mode, that's no disgrace," Father said, quite sharply.

Klymene blushed. "I did prefer it. And I thought you were cheating by turning your lyre over. I had no idea what Kebes was planning."

"Of course not," Father said. "No hard feelings. I don't know how it is, but you always manage to see me at my worst moments."

I looked at him in complete incomprehension. She had voted for his death by torture, and he must now understand what that meant. However little he minded being dead and returned to his proper divine self, he had said he didn't want to be skinned. How could he not have hard feelings?

Kallikles looked at his mother incredulously. "You voted for Kebes?"

"You didn't hear him play," Father said. "He had a syrinx. He was very good."

"But it wasn't just a musical contest!" sputtered Kallikles. "It was your life."

"Kebes was Klymene's friend," Father said. "And three of the Lucians preferred the Phrygian mode, as it turned out."

Kallikles shook his head.

"Son—" Klymene said, putting her hand on his arm.

"Don't talk to me," he said, shaking her off. "You voted for my father's death."

"We are not going to have a feud over this," Father said, firmly. "If Klymene has wronged anyone it's me, and I refuse to have this be the cause of trouble." Again I thought this was like something from Aeschylus, except that it was also my family. There was an awkward silence.

"The problem is what we're going to do about the Lucians now," Maecenas said.

"If all the Lucians were treacherous and prepared to break guest friendship we'd all be dead. It was just a minority of them. Many of them fought beside us in the colosseum," Phaedrus said.

"Auge and Timon restored order," I said.

Maecenas shook his head. "We'll have to take a mission home with us, and then at the very least bring them back. This will have to be discussed in Chamber, and voted on in the Assembly. It's too much for us." He looked at Nikias. "You can come with us. We've never stopped anyone coming back to the Remnant, there's clear precedent for that. And if you're a Christian, you can mix in with the New Concordance lot. They have a little temple down on the street of Hermes."

"I'm not bothered about religion," Nikias said. "I have useful skills. I'm a glassblower."

"You were a poet and a philosopher when you left us," Pytheas said.

"We've all grown up a lot since then," Nikias said, smiling.

"And you're not abandoning a family here?" Klymene asked, familiarly. I realized as she spoke that of course she knew him, even though they hadn't seen each other for longer than my entire lifetime. All the Children knew each other. Whatever city they lived in now, they had long complex histories of growing up together in the original Republic.

"No. I did, but we're separated. She went to Hieronymos." He looked down.

"You might like to know that as well as Neleus here you have a daughter in Psyche. Andromeda was pregnant when you left."

"I'm going ashore," Maecenas grunted. "I'll talk to Timon and try to sort things out."

"Is it safe ashore?" Klymene asked.

"Armor, and an armed escort." Maecenas sighed. "I'll take Dion and—no, by Hekate, not Phaenarete. Klymene, find me half a dozen trained unwounded Young Ones for a shore mission."

She nodded.

"I'm going to swim some more," Father said.

"Not alone you're not," Maecenas said. "Arete, Kallikles, stay with your father. Swimming is all right, but you're not going ashore, none of you. You're a provocation."

"And me?" Phaedrus asked.

"Keep helping the doctors, you're good at that."

Klymene looked at Kallikles again, but he didn't look at her. She caught my eye, and I spread my hands. I didn't know what to say to her. I was also horrified that she had voted against Father, but if he was prepared to deal with it, so was I. She was Klymene, Mother's friend, Kallikles's mother. I had known her all my life.

"Kallikles," she said.

He turned to her. "We won't have a feud, since Father doesn't want one, but you can't expect me to feel the same toward you."

"That's fair," she said. She turned and went below, moving as if she had aged twenty years in the last half hour.

25

ARETE

The voyage home was strange. On the voyage out, even during the storm, we'd had a sense of adventure, of the world opening before us. I know I wasn't the only one who felt like that. Ficino had wanted to find the Trojan heroes. We had all sung in the evenings. We were sailing into the unknown, and we looked forward to what we would find. It was a voyage of discovery. The voyage home was a journey through anti-climax. I stood my regular watch, but all the joy had gone out of it. The ship still felt alive, and the sky and the sea and the islands were still beautiful, but that was all. Erinna seemed to be avoiding me, after the conversation on the masthead. She was polite when I spoke to her, but uncomfortable. I wasn't sorry I had saved her life, how could I be? But I cried myself to sleep missing her, and missing Ficino, who might still be alive if I hadn't thrown myself into the fight. I had always been told that all actions have consequences. Now I was starting to understand what that meant.

We had envoys aboard to Kallisti from Lucia—to all the five cities. And we had people who wanted to go to other Lucian cities, and a handful like Nikias who wanted to come back to the Remnant. There were no more secrets about where the Lucian cities were. Timon had given Maecenas a map, a beautiful thing, drawn like an illuminated manuscript, embellished with dolphins and triremes, with all their cities neatly marked.

"Ah," Father said, when he saw it, and then when we looked at him curiously he just said "Beautifully drawn."

We called at the Lucian cities, one after another, where the news that Kebes was dead and the *Goodness* destroyed was met each time with shock and horror. Aristomache tried to explain to them that it wasn't really our fault, but it was hard to avoid feeling guilty nevertheless.

"The problem is that it's a subtle complex thing and hard to explain," she said to me as we sailed toward Marissa. "Matthias was in the wrong, and he started the attack. But you did destroy the *Goodness*, and that does destroy our civilization. And we were doing so much good."

"The *Goodness* would still be safe if Matthias hadn't attacked us," I said. It felt strange to call Kebes by his other name.

"Indeed," she agreed. "That attack was wrong and unprovoked. And you didn't destroy the *Goodness* on purpose. The wind changed. It was Matthias's fault for using a fireship and trying to destroy this ship. God punished him. But he has punished all of us for Matthias's hubris."

It was strange. I knew Kallikles had made the wind change. In one way that did make it unquestionably a divine action. But I was much less ready than Aristomache to see it as part of Providence, or being inherently just. To Aristomache, even though she had known Athene, the actions of the gods were something that happened on a different moral plane. To me they were not, they couldn't be. "Kebes—Matthias—was one of your leaders," I said.

"One of them, yes, but one among many. You saw how we didn't all follow him."

"I did. But he wasn't acting alone, either."

"The other conspirators, those who survived, were condemned

to iron for ten years. I thought you heard that." A cloud passed over the sun, and in the changed light Aristomache looked old and frail, though she was nowhere near as old as Ficino had been.

"I heard it, but I didn't understand it."

"They're reduced to iron, the fourth rank," she said.

"We have irons, but it isn't a punishment." The idea was very strange to me. "Do you mean that they'll be slaves?"

Aristomache winced. "Not slaves. But the irons do all the hardest work. They mine, and do all the things nobody else wants to. Especially in the new cities it's dangerous and difficult work."

I thought about it. It seemed almost like slavery. And the way Kebes behaved seemed like putting pride above the good, exactly as Plato said timarchy began. Sparta had been a timarchy, valuing honor above truth. But saying this to Aristomache would hurt her without helping anything, and she was among the best of the Lucians. I was glad she was coming to the City with us as one of the envoys, and glad that Auge was another—though poor Auge was seasick, even in these calm breezes.

We set people down and picked up more envoys at all eight Lucian cities. I wasn't allowed ashore anywhere, though I sometimes had a chance to swim. Maecenas wasn't taking any more risks with the ship.

I kept on grieving for Ficino. Maia missed him even more. She wasn't grieving extravagantly the way Father had. She withdrew into herself and never mentioned him. She spent hours standing at the rail in the wind. She avoided Aristomache much as Erinna was avoiding me.

"He always said he'd die when he was ninety-nine," I said, coming up next to her.

She jumped. "Arete, don't creep up on people that way!"

"I wasn't creeping up, you were completely locked in your thoughts."

"It's not true that I don't love people," she said, out of nowhere. She had Ficino's hat crushed between her hands.

"Of course it's not! Who said that?"

"Ikaros," she admitted.

"That idiot." I had never met Ikaros. "What does he know about it? You love lots of people. You love me." I put my arm around her.

Maia snorted, half way between laughter and tears.

"Come on, Magistra, you haven't taught me anything for days." It was the best way to cheer her up, giving her something to do. And besides, my birthday was coming the next month, and with it my tests and my oath. I wanted to be ready.

We sailed on among the islands, and I wished them unknown again and empty of consequences. I stood my watches and did lessons with Maia and had occasional conversations with Father and my brothers. We did not stop at Ikaria, but I looked longingly at the shore and the pine woods as we sailed past.

We struck the shore of Kallisti from the northeast, and so we saw the City of Amazons first, immediately recognizable with its immense statues on the quayside. We sailed on. "Home first," Maecenas said, decisively, and nobody disagreed.

We arrived home at sunset on the twenty-ninth day after our departure, though it felt as if we had been away for centuries. The mountain was rumbling and belching out red-black streams of lava as we sailed in. "Just a normal little eruption," Phaedrus said reassuringly.

"You know?" I asked.

"I do," he said, sounding a little awed.

It is a testament to how much had happened on the voyage that our gaining god-powers seemed such a minor part of it. And yet the story of what had happened to us wouldn't make an epic. Or would it? I thought it over. It seemed too ambiguous, but Homer embraced ambiguity. Homer had heroes on both sides.

I remembered Ficino saying he'd fight for Troy. How would people tell the story of Kebes? Would they tell how Apollo beat him in a contest and skinned him alive? Or would it all be forgotten as Father believed? But Father had said everything the gods did became art, and he was still a god. Maybe it was more like a tragedy, heroes overcome by their flaws.

We tacked in to the harbor and tied up, safe at the wharf, home at last.

It felt strange to be greeted by Baukis and Boas and Rhea, to see people I knew well who hadn't been with us. I had almost forgotten they existed, that home was still there behind us all the time. It must have been how Odysseus felt coming back to Ithaka.

26

APOLLO

I spent the voyage home composing a song. It was the song I had been reaching for for months, the song that wouldn't come, because I couldn't make any true art about Simmea's death while I didn't understand why she had chosen to die.

I had been maddened with grief, and now I was not. I still missed Simmea. But I understood now that she had died to increase my excellence and the excellence of the world, and I would increase it, for her, for myself, and for the world. I would savor this mortal life while I had it, learn and experience all I could. And when it ended, I would take what I had learned and be a more excellent god and make the world better. That was what I always wanted. That was why I had chosen to become mortal.

The song I had sung in the colosseum at Lucia had been a cold Platonic composition, perfect but passionless. This one was the opposite. It made the Dorian mode burn with passion. If I had been on Olympos my hair would have stood on end and glowed as I made the song. I would also have concentrated and done nothing else for however long it took until the song was done. As it was, onboard the *Excellence* I had to stand my watches, sleep, and eat, and beyond that I was constantly interrupted. There's no privacy on a ship, and it's hard to be alone. I couldn't so much as play a chord without someone stopping to listen, and I didn't want anyone to hear this song before it was ready. The ship was teeming with people—in addition to the surviving crew we had a whole slew of envoys. Maecenas was very firm that I wasn't allowed ashore. I don't know what he thought I was going to do, or whether he thought the Lucians would try to kill me if they had the chance. I wanted nothing more than to be quiet somewhere alone to work on the song, but instead I trimmed the sails and talked to people who wanted to talk to me. These frustrations too were part of mortal life, and fueled the song.

Every day I went up on deck to watch the sun rise, as the lyrics and music echoed through my head. One morning Maia was there by the rail, twisting Ficino's hat in her hands as she stared out to sea. Always thin, she was gaunt now, and her silvering hair wisped out of its neat braid in the sea wind.

"One thing I have learned about grief," I said to her, "is that nothing anyone says to you is useful, but it can still be comforting sometimes to know you're not alone and not the only person who cares about missing them. Ficino was my friend too."

She smiled through her tears. "Thank you, Pytheas. And Simmea was also my friend."

"We have to do the work they left undone," I said.

"I know," she said. "Oh, I know. But it makes me so tired to think of it."

"We have to stop the art raids, and come to an equitable solution with the Lucians, and bring up the next generation to be more excellent than their parents."

"The Lucians skin heretics, and have gladiatorial fights, and their irons are almost like slaves," Maia said. The edge of the sun showed red over the rim of the world.

"Nobody's perfect," I said. "The Romans had gladiatorial

combats, they dislocated the arms of heretics in Renaissance Florence, all of the classical world had slavery, and so did we in the City before we realized that the Workers were self-aware."

"Plato—"

"Plato was laying out an unachievable ideal, to spur people to excellence," I said. "What was it Cicero said about Cato?"

"That Cato acted as if he was living in Plato's Republic instead of the dunghill of Romulus?" She switched into Latin to quote it.

"That's it. Plato wanted to give people something to aspire to. That's why he isn't here, he didn't really imagine it as a possibility, just as something to encourage everyone to think, and to work toward excellence. In reality, while we aim for excellence, we're always living on somebody's dunghill. But that doesn't mean we're wrong to aim to be the best we can be. And the Lucians aren't all like Kebes. If they were we'd all be dead. We can find a way to help them toward excellence."

She sighed. "Everything is complicated and compromised."

"It is," I said. "That's the nature of reality." A gull swooped down low over the water.

"Ficino understood how to go on amid the compromise and find a way forward," Maia said.

"Yes. He took over the Laurentian Library for the Florentine Republic after Piero de Medici fled," I agreed.

"How do you know that?" she asked. "Were you there?"

I had frequently been there, but of course I didn't want to tell her so. "I've heard him talk about it," I said, truthfully. "I know nobody is supposed to talk about their lives before they came to the City, but everyone does."

"I don't think we were wrong to make idealistic rules," Maia said, her voice shaking a little. "I don't know, Pytheas.

I've been trying to make the Republic work since I was a young woman, and I'm getting old now. Ficino was always so delighted to be here, to be doing it. He loved everything, except when we divided after the Last Debate. When I came back from Amazonia he was so pleased to see me. I don't know how I can take it all up again without his enthusiasm to keep me going."

"I'm the worst person to ask," I said. "I only just worked out that what I'm supposed to do is keep on working and doing Simmea's share too, as best I can."

"I can't possibly do Ficino's share!" she said, horrified.

"You can do some of it, and I'll do some of it, and other friends will do some of it."

"You'll teach music and mathematics?"

I had been teaching gymnastics in the palaestra but diligently avoiding teaching music and mathematics, as we called all intellectual study. I had evaded it by taking a larger share of the physical labor we all had to share since the Workers left.

"And you'll serve on committees for Simmea?" she went on.

"Oh Maia!"

"You can teach Ficino's beginning Plato course, for the fourteen-year-olds," she said, relentlessly. "And you can teach the advanced lyric poetry class. I don't understand how you've got out of that so far."

"I always volunteer to judge at festivals, and I couldn't judge fairly if I were teaching them too," I said smugly.

"Well, that's been a good argument, but now you can teach them. You can do it better than anyone else, so it's your Platonic duty. And you can serve on the Curriculum Committee too, as well as taking Simmea's place on the Foreign Negotiations Committee."

I looked at her face in the glow of the sunrise. She had

stopped crying. "I believe I have actually comforted you a little," I said.

"And I you," she replied.

It was true. Taking on those responsibilities wouldn't be any fun, but knowing they needed doing and I could help do them in Simmea's name did ease my grief a little.

As for stopping the art raids, I was working on a song.

When the *Excellence* tied up at the City, the travelers who had been together for so long divided immediately. Kallikles went off with his girl, Rhea. Maia headed for Florentia to tell the sad news to Ficino's friends there. Arete was immediately embraced by her agemates. Neleus and Phaedrus headed for Thessaly. Everyone else went their separate ways. I was so desperate to be alone to get my song straight that I went straight to the practice rooms on the Street of Hermes.

I shut myself into one of the little rooms and worked nonstop on the song for several hours. The last time I sang it through I was happy with it, but a song isn't real until somebody hears it. I went home to Thessaly, and was astonished to find my son Euklides there, Lasthenia's boy, who lived in Psyche. Phaedrus and Arete and Neleus and he were sitting in the garden by Sokrates's statue of Hermes, under the lemon tree. They looked up when they saw me, and all of them tried to speak at once.

"Just listen to this first," I said, and drew my lyre into place.

It couldn't have been more different from the colosseum in Lucia, the banked rows of spectators, Kebes's hate burning hot, the judges uneasy in their seats, and my own soul longing to escape. Now I was at home, my soul was sure of the work set before it, and the audience were my own children, who loved me. In my memory Sokrates and Simmea and Kebes also populated the garden. Simmea sat intent, leaning forward, bursting with ideas; Sokrates was running his fingers through his hair distractedly; Kebes was frowning and drawing breath to speak. I smiled and let go of them. All of their souls had gone on to start again and learn new things. It was the solid and present Young Ones I wanted to reach with this song.

"Simmea asked me to write this song when we were fourteen years old," I said. Before she had met Sokrates, before we had discussed our agape, before we knew the Workers were people. "It's called 'The Glory of Peace.'"

I knew I had them before the end of the first verse. By the final chorus, they were all openly weeping. The best of it was, the song didn't mention either Simmea or the art raids directly. It was all about the things worth fighting to defend and being our best selves.

Neleus, who had fought in art raids, was the first to speak after the last chord had died away. His voice was choked. "Is that really what we were doing? Were we going against Plato and making ourselves worse?"

"Yes, we evidently were," Euklides said, wiping his eyes. I didn't know him well, and I hadn't known until that moment that he had fought in them.

"The art raids are a falling away from excellence," Phaedrus said. "Toward timarchy. Fighting for honor instead."

Arete looked at me with awe in her eyes. "Maybe you really could stop the art raids! If people hear that, they might understand. It gives us a different way to think about it. And it's really true. *The dreams shared with a friend*," she quoted.

"And that's what Mother died for," Neleus said.

They all looked a little stunned. "I'll have to sing it to harder audiences," I said. "But stopping the art raids is what this song is for. And that's the best thing I can do now in memory of Simmea."

"Not just stopping the pointless deaths, but bringing the City closer to excellence," Neleus said, seeing the point at once, as Simmea would have done.

"All the cities," Arete said.

I nodded. "All the cities. I want to teach you to sing the harmony, so you can sing it with me when we go."

"There's a harmony?" she asked.

"Yes. Why are you looking at me like that?" They were all staring at me with eyes wide open in astonishment.

"You never write songs with multiple parts," Phaedrus said. "You always write things you can perform alone."

"Well, this song can be sung alone, as you've just heard, and it will sound even better with Arete singing the harmony, and it also has an arrangement that can be sung as a choral ode with parts for a whole chorus, which I am planning to have sung before the conference. But you're going to have to rehearse them, Phaedrus, because Arete and I will be going around to the other cities to persuade them to come."

They still looked stunned. I smiled, and sat down and began to eat a lemon.

"Have you ever written something for a chorus before?" Neleus asked. "Ever, ever? I know you haven't done it in the City."

"I haven't, and it was an interesting challenge, especially without any privacy on the boat to work on it. But you wait until you hear the choral version, with the men's chorus singing low down *home and hearth and love and life* and the women's chorus singing high up *worth the cost of risking life* and the lines working with and against each other." I sang the lines as I quoted them. They kept on staring at me. "Yes, it's a new thing for me. But life is about moving forward and learning new things."

"You've stopped being cracked," Arete said.

"Yes, I think I finally have. I haven't stopped missing her. But I'm whole again. I'm finally doing what she wanted."

"Stopping the art raids?" Euklides asked.

"That's part of it," I said.

27

ARETE

In our absence, my brother Euklides had run away from Psyche and sworn a new oath to the Remnant City. He was staying in Thessaly and drilling with the Delphian troop. His armor stood on a stand in the corner, and he had moved things around in the house. He apologized for disturbing things, and said he didn't know whether he was host or guest, welcoming us back. It was wonderful to see him, but on the second day after our return he discovered that Kallikles and Phaedrus and I had powers.

"You have to take me to Delos," he said to Father, as soon as he understood how it had happened.

"It isn't an unmitigated blessing," Kallikles said. He hadn't found a way to tell Rhea about his powers yet.

Euklides looked at Kallikles with cold dislike. "Let me be the judge of that."

Phaedrus wasn't home because he was going around the city healing everyone. I missed his friendly presence in the family argument. Neleus wasn't home either, but then I'd barely seen him since the first afternoon when we came back, when Father had sung to us in the garden. He was spending a lot of time with Nikias, and also with Erinna. He was also working hard, with Maia and Manlius, on arranging the conference.

"If there's another voyage, and if I have any say, I'll make sure you get to visit Delos," Father said. "And Alkibiades and Porphyry if they want to go. And maybe I should arrange it for Fabius in Lucia too."

"If there isn't another voyage, could we get there anyway?" Euklides asked. "Could you fly that far with me, Arete?"

"I don't know. It's a long way."

"Could you fly to Amorgos and rest, and then to Naxos, and so on?" Kallikles suggested.

"I don't know. I've never flown carrying anyone for longer than that time with you by the rock. There's a big difference between flying for a few minutes and flying for hours. I'd want to try it somewhere I could land if I needed to rest, not over the open sea!"

"It's a possibility anyway," Euklides said.

"I hope it won't come to that," Father said. "They'll have to send the Lucians home at the very least. And I expect we'll have trade voyages, and missions of mercy helping the Lucians."

"I wonder what powers I'll have," Euklides mused. "It seems so random."

Perhaps it wasn't as random as it seemed. I couldn't quite see how my own powers fit together, but my brothers' were beginning to make sense to me. I had spent one morning up on the mountain with Phaedrus, standing on the edge of the lava ready to swoop down and rescue him if he got into trouble. It didn't bother me to see him walk through the lava, or when he diverted the flowing stream around himself. But I could hardly look when he lay down and sank into it.

"Didn't you need to breathe?" I asked, when he came up after what felt like a long time.

"I could tell when I needed to," he said. "And I did start to burn, but I healed myself." And he had been thinking about developing an excellence of volcanoes before we went to Delos.

As for Kallikles, lightning and weather working certainly fit together. "Perhaps Zeus will devolve weather to you," I suggested, when Kallikles demonstrated his lightning by blasting a rowan tree on the lower slopes of the mountain. There was nothing left of the tree but blackened roots at the edge of the little pool.

"I wish I could do that to Klymene," was all Kallikles said. He wasn't getting over his anger at his mother. He was having fun with electricity, though. He could make the light-beams in Thessaly come on without touching the switches.

My own abilities didn't seem in any way coherent. They also weren't very useful. Nobody on Kallisti spoke different languages, so I never had the chance to use that ability. I already knew Greek and Latin. And I could only fly when I was sure I was unobserved. The truth recognition was useful, and I think that was why Father decided to take me with him on his missions to the other cities. Well, that and wanting me to sing the harmonies to "The Glory of Peace."

Over the course of the next month I went on four embassies, accompanying Father on his new quest to end the art raids. His proposal was radically simple—everyone would return everything they had stolen, and then the art would be fairly distributed according to population. This had been Psyche's original proposition, which we had rejected with scorn the first time we had heard it. Mother had wanted to accept it, but back then she couldn't persuade enough people. Then the raids had started, and the honor of people and cities had become tangled up with them.

Father had three advantages in stopping the art raids now. First was the song, which really was a wonderful tool. It made people stop and think. We'd been trained to fight, but we'd also been trained to think and debate, and the song broke the cycle of raids and revenge by making people question why they were fighting and whether it was worth it. Secondly, because people generally liked and respected Father, and because he had been so vehemently in favor of vengeance for so long, his renouncing that now was very powerful—especially at home in the Remnant, where everyone had seen the force of his madness. Everyone had also heard what he'd done to Kebes, from those of us who had been there. To go from that to singing about peace and civilization and excellence made a powerful statement on its own. And thirdly, there were the Lucians. The specific way the Lucians were falling into timarchy was easy for us to see—the bloodsports and torture, and their focus on the physical side of life over the intellectual side. But their horror at our wars made us see that we were doing the same thing in our own way. The existence of the Lucians, and the need to do something about them, provided a new factor that made everyone refocus.

The people who really needed to be persuaded most were our own people at home in the Remnant. Most of the art was still safely there, and people had no desire to part with any of it. People tended to be especially attached to the art in their own eating halls. It wasn't difficult to get people to agree that the art in the temples and streets should be shared, but they tended to feel that the art in their eating hall belonged to them personally. I had heard Mother talking about this since the art raids began.

What Father proposed was that there should be an art conference, combined with a Kallisti-wide conference on deciding what to do about the Lucians. This was clever, because the Lucians were, or could be made to appear to be, a common enemy. Everyone in Chamber agreed on the foreign conference, and Father and Maia made the art conference seem like the thing that would make all the other cities agree to come.

We went to Sokratea first. Sokratea was our closest ally. They had never been much engaged in art raids against us, though they had raided the other cities. I had been there before, on a mission with Mother. This was not all that different. We sailed there on the *Excellence*, which remained in the harbor there while we stayed in a guest house.

Sokratea was a strange place. In some ways it was the least Platonic of all the republics, including Lucia's Christian Platonism. They didn't have classes, and they didn't separate out guardians from other people. They wanted to examine life, in the Socratic spirit, and they did that. They believed that Sokrates had been entirely right in the Last Debate. They read Plato, but in no very respectful spirit. They banned Masters from their city, but otherwise they had complete free speech and freedom of publication, and voted on everything, all the time. When Father addressed them he addressed the whole city from the rostrum in the agora—they had no Chamber and no committees.

"Doesn't public business get unwieldy?" I asked Patroklus, one of the Children whom I'd met the last time I'd been there. He came to our guest house and took us to eat with him in his eating hall, which was called simply "Six." Their streets too were numbered.

"It does get unwieldy. It takes a lot of time," he admitted. "But we find it's worth it." The food was good; they gave us fish and cabbage and pasta. They had plenty of Young Ones, and lots of Children of course, but because they had refused entry to Masters, no old people at all. Nobody was any older than Father and Patroklus, and that felt strange to me as soon as I'd noticed it.

Father and I sang to their Assembly. I was nervous, even though I knew the harmonies really well by then. I'd never performed to so many strangers—and as Briseis I'd been wearing a mask. Now it was just my naked face. I felt a little sick before we started. But once Father played the first chord the music carried me with it. And it was all true. Peace was worth fighting for, defending, and in some circumstances attacking—to help another city put down a tyrant, for instance.

The people of Sokratea were moved by the music, and by Father's arguments. They agreed to send envoys to the conference, and, after much spirited and public debate, to send their art. "Not the art we have made here!" one woman insisted.

"Nobody is asking for that," Father said. "Though some of it is excellent, and if you chose to circulate it I think everyone would be truly impressed by it."

I stood in the crowd after we'd finished singing, watching the speakers, ready to let Father know if they were lying. Apart from some forgivable hyperbole, they were not.

The next day we moved on to Psyche. Psyche had been built entirely by humans, with no Worker assistance, and it bore a certain resemblance to Marissa and the other Lucian cities. They had lots of art visible, almost all of it stolen from us. The city was arranged in concentric rings around a small hill, and consequently was very difficult to navigate. It was supposed to be the physical model of the soul, but if so my soul didn't understand it.

We were not offered guest-friendship—partly, we guessed, because of Euklides leaving. Psyche accepted applications for citizenship but did not allow emigration. We ate and slept aboard the *Excellence*. The ship felt strange. It had a different crew, people who had not been on the voyage, and who seemed like usurpers in the place of friends and familiar faces. A pimply ephebe only a year or two older than me kept sprawling on the coil of rope where Erinna and I had sat the night Kallikles told us about the Naxians, and I almost wanted to push him overboard for his effrontery.

In Psyche, Father had to meet what felt like an infinite number of committees. In direct opposition to Sokratea, Psyche was top-heavy with Masters. In addition, they denied women a place in public life, so everyone we met was male. Lots of them lied, though maybe I shouldn't call it lying when people blandly assure you that they understand and sympathize. They were frequently and habitually insincere. They were also obsessed with numerology. I knew a little of it from Ficino, whose loss the people of Psyche genuinely regretted. Eventually, after days of obfuscation, Father had a meeting with a man called Aurelius who seemed to have the ability to make decisions. Father persuaded him to send envoys to the conference. It then took days more to persuade them to send their art, and we had to agree that it would be sent under armed guard and with hostages pledged for its return.

They wouldn't let us sing before their Assembly, but we sang in the agora on the day we left. It wasn't official. We just walked through the agora and stopped and began to sing. People clustered around, naturally, more and more of them, women as well as men. Afterward everyone tried to hug us and touch us—it felt very strange. Father said it was because they'd been moved and they wanted to make a connection. Many of them came to the quayside before the ship left, so we sang it again standing on the desk of the *Excellence*. On the last chorus, they joined in on "When the time comes to defend," startling me.

"Wait until you hear the full choral version," Father said, afterward. "Phaedrus is rehearsing them. They'll sing it at the conference."

We moved on to Athenia. Athenia looked just like home, except smaller. We stayed in a guest house and spent a lot of time with my brother Alkibiades. I was so delighted to see him that I was prepared to forgive Athenia a lot of its formality and rigidity. Alkibiades was a gold, naturally; he had also been a gold at home. He took us to his eating hall, Theseus—all the halls were named after Athenian heroes. There was a bronze statue of Theseus with the head of the giant Kerkyon in the hall, which I remembered seeing in the Athenian eating hall at home years ago. Alkibiades had good advice for Father.

"Talk about what happened to Mother. They'll be sympathetic. We're sick of art raids too. The Amazons keep raiding us. Talk about Plato. They think you're compromised but essentially trying to do the right thing."

"That's about right," Father said.

That night he asked me if I'd talk to Alkibiades and Porphyry about going to Delos. "It would be easier for you. It happened to you. You can explain it better. I can't think how to bring it up. It was awkward with Euklides."

"I don't think it would be very easy, but I will if you want me to."

The Athenians didn't allow anyone under the age of thirty into their Chamber, not even envoys. Father said he'd have to sing alone, and that he could manage. Alkibiades and I went for a walk in the hills outside the city. They were planted with vines. "It's good volcanic soil and they thrive here," he said. "I've done a lot of work pruning them this year. We have vines and olives and barley, just as Plato says. No goats or sheep, though. We have to trade for all our cheese and leather. Fortunately, everyone wants wine."

"When we went to Delos, Kallikles and Phaedrus and I acquired god-powers," I said. I hadn't been able to see how to tell him, so I just blurted it out.

He stopped walking. "What?" I could tell he didn't believe me. Though he was fond of me, I'd been so much younger when he left home.

"Really. We can all do things. And Father says he's going to try to take Euklides there, and you and Porphyry if you want to go."

"What kind of powers?" He was still only half-believing.

"I can tell when people are telling the truth, so I can tell that you don't believe me. And Kallikles can change the weather and call lightning, and Phaedrus can heal people and control the volcano."

"It would be hard to demonstrate knowing the truth," he said, skeptically.

"Oh, and I can fly as well," I said. "Look." I swooped up into the air, and had the satisfaction of seeing my favorite brother's mouth fall open.

We discussed it as we walked on. Before we'd gone much farther he had decided he definitely didn't want any powers of his own. "It's not my kind of thing. I don't want to be a god. I just want to be an ordinary philosopher king, like everyone else." He intended to tease, but he was absolutely serious and meant it. That really was what he wanted. "We're trying to do Plato right here, as Athene intended, as Plato intended. And we're all volunteers—not the babies born here, but even they have the choice when they become ephebes to swear their oath or leave for one of the other cities."

"That's the same with us," I said.

"Yes, that's part of why we think you're essentially all right in the Remnant. I came here because I believed we should be following Plato more strictly, and I'm happy here."

"Even with the Festivals of Hera?"

"The Festivals of Hera are great!" He grinned at me. He was telling the truth. "No courtship, no ambiguity, no will-they-or-won't-they, everything organized simply for you, and most of the time no need to worry about it. Perfect!"

"And you haven't fallen in love with anyone or anything?"

"Oh, sure." He shrugged, a little too casually. "Agape. That's also great. I'll introduce you to Diogenes later. He's in my troop, but he's in Solon, not Theseus. He's originally from Psyche. He had to escape to get here, as they hate to have their Young Ones leave. You'll like him. I hope Father does."

"I'm sure Father will," I said, loyally. I felt a pang when I thought of Erinna, and pushed it away. A bird rose up singing from the vines, and we tilted our heads back to follow it up the sky.

"I'm happy," he said, looking back at me. "I like it here. I have

Diogenes and all my friends. I have my studies and my exercises and my troop. I enjoy my hobby work among the vines. When I'm thirty I'll be able to vote in Chamber, and when I'm fifty I'll be able to read the *Republic*. If you can stop the stupid art raids so that we only fight about important things, that would make everything better. But I don't want to change anything about my life. I don't want strange powers messing up who I am and all my friendships. I don't need to be able to fly like that bird to be happy watching it fly. I don't want something else I can't tell Diogenes."

"I'm so glad you're happy," I said. "It does seems strange to me that you don't want powers when you could have them."

"It's so pointless," he said. "Athene set us here to enact the Republic as best we can, to become philosopher kings and live the just life. We'll be destroyed when the volcano takes down this side of the island. There's no sense in going beyond that."

"Because there's no posterity," I agreed. "No future, except for our souls. But don't you feel you have a duty to Fate?"

"My excellence is here," he said. "I feel my best self isn't in acquiring divine powers and learning about them, it's in living the good life here in Athenia."

28

ARETE

I had heard so much about the City of Amazons and Ikaros that finally seeing them was almost a disappointment. The city was much like Athenia, like home only smaller, and not so well built. *The Naming of Crocus* was as impressive close up as it was from a distance—crouching Sokrates was bigger than a building, and Maia, younger but very recognizable, seemed to have her head almost in the clouds. Crocus himself was completely unrecognizable as anything, seeming equal parts Worker, human, and flowers. "It's even bigger than his *Last Debate*," I said.

"It was his first full-scale colossus," Father said. "Crocus's art has always been really interesting."

"And he's been making more of it," I said.

Father nodded. "He's one of the city's most unexpected successes as a philosopher king. Sixty-One's numerology confuses me, but Crocus is a true Platonist."

"His art shows good people doing good things," I said, gazing upward at the huge Maia. Her braid was falling down slightly, the way it did sometimes when she twisted it up before it was quite dry. I wondered what she thought of seeing herself this way.

Ikaros met us as soon as we stepped out onto the quay. He was a man in his early sixties, with a charming smile and a cloud of untamed silvery hair. He had a girl with him, an ephebe about my age, whom he introduced as his daughter Rhadamantha. My birthday had come while I was away. I would be cutting my hair and taking my tests when I got home again.

Ikaros kissed my hand and told me that I looked like my father, so I must have been blessed with my mother's brains. While this came out as a compliment to me, it was subtly insulting to Father, but he only laughed. "I'm not such a fool as you think, Ikaros, for I have been chosen as envoy on this mission, and so far all the cities have agreed to come to the conference we are arranging."

Athenia had agreed to send envoys to the conference, and to send all their art for redistribution on condition that all the other cities agreed to do the same. "They think the Amazons won't," Alkibiades had explained. "They're sure the Amazons have the head of Victory, and that they won't give their art back because they'll think it's a trick to find out who took it." Father had nodded thoughtfully.

Now Ikaros took both of Father's hands and kissed them. "I was so sorry to hear about Simmea. A loss to you, and to the world. She was a true philosopher." Astonishingly, he was sincere. He really had admired Mother.

"We need to stop fighting about art and concentrate on increasing our excellence," Father said, with no preliminaries.

"Yes," Ikaros said. Father's eyes flicked to me. I nodded quickly. He meant it. "Do you have a plan?"

"I do," Father said. "Shall we go somewhere and discuss it? Do you have a committee for me to meet? Or should we go aboard and share a cup of wine?"

"We're guest-friends already," Ikaros said. "I remember sharing lemons with you and Simmea in Thessaly when Sokrates was still with us."

"I have the other member of your debate team. Aristomache is back in the City," Father said.

"Wonderful!" Ikaros sounded delighted. "You rescued her from Kebes?"

"It's more complicated than that, and I don't want to discuss standing it on the harbor," Father said.

"Oh, be welcome to the City of Amazons, both of you, come share food and drink and tell me everything you know about everything," Ikaros said.

He took Rhadamantha's arm, and we all walked along the quay to a nearby eating hall which, as it was the middle of the afternoon and not anywhere near a meal time, was almost empty. He sat us down so that we were in sunlight from the window. Rhadamantha ran off to the kitchen and came back with rather good cold cakes spread with quince and red currant conserves, and wine.

"Now run and find Lysias, and your mother, and Damon, and Klio," Ikaros said. The girl nodded and ran.

"Our Foreign Negotiations Committee," Ikaros explained.

"Four Masters and one of the Children?" Father asked, sipping his wine.

"Three. We were so used to running things," Ikaros said, narrowing his eyes. "Children, and even some Young Ones, are on lots of committees. Your boy Porphyry is on the Farming Committee."

"How you run the City of Amazons is your affair," Father said. "But I do want to tell you that other people have equal significance—they're just as real as you are, and you have to allow them to make their own choices."

Ikaros blinked. "Why do you want to tell me that?"

"Because Maia said something that indicated that you might not know it," Father said, sitting back blandly. I frowned at him. Had Maia told him about Ikaros saying she didn't love anyone? But how did that relate to other people being real? Father bit into his cake. "Good quinces you have here."

Ikaros recovered his poise. "Tell me about Kebes. You found the Goodness Group? All we've had is rumors."

"Shouldn't I wait for the others?"

"Then what should we discuss while we're alone?" Ikaros was wary. There were a few people working in the kitchen, laughing together as they made an early start on dinner, and one old woman sitting drinking by the window, out of earshot.

"My plan for ending the art raids involves returning everything to the original city and redistributing it based on population, with a certain amount of the more portable art moving between the cities on a regular cycle. The other cities have agreed to this, which means that you have the head of Victory, because nobody who had it would agree, not to me, not about this."

"So it wasn't Kebes?"

"You know it wasn't. Stop playing games." Father didn't take his eyes off Ikaros for a moment. Ikaros was looking at Father, but he didn't seem to be focusing on him.

"You've been swearing blood and vengeance on whoever has the head," Ikaros said. "I'd be a fool to admit it if we had it."

"As you may have heard, I took vengeance on Kebes. That's enough. Besides, while there are some circumstances where it's appropriate, this isn't one of them. The important thing is to stop wasting lives and effort over this foolishness, not to make everything worse." Father was utterly sincere.

"Our Young Ones enjoy the art raids. It makes them feel important and gives them a chance to let off steam," Ikaros said. "And then they get out of control, and they feel important, and they have weapons. So you don't need to tell me, because I can see exactly and precisely how things disintegrate into timarchy from here, and so I want to stop this as much as you do. But if we had the head, and I'm not saying we do, what would you suggest we do with it? We couldn't return it with everything else."

He was telling the truth too, but Father didn't look away from him to see me signal.

"And you can't secretly keep it either, because then everyone will know that it wasn't returned, and if that was kept back then other things might have been." He hesitated, and continued in a lower voice. "And besides, she died for it."

"Sneak it back into the temple," I said. "Put it back where it came from, without admitting you ever had it in the first place."

Ikaros laughed, and looked toward me, but not quite at me. "Audacious. But how do you suggest we do it? A troop heading for the temple would be assumed to be raiding and attacked. And half of my problem is how wild the Young Ones in the troops are. I need to keep them under control, and they wouldn't respect me at all if I tried to stop them from fighting back if they were attacked. They might not even want to return it. And they have votes in our Assembly."

"Let me sing to them, and see whether that will help change their minds about the fun of art raids," Father said. "As for the head, get Rhadamantha to give it to Arete. Then Arete can quietly put it back. You and I won't be directly involved. I won't have to know officially who took it, or take any vengeance, and we can swear we didn't do it. It can be a divine intervention."

"An angelic one," Ikaros said.

"Kebes and the Goodness Group have been practicing muscular Christianity all over the Aegean," Father said, switching subjects smoothly.

"What?" Ikaros looked stunned.

"They have eight cities, mostly filled with refugees from mainland wars, mostly converts. It's not your New Concordance, nothing like that subtle. They say Athene was a demon, perhaps Lilith."

"What?"

"They've been teaching people to worship Yayzu and his mother Marissa, and revile Athene."

"In a Platonic context?" Ikaros asked, quite calmly, surprising me because I was expecting him to say "What?" again.

"Oh yes. But with torture for heretics, you'd feel quite at home."

"I would not! We don't do anything to heretics but debate with them. And we have *Saint* Girolamo in our calendar."

"Saint Girolamo, and the Archangel Athene too. You'll have to send missionaries," Father said, quite comfortably. "Nag them to death. Teach them your beautiful complex system. Let them know Christianity is all just fine up to a point, and torturing heretics is well beyond that point."

"I thought you wanted people to worship the Olympians," Ikaros said, frowning a little.

"I do, and so did Plato. I didn't say we wouldn't be sending out missionaries too."

Ikaros laughed, and just then the girl Rhadamantha came back with the others. She looked a tiny bit like Erinna, she had the same kind of hair and the same lean grace. I was glad when she stayed for the debate.

The debate was long. Father and I explained the Lucian civilization and the two conferences. I had heard it all before, but I had to stay to sing, when Father decided it was time, and also to let him know when people were lying. By dinner time, I had realized that there was something seriously wrong with Ikaros's sight, although he was trying to hide it. He didn't have cataracts, and he didn't peer and lean forward to see close up like Aristomache, but he never seemed to be focusing on what he was looking at. When Lysias passed him a note, he didn't even glance at it. He fumbled picking up his wine cup. He couldn't be blind. He had seen that I looked like Father. But that had been outside, in full daylight.

We had meetings with the committees, and then their Chamber, where we sang, several times. It took three days, but in the end they agreed to send envoys. They agreed to send their art back on the *Excellence*, too.

On the evening of the third day, after everything was agreed, I went for a walk up into the hills with my brother Porphyry, as I had done with Alkibiades. I didn't know Porphyry well. He had always lived in the City of Amazons, and only made occasional visits to us. "I'm sorry about your mother," he said, awkwardly, kicking at a stone.

"We're trying to stop the art raids in her memory," I said.

"Is it true that Father tortured Kebes or Marsias or whatever his name was to death?" he asked.

"Yes. And it was Matthias. But he was Kebes when he was here, so we always call him that."

"So does my mother. Matthias is a difficult name to get my tongue around anyway. So Father really killed him in that horrible way?"

"Yes. But Kebes was going to do it to him." I explained the competition, and the battle afterward.

"I suppose he had to." We were sitting down on the edge of a little stream, in the shade of a plane tree, dabbling our feet in the water. "But I think I would have cut his throat instead, even if that was their idea of justice."

"So would I, and so would Kallikles," I admitted.

"I've always been a bit frightened of Father, and this doesn't help," he said.

"Frightened of him? Why?" I couldn't imagine it.

"Oh, because he's so excellent. It makes it difficult to live up to. My mother always says he was just clearly the best when they were all growing up together. And she was beautiful then, of course."

"I think your mother is still beautiful," I said. Euridike had a lovely face and wonderful hair.

"She says she hasn't been the same since she had babies. And she says it has been better for her, because she used to be vain about it. But anyway, back then when she tried to be friends with Pytheas because he was beautiful too, he never had any time for anyone except your mother. And he's not just beautiful, he's so good at everything. I always felt that I wasn't good enough for him. Children are supposed to outdo their parents, but how could I ever outdo Pytheas?"

"You have your own excellence," I said. "You just have to develop it. I never heard we were supposed to outdo our parents, or compare ourselves to anyone else, just that we had to work to become our best selves, the best that it's possible for us to be." I looked up at him. Porphyry was tall. "Do you know about Father?"

"Know what? He's hard to get to know. Especially when I didn't see much of him."

I lay back and stared up at the blue sky through the dappled leaves. I had to ask him whether he wanted to go to Delos, but if he didn't know who Father was that made it very difficult. "If you could have divine powers, but you had to keep them to yourself, would you want to?"

"Would I have divine responsibilities too?"

"What a good question! What do you mean?"

"Well, what kind of powers are we talking about?" Porphyry asked, treating the whole question as an abstract Platonic inquiry.

"Flight. Healing."

"Right. So say I could heal people, would I have a responsibility to go around healing everyone all the time? Of course I would, nobody could have that power without. With flight I suppose I'd have a responsibility to take messages rapidly everywhere, and rescue people from burning buildings, and that kind of thing."

"Yes," I said. "Assuredly, Sokrates, that must be the case."

He laughed. "Your mother said Sokrates hated it if they said that."

"I know." I was thinking about whether I had a responsibility to take messages quickly around the world. If I did, it could explain where my language skills fitted in. But I didn't much want to be a messenger god. Besides, did the world need another?

"I don't know if I'd want divine powers. It would be so disruptive. But it could be fun. And it would give my life a purpose. I wouldn't have to worry about what my excellence was, I'd know."

"No you wouldn't," I said. "What if you had them and couldn't tell anyone."

"You mean I could heal people but they wouldn't know I was doing it?"

"Yes."

"That would be very strange. And how would that work with flight? I could only fly if nobody was looking? I'd have to stand by burning buildings knowing I could rescue people and let them burn to death?"

I started to cry. I didn't mean to, but I was remembering Erinna in the storm. Porphyry put his arm around me, not awkwardly like Father but as if he was used to being comforting to people. "What's wrong? Is the debate making you miss Simmea?"

"I do have divine powers, and I don't know what to do about the responsibility," I sniffed.

"What, really?" he looked down at me, astonished, but not disbelieving.

"Stand up and I'll show you," I said, getting to my feet. There was nobody around. I leaped into the air, and swooped down to scoop him up, as I had Kallikles. Porphyry went rigid for a moment, and then he started to laugh. My tears dried in the wind and in the face of his delight.

"Take me right up," he called. "Take me so high I can see the city from above, like an eagle."

"But then they'd see us," I said.

"How about over the mountain then? Could we fly over the crater? That would be so great."

"I don't think I can carry you for ten miles," I said. "I don't know. I never have and I don't want to risk dropping you." I went up, so he could see the stream and the hill it ran down and the City of Amazons in the distance. Then I made a series of loops around the tree and set him down again. "Sometime we could meet up on the mountain and I'd fly you over the crater, if you want."

"I'd love that! That was such fun. The wind on my face. It was amazing. How can you do that? And why can't you tell anyone?"

"I can do it because Father is Apollo, and I went to Delos and it woke my power."

Porphyry sat down again, and I sat down beside him. "Father is Apollo? Incarnate? Like Jesus?"

"Yes, pretty much exactly like, as far as I understand it," I said, pleased that he'd understood so rapidly. "But he doesn't want anyone to know except family. I didn't know whether he'd told you, but when we were talking about Delos he said he'd take you if you wanted to go. And he asked me to tell you about the powers."

"It makes so much sense that he would be Apollo. Why did I never think of that? And . . . how could I possibly try to compete! Did Simmea know? Of course she did." He shook his head in wonder.

"She figured it out herself," I said, proud of my mother. I'd heard the story of how she'd figured it out many times, from both my parents.

"And what happened on Delos?"

"Kallikles and Phaedrus and I found a spring and drank from a cup, and then we had powers. Different powers. Phaedrus can heal and control the volcano, and Kallikles has lightning and weather powers."

"Lightning? Amazing. But they can't fly?"

"They can walk on air, but I'm the only one who can fly properly."

"And why can't you tell anyone? Will you lose the powers if you do?" He seemed eager and enthusiastic.

"No, just that everyone will know we're freaks. Father says he wants to live a normal life as best he can."

"But my burning building question made you cry because in that situation you'd have to give yourself away?"

"Of course I would. I couldn't just stand there." I rubbed my eyes hard to stop myself crying again. "I don't know if I can live a normal life, with powers. It's going to be hard. I already used them, in the battle in Lucia. I flew over a man who was attacking me. People thought it was a leap, but really it was flight. And Phaedrus healed people. Aristomache had broken her arm, but he healed it and said it was just a bruise, that kind of thing."

"And Kallikles?"

"He struck an attacker with lightning, and he made the wind change so that the burning boat burned the *Goodness* instead of the *Excellence*. But people didn't know it was him. They thought it was Zeus."

Porphyry shook his head. "I don't see how you can keep powers like that secret, long term, if you use them. And you can't help doing it, when something happens like that. It would be better if people knew and could plan for it. And maybe Pytheas ought to talk to Ikaros about being Apollo. Ikaros would be so interested. He'd instantly work out a way to make it fit with the New Concordance."

"But then people would always be pestering him about it."

"And people would always be asking you to get kittens out of trees."

I laughed. "And taking messages between cities, like you said."

"If it turns out that you can fly that far."

"I don't know whether I can. I need to practice. But for now, do you want to go to Delos and get some powers of your own?"

He grinned. "Yes, definitely, as soon as I possibly can. It would increase my excellence, and also be a ton of fun. But I'm not going to promise to keep them secret and not use them for the good of humanity."

"I think you'll have to talk to Father about keeping it secret. And maybe to all of us. Because it doesn't just affect you. If people know you have powers, they'll want to know why."

"I'll talk to Father." He looked as if he was bracing himself for it. "And Kallikles and Phaedrus. And it will depend what my powers are, and whether they'd be useful. I wish I could choose what they would be. I'd love so much to be able to fly. Would you take me up again? Just for a little bit?"

"Of course." It was lovely to meet such enthusiasm. I swooped up with him in my arms. We went quite high, so he could see the landscape, and then I let him direct me along the stream toward a cove. I took him down again then and set him down gently on the black sand. I spiraled a few times around the cove before coming down in front of him, on the edge of the sea. Only then did I see a man sitting against the base of the cliff, with his arms wrapped around his legs, watching us. Ikaros.

He looked stunned and delighted. There was no point pretending it hadn't happened, because he'd clearly seen the whole thing, and besides there were no tracks in the sand. "Joy to you," I said.

Porphyry spun around. "Ikaros! Joy to you," he stammered. "We were just . . . that is I . . . my sister was just showing me . . ."

"She's an angel!" Ikaros believed every word he was saying, but that didn't make it true.

I flew over to him in one swoop and sat down in the sand beside him. I pinched the skin of the back of his hand. "Real," I said. "Not an angel."

"So was Sophia—Athene—as tangible and corporeal as anyone else," he said. "She never pinched me, but I brushed against her several times and touched her hands when we were acquiring art together. But if you're not an angel, explain to me what you are, and I'll figure out how it all fits together."

I opened my mouth, but Porphyry interrupted before I could. "Don't tell him anything."

He was standing, with his shadow falling over me. He had composed himself in the walk across the beach and no longer looked worried. "What? Why?"

"For one thing it's not only your secret, as you were just telling me. But I've just worked out the most important reason is that knowing for sure would break his heart."

I frowned up at him. "How? You said before he'd work out how it fit together, and that's just what he said himself."

"Yes. But I was wrong. I know Ikaros a lot better than you do. He's my sister Rhadamantha's father, so he's been around our house a lot all my life. He's my teacher. He thinks he wants to know, but—"

"I'm right here," Ikaros said, plaintively.

Porphyry looked at him and smiled. "Tell me truthfully you want Arete to explain it to you, instead of letting you work it out for yourself."

"Oh!" Ikaros put his hand to his heart. "A hit! And from my own disciple!"

Porphyry smiled and sat down. "What are you doing out here anyway? You shouldn't come this far alone. Your eyes aren't up to it."

"I keep telling you, I can still see perfectly well in full daylight." He was lying. "The debate ended earlier than I thought, and I came to get something that's hidden in the cave." That part was true.

Porphyry's eyes flicked toward the cleft in the cliff.

"If that's where you're keeping the head of Victory I can just go in myself and take it now," I said.

"And fly home to the City with it, and set it back in the temple," Ikaros suggested. "While I work on my theory of how it is that you're a girl born in the Remnant City and grown up at a normal speed, but you can fly. You say you're not an angel, and I admit it does seem unlikely. Maybe it's because your mother was such an exceptional philosopher and you're developing angelic abilities because of that. Maybe if we all study Plato hard enough the entire next generation will be able to fly."

I laughed, because while he was joking, he also half hoped he was right. "You really do believe in the perfectibility of humanity," I said.

"Despite everything, I keep hoping. And from time to time I find some evidence."

"Please don't tell anyone," I said. "Once everyone knows I can fly they'll always be getting me to carry messages and rescue kittens from trees."

"I won't tell anyone until I'm sure I have the right answer. But can I come to you with my guesses?"

"To me, or to Porphyry," I said.

"And even if and when you have it right, perhaps you could incorporate it in the New Concordance anonymously, as in saying that a girl born in one of the Republics, rather than giving Arete's name?" Porphyry suggested.

"But her name perfectly encapsulates what she is. As does yours, of course. But I won't use it. You can trust me."

I wanted to like him and trust him, but I couldn't. "Why were you so mean to Maia?" I asked.

Ikaros blinked. "Maia? I thought she accepted my apology?" He was sincere, which wasn't to say he was correct.

"You told her she doesn't love anybody!" I accused.

"Oh." He looked abashed. "She told you about that?"

"It's still hurting her."

"What happened was that Klio had been telling me about this German philosopher—"

"The Germans have philosophers?" Porphyry interrupted, astonished. I was astonished too. I'd read Tacitus. I imagined some hairy barbarian debating in the forests while avoiding the axes of his companions.

"This was later, after they were civilized," Ikaros said, waving away the distraction. "They conquered Italy and claimed to be the heirs of Rome like everyone else. Anyway, this German had interesting theories about how minds work, and I was interested in them for a time, as best Klio could remember what she'd read years before. And one of his theses seemed to me to explain Maia's behavior, and I was foolish enough to mention this to her. I can see now how it was unkind. At the time I thought she'd be glad of an explanation."

"You should tell her you were wrong," I said.

"I will. I'm sorry that's still upsetting her." He meant it. "Is that what Pytheas was talking about when he told me people have equal significance?"

"I don't know," I said. "But can I trust you that you won't tell anyone about me being able to fly?"

Ikaros laughed again. "You're safe even if you can't trust me. I've never seen anything so lovely as the two of you coming in to land just then. But while I've tried to keep everyone from knowing how bad my eyes are, they know enough to know I'm not a reliable witness on something like this."

"How much can you see, really?" I asked.

Ikaros sighed. "I can see shapes and colors, in sunlight," he said, truthfully. "No detail. And the middle distance is where I can see best. I could see you better when you landed than I can now. It's just strain from reading too much in bad light."

I wondered if Phaedrus would be able to heal him. I didn't want to raise his hopes without being sure.

"He doesn't want people to know. But I know, because I read to him and write things he dictates," Porphyry said.

"Some things," Ikaros teased, smiling. There was something about the way he said this that made me realize that he and Porphyry had the same kind of close teacher-pupil friendship that Ficino and I had had. "And I have a lot memorized. It's not so bad."

"I trust you not to tell," I said. "And Porphyry knows enough to tell you if your guesses are good."

"Get the head," Porphyry suggested to me, waving at the cave.

I went into the cave. It was dim after the bright sunlight outside, and I had to wait for my eyes to adjust. At first I couldn't see anything but the rippled volcanic rock, but then I noticed a shelf, just above my head. On it was a bundle wrapped in cloth. I pulled it down and unwrapped it. There was the serene and perfect stone face of Victory gazing up at me. What a stupid thing to die for, I thought, hating it. What a feeble recompense for all the years Simmea might have lived. And yet, how beautiful it was, even in this dimness. A masterpiece.

I wiped my eyes, tucked the head under my arm, and flew out of the cave. I circled the cove—I saw Ikaros's head move to watch me, and I settled to the sand again next to them. Ikaros took the head and ran his fingers gently over the contours of the face. He had tears in his eyes. He didn't even try to look at it. "Take it," he said. "Fly back to the Remnant with it. I'll come to the conference, and see you and it there."

"I'll help you back to the city," Porphyry said to Ikaros.

I took the head and flew up again. I had no intention of flying all the way home with the head, but I circled over Ikaros and Porphyry's heads and set off southward. I came down in the woods near the City of Amazons and walked in with the head carefully covered up. I took it to the *Excellence*, where I stowed it safely in my hammock.

Then I went to find Father. "Porphyry wants to go to Delos when you go," I said. "And I have the head of Victory, for what it's worth."

29

MAIA

We held the conference in the Chamber. The Chamber was the oldest building in the City. I could remember when it was the only building and all the Masters slept in it, uncomfortable and excited on the marble floor. I'd been in it thousands of times since then, and usually I took the steps and went through the pillared portico without thinking of anything but the day's business. The day the conference began, I walked in with Axiothea and remembered that early excitement, and my young bones that didn't ache. We had been among the youngest of the Masters, and now most of the older ones were dead, of time and attrition, or in Ficino's case a sword through the ribs. Once I had looked forward to a time when the older Masters would be gone and we younger ones could make decisions. But then I had imagined the Republic growing stronger and more secure every year. I had believed the Children would become philosopher kings. I was older now. I didn't know whether I was wiser.

The room was arranged for debate, with rows of benches facing the rostrum. It was packed, with all the envoys and all the Chamber members who wanted to participate. There must have been nearly five hundred people present. The envoys sat at the front, and it was agreed that they had precedence in speaking.

The conference began with a simple direct prayer to far-seeing

Apollo for clarity. It was given by Manlius, whose turn it was.
There had been some argument about this, with Ikaros and Aristomache both wanting prayers of their own, either as replace-
ments or additions. In the end this was a compromise—it didn't
mention Athene. Yet it was impossible, in this room, not to think
of her, not to remember her standing in front of us, nine feet
tall, with the owl on her arm turning its head to watch us all.

Then we elected a judge—a chair, a moderator, to control the
flow of debate. It had been agreed in advance that the voting for
this would be by simple majority of all present. Pytheas stood.
"I'd be a terrible judge," he began. There was a ripple of laughter. "The person I'd like to propose, our chair here since Atticus died, was killed in the fighting in Lucia. I'd like a moment
of silence for Ficino, missed now and always." Tears came to my
eyes. After the silence he went on. "I think our judge should be
someone who has experience of more than one city, who went
on the voyage, and has direct experience of the Lucian cities. I
propose Maia."

He hadn't warned me. Axiothea shoved me to my feet. "If
elected I will serve, and strive to be fair," I said. "It's an honor,
but also it will be very difficult."

To my astonishment, Ikaros seconded the proposal. (His hair
was entirely silver now, and shaggy like a lion's mane.) Somebody
proposed old Salutius, from Psyche; and Patroklus, from
Sokratea, proposed Neleus, on the grounds that he had been on
the voyage and was a Young One. Neleus declined, saying he had
no experience and he thought I'd do a better job. I was elected,
and made my way up to the front.

It was strange sitting where Athene had stood, where Krito
had sat, and Tullius, Cato, and Ficino. It was strange to look at
the hall from this perspective, the sea of faces. I had chaired committees, and even moderated plenty of debates, but none in
Chamber. I put my hands on the carved arms of the chair, grip-

ping them tightly. I had never imagined myself here. I had always seen myself in a support role, never imagined myself sufficiently respected to be chosen to judge an important debate like this. Well, I knew what Plato said about that. I took a breath and looked at Pytheas, who was still standing there. Neleus and I had been working on accommodation for the envoys and diplomatic issues. "Is there an agenda?"

Pytheas handed me a paper: 1. How to vote. 2. The Lucian question. 3. Choral ode. 4. Art raids. No more, no order of speakers or anything. I looked at him in exasperation. It was just like Pytheas: so generally excellent, with such unexpected lacunae. He shrugged.

"First, how to vote," I said, to the room.

It was a contentious issue. By number of cities the Lucians outnumbered everyone else. They had sent thirty envoys. About half of them were originally Masters and Children from the Just City. The other half were refugees rescued and converted to Christian Platonism. None of them approved of Kebes breaking guest friendship, but they were all devastated by the loss of the *Goodness*. They had different opinions on different subjects, but they were all united in their sense of mission. They wanted to rescue victims of Bronze Age wars and teach them civilization. That's what they had been doing all this time, and they wanted to keep on with it. And it was immediately apparent to everyone that if we used democratic voting by city, with their eight cities they'd immediately and unquestionably succeed in that aim.

Aurelius, of Psyche, suggested that the Lucians be considered one city, as we had imagined they were before they were rediscovered—the Goodness Group as we had called them, or the Lost City. "A hundred and fifty people left with Kebes. Calling them one city and giving them an equal vote with us seems generous. Calling them eight cities seems ridiculous."

"Each of our cities is bigger than Psyche, and though most of the people in them are volunteers, they have taken the oath of citizenship, they read and write, they know Plato," Aristomache countered. "Many of our leaders came from the *Goodness,* but others have arisen from the people we rescued. We make no distinction between us. Adrastos here is an example. We found him as a boy fleeing a war in the Troad. He's thirty now, and he has spent the last twenty years with us. He's a gold of Marissa, a philosopher and a stonemason."

"Like Sokrates," Adrastos said, shyly, standing up when he was mentioned.

Patroklus, from Sokratea, suggested that we should give cities votes by population, but aim for consensus—any motion would need a two-thirds majority to pass. (It would be total population, as citizens were too difficult to count, because we all had different criteria for citizenship. Psyche didn't count women, Athenia didn't count people under thirty, the Lucians didn't count bronzes or irons, and none of us counted children.)

There was much debate, and eventually this proposal was accepted, as being the closest thing to fair. I set up a hasty committee to come up with numbers over the lunch break. I fortified myself with soup and grapes in Florentia, while claiming that talking to anyone about the conference would violate my neutrality. "Ficino never said that," Arete complained.

"Ficino had more practice than I have. I need to clear my head."

On my way back to the Chamber, Neleus caught up with me. "You're doing well so far," he said. "I was terrified when Patroklus suggested me!"

"So was I when your father suggested me!" We smiled at each other. Neleus was one of the brightest of the Young Ones, and he had always been one of my favorite pupils, and one of Ficino's too. On impulse, I pulled Ficino's hat out of the fold of my kiton, where I'd been carrying it since Lucia. "I wonder if you'd like this. It's silly really, it's old and worn, and—"

"I'd really love it," Neleus said, tears in his eyes. He reshaped the hat in his hands and jammed it on his head. "Thank you. I don't know what to say." We walked along quietly together. Then to my surprise, Ikaros came bounding up through the crowd of people heading back into the chamber.

"Ficino! I'm so delighted—No. Sorry."

Neleus turned to him in astonishment. He didn't look a thing like Ficino, even in the hat. He was even darker-skinned than Simmea, and much broader-shouldered than Ficino.

"I did know he was dead," Ikaros said. "But there are others here I knew were dead. I saw the familiar red hat, on a street where I had seen him so often, and for a moment I thought it was him. Sorry, young man."

"How are your eyes?" I asked, remembering his eyestrain from translating Aquinas the day he apologized to me.

"Maia! You're doing a wonderful job so far. Could I talk to you this evening after the session?"

He hadn't known me, and he had thought Neleus was Ficino. And he hadn't answered my question about his eyes. I realized he must be nearly blind. I felt profoundly sorry for him. "Of course," I said. "I'll wait for you on the steps afterward."

We reconvened. Axiothea came up to announce the results of the numbers. Psyche was given five votes, the Lucian cities six each, Athenia and Sokratea twelve each, the City of Amazons fifteen, and the Original City twenty-five. "If all of Kallisti voted together, that would be sixty-nine, to Lucia's forty-eight," she said. Everyone laughed at the thought of all of Kallisti voting together.

"If the envoys from a city are divided, can the votes be split?" Aurelius asked.

"Certainly," I ruled. "The envoys can divide the city's votes as they choose."

"And who are the envoys who will vote for the Remnant?"

"The Foreign Negotiations Committee, with Pytheas representing Simmea," I said. "But no doubt they will listen to opinions."

The Chamber was less packed now. Some people were lingering over lunch, and others had realized that this would go on a long time and be boring. However, as soon as we started properly it began to move rapidly and became fascinating.

"The issue of the Lucians," I said. I'd been thinking how to address this. "First Pytheas will explain succinctly what happened on the voyage, and then Aristomache will explain what they were doing and what they want. Questions afterward. I'll open up the debate to the whole room and we'll have plenty of time for everyone. But let's hear this quietly first." I had caught both of them on my way to lunch and asked them to be ready.

Everyone in the room probably knew what Pytheas told them, but there were still some surprised gasps as he went through it. Then Aristomache came up and described the Lucian mission. "We have reading, plumbing, pottery, iron working, medicine, Yayzu, and Plato," she said "How can we sit safely on an island while there are people out there who have none of these things? Join us, and help us spread civilization."

Many agreed with her message, though some of us wanted to leave Jesus out of the lists of benefits. Kallikles spoke in support of Aristomache: "I was really shaken by what I saw on Naxos," he said, describing the ignorance and poverty of the village he had visited. "People shouldn't be living like that when we can help them. The Lucians like Adrastos prove it can be done. We should be doing it."

Others, especially the Athenians, were horrified at the very notion. "Athene put us here where the volcano would wipe out every trace of what we do. We can't go running around the Mediterranean interfering with everything! Who knows what harm it might do!"

I was sympathetic with that view myself. So was Klio. "We don't know how history works," she said. "But consider that it might be a wax tablet like the ones we use every day. After it has been written, it can be erased and rewritten. If we step out of the margins where Athene has set us, we could wipe out everything that comes after. What Kallikles said about helping those poor people sounds entirely good. But we don't know enough. What if the Trojan War needs to come out of the poverty and dirt we saw in the Kyklades? If so we would be wrong to change it, however painful seeing it may be. What if people handed the secret of iron-making will be content to make iron forever and never move on to steel, as they would have if they'd discovered it for themselves? And we don't know, we can't know, what matters, or what is and isn't safe to change. We have seen too much here of what comes from good intentions and ignorance. We should leave them alone to find their own destiny and stay here on our island."

Everyone had their own theory of history, and many aired them. Ikaros was absolutely sure that Athene wouldn't have put us here if there was any danger. He believed in Providence, and his argument was essentially that we could only do good by trying to increase excellence.

Finally Patroklus argued that the people of the Aegean had their own Fate and that we had no right at all to change that, or to judge them for living differently from the way we thought right. "You have described their art. What right have we to impose our ideas of art on them instead? Perhaps they have religions and philosophies that are equally valuable. I'm not arguing in support of Klio, that we don't know what it's safe to change. I agree with that, but my point is different. What right have we to judge and to say what is better or worse?"

I called an end to the day without calling for a vote. "Lots of people haven't had a chance to speak yet. We'll resume in the morning."

"You're not setting up a committee on the nature of time?" Pytheas asked as I stepped down.

"Why, do you have any pertinent information for it?" He was always such a funny mixture. I remembered him as a boy, so intent on everything, so serious. They were all my children.

"Nothing that I want to talk about right now," he said. "But it seems to me that the debate has been all about that, and only what Patroklus said was about whether we want to help."

"I think there would be a clear majority for helping if not for the worry about time," I said. "The suggestion that the Lucian cities are the cities Plato heard about was popular."

"I suspect it's what Simmea would have wanted." He sighed. "It's never easy, is it? But I think you're doing very well in the chair."

Ikaros was waiting on the steps when I came out. The sun was setting, and in this light I had to touch his arm to get his attention.

"Where shall we go?" he asked.

"Let's go to my house," I said.

"Oh marvelous!" he said.

"My house isn't so wonderful," I said, taking his arm to lead the way.

"But if you'll invite me there it means you have forgiven me. Some things your pupils said led me to believe you might not have. That's really why I wanted to speak to you."

I didn't want to say that he was old and almost blind and I felt sorry for him and not at all afraid any more. "Of course I forgive you. I forgave you years ago, before I left the City of Amazons. What pupils?"

"Pytheas said something very gnomic. And Arete said you were still upset about me saying you were afraid to love," he said.

"I do think of that sometimes, wondering if it's true," I admitted. We came to my house. I pushed the door open and turned on the light. "I think it made me uncomfortable because it was a little bit true. If it wasn't partly true it wouldn't have stung."

He stood inside the dim room. I guided him to the bed, where he sat, cautiously. "And it was my fault you were afraid," he said.

"Yes," I said, as I mixed wine. "But it was a long time ago, and I have forgiven you. And I realized when Ficino died how much I loved him all this time." I gave him a cup of wine, putting it into his hand.

"I'm sorry," he said.

"We can't undo the past. We go on from where we are." I sat down on a cushion on the floor, against the wall. "And here you are back in the original city, and in my house. Tell me about your eyes. How much can you see?"

"I do all right in sunlight," he said. "Though I mistake things even then, as you saw this afternoon. It's grown much worse this last year. But it's been three years now since I was able to read."

"Oh Ikaros, how terrible for you! I'm so sorry."

"It was Crocus's fault really, not yours," he said. I'd only meant to convey sympathy, not admit fault, but if it was translating Aquinas that had made him lose his vision it was indeed partly my fault. "I've wondered sometimes if it's Providence, if it's punishment for what I did to you and destroying your joy."

"No," I said at once, then wondered. Could it be? "I have had plenty of joy, even though I was afraid. And I still do." And I can read, I thought, looking at my bookshelves.

"I think it would have happened more quickly and more directly," he said. "If this is a punishment for anything it's probably for buying those books."

"Forbidden books," I said. "How did Crocus know you had them?"

"And he was there. I told Sokrates about them. Sokrates couldn't read Aquinas, because it was in Latin, of course." He hesitated, and sipped his wine. "Speaking of Latin and forbidden books, could I ask you to read something to me?"

"Of course," I said, with no hesitation.

He pulled a book out of his kiton. It was black and had a cross on the cover. I recognized it immediately as a Bible. "It's Jerome's Latin Bible," he said.

Written on the cover was *Versio Sacra Vulgata*. It was the Vulgate, the Latin Bible of the Catholic Church. I had heard about it but never seen it before. We didn't allow it in the Republic, of course, and I had only read the King James Version when I was young.

"I thought you allowed Bibles in Amazonia?"

"We have Bibles compiled from memory. It's surprising how much people knew, and of course I had this and could fill in some pieces nobody remembered." I took it from him and leafed through it. It was printed on the same Bible paper I remembered from my childhood, with the initials of verses printed in red.

"So what do you want me to read?"

"Jerome's prefaces. Of course nobody had memorized those." He smiled. "Nobody else. But ever since I heard about Ficino's death, I've been longing to re-read Jerome's preface to Job, where he talks about the difficulties of translation."

I turned the pages until I came to it. I had never read it, and reading it aloud now I laughed when I reached Jerome's comparison of translating to wrestling an eel, which gets more slippery the harder you try to hold on. When I came to the end of the preface, I kept on reading. I had not read Job since I was a girl, and I was surprised how much it still meant to me. We both had tears in our eyes when I stopped reading.

"Come to Florentia and have dinner," I said, handing him back the book.

"Keep it," he said. "It's no use to me now. Even if you don't want to read it, you can enjoy all of Jerome's snarky prefaces, where he calls people who prefer other translations barking dogs."

"Do you still think Athene's perfect?" I asked. "Because I find a great deal of comfort in thinking that she isn't, and that the gods have limited natures and limited reach. Believing that allows for things going wrong and not being part of anybody's plan."

"I keep trying to understand," he said, getting up. "If we became like angels, we would see how perfect she is. Don't you remember how wonderful she was when she was here?"

"Wonderful, yes, absolutely. But wonderful is not at all the same thing as perfect. Come on, let's go and eat before the food is all gone. I'll read to you some more tomorrow if you want. I assume you have plenty of people to take dictation."

By lunchtime the next day we had a consensus—a two-thirds majority—for helping the Lucians. We weren't prepared to give them the *Excellence*, though obviously we'd have to use it. Details remained to be agreed on, especially on religious issues. I set up a number of committees. I pushed Aristomache, Ikaros, Aurelius, Manlius and Pytheas onto the committee on religion, and swore privately never to go near it myself. There was also consensus that any individual Lucians who wanted to return to the Remnant City would be welcome, and any who met the immigration criteria for the other cities would be welcome to apply there. The Lucians offered reciprocal agreements, but I didn't think many of us would want to emigrate there.

After lunch came the choral ode. Pytheas had written it, and his son Phaedrus was conducting it. It took place out of doors, in the agora, so that as many people as possible could hear it. It was Pytheas's best work, powerful and moving, especially with the massed voices echoing around the space. The song was about peace. I'd never really considered that peace isn't just the absence of war but an active positive force. It must be one of Plato's Forms, I thought.

At the end of the ode, there was a consensus for hearing it again, so we did. This time many people were joining in with the final chorus, making the commitment to fight to defend peace.

We went back into the Chamber in a very different mood. I was preparing to begin on the question of art raids when a messenger came in to the Chamber. It was Sophoniba, a Young One, one of the Florentine troop. "The head of Victory is back," she said, panting. She had been running.

"Back?" I asked. "What do you mean?"

"Back in the temple of Victory just outside the walls, where it used to be. And the strangest thing is that the gravel courtyard was raked this morning and there are no marks on it at all. It's as if the gods brought it back."

"Was it with the returned art?" The returned art was on display in the agora and the colonnades around it, forming an impromptu art exhibition which everyone had been enjoying in their spare moments. I'd been spending my spare moments reading to Ikaros, so I hadn't had time for it myself.

"No," Pytheas said. "I looked closely, as you'd expect. The head of Victory wasn't there. But you say now it's back in the temple?"

"That's right," Sophoniba said. "It's the strangest thing."

We all trooped out to see it, and there indeed it was, where it had always been, serene, victorious, mysterious, in the niche against the back wall. Pytheas started to sing his ode again, and although the choir had dispersed many people joined in.

"It's a Mystery," Aurelius said to me as we were walking back.

"I certainly can't understand it."

"Do you think it was Sophia?" Manlius whispered behind us.

"I can't think who else it could have been," Sophoniba said. "There wasn't a mark on the gravel, and it shows every mark."

"If she's still paying attention, what must she think of us!" Manlius said.

Back in the Chamber, the debate on art raids then resumed.

Pytheas began. "After the Last Debate, when the new cities were founded, we all agreed that we couldn't divide the technology because we didn't understand it well enough to move things, and all of it was needed here to function properly. We might have agreed to divide it with our brothers and sisters in any case, had it not been absolutely necessary to the lives of Crocus and Sixty-One. Their vital need for electricity was more important than anything. Secondly, the electricity keeps the library at a constant temperature, which isn't just a comfort for us but a necessity for the preservation and safety of the books. That's why we printed additional copies for the libraries in the other cities but kept the originals here." He looked at the Lucians, all sitting in a group on the left-hand side now. "You weren't present for that debate, but I feel sure you'd have agreed if you had been."

There were nods among them, and some hands raised in other parts of the room, which I ignored. If people wanted to point out that the books were traded rather than given away, that would divert the argument. Let them wait.

"Then when the envoys of Psyche suggested dividing up our art, it seemed at first to be the same thing. It was an easy mistake to make. But it wasn't at all the same. Art can be divided in a way that technology cannot. We can travel to look at art. Nobody's life was being endangered if the art left the City, nor was the art itself endangered. We wanted to keep it because we loved it, but that was the same reason why our brothers and sisters in other cities wanted to own it. We fought over it. Nothing could have been more foolish than war over art. And we're all tired of it. All the cities have brought back what was taken, and we've been enjoying seeing it again. I propose that we distribute art to all the cities according to population, and bring it back here to redistribute it again every five years, at a great festival of art, where new art can also be seen and enjoyed. Simmea," he choked as he said her name, took a deep breath and said it again, louder. "Simmea always said that we should be making more art instead of squabbling over the art we have. She loved the Botticellis in Florentia with all her soul. But there are nine of them. If four of them had gone, one to each of the other cities, she'd still be here to love the five that were left."

He sat down. Among the forest of hands, only one was raised among the Lucians: Auge. Curious, I called on her.

"We didn't take any art on the *Goodness*. We made our own art in the Lucian cities. We haven't talked about it, but we're not here to demand our share of original art for our cities, and it might be at risk going by sea, and we wouldn't want that. I'm horrified at the art raids you've been describing. I can't believe Simmea died in one—actually died! Simmea, whose own original work was so wonderful. The kiton I wore when I lived here has long since worn out, but I cut off the piece of embroidery Simmea did along the hem and I still have it framed on the wall above my daughter's bed. But what I stood up to say is that I'm a sculptor. If you agree to share your art as Pytheas suggested, I'll do an original piece of stonework for each of your cities, on any subject you like. The people of Sokratea have already commissioned me to do a statue of Sokrates as he appeared in the Last Debate. I'll do that for free, and whatever else equivalently for the other four cities—statues or bas reliefs, whatever you want."

There was a roar of acclamation, and I had a lump in my throat. She was so sincere, and asking for nothing but instead offering to make and give. And her visible horror at the thought of the art raids helped us realize how barbaric they were. They'd been going on so long we'd almost become used to them.

Then Crocus raised one of his great arms. Neither of the Workers spoke often in Chamber. I called on him. He wrote his statement on a tablet, and Manlius read it aloud. "I will also offer free art equivalently, and extra work, whatever is needed, to stop the fighting."

There was another great cheer. More people began to offer the same. Then there were a few other speeches. Some citizens of the original city said how attached they were to the particular art in their own eating halls, and Aeschines and Sixty-one talked about how frescoes and mosaics couldn't be moved without damaging them. But nobody wanted to continue the art raids. When I called for a vote it was almost unanimous.

30

ARETE

When I came back from the missions I plunged straight into my adulthood tests, along with Boas and Archimedes, who were the other two people born in my birth month. When my brothers had become ephebes they had done it amid hordes of other Young Ones born in the same month, but for me there were only the three of us. Boas and Archimedes had been waiting more or less patiently for my return so that we could all do it together. They could have petitioned the Archons to go ahead without me, and I could have done it alone, but they had waited. Neither of them were philosophically inclined. Boas wanted to be a metal worker, perhaps a sculptor, and Archimedes loved growing things and was already working out at the farms for far more than the required time. We had very little in common but we got along well.

We all acquitted ourselves well in the palaestra, especially Archimedes, who was already getting broad shoulders. "They'll make you a silver," I said when scraping him off after the wrestling.

He shook his head and grinned. "They know where I belong."

Then the conference began. Alkibiades, with his friend Diogenes, came to town with the Athenian delegation, and Porphyry came with the Amazons, so Thessaly was full to bursting point.

I had no time to spend with them because I was being tested on the laws, and on rhetoric, and history, and music, and mathematics. It was an experience intended to be grueling, and it was. It was meant as a rite of passage. For Boas and Archimedes it unquestionably was. If I hadn't been on the voyage I would no doubt have felt it that way too. As it was, I felt grown up already, as if this were just a necessary marker.

I wanted to know about the conference. Maia wouldn't talk about it, but my brothers told me everything.

Ikaros had come to the conference. I asked Phaedrus to heal him while he was in town. He was reluctant. "He couldn't help but notice!" Father had talked to us seriously about not being caught using our powers.

"He already knows about me. We can arrange it so that he thinks I've healed him," I said. "Come on Phaedrus, think about it, he's nearly blind and he loves reading."

"He wouldn't tell anyone," Porphyry assured him.

"All right then. But not until after your initiation. You won't have time to pretend it's you until then."

I had to be content with that.

The day after the conference was the Ides, and therefore the day set for me to swear my oath to the Republic, and become an ephebe and be given my metal. It wasn't the grand affair it had been when the Children swore, or even five years ago when my brothers swore. Then there had been so many new ephebes that almost the whole city turned out to see them swear. But nevertheless, it was an occasion. Since all the envoys were still in town and many of them knew me and wanted to come, it was going to be a big public event, with a proper feast afterward, with a sheep roasted on a spit, and bannocks, and cream cheese, and plums stewed with honey. Hebe, one of my friends in the Florentine kitchens, told me about the preparations.

I had a new kiton, dyed orange and blue in the wool and

woven in ocean pattern. Mother had been embroidering the hem when she died, and I had thought I'd wear it with the pattern unfinished. But Euklides had finished it for me while I'd been away. I could see where he'd taken it over, the lilies and scrolls were less even, and the colors less precise than the ones Mother had done. But it was wonderful that he had taken the time to finish it for me. I felt loved as I put it on for the first time on the morning of the Ides. I kept my hair loose for the ceremony.

I went to Florentia for breakfast, and as always when I went in my eyes sought for Ficino, and as always now failed to find him. I wondered whether I'd always do that, whether when I was myself ninety-nine I'd still half-expect to see him somewhere about the hall. Before I could sit down, Baukis and Erinna brought me a crown of flowers they had made. "Neleus and I collected the flowers and Baukis wove it," Erinna said. It had tiny wild roses and long-stemmed daisies and little dark-blue hyacinths and their leaves. It was lopsided, but I didn't care. Baukis hugged me, and I looked over her shoulder at Erinna. "Welcome to adulthood," she said, awkwardly, and smiled. I put the wreath on, and then Maia came up and started to fuss with my loosened hair and straighten the wreath for me. I hardly had time to gulp down my porridge before it was time to go.

We walked to the Temple of Zeus and Hera in a big crowd. My whole family was there—Father, and all my brothers, including Porphyry and Alkibiades. Neleus was wearing Ficino's hat. In addition we had Rhea and Diogenes, and Nikias, who probably should have been counted as family. All my close friends came—Maia, Crocus, Erinna and Baukis, and Baukis's father Aeschines. Klymene showed up just as we were about to leave Florentia, wanting to be included in the family for the occasion. She hugged me, and I let her. Father didn't want a feud. Kallikles was still very distant with her, and she was clearly hurt by this and trying not to show it. I missed Mother sharply and specifically then, because she would have known what to say to make it all right.

I patted the bronze lion as we went past it, for luck, and because Mother always did. It looked at me today as if it were hoping for something.

"I can't believe how easily the conference went," Klymene said to Maia. "Or how fast either. I expected it to take six or eight days."

"Everyone was reasonable," Maia said.

"You were a great judge," Father said. Maia snorted.

We ran into Boas and Archimedes as we came into the plaza where the street of Demeter crossed the street of Dionysios, by the Temple of Demeter and Crocus's great colossus of Sokrates laughing. They too had garlands and new kitons and clusters of family and friends with them. I was very glad to see them. We walked in our separate family clusters, like a procession.

"We don't have all this fuss in Amazonia," Porphyry said. "We do it individually, on our actual birthdays, in the agora, and our names are written down."

"That sounds nice," I said.

"But our ceremonies in Athenia are ten times more formal, and take days," Alkibiades said. "And we have to do our examinations right there and then, with everyone watching, not quietly in advance the way you do. So think yourself lucky."

I laughed. "If I wanted to live in Athenia or the City of Amazons I'd go there. I belong here." Being away had made me realize how much I loved my city, every pillar, every word of the Workers' dialogues carved into the marble flagstones, every patch of flowers in front of the sleeping houses.

When we came into the square in front of the Temple of Zeus and Hera, the two Archons were waiting on the steps between the two great statues of the gods that flanked the temple. The altar stood behind them, smoke rising from the sacrifice. The square was packed with all the envoys, and with people who had just showed up, and for all I knew some crazy oath-enthusiasts who went to every single ceremony for everyone. I noticed Ikaros and Aristomache with Sixty-One, standing together, engaged in dialogue. Maia went over to join them. All our family and friends faded back into the crowd, leaving the three of us who were candidates standing together in the center. One of the Archons made a welcoming speech, talking about the significance of citizenship and Plato and the city. I wasn't listening properly. I was nervous. I felt it was hard to draw enough breath. I straightened my wreath, which was slipping into my eyes. The other Archon made a very similar speech, about the importance of young people and the significance of the community, and how the city was open to all and we had never turned anyone away—aimed at the visitors, I suppose. Then finally they got to it.

"Boas, bronze. Archimedes, iron. Arete, gold." I hadn't really doubted it, but it was a great relief nevertheless. Archimedes punched my arm, and I punched his back. We both had what we wanted. He was right, of course he was, we could trust them, they knew where we belonged. I could never have faced Father or my brothers if I hadn't made gold. I had felt confident that I deserved it, except for that moment when the speeches seemed to be going on forever. I went up the steps and took my pin, the bee Mother had designed when she'd been younger than I was now. I pinned my kiton with it immediately, and saw the gold gleam against the cloth, the only gold I would ever own. I was so delighted that I couldn't help smiling. Then I lifted off my wreath and knelt, with my back to the square, and the archon took the shears and cut off all my hair at the nape of my neck. I stood again and put the wreath back on. I felt odd without my hair; lighter. He had missed one strand, which tickled against my newly bare neck.

I went down two steps, as we had been instructed, and waited while Archimedes, and then Boas, were given their pins and had their hair cut in turn. Then the Archon took the mass of hair from all three of us and thrust it onto the smoldering fire on the altar. It blazed up at once and made a horrible stink, but she threw on some incense which soon masked that.

"You are no longer children," the other Archon said, his voice booming. "Come here and swear your allegiance to the City."

We went up one at a time in reverse order, Boas first and me last. I listened as the others swore. It was a great oath. I'd had it memorized for years, since my brothers took it. Boas swore, and the Archon marked his forehead with ash, then Archimedes did the same, looking awed and solemn now. Then it was my turn. I took the two steps up and moved just as they had done, so that I stood between the Archons. I was behind the altar for what would probably be the only time in my life unless I became an Archon. I set both hands palm-down on the marble top of the altar, careful to place them on either side of the sacrifice. The smoke of hair and incense was streaming straight up into a clear sky. I looked out through it over the crowd, seeing Father and my brothers watching, and Maia, who was wiping her eyes. I took a deep breath and spoke loudly and clearly, projecting to fill the space, as I had been taught when I was Briseis in the Dionysia.

"I swear by Zeus and Hera and Demeter and Apollo and Athene, by the figs and olives and barley and grapes, by the sea and the sky and the earth beneath my feet, that I will protect and defend the excellence of the Just City from all enemies, internal and external. I will fight bravely, judge fairly, and contribute to the best of my abilities. I will defend her laws and institutions, resist tyranny and foolishness, and the lures of wealth and honor, and strive ever to increase her excellence."

It had been a bright sunny morning, but it clouded over as I was speaking so that the last words came out under a dark sky. I looked up from the altar as the Archon marked my forehead and saw that I was mistaken, I was simply in the shadow of a very tall man. Then I saw that it was the great ivory and gold statue of Zeus, but it had moved and was standing in front of me instead of at the side of the steps. And then I realized that it was not the statue but Zeus himself standing there, frowning down at me. I remembered too late what Father had said about attracting the attention of the gods. I took my hands off the altar and stepped back, as if that might make him disappear again. Of course, it did nothing.

"Granddaughter," all-knowing Zeus rumbled, his voice like thunder. He looked around slowly, taking in the temple and the square and the people. Some had fallen to the ground. Most of them looked terrified. Ikaros looked absolutely thrilled and was bouncing on the balls of his feet with excitement. Father took a step forward, my brothers close at his back. Zeus nodded at Father, and thunder echoed all around. "Where is Athene?" Zeus asked.

She appeared on the steps in front of us. She had her helmet and her shield and her owl, and she seemed to be perfectly composed. I had never seen her before, but I would have recognized her anywhere. There were statues and paintings and bas-reliefs of her all over the city, many of them done from life. "Joy to you, Father," she said. "Be welcome to the Just City."

"And when did you intend to tell me about this folly?" We were speaking Greek, of course. But that last word held double meanings, in other languages. As well as meaning foolishness, and thus the opposite of the wisdom that was Athene's domain, it had the connotation of an anachronistic ruin built deliberately to enhance a landscape view. I bristled to hear the Republic described this way, not because it wasn't true but because it hurt.

Athene did not flinch, but stood looking up at her father calmly. "In the fullness of time, when there was something to report," she said.

"Come, let us discuss this," Zeus said. He pointed at Father and my brothers. "And you can come too." He pointed at Ikaros.

"Me?" Ikaros squeaked.

"Yes, you, Giovanni Pico della Mirandola, Count of Concord, Ikaros of the Amazons. You. Did you think I wouldn't recognize you when you profess to know so much about me? Come."

Maia had her mouth open, as if she was about to say something. Ikaros grabbed her arm.

Erinna was stepping forward too, and the Archon was reaching for me, and then they were gone and I was standing on a sloping mountain meadow, green with soft spring grass and dotted with strange blue and golden bell-like flowers, nodding in the gentle breeze. It felt like Delos, only much more so.

31

ARETE

Father was there, and my brothers, and Zeus, and Athene, and
Ikaros, and Maia, standing in a rough circle. I sat down at once
on the soft grass, and so did everyone else, almost simultane-
ously. There was something strange about how everyone looked,
as if perspective didn't work properly here. Zeus and Athene
both were and were not normal human sizes. They were much
too big to be sitting in a circle with the rest of us, yet there they
were, sitting right there, not taking up any more room, and not
far away. Zeus was big enough to fill the mountain and the sky,
and at the same time only a little taller than Phaedrus. It made
me feel a little dizzy when I focused on him and anything else
at the same time.

"Why did you bring Pico?" Athene asked Zeus.

Zeus raised an eyebrow. "He's the reason you did all this, isn't
he?"

I looked at Ikaros. He looked different, younger. His long hair
was chestnut brown and his face was unlined. He looked only a
few years older than my brothers. He was still clutching Maia's
arm. Maia also looked younger, very much the way she looked
in her statue in Amazonia. She was staring at Athene. Ikaros
opened his mouth as if he was about to say "Me?" again, but

Porphyry put a hand on his shoulder and he subsided. Athene didn't turn her head in his direction, but the owl was staring at him, and I felt she didn't need to look at him to see him. I could also tell by the way he was looking delightedly at everything that he could see properly.

"It's true I wanted somewhere interesting to take him. But he prayed to me for the Republic. They all did, all the Masters. And I could grant their prayers and help. It seemed like a good time and place for such an experiment."

"It was meddling for your own vanity," Zeus said, decisively. "And dragging Phoebus into it, where's the sense in that?"

"I wanted to become incarnate to learn some things," Father said. "Athene offered me the Republic as a time and place to do that. It was my free choice."

"And you've learned them, I see, and more besides. And you have a daughter. How very unlike you." Zeus looked at me, and I met his gaze as best I could. He looked a little puzzled. I felt as if I should be terrified, but I wasn't afraid at all. It wasn't like the time on Delos where everything I did was under the control of Fate and I was going through a prescribed and required set of motions. I was entirely free to act and choose for myself. But I didn't feel fear or anger, or anything at all really. Indeed, I felt preternaturally calm.

"My daughter Arete, my sons Kallikles, Phaedrus, Neleus, Euklides and Porphyry," Father said, indicating us. I realized for the first time that Alkibiades wasn't there, though he had been standing with the others. Was that because he had said he didn't want divine powers? How did Zeus know? And how was Neleus here? He wasn't really Father's son.

"A place women can be excellent, eh?" Zeus said, punning on my name of course, not even the king of gods and men was above that. He seemed to hear a lot more than was said, because while

I knew that Father usually only had sons because it was generally so unpleasant to be a woman, but the Republic was fair to both, Father hadn't said anything to Zeus about that.

"Plato—" Athene said.

"Don't start," Zeus said. "After what you did to Sokrates?" He stopped and looked at Ikaros. "To answer your unspoken question, I knew nothing about it until it was drawn to my attention by Arete just now, and now I know everything about it, as if I had always known."

"Thank you," Ikaros said. "And if you don't mind me asking, why are you taking the time to explain this to me?"

"Because it's better than overhearing your infernal conjectures," Zeus said. As he laughed the mountain seemed to shake. Then he looked at Maia.

"And yes, this is Olympos, and you are correct that we are not perfect. And yes, Pytheas is Apollo."

Maia nodded gravely. "Of course," she said. "And Simmea knew, of course." Father smiled at that.

"And you are here because Ikaros felt you were a deserving philosopher who had been right where he had been wrong," Zeus went on.

"And since I was wrong, why from all the assembled citizens did you choose to bring me?" Ikaros was being very polite, but he didn't seem afraid either. I wondered if calm was somehow in the air here.

"My wise daughter, in her chaste and foolish way, is in love with you. Only with your mind, I hasten to add. But I think it would be fair to say that she is in a state of unrequited agape with regard to you."

"Father, we all have favorites," my own father said. Maia laughed. Ikaros was staring at Athene in complete astonishment. "It helps to have conversations with them about it and find out what they want," Father went on.

Athene looked up from her shield and rolled her eyes at Father. "It wasn't that kind of thing. There's no comparison. I just—he was so bright and so young and he did pray to me for it, and lots of other people had too, and it all seemed as if it would be so interesting and so much fun," she said. "Nothing like your romances at all."

"Not unrequited," Ikaros said, passionately, as soon as she had finished speaking. "Never unrequited. I have loved and sought wisdom all my life—and you, Sophia, from the day I saw you."

"Then why did you betray me?" she asked, her gray eyes hard as flint.

"With Sokrates? Or by saying you were an angel?" he asked.

"That there are multiple possible occasions does seem indicative of problems," Zeus said.

"But I loved you all the time." He didn't look away from Athene, and he absolutely meant it.

"You betrayed me when, just before the Last Debate, you turned away from reason and said will and love could be enough, you didn't need comprehension!" Athene said.

"Oh." Ikaros looked abashed. "That was just a theory, and I was just wrong. Simmea said it was mystical twaddle, and I realized she was right as soon as I read Aquinas again. But even then I never stopped loving you."

"I *am* reason, you idiot," she said.

"I am human and make mistakes, but I always try again to serve you and be worthy of you," Ikaros said. "You have always been my goal and my delight."

"Touching as this is, we have serious business," Zeus interrupted.

"He is my votary. He prayed to me when he could have been burned at the stake for it," Athene said, turning to Zeus. "And others too. Ficino. Aristomache. Maia." She gestured to Maia, sitting primly on the grass listening intently. "They loved our world, and their own worlds held too little to fulfill their souls. I wanted to see what they would do with their imagination of our world, and Plato's vision."

"Plato's Republic," Zeus said. "Three hundred philosophers and classics majors. Ten thousand slave children. Lost artworks from all of time. Robots. The head of the Winged Victory of Samothrace."

"All the books," Ikaros put in. "We rescued all the books from the Great Library of Alexandria."

"Of course you did," Zeus said, his gaze still fixed on Athene. "You took Pico and Ficino and Atticus careering through time rescuing books and art, you turned Sokrates into a fly because he beat you in a fair argument, and you'd like me to regard this as something other than sheer unadulterated self-indulgence?"

"I have learned a lot I could have learned nowhere else," Father said.

"I have lived a life I could have lived nowhere else, and I shall always be grateful to Athene for giving me my life," Maia said.

"I accept your judgment," Athene said, inclining her head to Zeus.

"My judgment. Yes. But how shall I judge what I shall do with it? They've already left the island and started to reach out. I can't leave them there to tangle with history. For us, what's done is done. But for them, it might be kindest if—"

"No! Please!" Father said. He flung himself down before Zeus, flat on his face, with his hands on Zeus's knees. My sense of scale quailed, for in one way Zeus's knees were as huge as mountain ranges, and in another Father, who was the same size he always was, could comfortably clutch them. Also, the posture was ridiculous, but Father managed to make it seem not only graceful but entirely natural. "Not the darkness of the oak! Don't unmake them. I beg you, Father, not that."

I had never before heard of the darkness of the oak. But as

soon as I heard what Father said, I understood what it meant. Zeus had the power to undo time, to make things never have happened. He could do that with the city, unmake it. The Masters and Children would never have left their own times. The Young Ones would never have been born. The City would never have been more than Plato's dream. The darkness of the oak. I shuddered.

Fear is a strange thing. I had been afraid I wouldn't qualify as gold, but I had not been afraid when all-knowing Zeus had appeared before me and carried me off outside time. I had sat through the debate so far listening to Athene being chided and been calm and interested. But as soon as Father said "the darkness of the oak" I was terrified—and yet still a little detached from my fear, observing it rather than being swept off in it. Was this what it was like to be a god?

"But why, Phoebus?" Zeus grumbled. "You're outside time. You'd still remember what you've learned. Your children are here, even Neleus." Neleus straightened Ficino's hat as Zeus glanced at him. "And however much agape you felt for her, your woman is already dead. The whole thing is ludicrous. Their souls are going back where they came from. It has only been a few years. The darkness of the oak would be a mercy—"

"No," Father said. "Please."

"Bring down the volcano," I said, seeing it all at once as a solution. Zeus's eyes met mine over Father's prostrate form, and again I felt that I puzzled him. "If we can't go on, if you have to end it, bring down the lava and the fire and the death we have always known is coming, sweep it away, kill us all. But let it have happened! Wipe it out if you must, but don't make it never have been."

"Why?" Behind him lightning flashed around the snowy peak of Olympos.

"We were trying to do Plato's Republic," I said. "It may be

ludicrous and impossible, it may seem foolish to you, but we were trying. We made compromises and adaptations, but we were all trying to increase our excellence, to increase the city's excellence, and the world's. You heard the vow I made, that's why you came, because I called on you to hold the oath. We all made that vow. We may have fallen short, we may have made mistakes, we may have done it all wrong, but our goal was great. Athene set us there under the volcano so that we would have no posterity, and we accepted that—difficult as it is to accept. But we were what we were, we existed. We tried. Kill us now if that's what's necessary to preserve history, but leave us the effort we made, at least." I thought of Mother, Ficino, Erinna, Crocus, the everyday life of the Republic, Alkibiades showing me the vines and saying he didn't want divine power, the people of Psyche joining in raggedly on the last chorus of Father's ode to peace. "We might not have been philosopher kings as Plato intended, but at least we made the attempt."

Maia was smiling through tears. Neleus nodded at me.

"And would you go back and die with the city you care for so much?" Zeus asked, his great dark eyes fixed on mine.

"You know I would. I know how temporary death is. My soul would go on with what it learned in the Just City, as we all would. Don't take that away from us."

Ikaros was staring at me, his lips parted. "You said you weren't an angel," he said.

"God is a better term," Zeus said, absently. "She has free will, and limited knowledge. And there is no such thing as omnipotence, and omniscience is extremely overrated. As for omnibenevolence, I'm sure you realize by now that we're doing our best. And time is a Mystery, by which I mean you are welcome to make up your own theories and I'll be grateful if any of them come close to being a useful analogy."

"I'll work on it," Ikaros said. He looked at Athene. "I'll work on it with Sophia's help." Athene was smiling at him, but he looked away from her, to me. "And I will always pursue excellence."

Zeus's gaze ran over my brothers. He looked down at Father, who was still clutching his knees. "Get up, son. I won't do it. Though I can't see where, under Fate and Necessity, the place can go. She wants posterity, you know."

"Mortals all want posterity," Father said, getting up and settling back on the grass next to Zeus. "It's some compensation for forgetting when they go on to new lives. Mortality is so strange. You should try it sometime. It's so very different in practice."

"I look forward to hearing you sing about it." Zeus put his hand on Father's shoulder.

"They have equal significance, you know," Father said. "All of them. They all matter to themselves, to each other."

"I know. I wondered how long it would take you to figure that one out."

Father leaned back on his hands. "There will be songs. A lot of songs."

"Good. These are things the gods need to understand. If I am to send the lava—"

"Yes. Send me back to die with the city." Father didn't hesitate.

"And I," Maia said, instantly.

"And I," my brothers chorused.

"And I," Ikaros said, only a heartbeat later.

"It's not even your city anymore, you've just been given a research project by ever-living Zeus, you're on Olympos with the gods, and you're asking to go back to die?" Athene asked, incredulous.

"If it's going to perish that way, I should go with it. And all of Kallisti is the Republic, all the different cities are our own visions of the Just City, and choices we have opened up in our interpretations." Ikaros nodded to Porphyry, who grinned at him.

"Don't worry, he won't do that either," Porphyry said.

Deep-browed Zeus turned his gaze on Porphyry. "Won't I, grandson? How do you know?"

"You're trying to find a way, by Fate and Necessity, to give us posterity. And I see one!"

"Oh Porphyry, you have your powers! Are they prophetic?" I asked.

"I'd much rather be able to fly," Porphyry said. "And I don't know whether it's prophetic power, or just being outside time, but I can see time from the outside, and I see the threads and patterns of it, so I see where we could go."

"What useful skills your children have," Zeus said, to Father. "Did you think at all what you were doing with a whole clutch of them? Setting up your own pantheon? Will you go back with them even if it's not to fiery destruction?"

"I'll live out this life until this body dies, and then come home to Olympos," Father said. "When this body dies, whether that's in ten minutes from the volcano or in fifty years from old age."

"You'll be cleaning up this mess for a lot longer than fifty years," Zeus said. "And you too," he added, to Athene. "You'll be out there getting your hands dirty, not tucked away in your library."

"If that is your judgment," Athene said.

"Show me what you have found, Porphyry," Zeus said.

Porphyry stood up and walked over to Zeus. He put his hands together, then pulled them apart, as if doing a cat's cradle, but without string. Something glimmered between his fingers. I thought for a moment it was one of the blue and gold bell-headed flowers, but there was nothing there. "Here," Porphyry said, indicating the emptiness between his fingers. "And a little while before the ships arrive from Earth, do you see?" Zeus peered into the nothingness, then laughed. Thunder rolled around the mountain.

"That'll do," he said.

"What is it?" I asked.

"It's an era far in the future, in the twenty-fifth century, when humanity has just discovered faster-than-light travel," Porphyry said. "They're just rediscovering all the civilizations on planets that were settled more slowly than light. There aren't complete records of who went where. Some of them are very strange. We can be one of them. We won't look much odder than the others. It's long after the *Republic* was written, so why shouldn't a group of people have tried it?"

"Nobody ever has," muttered Zeus.

"We'd have a divine origin story, but nobody would have to pay any attention. And the ships will come, and they can discover us, and we can rejoin the human mainstream, with all our books and art and theories. It will be a mystery, but only a small one, nothing to prove anything."

"Why do you keep so secret?" Neleus asked. "Why can't we give them proof? People want so much to know and to understand."

"It's better for humanity to allow us to work out our own theories, our own destiny. If we *know* it changes everything," Ikaros said.

Neleus nodded slowly, recognizing that in himself.

"And knowing would fix one truth, and close off many paths to enlightenment," Athene said. "You're going to love the Enlightenment," she said aside, to Ikaros.

"Posterity," I said, to Zeus and Porphyry. "But another planet? I suppose a new world would be a fresh beginning."

"A new world won't be an empty blank any more than ten-year-olds are," Maia said.

Zeus smiled at her. "True, and well deduced." He looked at my brothers. "New planets need their own pantheons, and it seems we have one all ready." He turned to Ikaros. "It has to do with place. Place is much more important to deity than you've ever considered. You should get out more. Travel."

"On another planet?" he asked.

Zeus looked at Athene. "Were you planning to keep him as a pet?"

"There are a lot of wonderful times and places he hasn't seen on Earth," she said. "And then perhaps later other planets."

Zeus waved his hand, and thunder rumbled nearby. "Do what you want. You will anyway. You agree, Ikaros? You'll work with Athene?"

"If the City doesn't need me."

"The City will get along without you, on its new planet. And as well as going sightseeing with Athene, which I'm sure you'll enjoy, there are Mysteries here you can be working on." He looked at Maia. "How about you? Do you want to stay here or go on?"

"Go on," she said.

"Good. The Republic will need you. You'll be directing it in a few years, you know, you and Crocus. And then you." He indicated Neleus. Lightning danced around his head. "Philosopher kings. It won't be easy."

"It hasn't been easy so far," Maia said.

"I swore that same oath," Neleus said. "Fight bravely, judge fairly, contribute to the best of my abilities. We all did. We all want to go."

I was looking at Neleus, and so were my other brothers as he spoke for them, and for a moment it was the way it had been before the voyage, when we had seen that we were all one thing, and he was another. But now, on Olympos, we looked to him

for leadership. We had our powers. But he was the most philosophical. And that made him the best of us.

"But another sun?" Father asked, sounding worried.

"You can have it," Zeus said wearily. "Now, is there anything
else before I send the pack of you back where you belong?"

32

APOLLO

Euripides puts it very well: Zeus brings the unthought to be, as here we see.

Before we left Olympos I took Athene aside and took care of a few details. I scrawled *"Goodness"* on the parchment map they gave Maecenas in Lucia, and gave it to her to put into her armrest so that I could find it there. "Any time between the Last Debate and last autumn. And if you get the chance, could you possibly take the head of Victory and donate it to the Louvre so the poor thing can be back in one piece again? Oh, and for goodness' sake, get us some more robots," I said.

"Porphyry will get you robots," she said. "Father's going to be loading me down with work here."

"But you'll have Pico to help. He's going to love your library. And learning all the new languages." Behind us, he was hugging Maia, and Porphyry, and to my surprise, Arete.

"Thank you for speaking up for me," Athene said, stiffly.

"It was nothing," I said. I had felt sorry for her, exposed that way. "I know what it's like to love a mortal."

"It's not the same," she said, automatically. "Did you think of doing that with Simmea? Taking her outside time, where you could keep her young?"

"Sooner or later her soul would have wanted to go on," I said, gently, because it would happen with Pico too, sooner or later, unless he became a god. Perhaps he would. He had the right kind of mind. Father had noticed that at once. We could do with a god with an excellence of fitting facts together into complex theories, especially if he could generalize it to things other than metaphysics. Now that I'd seen it, it seemed obvious. Athene didn't have any children, so none of her areas of responsibility ever got passed along to anyone else. I really liked the idea of Pico as a god of synthesis.

"But did you want to?"

"I'm glad in a way that I didn't have to make that choice. Simmea's mortality was so much a part of who she was, and my incarnation so much a part of our relationship, that I don't know what it would have been if I'd brought her here." She'd have started to *analyze* everything. It would have been wonderful. I wished I had brought her, and Sokrates too. But mortal souls need to grow and go on, that's part of the marvel of them, part of what we love about them. If Pico became a god, which I was now sure was Father's plan all along, he would lose some of what made Athene love him, and lose the opportunities his soul would have had to transform. Who could tell what wonderful people Ikaros might become, given the opportunity? How much he might contribute to the excellence of the world? Still, there wasn't any point saying that to her and risking spoiling what they had for now. He had to make his own choices.

"But you knelt in supplication to Father rather than let her life never have been."

"Yes," I said, simply. I hadn't cared what it cost me.

She nodded. "Maybe it's not so different. Agape."

"Thank you for setting up the Republic, so I could learn what agape was," I said.

She smiled. "I'm glad it was worth it. Have fun on the new planet. They're bound to call it Plato. What else could they possibly agree on?"

I laughed. "Have fun with Pico. Keep learning everything, and let me know all about it when you have the chance."

"When you come back, I'll meet you in the Laurentian Library on the first day the orange tree blooms in 1564."

"It's a date," I said, touched, and turned back to where Father and Maia and my Young Ones were waiting.

The sun isn't literally a winged chariot with two fiery horses. It's literally a big ball of fusing hydrogen. But metaphorically and spiritually, it's a chariot. *My* chariot. My new sun, which had no name, only a catalog number, and which is literally a slightly bigger and redder ball of fusing hydrogen, is metaphorically and spiritually a racecar. *My* racecar. We called it Helios, "the sun," either because we're an unimaginative people, or because we instinctively recognized that it had metaphorically and spiritually the same driver as the old Helios we'd left shining on Earth. It zips across the sky. The day is only nineteen hours long.

Father set the five Republics of Kallisti and the eight Lucian Republics down carefully on the new planet, without so much as bumping any of their art or architecture. He also took all the people who chose to go, which was everyone except for a scattering of stubborn idiots who stood alone to see their cities and civilization disappear around them. (And who do you think has to be their patron and look after them forever after? Well, did you think Athene was going to get stuck with it?) He set the cities down the same distance apart they had always been. It didn't matter at all to Father that he put them on a rocky volcanic plain on the edge of a great ocean, or that many of them now had harbors that went nowhere. It looked exceedingly peculiar, but we coped.

Porphyry did indeed get us some new robots, and that helped a great deal.

Maia became the first leader of the City after the move, and she and Crocus were the first Consuls of the Senate of Plato, the council made up of representatives of all twelve cities. She helped lead us into the era of peace and exploration, and when the aliens came she was the first after Arete to learn their language. She was thrice Consul, and after she died we put that on her memorial stone, along with all her other achievements. As Father had predicted, Neleus led us after that. By then we were thoroughly involved with the alien confederation, and we'd persuaded a surprising number of aliens to strive for excellence and justice in a Platonic context before the human spaceships discovered all of us and things got complicated.

As for me, I kept writing songs, and learning things about myself, about mortal life, about my children and other people. I kept on striving toward excellence, for myself and for the world. All the worlds.

I could still see my chariot at night from our new home, a distant glimmer, shining to me across space and time, which are Mysteries, and in strange ways almost the same thing. I was glad I could see it. I would have been very sad without it. But I'd have managed. I managed without Simmea, after all.

Not even Necessity knows all ends.

THANKS

Ada Palmer gave the right answers to all my questions, lent me books, sent me useful links, and talked to me about Pico when she was supposed to be grading. Then, after all that, she read it and made brilliant suggestions. This book wouldn't exist without her. Buy her books and listen to her music. You'll be glad you did.

I'm very grateful to my husband, Emmet O'Brien, for putting up with me when I'm writing. Elise Matthesen spent much longer than she imagined we would in the Bronze Age Greece section of the National Museet in Copenhagen, not to mention snarky Apollo comments in Antwerp cathedral. Gillian Spragg and Lauren Schiller were a great help with references.

This book was read by Mary Lace and Patrick Nielsen Hayden while it was being written, and after it was finished by Bo Balder, Biersma, Maya Chhabra, Pamela Dean, Ruthanna and Sarah Emrys, Magenta Griffith, Steven Halter, Sumana Harihareswara, Madeleine Kelly, Nancy Kremi, Marissa Lingen, Elise Matthesen, Clark E. Myers, Kate Nepveu, Lydia Nickerson, Emmet O'Brien, Ada Palmer, Doug Palmer, Susan Palwick, Eliana Rus, Drew Shiel, Sherwood Smith, and Nicholas Whyte.

I'd like to thank Patrick for editing, his assistant Miriam

Weinberg for wrangling, Teresa Nielsen Hayden for her sensitive and thoughtful copyedits, and everyone in Tor Production and Publicity and Sales who work so hard at the unglamorous part of publishing, without which we wouldn't have any books.